Two Brothers

For years, bestselling author Linda Lael Miller has delighted readers with her passionate, evocative stories of life and love in the Old West. Now, with this innovative pair of novels, she creates two gripping stories of identical twin brothers, separated at birth, but drawn to each other's side. . . .

The Lawman

Marshal Shay McQuillan has a lot on his hands—stage-coach robbers to hunt down, a murdered fiancée to avenge. He certainly doesn't need an identical twin brother he never knew existed turning up out of the blue and telling him what to do. Even less does he want pretty Aislinn Lethaby trying to rescue *him* from danger. Because, to tell the truth, Aislinn is a sweet distraction from duty whom Shay just can't resist.

Aislinn Lethaby has a fine job at the town hotel. Soon, she'll have saved enough to buy the broken-down homestead she has her eye on and bring her young brothers west. She has no business jeopardizing everything when she sees Shay in danger. But something about the man makes Aislinn lose all the good sense she thought she had—and follow the longings of her heart.

About the Author

LINDA LAEL MILLER has written more than twenty-three novels, including the *New York Times* bestsellers *Princess Annie*, *The Legacy*, *Yankee Wife*, and *Daniel's Bride*. With more than six million copies of her books in print, she is considered to be one of the finest romance authors writing today. Ms. Miller resides in the Seattle area, where she is at work on her next novel for Pocket Books.

Linda Lael Miller

Two Brothers

The Lawman
The Gunslinger

POCKET BOOKS

New York London Toronto Sydney Tokyo Singapore

This book is a work of fiction. Names, characters, places and incidents are products of the author's imagination or are used fictitiously. Any resemblance to actual events or locales or persons, living or dead, is entirely coincidental.

An *Original* Publication of POCKET BOOKS

POCKET BOOKS, a division of Simon & Schuster Inc.
1230 Avenue of the Americas, New York, NY 10020

ISBN: 0-671-00401-8

First Pocket Books trade paperback printing October 1998

10 9 8 7 6 5 4 3 2 1

POCKET and colophon are registered trademarks of
Simon & Schuster Inc.

Cover illustration by Lina Levy
Cover handlettering by Ron Zinn

Printed in the U.S.A.

For Peggy Jean Knight,
who introduced me to a whole new world
and a lot of great people,
most especially, herself.
Keep on talkin' to strangers, girl.

1853

From the Journal of Mattie Killigrew

I have neglected this journal sorely, since leaving home. I shall try to do better, for no doubt I will find it interesting in future years.

September is upon us already, and I fear I shall not be able to ride one more day in that wagon without going mad from the jostling. Surely it is a marvel that I have not given birth before my time; I am enormous and unwieldy, like a corn-fed sow in autumn, and from earliest light until sunset, we roll onward, ever onward, over rutted tracks, uphill and down.

Surely it is impossible that a mere four months have passed since we left St. Louis, Patrick and I, our hearts full of hope and wonder, our foolish heads brimming with glorious visions of adventure. It seems ever so much longer, looking back. So many rivers crossed.

In those first joyous nights, we slept beneath our rig on the feather mattress that was our marriage gift from Patrick's grandmother, God rest her soul, and chattered on and on about the grand homestead we would have in the West. Three hundred and twenty rich and fertile acres, ours for the taking!

We have no living kin save each other, but it didn't matter so much then, for we had set our faces toward the Promised Land, and we could already taste the milk and honey. Patrick would ofttimes lay a hand on my belly, there beneath our creaky old wagon, and say we were a family, he and I and the babe. That together we were more than enough.

I love him so much.

I shall never tell him, of course, how I wish with all my will and spirit that we had never left Ohio, that we had made a life for ourselves there, on the little farm where Patrick was born. Instead, we sold our land and bought this accursed wagon, these plodding, sweaty oxen, and more dried beans and hardtack than any mortal should ever be required to eat.

Some families have turned back—three at the first river crossing, two more when smoke signals appeared on the far horizon. We lost four to cholera, and were forced to leave the Flynns and the Lingwoods to fend for themselves when the sickness overtook them as well. The wagon master said we were losing too much time, that we must put the high country behind us before the snows came and, anyway, we could not risk an epidemic. Whole trains had been lost that way, he said.

Still, Ellen Lingwood was my friend. I shall never forget the despair in her eyes when we abandoned her with her sick husband and four feverish little children, there beside the trail, as if they had no more value than the discarded pipe organs and china cabinets and cedar chests we come across on occasion.

I confess I fear that fate more than anything, even the red savages who occasionally watch us from a distance, spears in hand, their painted ponies restless, eager to give chase. More, in fact, than death itself. To be alone, surrounded by all this vast and uncaring emptiness—I can hardly bear to contemplate it.

Patrick says cavalrymen patrol these parts, that I mustn't fret, for the Lingwoods will surely be found and taken in, as will the Flynns. We have not seen a single soldier since we passed through Kansas; perhaps he thinks I haven't noticed. This land belongs to the Indians, and rightly so, and were it up to me I should let them have it for all of time and eternity!

I will set aside my writing, for now, although it comforts me mightily. I must conserve my ink, for I have only this one bottle, now partly gone.

*   *   *

Three days have passed since my last entry. We are climbing, climbing, higher and higher into the mountains. Sometimes the wagon is at such an angle that I can barely hold my seat at the reins, and our belongings slide and clatter behind me. Twice I have had to beg Patrick to climb up and drive, for I am too fearful. In the steep places, though, where the track is narrow, he must walk alongside the oxen, murmuring to them, guiding them, lest they panic and lose their footing.

How I thank God when eventide comes, and we can stop and take our rest! Patrick must hoist me down from the wagon seat now, for I am ever so great and awkward. Mrs. Chambers says my babe has dropped, that I will surely enter my confinement soon.

I am so afraid. We cannot stop, and unless my pains come in the evening, I shall have to bear my child in that infernal wagon. Mrs. Chambers says I am not to fret, for she has had experience in such matters, and will take me in charge and see us both safely through the ordeal. And an ordeal it is; other women have borne children during our passage west, and their shrieks of pain reached every ear, though most pretended not to hear. Some were hearty, and came through gamely, but others were buried beside the trail, with their infants cradled in their arms.

Patrick says it will be over quickly, and I will have a fine son or daughter to show for my travail. Love him though I do, I confess that sometimes I want very much to strangle him.

There are two babes inside me, I am sure of it. They are making war, one against the other, like Cain and Abel. When I told Patrick I thought I was carrying twins, expecting husbandly sympathy, he beamed and said God had blessed us.

I wonder if he would think that if he were the one facing the valley of the shadow, not once, but twice.

Perhaps I should have been a spinster.

Two Brothers

* * *

There is a great storm brewing—the sky has been ominously dark for days—but the summit is not far off, and the wagon master has been pushing us all to our limits, haranguing the stragglers. Patrick is grim-faced with the tension of it, and he thinks of little but driving the oxen to the verge of collapse. They bellow in protest, poor, wretched beasts, their hides lathered and steaming; no doubt they yearn for the quiet fields of home, and I feel great pity for them. At midafternoon yesterday, the Swannells' mules simply gave out. They lay down and would not rise and go on no matter how strong the urging.

The sight disturbed me prodigiously; I scrambled down from the wagon, though it was moving still, to retch in the bushes. I expected kindly words from Patrick; instead, he was impatient with me for causing a delay. My dearest husband, who has never spoken harshly in my presence in all the time I've known him, growled at me like a bear. (Of course he later apologized, as well he should have done.) It makes me sore fearful to know he is so worried; I am still smarting a little and will take my time letting him know that I've forgiven him.

It came today, the rain that has been burdening the dark and rumbling sky, and we are up to our axles in mud. The torrent pounds at the canvas top of our wagon as I write this, by the light of a kerosene lantern, and there is a heavy ache, low in my belly. Patrick is frantic, as are the other men, for the summit is still some distance ahead, a seemingly unattainable goal that must, nonetheless, be reached. I take an uncharitable measure of cheer in the knowledge that we cannot be left behind in this terrifying place, for the other wagons are stuck fast, too. Patrick has not upbraided me again, and last night before we slept, I let him know I had put aside my grievance with him. He is very fetching and very persuasive, my Patrick, and his kisses move me in a way that would not be seemly to record.

Still more rain. We remain stalled just short of the mountaintop, and this morning several Indians rode right into our camp, bold as brass, demanding horses and sugar and tobacco. I peeked out through the flap and saw their feathers and painted faces.

They were given everything but the horses, these savages, and it was plain that they were not satisfied when they left. The wagon master said they were renegades.

Later, I overheard Patrick telling Mr. Swannell that we, the company of travelers, are as vulnerable as ants in a puddle of honey. At the time I didn't give that remark much weight, thinking it was a fine and merciful thing that we'd been made to stop, for it gave those woeful mules a chance to rest.

Mrs. Chambers has been to see me twice. She said my babes are uncommon big, and shook her head once or twice, in response to some private thought. I am small; perhaps too small, and only eighteen. That seemed an advanced age, before we left Ohio, but now I feel very young.

They came back, the Indians, at first light. The rain had ceased, and our men were busy digging out the wagons, railing and cursing and pushing at the poor animals. I did not care a whit for any of it, as my pains were upon me.

I called for Patrick, but he did not come to me. That troubled me greatly.

The babes were born amidst savage shrieks and gunfire; even then I could think of naught but how they were tearing me asunder, these fierce, strong children, as though I were not flesh and blood, but merely some brittle shell to be broken open and left behind.

I have seen them, held them, all too briefly, for I am weak. Mrs. Chambers agrees that they are fine boys indeed, with their fair hair. Surely they will resemble Patrick when they are grown.

Something is wrong, for all that my travail is ended at last and the babes are here, safe and strong. Mrs. Chambers has tears on her face, and enjoins me now to put aside my pen and sleep. She has never seen anyone write at such a time, she says. The Indians are gone, she tells me, and I may rest in the assurance of safety.

I must not stop until my strength fails, however, for if I do, if I lie idle, then I cannot but credit the fact that Patrick has not come to the wagon, not even to look upon our sons. Perhaps I have shamed him before the company of travelers, with my screaming.

I hope that is it. Dear God, surely he did not die in the fighting.

Patrick is dead, felled by an arrow in the chest. I believe I knew he was no more when night fell and there was still no sign of him. And I shall perish soon as well; I have seen that bitter truth in Mrs. Chambers' kindly face. I have lost too much blood.

I have begged them to let me see Patrick, but they will not.

I am not afraid to die; no, without my beloved, it is life I fear. I know that he waits for me, somewhere just beyond the shadows.

Arrangements have been made. Margaret Saint-Laurent came to call, just a little while ago. She is a kindly lady, and educated, and she held my hand and spoke in a soft voice, and took down these final words for me when I asked it of her. She and her husband, John, will take one of my sons on to Oregon and raise him as their own. They mean to call him Tristan.

Shamus and Rebecca McQuillan have agreed to bring up the second babe, for they have only daughters, and are glad to get a son. They mean to christen our little boy Shamus, and California will be their home.

I am sorry that I was not stronger, for the sake of my children. I would surely have loved them as deeply as any mother could, had there been time. If there is a way, then let them know that I am buried in my rightful place, beside their brave, good and generous father, alongside the trail that led to our dreams.

The Lawman

1883

Shay

Chapter 1

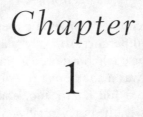

PROMINENCE, CALIFORNIA, JUNE OF 1883

*H*E DIDN'T EVEN ATTEMPT to draw on the intruder; it was far too late for that. The cold weight of a pistol barrel rested in the hollow of his throat, and he heard the click of the hammer as it snapped back.

"Don't move." The voice unnerved him almost as much as the situation in which he found himself, for it might have come from his own throat. The tone, the timbre, were his.

"I didn't plan on it," he answered. It was still dark in the jail cell, where he had made his bed after a night passed in the card room behind the Yellow Garter Saloon, and all he could make out, looking up through his eyelashes, besides the blue-black barrel of the gun, was a glint of light hair and an impression of wolf-white teeth.

Delicately, the stranger relieved him of the .45 in his holster, still strapped to his hip, spun it fancy-like on one finger, and laid it aside with a clatter. A match was struck, and Shay caught the sharp, familiar scents of sulphur and kerosene, mingled. Thin light spilled over the jailhouse cot and dazzled him for a moment, but he knew he was still square in the other man's sights.

The visitor whistled low through his teeth. "So," he said. "It's true."

5

Shay blinked a couple of times and then squinted. Except for a few minor differences, mostly matters of grooming and deportment, he could have been looking at himself. The other man's hair was a shade or two darker than his own; the stranger wore a full beard, too, and a cheroot jutted from between his teeth, but virtually everything else was the same—the lean build, the blue eyes, even the lopsided grin, tending toward insolence. "What the—?"

The specter chuckled. "Hell of a thing, isn't it? You always sleep in your own jail cell, Marshal?"

Shay ventured to sit up, and the other fellow didn't shoot him. Taking that for a good sign, he swung his legs over the side of the cot and made to stand, only to find himself looking straight up the barrel of the pistol.

"Not so fast."

With a sigh, Shay sat down again. "Who the devil are you?" he demanded. Now that he was sure he wasn't dreaming, he was beginning to feel fractious.

His antagonist grabbed the rickety chair in the corner of the cell, turned it around, and sat astraddle of the seat, all in virtually one motion. His left arm rested across the back, the .45 dangling idly from one gloved hand. An odd sensation prickled Shay's nape, but he forbore from rubbing it. "Maybe I'm you," the man said. It was downright irritating, the way he took his sweet time answering.

"I gotta quit drinkin'," Shay observed philosophically.

His reflection grinned. "The situation isn't *that* drastic, though I will admit you look as if you've been overindulging of late. How old are you?"

"I'm the one asking questions here," Shay snapped.

"I'm the one with the gun," came the easy reply.

"Hell." Out of habit, Shay polished the star-shaped badge on his vest with his right shirt cuff. "I turned thirty last September."

"So did I."

"Well, write-home and hallelujah. I hope somebody baked you a cake."

The response was a slanted grin that gave Shay a whole new insight into why his pa had felt called upon to box his ears now and again. "Somebody did. I believe her name was Sue-Ellen. How long have you had this job, Marshal?"

Shay put his foot down, figuratively, at least. "Oh, no," he said. "I asked for your name, and I'm not saying anything else until I get it."

"Saint-Laurent," was the crisp reply. "Tristan." Still holding the gun, Saint-Laurent used the thumb of that same hand to scratch his chin.

Shay pondered the revelation, mentally leafing through the piles of wanted posters on his desk for a match, and was relieved when he came up dry. "It's plain that you've got me at a disadvantage," he said. "So why don't you just go ahead and tell me how the hell it happens that a man comes awake in the middle of the night to find a gun at his throat and his own face looking back at him?"

Saint-Laurent watched him narrowly for a few moments, as though making some kind of calculation, then threw down the cheroot and ground it out on the wood floor with the heel of one scuffed and mud-caked boot. "Your folks never told you what happened? How you were orphaned and all?"

Shay shook his head. He had two older sisters, Dorrie and Cornelia, and they'd wasted no time in letting him know he was a foundling, but they'd been nearly grown when he came along, and secretive about the details, probably because it gave them power over him. Neither his mother nor his father could be persuaded to part with the story; in fact, they'd taken it to their graves, dying within a year of each other, and he'd left off wondering a long time ago. Mostly.

Saint-Laurent sighed. "You must have reasoned it through by now," he said. "We started out from the same place, you and me. We were born in the Rockies, to a couple named Killigrew—they were headed west with a wagon train, and both of them were real young. Our pa never even got a look at us—he was killed by Indians while our mama was in labor. She died of grief and blood loss before the day was out."

The tale was briefly and bluntly told, and it bludgeoned Shay in a way he wouldn't have expected. He was grateful he was already sitting down, since he reckoned his knees might have given out, and for the first time in eighteen months, he was sober clear through to the middle of his brain. He thrust a hand through his hair but said nothing, not trusting himself to speak.

"I didn't know about it either, until last year, when I learned my mother was failing and went home to the ranch to see her. She told me the story then, and gave me a little remembrance book our mama kept."

"And you set out to find me?" The question came out as a rasp.

Saint-Laurent chuckled, fished another cheroot out of the inside pocket of his long, dusty gray coat and leaned over to light it from the flame in the kerosene lamp. He replaced the glass chimney before troubling himself to reply. "I didn't give a damn about you," he said. "After all, if I wanted to know what you looked like, all I had to do was look in a mirror. I meant to go my own way. But then, as they say in the melodramas, fate took a hand."

"How's that?" Shay asked, mildly insulted that his own brother hadn't taken more of an interest. Folks either loved him or hated him, but they generally committed themselves wholeheartedly to one view or the other.

Tristan looked him over, drew on the cheroot, and expelled the smoke, all without speaking. When he did open his mouth, he left Shay's question hanging in midair. "That stagecoach robbery, over near Cherokee Bluff," he said. "Were you wearing that badge when it happened?"

Shay wished mightily that he were drunk again. A year and a half before, the driver, the guard and three passengers had been killed when a bridge blew up beneath the stage and sent the horses, the coach itself and everyone aboard crashing into a deep ravine. One of the victims, Miss Grace Warfield, had been his bride-to-be.

"Yeah," he ground out, after a long moment. "I was the marshal."

Tristan was mercifully silent.

Shay assembled words in his head and, with considerable difficulty, herded them over his tongue. "I rode out to meet them, when the coach didn't come in on time," he said. "Me and old Dutch Cooper, from over at the livery stable. We figured they'd broken an axle or one of the horses had thrown a shoe. We were maybe a mile off when we heard the explosion." He stopped, unable to go on, stricken to silence by visions of the terrible things he'd seen that day. Two of the horses were still alive when he and Dutch got there, and the dust had yet to settle. Bodies were scattered over both sides of the ravine, and the coach was in pieces, one wheel spinning slowly in the breeze. The splintered timbers of the bridge made a gruesome framework for it all.

He and Dutch had gone scrabbling down the steep incline, leaving their mounts untethered at the top. Dutch had shot the injured horses, while Shay had rushed from passenger to passenger—an old man, a middle-aged woman, and Grace. His gentle, funny Grace.

He hadn't expected her back from San Francisco for another week—she'd gone there to settle some business and buy a wedding dress, and apparently decided to surprise him by coming home early. Now she was lying on the ground, broken like a glass doll dropped from a great height.

He'd knelt there, gathered her up in his arms, rocking her, making a strange, howling sound that seemed to rise up out of the earth itself, through his knees and belly and chest. Just remembering wrung his stomach and brought out a cold sweat all over him.

"From the looks of you," Tristan observed, "I'd say you recall it, all right." He scratched his chin again. "I work for the man who owns that stage line," he said, at his leisure.

"There was a good-sized payroll on board, on its way to the bank in Silver City. My employer would like to know where that money wound up, among other things."

Shay rubbed his eyes angrily with a thumb and forefinger. "Five people were killed that day," he said. "Was your 'employer' ever interested in that?"

"There wasn't a hell of a lot he could do about it," Tristan pointed out coolly. "The money, on the other hand, might be salvageable."

"It's scattered from here to Mexico City by now."

"You make any effort to find out what happened— Marshal? Or were you already a drinkin' man by then?"

Shay spat a curse. "I raised a posse and tracked those bastards from one end of this state to the other. We never turned up so much as a nose hair."

"Could be they've been right here in Prominence, all along, blending in with the town folk. They didn't leave many clues behind, as I understand it."

"Just bodies and an empty strongbox," Shay said bitterly.

"You got a barber in this town?" Saint-Laurent shoved his .45 back into the holster and stood.

It took Shay a moment or two to catch up. "What?"

"If I'm going to live in polite company, I'd better get a shave and wash this walnut juice out of my hair. Do you have a home, Marshal, or do you just wear those same clothes every day and live right here at the jail?"

Shay stood, hands raised to chest level, palms out. "Wait just a damn minute, here. You may be my brother, but you're a might too free with your insults for my taste. And why in hell and tarnation would anybody put walnut juice in their hair?"

Tristan reached for the pistol he'd taken from Shay and handed it over. Shay might not have spoken at all for all the mind his brother paid. "It's going to be a shock to the town, I imagine, there being two of us. We'd best take things slowly. Roust the barber out of bed and fetch him over here. And borrow a washtub and some soap while you're about it."

"If you're through spouting orders," Shay said, passing his brother in the open doorway of the cell, "maybe I can get a word in sideways." He went to the stove, jerked open the door, and stirred the embers with a poker. The coffee in the blue enamel pot on top was two days old, by his reckoning, which ought to give it some kick. "First of all, if you want a bath and a barber, you just take yourself down the street to the hotel and hire a room. And don't be trying to give anybody the impression that you're me, if that's what you've got in mind. I've lived in this town all my life and these folks know me. They'd see right through you."

"What good is being a twin if you can't fool a few people now and then?" Tristan smoothed his beard, sighed and grinned again. "I imagine you're right, though. They've probably forgotten what you look like sober. And when was the last time you took a bath?"

Shay added fresh grounds to the moldering brew in the coffeepot, grasped the handle, and gave it a shake for good measure. "I've taken all the guff I want from you," he said.

"You got a woman?" Tristan watched him with interest, waiting for an answer.

For no earthly reason, Shay thought of Aislinn Lethaby, over at the hotel dining hall, where he took his supper whenever he couldn't cadge a meal from one of his sisters. She was tall, with dark hair and whiskey-brown eyes, and about as different from Grace as one woman could be from another. She belonged, as it happened, to the growing and outspoken faction that found him objectionable, and she seldom missed a chance to let him know it. "No," he said. Since Grace's death, he'd taken his none-too-discreet comforts with a certain widow of faulty reputation and left off courting altogether.

But he thought about Aislinn, all right. He thought about her a lot.

Tristan stood in the doorway to Shay's office now, arms

folded, leaning against the woodwork. He looked like a trail bum, and it nettled some to know he counted himself too fancy to be taken for Shay. "Damn, but you feel sorry for yourself, don't you?" Tristan asked. He blew out a brief, disgusted snort. "You know, little brother, before I leave this hind-tit town, I'm going to make a point of kicking your ass from howdy-do to farewell. It's long overdue, I can see that."

Shay had been stuffing more wood into the stove, in hopes of heating the sludge in the coffeepot. At Tristan's words, however, he straightened, and let his hands rest on his hips. "Maybe you'd like to start right now," he said evenly. He could do with a good brawl, no holds barred, and since Prominence was mostly a quiet town, he didn't get many such opportunities. "And I'll thank you not to call me 'little brother.'"

Tristan thrust himself away from the woodwork, strolled over, and reached for the coffeepot. Flipping up the lid with a motion of his thumb, he peered inside and grimaced. "You aren't much of a cook, either." With that, he took the pot to the door and flung the contents into the street. Then he returned, ladled in some water from a bucket on a bench near the stove, sloshed it around in the pot and threw that water out, too. When he'd assembled a fresh batch and put it on to brew, and only then, he addressed Shay again. "Just think," he said, "how much you might accomplish if you could be in two places at once."

Shay was intrigued, in spite of himself. The prospect of finding the men who'd murdered Grace and the others in the course of the robbery had new appeal, now that his head was clear, and it didn't seem quite so hopeless as before. Somehow, he'd gotten stuck behind that incident, and he knew it had to be resolved before he could move on. "We'd never be able to keep something like this a secret," he pointed out. "Prominence is a small town."

"I just want to keep folks guessing, confuse them a little. Stir things up and see what happens." He paused thoughtfully, then flashed an amicable grin. "Tell the barber I'll shoot him in both knees if he says a word about there being two of us," he said. "That's news I'd like to break in my own time." Spotting the shaving mirror next to the stove, he stooped to peer into it. "And don't forget to bring me a bathtub."

He looked halfway decent for a change, Aislinn thought uncharitably, as she set a plate of bacon, eggs and fried potatoes down in front of Marshal McQuillan. He'd had his hair trimmed up, and there was a pinkish glow about him, as if somebody had scrubbed him down with a wire brush.

"Thank you, ma'am," he said, with that tilted grin that always made Aislinn mad enough to spit. It wasn't so much the audacity it conveyed that stirred her temper as her own involuntary response, a warm, aching shift, somewhere deep down, in a place nobody had any business affecting. Shay McQuillan in particular; he was trouble, and every woman in town knew it, though some were not dissuaded by this simple wisdom.

She'd already reached up and patted her dark hair, in back where the pins usually came loose, before she caught herself. She felt color sting her cheekbones, and turned around so fast to make her escape that she nearly collided with Cletus Frye, the undertaker. She thought she heard the marshal chuckle under his breath, but she couldn't be certain.

"Good morning, Miss Lethaby," Cletus said, removing his hat. Cletus was unfailingly polite, and not hard to look at, either, with his thick, russet-colored hair and earnest brown eyes, but he was courting one of the other girls, Suzanne. Aislinn wasn't looking for a husband anyway.

"Cletus," Aislinn replied, with a distracted little nod. The morning stage had just pulled in across the street, and there were cattlemen in town, too, since several ranches in the area were hiring. There was no time to dally.

Throughout the coming hour, as she rushed from kitchen to dining room, carrying trays and coffeepots and bearing away dirty dishes, however, her gaze kept straying to the marshal's table, where he lingered, reading a newspaper and sipping his coffee. What was worse, he somehow managed to intercept every single glance and smile at her, each time, slow and easy. By the time he left, her nerves had all congregated in the pit of her stomach, where they bounced like a handful of acorns dropped into a bucket.

She took momentary refuge on the porch off the hotel's kitchen, bunching her long apron into one hand and blotting her face and the back of her neck with it.

"What's got you so riled, girl?" demanded Eugenie, the sturdy, rough-voiced woman who ran the kitchen. "You look like somebody what's been throwed headfirst into a nettle patch and dragged back out by the ankles."

Aislinn took a deep breath and smiled. The work at the hotel was hard, but Eugenie looked after her "girls," made sure they didn't go astray and genuinely cared about their well-being. They were required to attend church on Sundays, write to their folks once a week if they had any, keep their shoes polished and their pinafores starched crisp and mended, and return to the dormitory in the stuffy hotel attic before eight P.M., provided they weren't working the supper shift. In that case, they had until ten. "I'm all right," she said. "Really."

Eugenie grinned, revealing one or two gaps in an otherwise substantial set of teeth. "That McQuillan boy cleaned up pretty good," she commented. "If I was thirty years younger, I might just lasso him for myself."

Aislinn ran the sleeve of her dress across her forehead. It was hot, and her white pinafore, fresh and perfect just a few hours before, was now wilted and smudged. "I'm surprised at you, Eugenie. You're one of the smartest women I know. I wouldn't have thought you could be fooled by such a man."

"What do you mean, 'such a man'?" Eugenie retorted.

She seemed disgruntled, but then, that was a part of her usual countenance.

"Well, look at him," Aislinn whispered. "He's drunk more often than not. He doesn't shave for days at a time, and nobody ever sleeps in that jailhouse but him. He'd be nothing more than a saddle bum if he weren't too lazy to mount a horse. If you ask me, he's a disgrace to the badge!"

"He's a good man who got his heart broke real bad," Eugenie said quietly. "The woman he meant to marry was killed less than two years back, and a thing like that can be mighty hard to get over."

Aislinn could have argued that other people faced tragedy and went on; she'd done so herself, after the fire, and so had her two young brothers, but she saw by the expression in Eugenie's eyes that it would serve no purpose. Besides, she was private about her past, and she hadn't confided in anyone. "I'd better get back to work," she said, and hurried inside.

The kitchen was sweltering, and the dining room, brimming with hungry cowboys and other wayfaring souls, wasn't much cooler. After a quick trip upstairs to change her pinafore, Aislinn threw herself into waiting tables and, by midafternoon, when her shift ended, she was tuckered out.

While the two other young women who'd served breakfast and dinner with her stripped to their petticoats and collapsed onto their cots, however, Aislinn untied her shoes, kicked them off, and put on a plain brown calico dress. After hanging her garments carefully on their allotted pegs, she took down her hair, brushed and wound it into a single heavy plait, splashed her face with tepid water, and started for the door.

"Aislinn Lethaby," scolded her friend, Eloise, from one of the narrow beds, "I swear it makes me weary just to know you. Where are you off to on such a hot afternoon?"

"I just need a walk, that's all."

"A walk?" scoffed another of the serving girls. "You're

not even wearing any shoes. Besides, you've been on your feet all day.''

Aislinn didn't pause to explain that she never wore shoes if she could help it. She and her brothers had grown up wild as renegade Apaches, back in Maine, and they'd gone barefoot from the day school let out until the first hard frost. She still loved the feel of green grass and good dirt under her feet better than most anything else, and when she was outside, she could be that other, younger Aislinn, with parents and at home.

She left the hotel by a rear door, and followed a narrow alley that ran parallel to Prominence's main street, gnawing on an apple snatched from the pantry as she passed.

Dorrie McQuillan, the marshal's sister, was sitting on the little porch behind the general store, calmly smoking a long, slim cigar. Miss Dorrie, with her dishwater-blond hair and thin-lashed brown eyes, was not a handsome woman, being tall and thin and somewhat dour of expression, but it was rumored that she'd once run away with a peddler. Her father, Shamus the elder, had caught up with them just in time, folks said. He'd beat the daylights out of the rascal, had him jailed and dragged his daughter home by the hair.

Aislinn nodded cordially, and Miss Dorrie returned the favor, blowing out a shifting cloud of blue smoke. You didn't have to live in Prominence too long to learn that Miss Dorrie was a great trial to her sister, Miss Cornelia, who had a head for figures and had never eloped, taken strong spirits or smoked a cigar. No doubt having the marshal in the family circle was an additional cross for Cornelia, who was a very beautiful woman, for all her coldness of manner, with clouds of auburn hair and bright green eyes.

Aislinn smiled to herself and picked up her pace. She passed the feed store, the telegraph office, and the doctor's, and then there was nothing between her and the open countryside but the saloon. She moved to the farthest side of the alley and walked purposefully, with squared shoulders, her eyes fixed straight ahead.

She had cause to give the place a wide berth—once, she'd seen a man relieving himself through the open door, and another time, she'd been forced to fend off the advances of a drunkard. Still, it was better to pass behind the saloon, because the front was far more perilous, with cowboys and drifters and gamblers constantly trailing in and out in various states of temper and inebriation. The very men who treated her politely in the dining room could turn into fiends, whether filled with drink or just the prospect of it.

"Probably not the best place to take a stroll, ma'am," observed a familiar voice, just when she thought she'd passed by unnoticed. She didn't need to look at the marshal to know he was the one talking to her. She turned her head, a quelling glance at the ready, but at the mere sight of him, it seemed that her heart slammed itself into her throat. His badge shone in the sunlight and his clothes were clean, if well worn. How could a bath and barbering change a man so much?

"I appreciate your concern, Marshal," she said. "Of course, if you would do something about the criminal element in this town, a woman could walk safely anywhere."

He grinned that grin—he should have had a license for it, in her opinion, because it was unquestionably as lethal as the gun on his hip. "You're right," he said, with a touch to the brim of his hat. "I've been remiss in my peacekeeping." He was chewing on a matchstick, and he rolled it from one side of his mouth to the other as he pushed away from the saloon doorway to approach. "I'll escort you wherever you're going. Make sure you get there all right."

Aislinn felt her neck heat up, and hoped the flush wouldn't climb into her face. "No, thank you," she said. "I'm fine on my own."

"I'm afraid I can't take no for an answer, ma'am," he

replied, with a note of genial regret. "Why, how could I sleep at night, knowing I'd let a poor, helpless little thing like you walk past a *saloon* without the full protection of the law?"

She expelled a sigh. "Helpless? Believe me, Marshal, I can look after myself." If he only knew, she thought, and was tempted to enlighten him, as to all she'd survived in her life. All she'd overcome.

"I reckon if that were the case," he said, showing no inclination to retreat, "you wouldn't have felt compelled to mention your concern about the safety of our female citizens."

The end of the alleyway was in sight; the graveyard next to the Presbyterian church was just ahead, set apart from the scourge of commerce by a split-rail fence. Beyond the church was a spring-fed pond, and a big, sunbathed rock where Aislinn loved to sit, dreaming and dangling her feet in the water.

Her patience was hard-won, but she managed to speak calmly, and with dignity. She turned and looked up into McQuillan's face. "You have made your point," she said firmly, and she knew her eyes were flashing. "Now, kindly let me go my way. There are those of us who work for a living, and our free time is precious."

He laughed, swept off his hat and struck himself in the chest with it, as if to stanch a bleeding wound. His hair was the palest gold and at once ruffled and sleek, though in need of trimming. It glinted in the sunshine, like stuff spun from a sorcerer's spindle, while his eyes were so dark a blue as to seem almost purple. She'd been serving him meals most every day for a year. Why hadn't she noticed, in all that time, just how devastatingly, dangerously good-looking he was?

"I can see I'm going to have my work cut out for me, ma'am," he said, "but I'm determined to win your confidence. Yes, indeed, I am determined."

Aislinn turned, hoisted her skirts as far as she dared,

and started up the cemetery fence. "Please don't trouble yourself," she said, perched astride the top rail. "Good day, Marshal." Having so spoken, she made to jump down on the other side, caught her dress on a splinter or some such, and landed in the grass in an ungainly heap, her skirts over her head.

Face aflame, heart pounding with humiliation, Aislinn scrambled to her feet, just as the lawman vaulted over the fence. He was making a downright heroic effort not to laugh, but she was in no position to appreciate the sacrifice. "Are you all right?" he asked, touching her cheek with the backs of his fingers in a curiously gentle way.

Aislinn busied herself, brushing off her skirts and smoothing her hair, which had begun to come loose from its careful braid. When she looked at him, her eyes were full of angry tears, and she would have choked if she'd tried to speak.

"You *are* hurt," he said, and he sounded genuinely worried. He shifted, so that they were very close, and she felt the heat and easy, restrained power of him. For one wonderful, dreadful moment, she thought he was going to kiss her. Then, in the next instant, he stepped back. "Guess it's mostly your pride that's smarting right now." He put his hat on, and she saw a wicked humor in his eyes, though he had the decency not to grin. "I'd best be getting back, I suppose."

Back to the saloon, Aislinn thought ungenerously, but at the same time she was feeling a tenderness toward this man that she couldn't account for, even to herself. Maybe Eugenie was right, and Shay McQuillan really was a good man, through the worst of his grieving and ready to go on.

"Did you love her?" She had never planned to ask such a bold and impertinent question; the words came out by themselves. "Grace, I mean?"

He turned, thumbs hooked into his gunbelt, eyes hidden in the shadow cast by his hat brim. "Yes," he answered, seriously and without hesitation. "Very much."

Aislinn stood for a moment, taking a new measure of Shay McQuillan. She'd been so certain, until he'd spoken those few telling words, that she understood the workings of his mind and the substance of his spirit. While she watched him, he climbed over the fence and walked away, headed toward Main Street.

When she reached the pond, she found it peaceful, dappled with sunlight and windblown leaves. As she climbed onto the favored rock and settled herself there, she saw a deer approach the water's edge on the opposite side. After studying her intently, the animal lowered its graceful head to drink, sending delicate, silvery ripples fanning out over the surface.

Aislinn slid to the stone's edge and slipped her feet into the water, and the sensation was so delicious that she let her head fall back and gave a long sigh. Then she unraveled her braid and combed her hair with her fingers, letting it tumble down past her shoulders to reach her waist.

The moment might in fact have been perfect, had it not been for the disturbing, persistent awareness that by changing something in himself, Shay McQuillan had changed something in her as well.

Chapter
2

༄

$\mathscr{F}$OR SOMEBODY WHO'D BEEN so concerned about keeping his presence in Prominence a secret until the right moment came, Saint-Laurent wasn't making much of an effort to stay out of sight. When Shay got back to his office, following the encounter with Aislinn, he found his twin sitting in the best chair in the place, flipping through a pile of wanted posters. His feet were propped on the desk.

The usurper assessed him thoughtfully, then broke into a grin that belonged on Shay's own face. Damn, but it was peculiar, looking at Saint-Laurent, like being haunted by his own ghost. "Anybody ever tell you you're a handsome devil?" Tristan asked, sober as St. Peter guarding the Gates.

Shay glared at him, stormed over to the coffeepot, and poured himself a dose. He'd been sober less than twenty-four hours, he was still trying to make sense of what he'd felt, seeing Aislinn, touching her, and he'd been confronted with a long-lost brother who might have been peeled off the surface of a mirror. By God, there should be a limit to what one man was expected to deal with in the course of a single day.

"You happen to have another badge lying around here

someplace?'' Tristan asked. He didn't stand on ceremony, you had to say that for him.

Shay slammed his cup down on top of a bookcase crammed full of ancient volumes, papers, and clippings from half the newspapers published west of the Mississippi. ''If I did, I sure as hell wouldn't hand it over to you. For all I know, you're an outlaw.''

Saint-Laurent swung his feet to the floor and stood. ''If I were, I'd have put a bullet through your head last night, when I had the drop on you. It would have been an easy matter to pin on that star and step right into your boots.'' The slight stress he put on the word ''easy'' did not go unnoticed.

Still, Shay had to admit, it was true that Tristan could have killed him, if that had been his intention. He'd been chewing on the fact, in one corner of his mind or another, since the night before, when he'd woken up with a gun at his throat. On the other hand, though Saint-Laurent was clearly a blood relation, that didn't mean his story was true, or that he could be trusted. He could be a distant relative, instead of a brother, or just a man who happened to bear an uncanny resemblance to Shay himself.

''If that's what you're figuring on doing, you'd better shoot me right here and now,'' Shay said. ''If you can.''

Tristan perched on the edge of the desk, arms folded. He rolled his eyes and glanced at the .45 riding low on Shay's hip. ''Relax, Marshal. I may not be your friend, but I'm not your enemy, either. I just want to recover the money from that robbery and ride out of here. That's all.''

''Fair enough, but I've got one question. What do you need me for?''

''I guess I must be the smart one, as well as the firstborn. I told you before, Marshal—you make it possible for me to be in two places at once. I like that idea; it ought to keep everybody off balance.''

''Maybe I'll agree to cooperate, and maybe I won't,''

Shay replied. He had a headache, and his nerves were raw. He wondered if Aislinn would have slapped him, if he'd kissed her. "Why should I?"

"You're a lawman. It's your job to bring in those outlaws. Besides, something in my gut tells me you've got another stake in seeing them hang. I can find out what it is easily enough, if you don't feel inclined to tell me."

Shay turned his back on this brother he had never known, never even imagined, and wondered for a fraction of a second what it would have been like if they'd grown up together. For a moment, he felt the loss of those years spent apart. "The driver of that coach was a friend of mine," he said gruffly. "A fine, decent man, with a family."

"No doubt he was," Tristan said mildly, "but you'll have to do better than that if you want me off your back. A thing like that's a tragedy, any way you look at it, but it wouldn't undo a man like you."

It felt like every word was torn from his throat, a separate strip of hide. "There was a woman on board— Grace Warfield was her name. She and I planned to be married."

Tristan was silent for a long time. Then he laid a hand on Shay's right shoulder. "I'm sorry," he said.

Shay turned around, unable and unwilling to say more about Grace. "What makes you think we could find those desperadoes, after all this time? It isn't like we didn't look, me and that posse—we did. We turned out every hayloft, every rat-hole saloon and whore's nest for fifty miles around."

"So did I," Tristan said gravely. "They're not out there, whoever they are. And that means they've got to be around here someplace. Think, damn it. Who do you know who might figure they had cause to blow a bridge out from under a coach full of innocent people? Why do that instead of just holding up the stage and riding off with the loot?"

Tristan's reference to the innocence of the victims was calculated to get under his skin, he knew that, but the ploy was effective all the same. Shay's right hand knotted into a fist at his side, but he couldn't quite bring himself to smash a face that looked so much like his own.

"Go ahead," Tristan said quietly. "Hit me, if it'll make you feel better. Then maybe we can get on with what we've got to do."

Shay uncurled his fingers.

Tristan folded his arms and grinned. Again. "Maybe you're smarter than I've given you credit for, up to now," he said. "If you'd blacked my eye, and then seen the sense in what I'm proposing—which you inevitably would have—I'd have had to give you a shiner to match mine. For the sake of appearances, you understand. I'd have been happy to oblige, of course."

Shay huffed out a heavy sigh. "It would almost be worth it. What do you have in mind?"

"Have a seat, Marshal," Tristan answered, with a grand gesture toward the desk and, presumably, the chair behind it, "and I'll explain."

Shay sat down, barely resisting the urge to swing his feet up onto the desktop, as Tristan had done. As he himself had done, ever since the day he was sworn in as the marshal. He folded his hands instead and waited.

Tristan began to talk, pacing back and forth before the desk like a big-town lawyer in front of a jury box, and damned if his ideas didn't make a certain amount of sense. Folks would soon guess that there were two of them, but the resultant confusion was sure to provide certain advantages.

When the speech was over, Shay opened a drawer and reluctantly took out a badge that had been worn by his predecessor, Big Dan Collins. He'd been Dan's deputy for five years, until the older man was killed breaking up a brawl down at the Yellow Garter Saloon, and he'd never admired anyone as much, before or since.

He polished the nickel star against his shirtfront before handing it over. "If you're going to get yourself shot," he said, a little hoarse all of the sudden, "make sure you get hit someplace where this badge won't be marked up. I want it back looking just like new."

Tristan pinned the star to his chest in precisely the same place Shay wore his, without looking. "I'll need some practice at being you," he said, letting Shay's warning go unremarked, as usual. He cocked a thumb toward the far end of the street. "You're clearly a man who likes his whiskey. What brand do I drink?"

"You don't," Shay said, with a grin that was all his own. He leaned back in the chair, his hands cupped behind his head. "You've decided to redeem yourself. Why, you might even want to go forward during Sunday's church meeting and give your heart to Jesus."

Tristan let that pass, drawing a cheroot from his shirt pocket, along with a match, which he struck against the outer edge of Shay's desktop.

"I don't use tobacco, either," Shay pointed out. He paused, considering Tristan's several allusions to his status as the elder brother. "What makes you so sure you were born first?"

None too cheerfully, Tristan shook out the match and tossed it, put the cheroot away. "I've got a birthmark on my right thigh. You don't. According to my mother—the woman who raised me, that is—the midwife on the wagon train took note of the fact."

Shay put his feet on the floor and leaned forward as a thought struck him. "Where's your horse? Somebody must have seen you ride in."

Tristan laughed grimly. "I hope it doesn't take much longer for your head to clear, because, God help me, I've got to depend on you. It was pitch black outside when I got to town, and I was wearing a hat and a long coat. You'll remember that I had a beard, too." He made to stroke the absent whiskers with one hand, obviously a habit of long-standing, then glanced ruefully toward the stove, where the sleep-addled barber had disposed of a pile of walnut-colored hair early that morning. "I told the man at the livery stable that the horse was yours, a gift from an old friend."

"He must have been drunk, half asleep, or both."

"He did say I put him in mind of somebody, though he couldn't rightly think who it was." Tristan smiled at the memory, then cast a glance toward the window. "It'll be dark in a couple of hours. Start talking, Marshal. Who am I going to meet when I walk out of this place, and what will they expect from me? Are you a chatty sort, or a man of few words?"

"What do you think?" Shay challenged. He was hungover, he couldn't chase Aislinn Lethaby out of his head, and he was still getting used to the fact that Saint-Laurent existed at all. And then there was the implication that he, Shay, wouldn't be able to bring the robbers to justice without his brother's help. He didn't have the patience to be cordial on top of all that.

"I think you don't say much—you like to watch and listen and work things through before you put in your two bits. You're at home on a horse, and probably fairly fast with that forty-five, when you're sober. As a kid, you got good marks in school, but you spent a lot of time staring out the window, wishing you were somewhere else. You liked to read, still do, and you're a good pool player, at least early in the day. Course, the way your hands shake, we'll be lucky if you don't get yourself killed in a shootout before this is over."

Shay ignored the reference to his unsteady hands— mostly because it was true—and studied his brother with calm amazement. Tristan's assessment had been uncannily apt. "How did you know all that?"

"Simple. Except for the pool playing—poker's my game—and the liquor palsy, I could have been describing myself. You've got a callus between the first and second fingers of your left hand, the kind left by the slide of a cue stick. Tell me about your sisters."

It was Shay's turn to grin. "They hate me," he said. "Or, at least, Cornelia does."

When the mosquitoes came out and the sun was going down, Aislinn reluctantly made her way toward the hotel. It was early evening, and bawdy music spilled out the back door of the saloon as she passed, but there was no sign of the marshal. She didn't attempt to convince herself that the disappointment she felt was really relief.

For her, twilight was the loneliest part of the day. Folks were locking up their places of business and heading home to supper, and in the lull before the night's revelry would begin at the Yellow Garter, she could hear the voices of women on the doorsteps of the town's barewood houses, calling their children in.

She bit her lower lip, remembering her own gentle, harried mother, her hardworking father, a country doctor. They'd both perished in a hotel fire, during a rare visit to the city, where they'd gone to celebrate an anniversary.

Aislinn and her small brothers, Thomas and Mark, had been at home when the news came. She could still see the expression on the constable's kindly face, when he'd stopped by, first thing one bright summer morning, carrying the weight of the news in his eyes as well as upon his shoulders.

They'd had no kin, she and her brothers, and there was very little money. The house was mortgaged, and even though Aislinn managed to sell it right away, it took all but a few dollars of the profits to pay their debts. Several men had come forward with offers of marriage, and she supposed accepting would have been the simplest solution, but something in her had rebelled against a loveless union, undertaken for the sake of expediency. Too, being a doctor's daughter, she'd known what was expected of a wife, and being just sixteen at the time, she hadn't felt ready to give that.

In the end, she had enrolled her brothers in a boarding school in Portland, Maine, using most of the remaining funds to pay for their room and board, and then gone to an agency, seeking employment in the West. She planned to save her wages, buy a little piece of land, and send for Thomas and Mark as soon as she could put a proper roof over their heads.

She'd found work immediately, serving food in a railroad dining hall in Kansas City, and she'd left there only when a certain unwanted suitor had become too persistent. She'd been moving from one town to another ever since, traveling farther west each time.

She was nineteen now, with a fair sum saved, and she'd found an abandoned homestead a few miles out of town, and hoped to make an offer of purchase very soon. Once the transaction was complete, she would send for her brothers, who waited anxiously to join her.

She hoped to marry one day, and have children of her own, but life had made her wary, and the more independent she grew, the less willing she was to settle for anything less than precisely the right man.

Nearing the entrance to the hotel's kitchen, she heard the clatter of stove lids and kettles and heavy china plates, the brisk, busy conversation between the cook and the serving girls, and, beneath it all, the bedrock of Eugenie's authority. It was, in a small way, a homecoming, and Aislinn found herself smiling a little as she went inside, toward the wavering light of the lanterns.

"There you are," Eugenie said, up to her elbows in a pan full of hot, soapy water. Beside her were stacks of crockery, waiting to be washed. "I was just about to send Mathilda out looking for you. Get yourself a plate of supper and don't give me any sass, miss. I won't have it said that we don't feed our girls proper."

Aislinn was hungry, and glad that someone had been

awaiting her return; that she belonged, however tenuously, in this place. The kitchen was warm, and so was Eugenie's affection, and her spirits rose as she obediently helped herself to a slice of venison roast, a mashed turnip with butter, and a corn biscuit. She took a seat at the trestle table, within the golden glimmer of a lantern, and began to eat.

Eugenie was in an unusually talkative mood, even for her. "Shall I put on a kettle of hot water for you?"

"Please," Aislinn said. Everyone knew she was fussy about cleanliness; each night, behind the rickety changing screen in the attic dormitory, she took a sponge bath. To the other girls, such behavior seemed as eccentric as going barefoot at every opportunity. "It looks as though the dining room's been doing a lively business tonight." She indicated the stacks of dishes with a nod. When she was finished eating, she would elbow Eugenie aside and take over the dishwashing task herself.

"Shamus's boy was here," Eugenie said, with much portent, and it was a moment before Aislinn realized she was talking about Shay McQuillan, the marshal. The word "boy" was a misnomer of monumental proportions; McQuillan was all man, with no apologies offered. "I believe he hoped to see you."

Something foundered in the back of Aislinn's throat and flailed its way to the pit of her stomach, like a bird falling down a chimney pipe and fluttering in the ashes of a cold stove. "Nonsense," she said, shakily. "One woman is the same as another to him. Everybody knows that."

Eugenie left her dishwashing to pump water into a large kettle and set it on the stove with a ringing thump. "Do they?"

She remembered looking up into those too-blue, too-knowledgeable eyes, and her throat closed so tight that she nearly choked on her food. After a few moments of recovery, she stood, meeting Eugenie's challenging gaze directly. "I'm sorry," she said, in even tones. "I guess the marshal is your friend, and you're right to stand up for him. But I'm entitled to my own opinion, and I think he's bad news, pure and simple."

Surprisingly, Eugenie chuckled. "Oh, he's that for sure. But there's such a thing as the right kind of misery, gal. I hope you find that out before it's too late."

The cook guffawed. "Lawd, Eugenie, you sure are right about that."

Aislinn scraped her plate into the scrap bucket, which would be set out by the back step for a scrawny dog named Bert at closing time, and took over the task of washing the dishes. She had to wait for her bathwater to heat anyway. Eugenie and the cook busied themselves preparing for the morning, giggling like a pair of schoolgirls, and Aislinn just shook her head.

When she went upstairs, the attic room was sweltering, as usual, so she pried open the single window, being as quiet as she could, since some of the girls were sleeping.

She bathed, as always, put on a nightgown, unplaited her hair, brushed it thoroughly, and braided it again. She'd crawled into bed, and was silently repeating her nightly prayers, asking God to keep Thomas and Mark safe and well, when she heard someone weeping.

At first, she thought it was one of the other serving girls—the new ones, frightened and far from home, often cried themselves to sleep at night—but the sound was thin, and seemed to rise on the hot summer air.

No one else stirred, and Aislinn honestly tried to ignore the soft, snuffling sobs, but in the end, she couldn't. She got up and went to the window, peering into the thick darkness. The night was a thrumming cacophony of saloon music, one or two barking dogs, a braying mule, the celebratory whoops of cowboys and even the occasional gunshot—she knew a moment's piercing fear for the marshal's safety—but underlying it all was the weeping, sorrowful and hopeless.

Far below, in the narrow space between the hotel and

the general store, a small figure crouched. Aislinn started to call out, then decided that would be a bad idea, for the girls sharing the room with her worked hard all day, and needed their rest. Exasperated, she pulled on a wrapper and made her way down the rear stairs in cautious haste. In the kitchen, now empty, she lit a lantern and un-latched the back door.

The brindle dog was taking a noisy supper from the scrap pail; he looked up at Aislinn and then went on lapping up leftovers. Hoping no one would come along and fasten the door behind her, she moved carefully around the corner of the building.

"Who's there?" she called softly, holding the lantern aloft in an effort to make out the other person's identity.

The figure was a small, trembling bundle, garishly dressed in purple and red taffeta and young, judging by her voice. "Go away and tend to your own business."

Aislinn crept closer. "I'm afraid I've never been very good at that," she said. "Are you hurt?" She had an impression of fierce, glittering eyes and terrible fury, barely held in check, and was reminded of a small animal, struggling in a trap. "Shall I fetch the doctor?"

"I told you, just go away. There's nothing you or that rummy old sawbones can do for me."

Light spilled over the tumble of taffeta and feathers and fear, and a small thrill of excitement went through Aislinn as she realized that the young woman was one of the dancing girls from the Yellow Garter Saloon. Her curiosity was overwhelming, and exceeded only by pity. "I'm not going to leave you. It's obvious that something is wrong."

The woman gave a hoarse, despondent laugh and wiped her nose with one hand. "You're one of those women who pours coffee and serves flapjacks in the hotel restaurant, aren't you?" she challenged.

It occurred to Aislinn that if she and the others could wonder and whisper about the soiled doves at the Yellow

Garter, the reverse might be true as well. "Yes," she answered, crouching down beside the fallen woman. "My name is Aislinn Lethaby. What do they call you?"

Another bitter laugh. "You don't want to know what they call me," she said. "It would singe your pretty little ears." She paused, then went on with a sort of forlorn defiance. "My mama and papa called me Liza Sue, but I've been somebody else for a long time. What kind of name is 'Aislinn'? You a foreigner or something?"

Aislinn smiled, set the lantern down, and reached quickly to steady it when it tilted. "My mother took the name from a book. It's Irish, I think. I was born in Maine, and so were both my parents."

Liza Sue sniffled. "That's a whole lot more than I asked you," she said. In the dim, wavering light, Aislinn could see that the other woman's face was badly bruised, as were her upper arms. Her cheeks were streaked with kohl, and the feather on her hat bobbed with a sort of pitiful gaiety. "Listen, I got beat up by a drunken cowboy. Are you satisfied? I'll be all right by tomorrow."

Aislinn gaped at her, horrified. "We have to go and complain to the marshal. Whoever did this should be arrested!"

The prostitute shook her head, marveling. "If I did that, I'd just get beat up all over again."

"Surely the marshal wouldn't—"

Liza Sue's smile was grim. "It isn't Shay McQuillan I'm afraid of—he'd throw the feller in jail right enough. The next day, he'd get out, and come after me again, only it'd be a whole lot worse the second time. No, ma'am. If Marshal McQuillan asks me how I got myself all black and blue, I'll tell him I fell down the stairs. You say different, and I'll swear on the preacher's prayer book that you're a liar."

"Surely you don't mean to go back to that place?"

"Where else would I go?"

Aislinn flung out her hands in frustration and nearly

overset the lantern. "I don't know. I could speak to Eugenie—somebody runs off to get married at least once a month, and they always need help—"

"You really are addlepated," Liza Sue scoffed, but her tones were hollow and her smeared eyes were enormous with a yearning she couldn't quite hide. "I step foot over the threshold of that place and they'll toss me right out again, quick as they would that old dog by the back step. Quicker, probably."

Aislinn considered the dilemma. Liza Sue had certainly strayed from the fold, but she was well spoken and obviously intelligent. "Do you have any other clothes? If we scrubbed that stuff off your face—"

"We'd never fool anybody."

"I can't solve the whole problem myself, you know," Aislinn pointed out. "For my part, I don't see where you've got a whole lot to lose."

"You'd lie for me? Why?"

"I wouldn't be lying, you would."

Liza Sue giggled tentatively. "It won't work. I've got these bruises, and somebody's sure to remember me from the Yellow Garter."

"There are a lot of ways to get hurt—you said as much yourself. And if someone recognizes you, well, it seems unlikely to me that they'd want to admit to frequenting the saloon, not in respectable surroundings like the hotel dining room, anyway."

The other woman was silent for a few moments. "I don't have any clothes. Jake Kingston took them away from me when I signed on at the Yellow Garter."

"Then I'll give you one of my dresses. I have two to spare." Another silence. The brindle dog came around the corner and tried to lick Aislinn's face. She pushed him away in a distracted motion of one hand.

"Why would you want to do this?" Liza Sue asked. "When those hotel folks find out, they'll send you packing, right along with me."

"That's probably true," Aislinn confessed. "But I've got somewhere to go." She was thinking of the homestead, with its sagging roof, broken windows and overgrown vegetable patch. She *almost* had somewhere to go, and in another month, if she scrimped, she'd finally have the funds to send for her brothers.

"Pardon me, but that doesn't answer my question."

Aislinn sighed. "I'm not sure," she said. "It's not that I'm particularly noble or anything like that . . ."

"I didn't say you were."

"I can't leave you like this, Liza Sue. My conscience will chew me up alive if I do." Aislinn stood, resigned to her duty. "If you don't come with me, I swear I'll go and report this whole incident to the marshal. You can say I'm lying, but it will be your word against mine."

"Hellfire and spit," Liza Sue muttered, getting up. "You just don't listen, do you?"

"Come on. You can hide in the pantry while I go upstairs and find you something to wear. We'll stuff those clothes into the stove and burn them."

"You won't either," came the protest, but Liza Sue tottered along behind as Aislinn led the way toward the back door. Mercifully, no one had bolted it.

"Hush, now," Aislinn warned, as they crept inside. Every board in the kitchen floor seemed to creak as they crossed the room, but soon Liza Sue was safely tucked away in the pantry, with the smoky stump of a tallow candle for light. She looked small and fearful in the gloom, like a bit of colored paper crumpled up and discarded.

"You'll come back, won't you? You won't forget I'm here?"

"I won't forget," Aislinn assured her. "Just be quiet."

She was halfway up the rear stairs, the lantern in one hand, when Eugenie appeared on the landing with a lamp of her own. "Aislinn? What's the matter? You feelin' peaky?"

Aislinn's heart pumped with sudden and painful force. "I was hungry," she said, and hated herself for the lie. Eugenie was kind, for all her gruff words and ways, and she might have sympathized with Liza Sue's situation. In the end, though, Aislinn couldn't take the risk of explaining; there was simply too much at stake. "I'm sorry if I disturbed you."

Eugenie assessed her in silence, as though weighing what she'd said. Then, with a weary sigh, she nodded and went back to her own room.

Aislinn got out her spare dress, a plain green gown of lightweight wool, praying no one would recognize it, and took the stairs one step at a time, barely daring to breathe. Liza Sue was still cowering in the pantry, but she'd found a piece of bread and was nibbling on it. She looked hungrily at the woolen dress.

"Put this on," Aislinn whispered crisply. The lamp was burning low and the candle had already guttered out. Soon, they'd both be in the dark. "I'll get you some water and soap."

"How are you going to account for me just appearing all of the sudden?" Liza Sue demanded, but she was stripping off her disreputable gown. "This whole plan is plain crazy—"

"Maybe so, but it's the only one we have. You'll sleep in the storeroom next to the dormitory. In the morning, we'll pretend that you've just arrived in town. You can present yourself at the kitchen door and ask for work."

"What if they say no?"

"Oh, for mercy's sake," Aislinn hissed, "stop fussing. We'll worry about that when and if it happens. I told you, Eugenie's always looking for help." She brought a basin of cold water, a sliver of soap and an old dish towel from the kitchen. "Here. Wash your face. Have you eaten? There are some corn biscuits left from supper, and there should be some cold venison, too."

Liza Sue was already scouring industriously, and it

must have hurt plenty, she was so badly bruised. "I'd be obliged for a biscuit," she said.

The second trip up the stairs was more harrowing than the first, for this time Liza Sue was right on Aislinn's heels. They'd left the lantern behind, on the kitchen table, and outside, the brindle dog began to howl plaintively, calling to the absent moon.

There was a line of light under Eugenie's door, and as they passed Aislinn could hear the steady squeak of a rocking chair within. She held her breath and did not release it until they'd reached the threshold of the storeroom.

"Good night," Aislinn whispered, after fetching the blanket from her bed.

Liza Sue's eyes glittered in the gloom. She nodded and slipped back into the darkness.

Chapter
3

$\mathcal{T}$HE MARSHAL CAME TO BREAKFAST the next morning, looking all scrubbed and spit-shined, and put in an order for ham and eggs. That wouldn't have been strange, but for the fact that he'd already been in, an hour before, and consumed a double portion of corned beef hash.

Aislinn, preoccupied with the logistics of getting Liza Sue from the storeroom to the back door, where she could ask for work without arousing too much suspicion, put it down to a hearty appetite. After all those months of seedy living, Marshal McQuillan was surely in sore need of nourishment. Out of loyalty to Eugenie, who thought highly of the man, she even managed a hasty, fretful smile.

"You are a lovely creature," the marshal drawled, rising to leave. He flashed that infamous grin, but to Aislinn's surprise and relief, it didn't affect her as it had before. "Maybe I'll see you tonight, at the dance?"

Aislinn bit her lower lip. The hotel manager put on a social, with music and fruit punch, the first Saturday of every month, but the maids and kitchen and dining room employees were not allowed to attend, lest there be an implication of impropriety. "I'm afraid that's against the rules," she said.

"That," he replied smoothly, taking up his hat, "is a pity. In fact, I'd say there ought to be a law."

Nearby, a red-eyed cowboy with bad teeth slammed down his china mug. "I need more coffee," he barked. "Right now."

The marshal took the large blue enamel coffeepot from Aislinn's hand with easy grace and refilled the cowboy's cup, bending low to speak to him. "What you need," he said mildly, "is a lesson in manners. Talk to the lady that way again, and you'll get one that'll stick with you till your dying day."

The other man backed down, but he didn't look happy about it.

"Thank you," Aislinn said uncertainly, taking back the coffeepot.

"Anytime," said the marshal, and left the dining hall. A glance around the room showed that every woman in the place, whether serving or being served, watched him go. Including Eugenie, though her expression was markedly different from those of the others.

"What do you suppose has gotten into him?" she inquired, under her breath, when Aislinn passed her on the way back to the kitchen for another pot of coffee.

"I don't know," Aislinn answered honestly, "but I think I like him a little better than I did yesterday." For the first time since she'd come to Prominence to work, she found herself lamenting that she couldn't go to the hotel dance. Now that the marshal had apparently lost that irritating ability to slay her with a single, lopsided smile, she wasn't so eager to avoid him.

Sometime during the busy clean-up process between breakfast and dinner, Liza Sue must have seen her chance and slipped downstairs, for when Aislinn went into the kitchen for a rest and a cup of tea, the other woman was there, seated primly across the trestle table from Eugenie, lying like a snake-oil salesman. She'd been in Prominence awhile, she said, staying with relations, but she'd worn out her welcome and they couldn't keep her anymore. The bruises? Yes, well, she was some marked up, wasn't she? She'd caught her toe in the hem of her dress while going after a jar of apricot preserves and fallen right down the cellar stairs. It was a lucky thing she hadn't broken her neck.

Eugenie listened inscrutably, and pondered for a while. Aislinn knew then that she didn't believe the story; Eugenie had made her own way in the world for a great many years, and by her own admission, she'd "come up hard," with no folks to speak of. She glanced Aislinn's way once, making it known that she was nobody's fool, and then cleared her throat.

"Well, girl," she said to Liza Sue, "if you don't mind making up beds and emptying slop jars of a morning, there's a place for you here. You'll have your room and board and four dollars a month. We'll provide you with proper work clothes."

Liza Sue's poor, swollen and discolored face was suffused with color, and her eyes shone with startled excitement. "Oh, thank you, ma'am," she said. "Thank you."

"Humph," Eugenie replied. "We'll see how happy you are after a day of hard work. Cook here will give you some breakfast, and Aislinn can show you where you sleep." She hauled her bulky body up off the bench at the trestle table. "Oh, and one more thing. We abide by stern rules around here. You're free to socialize if you have the inclination, but we expect you in by eight o'clock at night. You got courting to do, you get it done afore then. You'll go to church on Sunday mornings whether you've a mind to or not, and write to your people once a week if you have any. There's no smoking, no swearing and no drinking permitted, and if I ever catch a man above the second-floor landing, day or night, there'll be hell to pay. I reckon I've made myself clear."

"Yes, ma'am," Liza Sue agreed, with an eager nod. She might have been pretty, though it was hard to tell, her features were so distorted.

Eugenie gave Aislinn another long and thoughtful assessment. "See your friend gets settled in proper," she said, and went on about her business without another word.

Aislinn led Liza Sue up the rear stairs and showed her the small dormitory, where there were two empty cots to choose from. The newcomer selected the one nearest the window and stood with her hand resting reverently on the plain iron bedstead, as though it were something grand. When she looked at Aislinn, there were tears shimmering in her eyes.

"I wouldn't have believed it was possible," she said, in a small, tremulous voice. "I thought she'd see right through me, and show me the door."

She saw right through the both of us, Aislinn thought, still mystified. "Eugenie is like a mother hen—she'll squawk and flap her wings now and then, but heaven help the rooster who tries to get to one of her chicks. And Liza Sue, she means what she says about following the rules— a few months ago a girl stayed out all night after a town picnic, and Eugenie bought her a stagecoach ticket home and sent her packing. No amount of crying and begging would change her mind about it."

Liza Sue wiped her cheeks with the back of one hand. "I won't do nothing to ruin my chance," she vowed. "I mean to work like nobody she's ever seen, save my money, and get a new start someplace far away from here."

Aislinn had dreams of her own, and they centered around bringing her brothers out from Maine before winter came to the far West, and making a home out of a tumbledown cabin and a few acres of good land. If Thomas and Mark did odd jobs around town, and she kept her position with the hotel until spring, when they could put in a garden, they might just make it. She certainly understood Liza Sue's determination and high hopes, and she respected her desire to make a decent life for herself. "You'd best go and find Eugenie," she said. "She'll have a list of things for you to do."

"One of my girls is missin'," Jake Kingston bellowed, breathing sour whiskey fumes in Shay's face. "She was a good'un and I want her back!" The interior of the Yellow Garter was dim, the air flecked with dust particles and clouded with stale smoke. The sawdust on the floor was in sorry need of a rake, and a few women had wandered downstairs, half-dressed, hair askew, eyes full of brass and sadness. The poker game in the far corner had been going on since sometime yesterday afternoon and showed no signs of winding down.

Shay rubbed the back of his neck, wondering how he could have spent so much time in a place like this; it was like the colon of hell. Silently, he wished the missing woman Godspeed. "There's no law against taking to your heels, Jake," he said reasonably.

Jake set a bottle and a glass on the bar; Shay ignored them. He was watching the murky mirror behind the bartender's broad back, remembering the night Big Dan was knifed between the shoulder blades. Dan had gotten careless. "You gotta find her," Jake whispered the words, and he sounded desperate.

"You've had girls light out before. What's so special about this one?"

Jake wet his fat lips with an even fatter tongue. He was sweating, and his deer-colored hair was stuck to his square head like a threadbare cap. "She was Billy Kyle's favorite, damn it. He comes back and finds out she's gone, he'll put a bullet 'tween my eyes!"

Shay sighed. Billy was the only son of the richest

rancher within a hundred miles of Prominence, a mean-eyed, pimply little prick with a bowie knife, a penchant for cheap whiskey, and a poor outlook on life. He wouldn't be a bit above shooting Jake Kingston, which only went to prove that everybody had at least one redeeming quality, if you just looked for it hard enough. "You let me know if you have any trouble with Billy," he said, "and I'll take a razor strop to him."

Jake missed the irony. His Adam's apple bulged like a hard-boiled egg when he swallowed. "How'm I supposed to do that, if he shoots me in the head? I'm tellin' you, she was his *favorite,* and he won't take nobody else!"

"Then I guess he's in for a long dry spell," Shay reasoned, "since he hasn't got a hope in hell of getting any woman he doesn't have to pay for."

The bartender narrowed his pig-bright eyes. "You know somethin'? I don't think you're showin' much sympathy here."

"Nobody quicker than you, Jake," Shay answered. Then he tugged at the brim of his hat, scanned the room once, and headed for the swinging doors. Since his brother was out in the countryside somewhere, and he could turn a corner without fear of running into himself, he figured he'd make the rounds and let the good folks of Prominence see that they had a marshal after all.

He hadn't even gained the sidewalk when one of the saloon girls caught hold of his arm. In the sunlight, her hair was an unlikely straw color and her face paint was on crooked, resembling an ill-fitting, tawdry mask. She couldn't have been any older than twenty, but in her eyes he saw something ancient. She glanced back over one bare shoulder, well aware that Jake was watching her.

"If you see Liza Sue," the prostitute whispered, "you tell her never to come in here, not for nothin'. Billy'll kill her for sure if he sets eyes on her again. He damn near did last night—beat her half-senseless. If me and the piano player hadn't drawed his notice away, he'd 'ave smashed her face in.''

"I guess I'd better look Billy up and explain that I don't take kindly to that sort of behavior," Shay said calmly. He glanced back at Jake, who was oozing along the back edge of the bar, like the spill of something noxious, evidently ready to grab the girl if she made a run for it. Jake was too stupid to realize what Shay could see plainly in the woman's face; she'd long since run dry, where hope was concerned. She was just trying to stay alive, and that out of habit.

"She's hidin' out someplace," the woman murmured, and her fingers dug into his arm like the talons of a she-owl. "Marshal, you've gotta find her before Billy does, and put her on the next stage out of here."

Jake was within earshot by then, and Shay knew she wasn't going to say another word if there was a risk that he'd overhear it.

"Belle, you just get yourself back in here," the bartend-er called out. "I don't pay you good money to stand in the doorway barrin' my customers from comin' in."

"That's right, Jake," Belle snapped back, with uncommon spirit. "You don't pay me good money." She hung on to Shay for a moment longer, then turned and sashayed over the sawdust to stand behind a trail-weary cowboy, kneading his shoulders with her strong hands. Her gaze linked hard with Shay's, then she drew back inside herself with a harsh laugh. "This here handsome drover wants to buy me a drink, Jake. Make it whiskey, and hold the water."

Shay stepped outside, still turning the conversation over in his head, and nearly collided with Dorrie, out in front of the general store. When he'd told Tristan that his sisters hated him, he'd been stretching the truth a little. While Cornelia wouldn't have spit on him if he was roasting on a stick, he and Dorrie got along just fine.

She'd had a gift for stirring up scandal when she was younger, and Shay missed those entertaining days.

"Hello, beautiful," he said.

She'd been scouring the display window with vinegar water and crumpled newspaper and, seeing Shay, she beamed, drew back one fist, and punched him square in the belly. Fortunately, by dint of long experience, he'd been ready. She laughed and squinted at him. "I do believe you're sober, Shamus McQuillan," she said. "Just wait till I tell Cornie. It will spoil her whole day."

Shay rolled his eyes. Maybe he hadn't been at his best these past eighteen months or so, but he hadn't been lying around in the gutter, either. The way folks acted—his own sister, no less—he might have spent every day of that time facedown in the sawdust at the Yellow Garter. He got a prickly sensation at the back of his neck and glanced toward the saloon again. "You know anything about a girl running away from Jake Kingston's fine establishment?" he asked.

"If I did," Dorrie replied, "I wouldn't tell you." She frowned. "I thought I saw you riding out of town a little while ago, as a matter of fact. You were mounted on a black gelding with three white stockings."

Shay grinned and touched the back of his hand to her forehead, as though testing for a fever. "You're getting old. Seeing things."

"Go to hell," Dorrie said cheerfully. "I'll outlive you and Cornie both."

"Theodora." The voice was shrill and female, and it came from inside the store. "I am depending on you to wash that window."

Dorrie sighed. "God, I hate that woman," she said, with no attempt at a moderate tone.

"Then why do you stay?" Shay was honestly puzzled. Shamus and Rebecca McQuillan had never been rich, but they'd left a thriving business behind, and the only painted house in town, a two-story mail-order structure with a picket fence around it. It wasn't as though Dorrie didn't have choices.

"Because I won't give the old biddy the satisfaction of driving me off, that's why. Go dunk your head in the rain barrel, Cornie. I'm talking to my baby brother." Dorrie slowly descended to a stage whisper. "I mean to wait her out, Shamus. When she's toes-up in the Presbyterian cemetery, we'll sell this place, you and me, and split the takings."

Shay kissed Dorrie's earnest forehead. He hadn't been interested in the family business before and he wasn't now; store keeping wasn't for him. "Don't wait," he counseled. "She'll live another fifty years on sheer meanness alone."

Cornelia appeared in the doorway, a stunning woman of nearly fifty, with wide green eyes, hair the color of darkened copper, and a soul the devil wouldn't have taken in trade for a square acre of sulphur fumes. "What do you want?" she demanded, glaring at Shay. She had resented him as an intruder for as long as he could remember, and he'd long since gotten used to her rancor.

He touched his hat brim and treated her to the mocking grin he knew she had always despised. "Not a thing," he said. "I'm a contented man." It wasn't true, of course, but the thought that he might actually be happy was clearly enough to gall Cornelia, and that made the lie worth telling.

"You could come back home any time you wanted, Shamus," plain, fanciful Dorrie announced, putting a point on each word, for Cornelia's benefit. She was just a year or two younger than Cornelia; they'd both been nearly grown when Shay was born. "Mama and Papa would want that."

In truth, Shay often missed that spacious old house, with its shelves full of precious books, its clean white walls and cool, shining wooden floors. He'd had a small room, under the slant of the roof, with a window that opened to let in the stars on clear nights, and he had fond memories of lying in bed when the wet weather came, listening to the music the rain made on the shingles. He'd loved Shamus and shy, fretful Rebecca, never dreaming they were mortal until they were gone.

"Thank you, Dorrie," he said, "but I'm fine over at the boardinghouse. I'll be moving along now."

"None too soon," snapped Cornelia.

Dorrie bent, hoisted the bucket of dirty water and flung it toward her sister. Cornelia leaped back with a gasp and a poisonous look, and just missed getting drenched. Some days, there just wasn't any luck to be had, no matter how you might beat the bushes trying to scare it up.

Shay smiled at Dorrie and walked away. Behind him, his sisters flew at each other like two cats with their tails tied together.

He looked in on the banker next, then moved on to pay a call on Dutch Cooper, over at the livery stable. His presence aroused no little consternation, probably because Tristan had been there to collect the gelding not long before, and made a show of riding out of town. Shay enjoyed the bewildered looks and scratching of heads, though he knew the game couldn't last. Prominence was too small for that.

It was shaping up to be a dull day, and Shay was beginning to wonder why he didn't just hand in his badge and take to the trail when Billy Kyle came riding down the middle of the road, raising dust, flanked by four or five of his friends.

Shay walked out into the center of the street and waited.

Billy drew up at the last moment, his eyes as hard and cold as marbles. "Well," he said, and Shay figured he'd earned some of the contempt he saw in that homely, pockmarked little face, "if it ain't the marshal."

Shay took hold of Billy's horse's bridle. "I believe I've mentioned that I don't like you boys to run your horses through town, especially at this time of the day. Somebody might get hurt.''

Billy's thoughts were as plain as if his head had been made of glass; he weighed the pleasure of spitting in Shay's face against the likelihood of getting his ass kicked right there in front of God and everybody, and wisely elected not to indulge his baser instincts. "You ought to keep that in mind, Marshal. That somebody might get hurt, I mean.''

Shay entertained a brief, sweet reverie of his own, in which he dragged Billy down off that horse, took the little runt apart limb by limb and stuffed the pieces into the appropriate orifice, but he was a patient man. He could wait.

He acknowledged Kyle's henchmen with a cordial nod. "Billy and I have things to say to each other," he said. "You boys go on about your business.''

A flush climbed Billy's neck and pulsed behind his spindly beard. His eyes flashed with venom, and his hand made a fidgety move toward the hogleg shoved through his belt. When he spoke, his voice was tight with bravado and hatred. "Head on down to the Garter and make a place for me at the poker table," he told the others. "I'll be there shortly.''

With barely disguised relief, the riders guided their horses around Shay, moving at a cautious pace. Shay reached up, grabbed Billy by the shirtfront, and wrenched him out of the saddle. "Go ahead and draw," he said, through his teeth, when Billy made an abortive move for his pistol. "Nothing would make me happier than shooting you.''

The kid's hat flew off into the dust; he didn't try to recover it or to break Shay's hold on his shirt, but he looked mad enough to turn himself inside out. "My daddy ain't gonna like this," he said.

Shay backed him out of the street, leaving the gelding behind. "We're not talking about your daddy," he drawled, hoisting Billy onto the balls of his feet and letting him dangle there like a scarecrow in a brisk wind. "I hear you took some hide off one of Jake's girls yesterday evening. I don't want to believe such a thing of a fine, upstanding citizen like you, Billy-boy. Say it isn't true, so I can sleep nights."

"This is about that whore?" Billy went from crimson to the bluish white of strained milk, but his eyes were hot as acid. "Hell, McQuillan, I paid good money for what I done to her."

"You haven't paid," Shay answered. "Not yet." He kicked Billy's feet out from under him and watched as he sank into the slimy water of a horse trough out in front of the undertaker's.

Billy's temper, admirably restrained until then, finally gave way, and as he flailed in the water, splashing and spitting, he drew the hogleg and raised it, barrel dripping. Shay's own pistol was already out and pressed into the indentation between Billy's nose and upper lip. For a long moment, they just stared at each other, he and the Kyle brat, both of them a heartbeat, a hair's breadth, from firing.

Shay was under no illusion that it made a difference, Billy's gun being full of horse spit and rainwater. At that range, a bullet would shred his insides. He didn't give a damn about that, either.

"You ready to dance for the devil, Billy?" he asked, his thumb on the hammer.

Billy gulped spasmodically and lowered the hogleg. "She was just a whore," he whined.

"Shut up," Shay breathed. He jerked the iron out of Billy's hand, flipped open the chamber, and let the shells fall into the mud surrounding the trough. "I'm talking to you. You lay a hand on a woman, whether she's a whore or a saint, I'll hurt you, Billy. Real bad."

With that, he shoved the confiscated pistol into his belt

and strode off down the street, fury thrumming in his head like a drumbeat.

"I'll kill you, you son of a bitch!" Billy shrilled after him. "Do you hear me? I'll *kill you!*"

Shay just kept walking, because he knew if he turned around, if he spoke at all, he'd wind up handing back Kyle's gun and facing the little weasel down, right there in the middle of the street. And that would be nothing short of murder.

The music rose through the floorboards of the hotel like sweet smoke, and Aislinn, usually content to spend such evenings writing to Thomas and Mark, or reading a book obtained from the small lending library at the general store, yearned to put on dancing slippers and lacy petticoats and a silken gown.

She and Liza Sue were alone in the dormitory, since the other girls were either working or watching the dancers from the rear hallway, and Liza Sue was pacing. She kept going to the window, pushing the curtain aside, peering out into the sultry summer night.

"What is the matter?" Aislinn asked, with some impatience, wondering at the same time if Shay McQuillan was downstairs, holding some woman in his arms. Wondering why she cared what he was doing in the first place.

"He'll find me," she said. "He won't stop until he finds me."

"Who?"

"Billy Kyle, that's who," Liza Sue snapped. Her bruises were beginning to fade, turning pale green at the edges, but she looked very small and fragile in the black sateen dress Eugenie had given her, and even younger than Aislinn had feared she was.

Aislinn set aside her half-finished letter, which gave yet another glowing account of what a wonderful life she and Thomas and Mark would have together, once the boys got to Prominence. She felt shaken and sick. "How old are you?" she asked.

Liza Sue was silent, gnawing at her lower lip. "What does it matter?"

"It matters," Aislinn insisted softly.

"Fifteen," Liza Sue confessed. "I was thirteen when I came to Prominence."

Aislinn thought, briefly, that she would be violently ill. "Dear God."

The girl's eyes gleamed with desolate pride. "Don't you go feeling sorry for me! I ain't pretty like you, nor smart. I had to make my way as best I could."

"Of course," Aislinn said gently. She wanted to embrace Liza Sue, hold her the way she might have held Thomas or Mark, when they were smaller, and frightened or hurt, but she didn't dare.

"I'd like to go down there and dance and dance until my feet were wore out," Liza Sue burst out suddenly. "Wouldn't you?"

Aislinn sighed. "Yes," she said. She felt like weeping, for a multitude of reasons—because her mother and father were dead, her brothers far away. Because her feet hurt from wearing shoes, and because now that she was up close to her dream, she could see the cracks in it. She wasn't at all sure that she could fix up the homestead cabin and grow enough food to keep starvation at bay. Because there were young girls like Liza Sue in the world, lost souls who had to sell themselves to survive.

"Let's go down there and watch for a while." Liza Sue spoke dreamily, as though being at the fringe of gaiety could appease their longings. "We can't be sent away for just watching, can we?"

"No," Aislinn admitted, "probably not."

Five minutes later, she was peeking through the fronds of an enormous potted palm, looking on while the fiddlers played, and men and women in their best clothes waltzed round and round, smiling. It was some consolation, at least, that there was no sign of Marshal McQuillan.

Soon, the room grew stuffy, and Aislinn left Liza Sue to her watching, passing quickly through the lobby and out onto the porch. The night air was heavy and hot, but here Aislinn could breathe.

She had been standing at the porch rail for some time, looking up at the spill of stars littering a blue-black sky, when she became aware of a creaking sound behind her, in the shadows. She stiffened, but did not turn around and look, for her senses had already told her who was there.

"Evening," the marshal said.

His voice, his presence, made Aislinn aware of her loneliness, an affliction she could usually outrun, and she did not like him for it. "Why aren't you inside, with the others?"

The creaking stopped; he was out of the porch chair and beside her at the railing. Very close beside her. "Now, why would I want to be there," he countered, "when I can be here instead?"

Aislinn didn't, couldn't, answer. Inside, the fiddles took up a new and poignantly sweet tune, and she thought her heart would break, just from being young and having so many dreams and hopes and secrets. She had thought herself immune to this man earlier in the day but now she knew with bittersweet certainty that she was not.

He turned her gently to face him and for one jubilant, terrifying moment, apart from all the rest of time, she believed he meant to kiss her. Instead, he took her into his arms, and they moved slowly around in a small, graceful circle, a private waltz, draped in shadow. It might have been better, kinder, she thought, with a sort of frantic joy, if he *had* kissed her. That would have been a mere touch of the lips, but the dancing—the dancing was intimate, infinitely tender, almost a form of lovemaking.

Shay rested his chin on top of her head, and she could

feel the warmth of him, the hard strength of his chest and arms. He smelled of soap and summer and very cold water.

Aislinn found her voice, but just barely. "I'm scared," she said, to him, to herself. She could not credit the tumult she felt; the change was as sudden and profound as an earthquake, and it would leave her forever altered.

His laugh was low and throaty and utterly masculine. "Me, too," he replied. "Me, too." Then, without another word, he sought her lips with his own, found them, claimed them.

A fiery response shot through Aislinn's system, searing away a great many false perceptions of what it would be like to be held and kissed by a man. She felt her knees weaken and might even have swooned, if Marshal Shay McQuillan had not been holding her upright.

Chapter

4

SHE TURNED FROM HIM, at last, out of desperation, dazed and profoundly shaken. Shay made Aislinn face him again and raised her chin with a curved finger—his trigger finger, she reminded herself, though it didn't do a lot of good. Pragmatism, normally her most stellar quality, was quite beyond her. Her earlier conviction that she'd somehow grown immune to Shay's very questionable charms was nothing but a mockery now; she was ablaze with a welter of sweet, frightening feelings and vast, unchartable needs. The music from the dance inside the hotel seemed to roll out through the windows and the doors, pounding in her veins, a blood spell cast by some mischievous wizard.

"Are you spoken for, Aislinn Lethaby?" he asked gruffly. "If there's a husband or a beau tucked away somewhere, or a man headed out West to join you one of these days, you'd better say so now."

Color stung her face. She might have stepped back, since he wasn't holding her, and yet she could not make herself move away. "A husband? Of course not! Why, what sort of woman do you take me for, Marshal?"

He laughed, and the low, rumbling sound mingled with the music in her blood, became the breath in her lungs, formed a swift counterbeat to the pounding of her heart. As simply, as quickly, as deeply as that, he was a part of her, like a fever or a memory or an inherited trait. "Now don't take offense, darlin'," he said. "I meant the question honorably." Having so spoken, he bent his head and touched his lips to hers once more.

Aislinn had been kissed before that night, mostly by shy boys back at home, though once when she was serving coffee in Kansas City, a cattleman with a waxed mustache had jumped up, declared himself to be an ardent admirer, thrown his arms around her while she was still staring at him, dumbfounded, and planted a big smack on her mouth.

None of those kisses had been anything like the ones Shay McQuillan gave her that evening on the shadowy veranda of the town's only hotel, with music flowing around them like an unseen river. None of them had bolted through her like hot lightning, taken the starch out of her knees, rendered her light-headed, left her breathless and blinking and utterly mystified.

"My goodness," she gasped, when the faculty of speech returned.

He laughed again and, holding her shoulders in those strong hands, kissed her forehead. "I guess you'd better get back inside, Aislinn, before Eugenie comes out here with that shotgun of hers."

"I reckon that's good advice," Eugenie put in. The light in the open doorway framed her ample figure, but her features were in shadow and her voice gave away nothing of what she was thinking.

Aislinn's lungs deflated instantly and took their time filling up again. If Eugenie let her go now, she'd have no hope of bringing her brothers west anytime soon. She cast a frantic look up into Shay's eyes, then turned to flee.

He caught hold of her arm, and the motion, though fast, was gentle. "Good night, Aislinn," he said calmly. "Sleep well."

Sleep well? She probably wouldn't close her eyes before dawn, whether Eugenie allowed her to stay on at the hotel or ordered her to leave as soon as she'd made suitable arrangements for herself. She nodded hastily and made her escape, slipping past the other woman as she hurried over the threshold.

Shay watched Aislinn vanish, feeling as hot and hard as a desert rock, and waited, bemused, for the lecture that was surely forthcoming. Everybody in Prominence knew how fiercely Eugenie guarded her "gals," and close observation during recent meals in the dining room had convinced him that Aislinn was a particular favorite of the clientele.

"Where's your shotgun?" he asked, when Eugenie did not follow Aislinn inside, but instead came to stand beside him at the porch railing.

She was about as gracious as a mama grizzly with a snout full of wasps, but she had always treated Shay with a certain rough kindness, and he liked her. "Don't think I wouldn't shoot you, just because you're wearin' that star," she barked.

Shay chuckled. "I'm not expecting any special treatment," he said.

"Good," Eugenie retorted, with a huff, " 'cause you ain't about to get any such thing from me. You want to court that girl, you do so proper-like, and come callin' for her at the kitchen door, between suppertime and eight o'clock, or on Sunday afternoon." She paused and searched his face, her eyes bright even in the gloom. "Aislinn's worth ten of any of the others, and even though she's had some grief and made her way in the world alone, she's an innocent little thing. Sees things in the light of her own high principles. She'll believe what you tell her, and if you know what's good for you, you'll either behave in a manner befittin' that kind of trust or head the other way, fast. If you've a mind to entertain yourself at cost to her, I'll advise you to take your devilment someplace else.''

Shay regarded his old friend with respect and a certain tenderness, too, though the latter was well and wisely hidden. ''I can't tell you what I feel for Aislinn, exactly, because I don't really understand it myself,'' he said. ''There's something happening here, though, and believe me, I'm not taking it lightly. I never expected to care about anybody again, including myself, after Grace was killed, but all of the sudden . . .''

Eugenie offered one of her rare, flinty smiles, a mere twitch of the lips, gone as quickly as it appeared. ''I figured you'd be ready to get on with things in time, and I was right. But you remember my warnin'. If all you want is a tussle in the hay, you just stick with that widow-woman of yours, and leave this girl alone. There's an old homestead she wants to buy and prove up on, and she's got two brothers to raise as well. She needs a man who's willing to take hold and make good on his bargain.''

He hadn't known about the brothers or the land, but there was no sense in getting ahead of himself. He'd worry about them when and if they became his concern. His attraction to Aislinn was sudden, and it was strong, and for the time being, he had all he could do to grapple with that. And then there was Tristan. ''You don't think I'm a good man?'' he asked mildly. He wasn't looking for flattery or pretty reassurances, not from Eugenie. He just wondered.

''You're all right,'' she said, and gave him a punch in the upper arm that would probably leave a welt. ''For a while there, though, I was scairt the Irish Curse had got hold of you.''

He'd been afraid of that himself, on more than one morning, when he'd awakened with spasms in the pit of his stomach, drenched in cold sweat and feeling as though somebody had dropped one end of a pool table on his head. He might or might not be cursed, but he wasn't at all sure he was Irish, though he supposed Killigrew was a name sprung from the old sod. He hadn't thought to ask Tristan about such things as that, taken by surprise that way. "The drink doesn't seem to hold much appeal," he said. "I'm not sure why." Privately, he suspected that his brother had shocked the craving right out of him, looking the way he did and introducing himself with the tip of a pistol barrel in the middle of the night.

"Maybe it don't matter why," Eugenie said, squinting at him. The noise at the Yellow Garter was rising and getting wilder, like a creek swollen with melted snow and spring rains. Had been for several minutes. "You know," she mused, "if it weren't a crazy notion, I'd think there was two of you."

Shay had been on his way to retrieve his hat from the porch bench, where he'd left it when Aislinn came outside, but Eugenie's comment stopped him in midstep. He repressed a grin. "What?"

She sounded pensive. "It was odd, your comin' in twice for breakfast this mornin'. And the second time, well, there was something real different about you."

Shay grasped his hat and let out a long breath. He was on the verge of explaining when shots sounded from the direction of the Yellow Garter. "Hell," he said, automatically checking the cylinder of his .45. "I'd better get down there and find out what's going on."

"You take care," Eugenie commanded, as he sprinted past her.

"Yes, ma'am," he promised, without looking back.

Aislinn sat alone in the kitchen, her chin propped in one hand, watching the light of a single kerosene lantern flicker over the checkered oilcloth covering the table. She would have been the first to admit that she should have been thinking about the possible consequences of being caught breaking Eugenie's rules, but she could not seem to get beyond the impact of Shay McQuillan's kisses. She was startled when Eugenie spoke, for she hadn't heard her enter the room.

"You'd best get to bed, miss. Breakfast time comes around early."

Turning on the bench, Aislinn looked up into the older woman's face. "You're not sending me away, then?" She held her breath, waiting for the answer.

Eugenie got a mug and poured some cold coffee, left over from the supper trade. "I don't turn my girls out into the street," she said, in her own good time, after several unself-conscious slurps. She was looking out the window over the cast-iron sink, and that was a mercy from Aislinn's standpoint, because she needed some time to recover her composure.

Aislinn closed her eyes as relief swept through her. She'd taken a big enough risk, helping Liza Sue to escape the Yellow Garter Saloon. Letting Shay McQuillan kiss her in front of God and everybody had been downright reckless, given Eugenie's strict standards. "I—I don't know what came over me," she said, and she was telling the absolute truth. "I've always been so—so sensible."

Eugenie ignored that. "How's that little Liza Sue gal fittin' in?"

Aislinn stiffened. "Fine," she said, in a thin voice. She hated lying, especially to Eugenie, who'd been so unfailingly kind, but she'd been left with little choice in the matter. Liza Sue had nowhere to go but back to the Yellow Garter, if things didn't work out there at the hotel.

At last, Eugenie turned, still holding the cup. "I reckon she's glad to get away from Jake and that bunch over in that hellhole saloon."

"J-Jake?" Aislinn's heart was beating fast, and the music in the small ballroom seemed farther away than before.

"That's a mighty hard life," Eugenie said sadly. "There ain't anybody bad enough to deserve that kind of suf-ferin'."

Misery threatened to swamp Aislinn: the thing she had most feared had come upon her; she'd been found out. Eugenie was sure to change her mind about sending her packing, and she'd have no choice but to move on, leaving the homestead behind, for someone else to purchase. Thomas and Mark, counting the days until they could leave their school and board a westbound train, would be bitterly disappointed, and her own dreams, so close as to be almost within her grasp only the day before, seemed hopelessly out of reach. She started to speak, swallowed, and fell into a wretched silence.

Eugenie approached, sat down beside her at the table. "Thought you had me fooled, did you?"

Aislinn imagined herself writing to her brothers, telling them they couldn't come to California after all. Imagined herself leaving Prominence. "I was hoping so," she admitted. "But plainly I was wrong. How did you know?"

Eugenie smiled and patted Aislinn's cold hand. "Well, for one thing, the girl didn't have no belongin's with her. For another, you don't get bruises like that fallin' down steps. Them sort of marks, they almost always come from a man's fist, and even when they fade away, you can still see the shadows of 'em in a woman's eyes. And you ain't got so many dresses that I don't know 'em all as well as my own."

"Are you going to send her away?" Her own situation was serious enough, but Liza Sue's was dire. With no roof over her head, and no money to buy stagecoach passage out of Prominence, the other girl would surely end up back in the saloon, worse off than ever.

Eugenie sighed heavily. She sounded exhausted, like someone who's just come to the end of a long and difficult journey. "That's what you're afraid of? That I won't let that little gal stay here?"

Aislinn nodded. "That man who beat Liza Sue—she says he'll kill her next time, and I believe her."

"That's most likely so," Eugenie agreed, and she seemed to be staring through the kitchen wall, through the night itself, toward something far off in the distance. "She's not goin' anyplace, Aislinn, and neither are you. Not tonight, anyhow. You just get on up to bed. I expect a good day's work out of you tomorrow."

Tears sprang to Aislinn's eyes, and she blinked them back, rising from the bench. "Thank you," she whispered. "Thank you!"

Eugenie turned to look up at her. The lamp was burning low, and in that moment the night seemed especially dark, pressing at the window like some diabolical fog. "You're a fine girl, Aislinn, and I confess I'm inclined to favor you over the others, just a mite. But I made them rules of mine for a reason, and I've got to see that they're kept. You understand what I'm sayin' here, don't you? You'll have to find yourself another place if you don't behave yourself proper."

Aislinn nodded. Eugenie liked her, but she wouldn't turn a blind eye again; it was a matter of principle. "I understand," she confirmed. Then she hurried up the rear stairs, never bothering with a lantern, and let herself into the dormitory. The room was black, and the girls were all asleep, except for Liza Sue, who sat bolt upright on her cot, bathed in a single beam of moonlight, her arms wrapped around her knees.

"She knows," Liza Sue whispered.

"Yes," Aislinn answered, just as softly. "But it's all right."

"You mean that?"

"Eugenie will protect you. Now, go to sleep." Aislinn snuggled down, and was just about to doze off, when Liza Sue spoke again, very softly.

"You hear that racket, down at the saloon? A little while ago, there were some shots fired."

Aislinn hadn't noticed the noise until then. The only law in town, Shay was almost surely square in the middle of the situation, whatever it was, and the realization was terrifying, now that she cared about him so much. She sat up again, listening. A popping noise punctured the night.

"Was that a shot?"

"I don't know," Liza Sue said. "Billy's probably kilt somebody. Maybe that good-looking marshal, for making such a fool out of him in the street."

Some demon took Aislinn over in that moment. Tossing back her blanket, she scrambled got out of bed. "Where's that dress you were wearing?"

Liza Sue didn't reply until they were both out in the corridor. "It's behind that big crate in the storeroom," she hissed. "Why?"

Aislinn headed for the door across the hall. "Never mind. You just go back to bed."

The former prostitute stayed on Aislinn's heels. "That's my dress, and I have a right to know what you mean to do with it," she insisted.

Inside the small, stuffy room, Aislinn groped and searched until she found the crumpled gown. She shed her nightdress and wriggled into the garment, which was slightly too small and smelled of sweat, cheap perfume and stale whiskey. She suppressed a shudder. "In this instance," she answered, however belatedly, "ignorance is most certainly bliss."

"You're not actually planning to—to go down there, to the Yellow Garter? In that dress? Why, you'll stand out like a sore thumb!" Liza Sue stopped, struggled to bring her rising voice under control. "Are you touched in the head? If you don't get shot or beaten or arrested, you're bound to be thrown out of this place once and for all!"

Aislinn was well aware that what she was doing was pure lunacy, and she'd meant her implied promise to Eugenie, that she'd abide by the rules from then on and look for no special dispensation if she broke them, but she couldn't ignore the very real possibility that Shay was in terrible trouble. She knew, everybody knew, about his confrontation with Billy Kyle that afternoon, out in front of the undertaker's, and the rancher's son had probably been fueling his indignation with liquor ever since. How could she lie there, in that stuffy attic room, throughout the night, wondering if the marshal was alive, or if he'd been gunned down?

As for the dress, well, she was headed for a saloon, not a church social. By her reckoning, she'd have been a lot more obvious in one of her prim calicos.

She made for the stairs, began a careful but quick descent. Liza Sue hovered at the top, like a disgruntled guardian angel, but she didn't follow.

On the second-floor landing, Aislinn collided full speed with an immovable object—Eugenie. The older woman, the sentinel, struck a match to the wick in a brass wall sconce.

Her gray hair was wound into a bristly plait and dangling over one shoulder, and she was clad in a high-necked nightgown and a plaid wrapper. Her eyes pinned Aislinn to the wall as effectively as a spear.

"I have to go," Aislinn gasped.

Eugenie took in the ridiculous dress for a second time, slowly. "I don't reckon I need to ask where you're headed, but I sure as hell want to know why you're headed there, and in such a getup as that one."

"I've got to see for myself that Shay's all right. That's all. Billy Kyle swore to kill him and I'm sure he's in the Yellow Garter, and I heard shots—"

"I won't let you do it," Eugenie said. "He's a grown man, Shay is, and a United States marshal to boot. He's fought his own battles for most of his life and he can fight them now. Fact is, he won't thank you for interferin'."

"I have to go," Aislinn repeated, and moved to step around Eugenie.

The other woman swore quietly. "Just hold on for a minute, then. I got somethin' you'll need."

Maybe it was curiosity, maybe it was an instinct for

self-preservation, but Aislinn waited while Eugenie went back into her bedroom, returning only moments later to offer a small object in one extended hand.

Aislinn accepted the tiny pistol shakily.

"It's loaded," Eugenie said. "If you have to use it, step in close and make the shot count. You only got one bullet."

Aislinn didn't ask any questions; she just took the pearl-handled, nickel-plated derringer and sped down the steps, through the lobby. The dance was over, and the music was only an echo. The night clerk looked at her with popping eyes, and if he said anything, she didn't hear. She was outside, racing down the wooden sidewalk, her whole being attuned to the cacophony belching out of the saloon, like smoke billowing from a corridor to hell.

The street was empty, except for horses tied to various hitching rails, and a drunk sleeping in a trough, up to his chin in water. Reaching the Yellow Garter, Aislinn took a deep breath, prayed that God would look after Thomas and Mark if anything happened to her, and burst through the swinging doors.

She was well inside, and ankle-deep in filthy sawdust, before her eyes adjusted to the brighter light and the blinding sting of burning tobacco. Cowboys and gamblers looked at her with scurrilous interest, but she paid them little mind.

Shay was in the middle of the saloon, engaged in a game of pool, his pistol lying close at hand on the table's edge. His opponent was a man she didn't recognize, tall and thin and pockmarked. His holster was empty but his firearm, like Shay's, was within easy reach. Billy Kyle sat on the floor, his back to the bar. He was handcuffed to the boot rail, red-faced and rumpled, and even from a distance, Aislinn could see both his temples throbbing with fury.

She hardly dared to look at Shay again, for she could

already feel his gaze boring into her, every bit as ill-tempered as Kyle's was, but she made herself meet his eyes. She'd pegged his expression just about right, which was no consolation, of course. She'd been rash, and made a terrible mistake because of it.

Laying down his cue stick, his blue eyes narrowed, Shay took in the borrowed dress, the derringer and her face, in a slow, scathing sweep.

"Maybe the little lady would like a dance," a hapless cowboy speculated, swerving in Aislinn's direction.

Shay never looked away from her, although he recovered his pistol with an unerring motion of one hand and slipped it back into its holster as easily as if it were slathered in bear grease. "Anybody moves," he said, in a deathly quiet voice that nonetheless seemed to carry to every part of that godforsaken monument to sin and depravity, "I'll plug 'em."

The stranger at the pool table smiled, leaning on his cue stick now, both hands clasping it like a pole he meant to climb. The piano jangled to a discordant, echoing stop, and the cowboy who'd wanted to dance stood unsteadily, but still.

Aislinn took a step backward, and Shay advanced.

"I guess this was a reckless thing to do," she said, with a hard swallow.

That statement brought a nervous laugh from the assembly of revelers, prostitutes and general ne'er-do-wells, and Aislinn, while still painfully conscious of her blunder, was also indignant. She felt hot color pulsing beneath the flesh of her face. She'd come here on a heroic mission, after all, however misguided, and she deserved some understanding.

Reaching her at last, Shay snatched the derringer out of her hand and dropped it into his shirt pocket. He bore little resemblance, at least in manner, to the man who had kissed her so thoroughly on the hotel veranda, that very evening. His voice was low, pitched for her ears alone, as hard and as burning cold as a pump handle in a prairie blizzard. "You're under arrest," he said.

That was just about the last thing Aislinn had expected him to say. She stood there, her vocal cords paralyzed, while he strode over to Billy Kyle, bent down to take him by the hair. "You wait here for me, Billy. You hear?"

Adam's apple bobbing, a muscle jumping in his cheek, Billy looked as though he'd sooner spit on Shay than draw his next breath, but after a long and awkward moment, he nodded. Not that he could have gone far, cuffed to that foot rail the way he was.

Shay straightened then and, sparing not so much as a look for anyone else, returned to Aislinn, took her firmly by the arm and propelled her across the floor, with its disgusting clumps, toward the doors. The moment they gained the sidewalk, a roar of laughter arose inside.

Aislinn closed her eyes tightly. "I'm sorry," she said.

Shay headed for the street with barely a pause, dragging her along behind him. She didn't need to be told that he was too furious to speak.

"I think you're being unreasonable about this," she pointed out breathlessly. She was in good shape, but he was walking so fast that she had to take three steps for every one of his. "It should be obvious that I was merely trying to help."

They were not going toward the hotel, as Aislinn had expected, but toward the jailhouse. Apparently, he'd meant what he said, about her being under arrest. She couldn't believe he was serious.

"What, precisely, is my crime? You can't just throw me in jail because you want to, you know. I have rights!"

Shay hooked an arm around her waist and hoisted her off her feet, carrying her against his side like a rug loosely rolled. When they reached the door to the jail, he kicked it open, a gesture Aislinn thought was a bit excessive, not to mention hard on the nerves. It wasn't as though she'd robbed a bank, after all.

"I demand that you answer me!" she cried.

He carried her across his small office and into a cell, flinging her down onto the narrow cot inside. It didn't seem odd to her, in the chaos of the moment, that there were lamps burning here and there, spilling unsteady light over the rough board floors. "You can demand all you want," he growled. "Course, there won't be anybody around to listen to you." He went out before she could scramble off the cot, slammed the cell door, and locked it with a heavy key.

Aislinn rushed after him, arriving too late, clasping the bars in both hands. "Wait!" she called, to his retreating back. "You can't leave me here like this . . . I haven't broken any laws!"

Shay turned on his heel and glared at her. He'd left his hat behind at the Yellow Garter, and his bright hair was mussed in a way that, despite her angry frustration, made her want to comb it with her fingers. "Get a lawyer, then!" he yelled, jabbing a finger at her. "Sue me!"

She sagged against the bars, near tears, and only then saw the man sitting behind the desk, booted feet up and crossed at the ankles, an open book resting on his chest, the faintest possible grin perched at one corner of his mouth. Aislinn blinked, looked at Shay, looked back at the cheerful observer. He might have *been* Shay, so perfect was the resemblance, except for an indefinable something in his aspect or his manner that set him apart.

Seeing the other man at last, Shay swore succinctly. "What are you doing here?"

His counterpart ignored the question, stood, and approached the cell. With a little bow, and a grin as cocky as Shay's, he said, " 'Evening. I'm Tristan Saint-Laurent. Who are you?"

Shay was in front of the desk, leaning against it, his arms folded, his face rigid. Aislinn felt an actual jolt when their gazes connected, a shuddering impact, like two trains meeting on the same track.

"My name is Aislinn Lethaby," she said, drawing herself up. It was hard to be dignified in that dress, but she made a valiant attempt, and felt a distinct need to clarify her identity. "I am employed at the hotel, in the dining room."

"Somebody ought to speak to them about the gear they make you wear," Tristan observed, and though his voice was dry, his eyes twinkled with knavery. "Folks might get the wrong idea."

Up close, Aislinn could clearly see the differences between the two men, although she couldn't have defined them for the life of her, and she realized that it was Tristan she'd seen that morning, not Shay back for a second breakfast. It explained, if nothing else, why she'd been unmoved by him.

"Stop bothering the prisoner," Shay snapped. Aislinn had had the distinct impression that he'd planned to get back to the saloon as soon as he'd locked her up, but he showed no signs of leaving now.

Tristan winked at Aislinn before turning to face Shay. His twin, of course. There could be no other explanation. "What's the charge, if you don't mind my asking?"

"I *do* mind your asking," Shay retorted. "It's none of your damn business."

"I was merely trying to save you from getting shot!" Aislinn spouted. He'd ruined her, Shay McQuillan had, throwing her in jail that way. Even if Eugenie forgave her again, by some miracle, the church ladies would run her out of town on a rail.

"That's a crime?" Tristan inquired, arching one eyebrow.

"Stay out of this!" Shay yelled.

"I think he asked a legitimate question!" Aislinn cried.

"I don't give a damn what you think!" Shay bellowed back, shaking his finger at her again. "I'm the marshal here. You're under arrest and that's that."

"For what?" Aislinn insisted. If he was going to lay

claim to the last word, he'd have to fight for it. After all, it wasn't like he was in the right or anything.

"For wearing that dress!" Shay replied.

Tristan laughed. "If it was up to me, I'd give her a commendation—that's some dress—but you're right, little brother. It ought to be illegal for any woman to look that good in something that ugly." He cast an appreciative look back at Aislinn and winked again, and she found herself liking him tremendously, despite his next words. "That's a case of indecent exposure if I've ever seen one."

Shay emitted a loud sigh, closed his eyes, and held the bridge of his nose between two fingers, as though his head hurt. "That's the charge," he said. "Indecent exposure."

Aislinn wasn't about to stand still for such a thing. "If I'm guilty, so are all those women over at the Yellow Garter. Why aren't *they* behind bars?"

"Would you like to share a cell with them?" Shay countered, in ominously quiet tones. "It can be arranged."

"That will teach me to try to help!" Now it was Aislinn who paced.

Shay smiled grimly. "We can only hope," he said. Then, after exchanging a look with Tristan, he tossed the cell key into the air, caught it in his palm, and dropped it into his shirt pocket, with the derringer. Without another word, he turned and left the jailhouse.

Chapter
5

*A*ISLINN SLUMPED FORLORNLY to the edge of the jailhouse cot—God knew who'd slept on it, and what sort of vermin they'd left behind—rested her elbows on her knees and propped her chin in her hands. The skirts of Liza Sue's dress made a tattered froth of ruffles all around her, and she might have wept, but for the knowledge that she had only her own foolish and reckless self to thank for the predicament she was in. Much as she would have liked to blame Shay McQuillan for everything, she knew it wouldn't be right or fair. Sure, he'd proved himself downright ungrateful for her concern on his behalf, but then, he hadn't asked her to come to the Yellow Garter in the middle of the night, dressed in somebody else's clothes. Eugenie had been right: he hadn't needed—or wanted—rescuing. He was not, after all, one of her younger brothers.

She sniffled miserably. She'd let impulse dictate her actions—something that was quite unlike her—and now her job at the hotel was well and truly gone, for even if Eugenie were willing to let her stay on, it would be dishonorable to do so. The older woman's authority would be forever undermined; her rules would mean nothing.

She sighed. She might be able to live on her savings for a while, but she couldn't buy the homestead, and sending for her brothers was out of the question. They were unhappy at the school in Maine, but they were getting regular meals back there, and had decent clothes to wear, and clean beds to sleep in. For the time being, at least.

"He's trying to protect you, you know."

She looked up to see Tristan standing on the other side of the bars, wearing a half-smile and holding out a steaming cup as a peace offering. She'd forgotten he was there, and a moment or two passed before she worked out that he was explaining why Shay had thrown her into jail.

She nodded glumly and let out a sigh of resignation.

"Have some of this coffee," Tristan urged. "It might raise your spirits just a little."

She rose, crossed the small space between the bed and the impenetrable iron bars, and accepted the cup. She took a sip of the brew and found it surprisingly good. Even the aroma was restorative, a nutty vapor that brought back pleasant memories of her dear father, who had always enjoyed a stout blend of coffee with his breakfast.

"Who are you?" she asked.

"I told you," he answered. "My name is Tristan Saint-Laurent."

"And you're the marshal's twin brother?"

"That's a fact," Tristan confessed, with a sigh of his own. The grin flashed, blinding as sunlight on a bright surface. "Personally, I don't see the resemblance."

In spite of everything, Aislinn laughed.

"That's better," Tristan said gently. When she went back to perch on the side of the cot, he dragged over a chair and sat down, facing her from the other side of the bars. He rested one foot on the opposite knee and settled back, regarding her thoughtfully. When he spoke, there was no hint of accusation or judgment in his tone, only bewilderment. "Just exactly what were you planning to do, going into a saloon dressed like that?"

"The idea made sense when I first thought it up," she answered ruefully. "I knew Shay—Marshal McQuillan—had gotten into it with Billy Kyle today, out on the street. Billy's wiry as a snake, and he's mean, too. Anyway, we—Liza Sue and I—heard shots from the saloon, and all of the sudden I was just sure Shay was going to die. And—" This part was hard to say, "I couldn't bear knowing that, and not trying to do something about it."

Tristan was plainly trying not to grin again. He raised one eyebrow and said nothing. The silence itself was eloquent.

"I know it sounds like a paradox," Aislinn went on, "but I figured I'd attract less attention, in a place like the Yellow Garter, if I was dressed like the other women. So I put on Liza Sue's dress and set out. I was going to decide what to do when I got there."

"And when you did? Get there, I mean?"

Aislinn blew out a loud breath. "Shay was perfectly fine. He'd handcuffed Billy to a rail in front of the bar and he was playing pool."

"Ah," said Tristan, with portent, as though some great dilemma had been resolved. His chair creaked when he leaned forward. "Who's Liza Sue?" he asked.

Aislinn explained how she had found her friend huddled between two buildings only the night before, sobbing and injured, smuggled her into the employees' dormitory at the hotel, helped her land a position as a maid.

"You make a habit of this sort of crusade?" Again, there was no derision in Tristan's voice; he was merely curious, sifting coolly through an assortment of facts.

"No," she answered, and lowered her head. While it

was true she went out of her way to help other people whenever she could, she mostly had her hands full looking after her own concerns. She'd felt sorry for Liza Sue—who wouldn't have?—and as for the march upon the Yellow Garter to save Shay, well, she still didn't completely understand the forces that had compelled her to do that. It was as if something had taken her over from the inside and driven her to it.

Tristan got up, went to the potbellied stove, and poured a mug of coffee for himself. He held up the pot and Aislinn, knowing he was asking if she wanted more, shook her head. It was odd, having someone offer to wait on her; in the last three years she'd worked ten and twelve hours a day, six days a week, filling cups and carrying plates, and no one had served her anything.

Returning to his chair, Tristan swung it around backward and straddled it, his right arm draped across the high back, the cup in his other hand.

"How long have you felt the way you do toward my brother?" he asked.

Aislinn stared at him. "What way?"

He leaned forward again and widened his eyes at her in good-natured mockery. "The way that makes you put on duds like those and charge into a saloon with a derringer in your hand."

Aislinn subsided a little, pondering the undeniable implications of what the man had just said. "I don't know," she answered, at some length. "Yesterday, I didn't even like him."

Tristan chuckled appreciatively. "I see," he replied. He got up, returned the chair to its place by the wall. "Is there anything I can get you from the hotel? A change of clothes, maybe?"

She looked at him in weary appeal. "If you want to help, you can persuade your brother to let me out of here, tonight. I'm in enough trouble as it is, without the whole town seeing me leave the jailhouse in the bright light of day."

He seemed genuinely regretful. "I don't know Shay too well," he confided, "but it seems to me that there's a stubborn streak in him. When he turns you loose, ma'am, it will be because he's decided that's the right thing to do, and for no other reason."

"You're probably right," Aislinn agreed, dejected. "What about the clothes?"

She shook her head. She yearned to change out of the ruffled dress, but by now Eugenie and most everyone else who worked at the hotel would be fast asleep. Sending Tristan to awaken them could only make bad matters worse. "If there's another blanket around someplace—"

He found one of scratchy wool, but clean, and handed it through the bars. Then, after bidding her a courtly good night, he went back to the chair behind the desk, settled himself there, and began to read the book he had set aside earlier.

Aislinn was full of questions about Shay and Tristan— had been ever since she'd first seen them together—but it wasn't the time to make inquiries. She was exhausted, both emotionally and physically, and reluctant to pry, though she suspected that last was a temporary state.

She spread the blanket Tristan had given her over the cot and, with a little grimace, lay down upon it. She supposed stretching out on a jail mattress was no worse than wearing that particular dress. The garment surely had a history of its own; one she didn't care to examine.

"Do I have to dunk you in the horse trough again, Billy, or are you going to conduct yourself like a gentleman?" Shay asked, crouching beside the youth with the key to the handcuffs at the ready.

"I just wanna go home, that's all," Billy whined. He kept his eyes averted, but Shay knew what was in them all the same: the hope of murder. The converse and bitter realization that, for the moment at least, he was outmatched. "Just let me go home. My pa will be gettin' real worried long about now."

Shay blew out a breath and rubbed his chin in a show of deep contemplation. His beard was coming in, and it itched something fierce.

"I'll see he gets out to Powder Creek all right, Marshal," volunteered the man Shay had been beating at pool earlier in the evening. Jim O'Sullivan was the foreman on the Kyle ranch, and the old man often sent him along to town to play nursemaid to the boy. Not that it appeared to do much good.

"Well, now, Jim," Shay said, "I'll hand him over to you on one condition: that you keep him out of Prominence for a while. Me and Billy here, we're not on cordial terms these days. We need some time apart."

O'Sullivan nodded his agreement quickly; no doubt there would be hell to pay if he went back to the Powder Creek spread without the joy and delight of William, Sr.,'s heart.

Shay pretended to consider that, knowing all the while that he couldn't lock Billy up, since Aislinn was already occupying the only cell. "You got your temper under control?" he asked, and examined the small key between his fingers at great length, as if he'd never seen it before. Billy'd come at him with that bowie knife of his as soon as he'd stepped through the saloon doors earlier that night, after the first encounter with Aislinn, there on the hotel porch. There'd been a scuffle, and Shay had subdued Billy, with more effort than he liked to recall, and finally cuffed him to the boot rail.

During the pool game, which Aislinn had interrupted at the worst possible time, he and O'Sullivan had been discussing the wreck of the stagecoach eighteen months before. The Powder Creek foreman had been getting steadily drunker with every break of the balls, and even though he'd never admitted to knowing anything about the robbery and murders, it had been plain from the sheen of sweat glistening on his forehead and at the base of his throat that he had some idea who'd been behind it all.

Shay had been real interested in O'Sullivan's opinion on the matter, but when Aislinn appeared, wearing that god-awful getup and looking scared and defiant, both at the same time, the confessional mood was broken.

He opened the handcuffs and stood, dragging Billy along with him. He flung the boy forward, into O'Sullivan's arms. "Get him out of here," he growled.

Billy started to say something he shouldn't, but O'Sullivan took him by the elbow and headed for the doors.

"That boy's the sort to shoot a man in the back," Jake observed, from behind the bar. He was smearing a dirty glass with an even dirtier rag, and when he met Shay's eyes, it was clear enough that he had a few specific prospects in mind for the honor of receiving Billy's bullet.

Shay rubbed the back of his neck. It had been a long day, and he was ready for it to be over and done with. He ignored Jake, scanned the saloon in case anyone else was of a mind to offer up their view. To his relief, nobody did so.

The night air was sultry when he stepped outside, and the stars hung low, gleaming like a shower of silver coins fixing to rain down on the earth. Shay smiled at the fanciful thought and headed for the jailhouse.

Tristan was at the desk, reading by the light of a kerosene lamp. At Shay's entrance, he put a finger to his lips, then pointed toward the cell, where Aislinn lay in a pile of frayed purple ruffles. He crossed to the bars and looked in, and something happened inside him, all of the sudden, a sort of shifting slide that changed the terrain of his soul. He suspected the sweet pain he felt was a lasting and elemental proposition, as much beyond his control as that spill of stars he'd admired moments before, and that scared him more than anything ever had. This was an impervious force, beyond the reach of his wits or his fists or his .45.

After a while, he turned, resigned to utter mystification, and went back to the desk. "You'd better go and get some sleep," he said to Tristan. "It's late."

"Thanks," Tristan said, low, and with a small grin. "You want to read me a story and hear my prayers?"

Shay didn't bite the hook; it was too late and he was tired to the bone. He tossed a brass key onto the desk. "My room is on the second floor, over at Miss Mamie's boardinghouse. In the back, to the right of the landing. She's used to me coming in late, so she won't bother about you."

Tristan looked at the key for a moment, then shrugged and picked it up. "I guess one of us might as well get some rest," he said, and stood. "You have any luck over at the saloon?"

Shay glanced ruefully toward Aislinn, slumbering so peacefully in the cell, and couldn't forestall a brief twitch at the corner of his mouth. "I was making a little progress," he said, "until Miss Lethaby decided to save me from the forces of evil."

Tristan laughed quietly and slapped his brother's upper arm. "Don't worry," he said, in an exaggerated whisper. "I think that was Saint Aislinn's last miracle."

"Get out of here," Shay said. He hoped Tristan was right—he didn't want or need Aislinn or any other woman taking stupid chances on his behalf—but he knew stubbornness when he saw it, and she had a plentiful supply of that.

Shay blew out the lamps, settled himself in the desk chair, put his feet up and closed his eyes. "Night," he said.

"Night," Tristan responded, and went out, closing the door behind him with a soft click.

Shay meditated on the fact that if it wasn't for Aislinn, he'd have been sleeping in his own soft bed, sober as an angel, instead of that hard chair. Miss Mamie kept strict rules in her establishment, and she could smell whiskey on a man from an alarming distance, which was why he'd passed many a night on the jailhouse cot. He shifted in the chair, trying in vain to get comfortable, and sighed, listening as the town settled down around him like a creaky old house.

He hadn't been asleep long when the sound of the back door being forced open brought him back to the surface of consciousness. He swung his feet down from the desk top, silent as an Indian, and rose. The .45 was in his hand before he thought to reach for it.

"You must be loco, messin' with that marshal," whispered one of the two shadows lurking back by the cell. Shay couldn't make out their features, just the shape of their framework, but he knew who they were all right.

"You saw him leave," Billy told O'Sullivan impatiently.

"I still don't like this. I'm tellin' you, it ain't right."

There was, Shay reflected, a moralist in every bunch.

"We'll get the girl and leave. That'll teach McQuillan a thing or two."

"Teach him? You're the one with a dick for a head, Billy. You didn't learn nothin' that other time, apparently."

That other time. The phrase was a crooked twig, shoved through Shay's gills. He waited, hoping the exchange would continue, but once again Aislinn got in the way.

"Who's there?" she demanded crisply. There was a tremor of fear in her voice, but it was so faint you had to listen hard to hear it. Shay admired her grit even as he suppressed an intense desire to put a gag on her.

"Hell," said O'Sullivan. "What if she screams?"

Billy ignored the question. "It's your new beau, ma'am," he said, with what he probably conceived of as ironic charm, "come to take you home. It won't do, a pretty little thing like you, sitting here by her lone-self, all dressed up for a party."

Shay's palm sweated where he gripped the handle of the .45, but his hand was steady.

"Damn it, Billy," O'Sullivan grumbled. "Have you lost your brain someplace along the line? Let's get out of here before the marshal shows up. Swearin' off the bottle ain't done his disposition any good, in case you didn't notice."

"We couldn't leave the girl here even if we wanted to," Billy argued, making sense for once in his life, "now that you went and said my name." There was a brief, thoughtful pause. "Where do you suppose he keeps them keys of his?"

Shay cocked the .45. "Right here in my pocket, boys," he said, all friendly and accommodating. "Drop whatever you're carrying and put your hands up. I'd hate to have to shoot you just because I wasn't clear on your intentions."

"Son of a bitch," O'Sullivan groaned, and there was a clunking sound as his pistol hit the floor.

"Damn it," Billy added, after adding to the clatter with his own weapons, "I watched you leave here an hour ago!"

He'd seen Tristan, of course, but Shay felt no compunction to clear up the misconception. His brother had been right: having an identical twin had its advantages, disturbing as it was to find out that even though you were a whole man in your own right, you were also half of something else. Keeping the .45 trained on the visitors, he used his free hand to take the glass chimney off the kerosene lamp on his desk, strike a match and light the wick.

Billy and O'Sullivan made a miserable pair, standing there by the cell door, with their weapons at their feet. Billy had been carrying a virtual arsenal: his knife, a .38 revolver and a smaller handgun similar to the derringer he, Shay, had taken from Aislinn in the saloon. He hadn't known about that last piece, but there it was, in plain sight. That was Billy for you, honest to a fault.

He gestured with the barrel of the pistol. "Over here in the middle of the floor," he said. "Lie down on your bellies and please, for the sake of my immortal soul, don't give me call to shoot you. The temptation is nearly more than I can bear as it is."

The miscreants looked at each other, gulped in unison, and laid themselves down. Shay stepped over them, pulled the cell key from the inside pocket of his vest and unlocked the door.

Aislinn scurried past him, giving the new prisoners ample territory to themselves, and hovered over by the desk. In a sidelong glance, Shay saw that she was trembling, and her eyes were taking up most of her face.

Shay kept the .45 aligned with the back of Billy's head, searched him quickly, then picked him up by the scruff of the neck and tossed him into the cell with such force that he bounced off the inside wall. O'Sullivan followed a minute or so later, after undergoing a similar pat-down, and Shay slammed the door on them and locked it.

"What are we supposed to do in here, with just one bed?" Billy wanted to know.

"Cuddle," Shay answered, and turned his back on them.

Aislinn was still staring at him. He didn't think she'd be fool enough to ask about Tristan in front of Billy and O'Sullivan, but he couldn't take the chance. "This is no place for you," he said quickly, taking her arm. "Come on. I'll walk you over to the hotel."

She was pale, and scraped her upper lip once with her teeth. "What about the back door?" she asked. "They broke it down."

"There's only one key to that cell," Shay replied, "and I've got it. Let's go."

They stepped outside. "Did you hear what that man said to Billy Kyle?" she asked, almost immediately, in an unnecessary whisper. That bright spangle of stars hung almost within reach. "About how he hadn't learned anything the other time?"

Shay nodded grimly. He was still assimilating that, and didn't want to discuss it with anybody just yet. "I heard," he confirmed.

"Do you think he was talking about beating up Liza Sue?"

"No," Shay answered, after taking a long breath. He was remembering the scene of that coach wreck, the screaming horses, the shattered bodies. Grace, lying there in his arms, stone dead, her delicate limbs broken and askew. He had no doubt that Kyle was mean enough to wreak that kind of havoc—most men would simply have taken the strongbox and fled—but he couldn't imagine him conceiving such a scheme on his own, or carrying it out without help. He was sure now that Billy had been involved, and so had O'Sullivan, but there was a deeper question—who had they been working for? Had the gold been the only objective, or had there been a deeper reason?

He started up the steps of the hotel veranda, where he and Aislinn had danced together, and kissed. It seemed that those things had happened a long time before, instead of just a few hours ago, and he was caught off-guard when she suddenly stopped and dug in her heels.

"I can't ask Eugenie to take me back," she said. "It wouldn't be fair."

Shay looked down at her, standing there on the road, gazing up at him, looking earnest as a wayfarer before the gates of heaven. "Come on," he said. "You've got to sleep somewhere." He pulled on her hand, but still she resisted, shaking her head.

He sighed. "Then I'll get you a room."

"Unaccompanied ladies are not welcome in this hotel," she told him. "Besides, look at me. I couldn't get past the desk clerk in these clothes if I were escorted by the president of the United States."

Shay began to fear that she was right, which begged another set of questions. What was he to do with her— sneak her into Miss Mamie's place and tuck her in beside Tristan? Take her back to the jail, to enjoy the company of O'Sullivan and Billy Kyle? He swore and resettled his hat with a yank.

"I can go down to the church," she said, "and sleep on one of the pews."

"In that getup? The roof would probably cave in."

"Well, then, I'll just sit out here, on one of the veranda benches. Maybe they won't notice."

Shay took in the dress. "They'll notice," he said. Then he tightened his grip on her hand and started off down the street, pulling her along behind him. He'd never asked anything of either of his sisters, since the day he'd left his father's house, and he wouldn't have done so now, if the situation weren't desperate.

"What are you doing?" Aislinn hissed, five minutes later, when he opened the front gate of the big white house at the far end of Main Street and dragged her through it. Up until then, she'd evidently been too busy keeping up with him to ask questions.

He looked up at the two-story structure, and thought with nostalgia of his old room under the slant of the roof. "Getting you a place to sleep," he said. Then, swallowing his pride, he headed straight for the front door. With Cornelia, you had to be direct, even blunt. Diplomacy and pretty manners would get you nowhere.

"Shay—who—what—?"

He closed his free hand into a fist and pounded on the heavy leaded glass in the front door with such force that the whole thing rattled on its sturdy hinges. "Cornelia!"

he yelled. "Get down here, or tomorrow morning I'll stand in front of the general store and read out the contents of your father's will!"

A light appeared at the top of the stairs; he saw its wavering reflection as someone hurried down to the door.

"Shamus," Cornelia cried from the other side, "leave my property this instant or—or—"

"Or what, Cornelia? You'll turn me over to the law?"

The lock clattered, then the hinges squealed loudly as the door swung open. There was Cornelia, in a nightgown and wrapper, with her resplendent hair tied up in rags and her face slathered in cream. She looked mad enough to bite through a horseshoe and spit the splinters. "What do you want?" she demanded, in a furious whisper. She saw Aislinn in the next instant, dressed like a soiled dove, and moved to slam the door, but by then Shay had already put his foot in the way.

He grinned endearingly. "I'll tell you what I want," he said, "since you were so kind as to ask. My friend here needs a place to sleep and a decent dress to put on in the morning."

Cornelia's glance moved over Aislinn like acid, fit to raise blisters. Shay was still holding tight to her hand, otherwise she would have bolted for sure.

"I'll see you in hell first," Cornelia said. It wasn't clear who she was addressing.

"Now, that isn't very Christian," Shay observed. He didn't move his foot, and though Aislinn was now pulling frantically to get away, he wouldn't let go.

"She can stay," Dorrie put in, from behind Cornelia's rigid back. "Step aside, Cornie, and let the poor girl pass."

"Why should I?" Cornelia snapped.

Dorrie elbowed her aside and smiled fondly up at Shay, then lifted the lantern she carried for a better look at Aislinn. "Because I know what Papa's will says," she answered, without sparing her sister so much as a glance.

She was apparently enchanted by Aislinn's borrowed dress. "My, my," she said. "Tell me, dear—do you sing? We have a need for sopranos in the church choir." All the while she was talking, Dorrie was pulling Aislinn over the threshold, into the house. "Haven't I seen you somewhere before?"

"Not unless you've been bending your elbow down at the Yellow Garter Saloon," Cornelia said, without charity, but she was standing back, out of the way.

Aislinn's backbone straightened visibly, and her eyes flashed with ferocious pride as she looked at Cornelia. "I am—was—a waitress in the hotel dining room. Until tonight."

Shay felt a stab of shame, standing there in the entryway of the house he had always thought of as home, even though he knew it wasn't his fault that Aislinn had felt compelled to give up her place at the restaurant. Not exactly, anyway.

"What about you, Shamus?" Dorrie asked hopefully, smiling up at him. "Will you spend the night, too?"

Cornelia made a horrified sound, but she kept her distance.

"I've got prisoners to look after," he said, "but I'm grateful for the invitation." He glanced at Cornelia, hat in hand. "I trust my friend will be treated kindly under this roof?"

"Humph," Cornelia said, candle in hand, and turned away to stomp up the stairs.

Dorrie looked about ten years old in her long nightgown, bare feet and braids. "Don't you worry, Shamus. I'll look after—after—?"

"Aislinn," said the guest, offering a grubby hand. "Aislinn Lethaby, of Livingston, Maine."

Shay might have laughed at the warm formality of her introduction if he hadn't realized that it was a desperate attempt to hold on to the last tattered shreds of her dignity. "Come by the office in the morning, Aislinn, and we'll work out what to do. Maybe if I speak to Eugenie—"

She whirled on him, her tired eyes full of fire. "Don't you *dare* interfere, Shay McQuillan. I've no right to expect my job back, after all that happened tonight. I'll just have to make my own way."

"And how do you propose to do that?" he asked, leaning in close. His temper was coming to a simmer.

Dorrie stepped between them. "Now, now," she trilled, "it's very late and we're all feeling a bit fractious!" She gave Shay a good-natured shove in the direction of the door. "Good night, Shamus."

Before he knew it, he was out on the porch, with the door shut in his face and the lock engaged. He stood there for a moment, dealing with things that had nothing whatsoever to do with Aislinn and the fix she'd gotten herself into, then turned on his heel and walked away into the night.

Chapter
6

$\mathcal{T}$HE ROOM AISLINN WAS GIVEN was under the eaves of the house, with a slanted ceiling and sparse furnishings composed of a spool bed covered with a faded quilt, a plain bureau topped by a ripply mirror and a washstand holding a bowl and pitcher of dented white enamel, rimmed in red. There was a lamp on the bureau, which Dorrie lit, and an old rag rug lay on the floor beside the bed.

"Now, just you just never mind Cornie," Dorrie prattled, having set her lantern on the bureau top beside Aislinn's. She was rummaging through the middle drawer as she spoke, and soon produced a man's blue chambray shirt. "You can wear this for a nightgown."

Aislinn accepted the shirt and caught Shay's singular scent from it, along with those of laundry soap, fresh air, and the orderly passage of time, all without raising the garment to her face. She looked around again, her heart beating a little faster than before. This room had been Shay's, once upon a time. She tried to imagine what sort of child he must have been, but the man he had become filled her mind and overshadowed any idea of the boy.

Dorrie turned to regard her kindly, taking up her lamp again. "Sleep well, missy," she said. "Things will look better in the morning. They always do, you know. My mother used to say that.''

Aislinn merely nodded, and when Dorrie had gone, closing the door behind her, she tossed a sorrowful look toward the washstand. Water was too much to hope for, as was soap, and she longed to perform her normal ablutions. It was not to be, however, so she put the latch hook in place, fearing a vengeful visit from the inhospitable Cornelia during the remains of the night, and stripped off the dress. Wrapping herself in Shay's shirt, she found that she was comforted, and the bed, though long unused, looked like a definite improvement over the cot at the jail.

She blew out the lamp, then turned back the coverlet and top sheet to crawl in. Expecting sleep to elude her, she lay there, once again attempting to get a sense of Shay in this place—the youth he had been, the reasons for his obvious estrangement from his eldest sister. Something about a will, she recalled, turning onto her side.

The mattress was firm, but gloriously comfortable, and the sheets, though worn, were starched and smooth. Aislinn changed positions again, landing on her back this time, and the instant she did so, a visceral memory of Shay's kiss swept through her like a brush fire devouring dry grass. She squeezed her eyes shut and a small, involuntary whimper of frustration escaped her.

She rolled onto her other side, but that changed nothing, of course. She was still possessed of that same sweet, poignant misery that made her exult in her womanhood and, at one and the same moment, wish devoutly that she had never been born. In just this state of confusion and clarity, affliction and bliss, Aislinn gave herself up to the healing mercies of sleep.

She awakened to a stream of sunlight pouring through the single window and the sound of raised voices downstairs. That she was the topic of sisterly discussion she had no doubt, and she pulled the covers over her head, longing for a home and a life of her own, a place where she belonged and would always be welcome.

Presently, the disagreement subsided to the clanking of stove lids and the slam of a door. Aislinn was trying to persuade herself to climb out of bed and face the world when she heard someone in the corridor outside her room.

"Aislinn?" The voice, blessedly, was Dorrie's. "Do let me in, dear. I've brought you some hot water and towels. A nice cake of lavender soap, too. While you're having a wash, I'll find you something proper to wear."

Grateful beyond measure for the woman's kindness, not to mention her generosity, Aislinn crossed the room and admitted Dorrie with a flimsy smile. The ruffled dress she'd borrowed from Liza Sue with such fateful consequences lay in an innocent if tawdry heap on the floor.

"Good morning!" Dorrie sang, sweeping past with a steaming bucket of water, a fragrant bar of pale purple soap and a towel. "Here you are, then," she said, filling the washstand pitcher and then setting the bucket, which was still half full, near at hand. "Did you rest well?"

Aislinn nodded. "Yes, thank you," she said, well aware that she was an intruder, for all Dorrie's cheerful compassion. "This was Shay's room." It was a request for confirmation of what she already knew, rather than a question.

Dorrie looked sad for a moment. "Once upon a time, yes," she answered, at some length. By then, she was back at the door, poised to search out proper attire for her houseguest. She sighed. "I miss those days very much," she said. "Cornie was far more charitable back then. When she thought William Kyle would make an honest woman of her, I mean."

Aislinn was already pouring the water into the basin, smelling the lovely, finely milled soap, a luxury she had not enjoyed since before her parents died; she normally used the strong yellow stuff Eugenie bought from a widow at the edge of town. Surprise stopped her in midmotion. "William Kyle? Would that be Billy's father?"

Dorrie's expression grew anxious; she stuck her head out into the hallway and peered in both directions before meeting Aislinn's curious gaze again. Her voice was pitched only slightly above a whisper. "I shouldn't have said anything. Cornie thinks no one knows how William, Sr., spurned her so cruelly. Lately, though, I've suspected that the two of them are on speaking terms again." She indulged in a wistful, tentative smile. "Wouldn't it be wonderful if they fell madly in love, and Cornie could be happy after all? Like I was with my Leander, before Papa had him thrown in the hoosegow and brought me home?"

Aislinn held her breath, torn between a good story and the deliciously hot, clean water awaiting her. "Yes," she said thoughtfully. "Wonderful."

At that, Dorrie vanished, and Aislinn closed the door, latched it and engaged in a hasty wash. She was wrapped in the towel when her benefactress returned with a brown calico dress, petticoats, a pair of drawers and a camisole. Left alone to put on the clothes, which were clean, only slightly too large and well worn enough to be comfortable, Aislinn pondered what Dorrie had revealed about Cornelia's love for William Kyle the elder. The information was probably significant, she thought, though not to her. Like virtually every other decent woman in Prominence, she'd taken care to avoid the men from Powder Creek Ranch, father and son, for the man was known to be as ruthless as the boy, only far keener of wit. And thus more dangerous.

A match between Cornelia and the notorious rancher, given that lady's surly disposition and Kyle's devious and unconscionable ways, would be nothing less than the work of dark angels.

"You won't say anything, will you? About Cornelia and Mr. Kyle?" Dorrie asked fretfully, minutes later, when Aislinn descended the rear stairway, looking for a way out of the house, and found herself in the kitchen instead. Miss McQuillan was at the table, pouring tea, and there were scrambled eggs warming in a copper chafing dish. Slices of toasted bread, well buttered, stood in a silver-plated rack, and Aislinn's empty stomach betrayed her with a loud rumble.

She shook her head, in answer to Dorrie's question, and sat down to eat. Her mind was divided between the conversation at hand and her own dismal prospects. Although Eugenie would surely forgive her, Aislinn's sense of fairness prevented her from asking to keep her position in the hotel dining room. After all, if Eugenie relaxed the rules for one, she would have to do so for others, and the inevitable result would be chaos. Thus, it seemed to Aislinn that she was fresh out of choices, unless she was prepared to move on to yet another town. Which she wasn't.

She might as well forget about buying the homestead, that much was clear.

"You look so worried, dear," Dorrie commiserated, reaching over to squeeze Aislinn's free hand.

Aislinn blinked a couple of times, on the verge of weeping inconsolably. She had fought the good fight, but she was tired and discouraged and the situation she faced seemed hopeless. She had no idea where to turn, what to do. "I'll be all right," she said, out of long habit, rather than conviction.

"Are you all alone in the world?"

Aislinn shook her head. She'd lost her appetite by then, ravenous as it had been, but she was forcing herself to finish her food. She would need her strength in the days to come. "No, I have two younger brothers, Thomas and Mark. They're in school, back in Maine."

"What about your folks?"

She took a steadying gulp of tea. "They're gone."

"And you have no aunts or uncles or grandparents?" Dorrie's narrow, homely face was the picture of sympathy and shared suffering. Ironic, Aislinn thought, given the woman's scandalous reputation; she was a far better person than the much-respected Cornelia, pillar of the church in general and the community at large, for all that she'd run away with a peddler, Dorrie had, and been dragged home in disgrace by her outraged father.

Again, Aislinn shook her head. "We'll make a family, my brothers and me, when we're all together." That day certainly seemed more distant than ever now, despite her small bank account, her intelligence and determination, and her good, strong back. She might well have to spend her savings just to survive, and that of course would leave nothing for buying the cabin and land, let alone for tools or seed or food for the winter, nothing for a milk cow and the boys' train and stagecoach fare from the East, and the many meals they'd need along the way.

"You must stay here, then. You can work with us, in the store."

Aislinn didn't allow herself to hope for that for so much as a moment. "Cornelia would never allow it," she said. "Why, she wouldn't even have let me sleep here last night if she'd had a choice."

"Cornelia gets above herself, now and then. Papa used to say she was like a stubborn mare, taking the bit in her teeth and running. All the same, in the eyes of the law, that store is mine and Shamus's, as well as hers. Same as this house. We've let her bully us, Shamus and I, each for our own reasons." Splotches of red conviction appeared on Dorrie's otherwise gaunt cheeks, and her eyes practically threw sparks. "I reckon neither of us cared enough about the store and the house to fight back—I was grieving for Leander and Shamus never wanted to be anything but a lawman. Wasn't worth a plug nickel after Grace died, either." She regarded Aislinn speculatively for a moment. "Things are different now, though. One of these days, my Leander will come back to collect me, just you wait, and I'll be gone from here forever. And Shamus seems to be putting his sorrows behind him. Before I leave this town, I mean to put a stop to Cornie's tyranny. Shamus will have his rightful share, and so will I. Leander and I will need a good stake to start over someplace else."

Aislinn leaned forward slightly, intrigued. "Leander is coming back?" If the story was true, and not merely the far-fetched fantasy of an aging spinster, it was far and away the most romantic thing she had ever heard. "Have you had word from him?"

Dorrie's eyes, snapping with ire only a moment before, went all soft and dreamy. "I have his solemn promise to return. Soon as he's out of jail, he's coming here to fetch me. That's what he said the day Papa had him arrested for kidnapping, and I know he was telling the truth."

Aislinn's mouth dropped open. And she'd thought *she* had problems. It just went to show that there was always somebody with a better reason to feel sorry for herself. "He's been in prison all this time? And your own father put him there?"

Dorrie nodded. "But I send him letters right along. In secret, of course."

A memory flicked at the edge of Aislinn's mind: Eugenie, passing fat envelopes to the stagecoach driver, having slipped them from her apron pocket. Making for the general store when there was a lull in the round of hard work that was her lot.

"Eugenie!" she said, smiling. "Why that old darling!"

Dorrie looked surprised, then pleased. "You mustn't tell anyone. Cornelia would probably have me locked up if she knew, and I can't be sure what Shamus might do. He's very like Papa, for all that we adopted him on the Oregon trail." She paused, plainly sorry for betraying a family secret, then went hastily on. "I don't mind going over to get your things for you. We'll put them in your room, and then the two of us will go to the store and I'll show you how to stock shelves and measure out sugar and flour and the like.''

Aislinn dreaded any further dealings with Cornelia, but she was too desperate to refuse the chance Dorrie was offering. If she could just stay out of the elder sister's way, and work hard, as she had always done, she might still be able to send for her brothers and proceed with her plan to make a home for them and for herself. At last.

"I can't thank you enough," she said, seeing that Dorrie had finished her breakfast and rising quickly to begin clearing the table. "If it weren't for you—"

"Here, now," Dorrie interrupted, blushing. "I might just need your help one day. When Leander comes back, I mean. Cornie will fuss like a Philistine when she sees him ride into town."

Impulsively, Aislinn gave Dorrie a brief hug. "When the time comes," she promised, "we'll find a way to deal with Cornelia, and Shay too if need be. I promise you that."

Dorrie beamed, her eyes glittering with tears. "Friends," she said, exuberantly, putting out her hand.

Aislinn took the other woman's hand and shook it energetically. "Friends," she agreed.

William Kyle, Sr., made an impressive sight, with his formidable height, dark hair, muttonchop whiskers and apparently inexhaustible supply of money, and he looked fit to pull up railroad spikes with his teeth as he stood facing Shay across the desk in the jailhouse.

"What do you mean by arresting my boy?" he demanded, in that low, thunderous voice of his. He didn't need to raise it; Zeus-like, it caused the mountains and the valleys to tremble just as it was.

Shay stood his ground. "I've had no end of trouble with Billy lately," he said. "Last night, I told O'Sullivan to take him home. Instead, the two of them sneaked over here and broke in through the back door, planning to abduct a prisoner I was holding. I just plain ran out of patience then.''

Kyle tried to stare him down for a few moments then, when that failed, took his billfold out of the inside pocket of his fancy Eastern-style waistcoat. "How much?" he asked.

"No bail's been set," Shay said, well aware that the offer had been intended as a bribe, not an honest bond. "It's the circuit judge's place to decide the matter, not mine."

"We don't need the circuit judge, unless you refuse to drop the charges." Kyle's thick eyebrows bobbed in plain consternation; he wasn't used to people turning down his requests, whether he considered them to be reasonable or not. He appeared to think this one was eminently just.

Shay hoped his smile seemed sympathetic. "That's right," he said. "Trouble is, this wasn't ordinary mischief. Billy and O'Sullivan there entered an official agency, the office of a U.S. marshal, unlawfully. They planned to carry out a kidnapping, and that's a serious matter; I personally know of more than one man doing time in the penitentiary right now because of it."

Kyle's rugged, time-beaten face went crimson, then pale as milk, beneath the leathery bronze of his flesh. "The boy meant no harm," he insisted, through ill-fitting teeth that he'd probably ordered from some mail-order company back East. "Maybe the reason you have it in for my Billy is that you wanted that saloon woman all to yourself."

It never ceased to amaze Shay how fast news got around in that part of the countryside; the Powder Creek spread was a good ten miles outside of town, he hadn't even worked up a good appetite for breakfast yet, and already the old man knew about Aislinn. Since Kyle hadn't had a chance to discuss the situation with his son, someone had either met him at the edge of town with the details, or carried them out to the ranch before the sun came up.

Shay polished his badge with the cuff of his shirt. The action always calmed him a little, when his mood was leaning toward the testy side. "And if I didn't have an interest in this 'saloon woman,' as you put it, I'd just have let Billy take her out of here, is that it? Boys will be boys?"

Kyle didn't answer, but the muscles in his bull neck were corded.

"You gotta get me out of here, Pap!" Billy wailed from the cell. He looked as pitiful as a shaved dog, peering through the bars that way. His thin beard was coming out in patches and there were big circles under his eyes. "He's gone loco since he sobered up—handcuffed me to the boot rail over at the Yellow Garter last night and left me there practically the whole night."

The rancher turned to regard his son, and Shay would have sworn he felt a chill coming off the man, as cold and dank as the breath of a cave. "Be quiet," he said, and though the words were spoken softly, they conveyed an unmistakable warning. "If I have to speak to you again, I swear I'll horsewhip you myself."

Billy gave up his sweaty grip on the bars and shrank back, gulping as though he'd just swallowed the slippery skin of a raw chicken. O'Sullivan looked nervous enough to skitter up the wall like a spider dodging high water.

Shay kept one eye on the prisoners, but the better part of his mind was occupied with Kyle's reasons for rushing into town, bright and early, to fetch home his baby boy. He was clearly worried that Billy might say something he shouldn't; a distinct possibility, given the fact that the boy had all the grace, intelligence and discernment of a horse turd.

"If you want to send somebody out looking for the circuit judge, that's your affair," he told Kyle. "When he sets bail and you pay it, I'll release your son. In the meantime, I'm holding both these men for breaking into this office with the clear intention of kidnapping one Miss Aislinn Lethaby. God knows what the charge would be if I hadn't been here to stop them."

Kyle just glared at him for a few moments. The alarming tide of color receded from his face, but he was still agitated. The muscle jumping just beneath his jaw-bone was proof enough of that, even without the feverish glint in his eyes. "I would like a private word with my son," he said, paying dear for every word. "You can grant me that, I suppose?"

Shay rubbed the back of his neck. He was fighting a battle of his own, to keep himself from diving over that desk and throttling the truth—the whole truth and nothing but—out of Billy *and* his daddy. One hand for each throat would have sufficed. "Go ahead," he said.

"He'll kill me, Pap!" Billy cried. "You leave me here, and he'll kill me for sure!" He had a very short memory, Billy did. He even looked startled when his father reached through the bars, grabbed him by the shirtfront, and slammed him hard into the iron rods that stood between them.

"Shut up," the old man growled. Or, at least, Shay was pretty sure that was what he said. Kyle had dropped his voice down low, but it was too late for secrecy.

Shay perched on the edge of his desk, arms folded, head lowered. He'd been a damn fool, he reflected, with new bitterness. A whiskey-fogged idiot. The slowest kid in the schoolhouse could have figured out who was responsible for the explosion that killed Grace and the others on that stagecoach eighteen months before. He would still have to prove his theory, because knowing in his gut what had happened wasn't enough to get the guilty parties tried and hanged. While Billy might blow up a bridge, murder five people and carry off the contents of a strongbox out of pure meanness and stupidity, the old man probably hadn't made an impulsive move in thirty years. Either he'd known in advance and supplied the dynamite and the plan, with some end of his own in mind, or he'd found out right after the fact, and made up his mind to protect Billy from the law.

Shay was placing his bets on the second of those two possibilities. Kyle had given his boy practically everything a young man could want, and looked the other way when he did wrong. In some people's minds, that was fatherly love. To Shay, raised by a decent, honest man who praised him when he was in the right and made him accountable for his mistakes, it was something else entirely: plain disinterest seemed the most likely.

To his amazement, he felt a degree of pity for Billy Kyle, which didn't mean he wouldn't make him pay for what he'd done.

The old man finally finished his conversation with Billy and turned back to Shay. He approached, stood in the middle of the floor, his gaze direct, his hands relaxed at his sides.

"You won't reconsider." The words were probably meant as a question, but they came out sounding more like a statement. Even an accusation.

Shay shook his head. "No, sir," he said, and knew that nobody in that room, not Billy or his father or Jim O'Sullivan, was under the misapprehension that the term conveyed respect. "They stay right here, both of them, until a judge says different."

Aislinn was in the general store, sitting on the floor behind two large barrels full of nails and unpacking a crate of new books, when she saw the elder Mr. Kyle stride across the street, looking neither to the left nor the right, but straight ahead. Which was fortunate, because he might have seen Aislinn through the window otherwise. He mounted the steps and came over the threshold in a pace or two, and his face looked hard as granite.

Without removing his black, round-brimmed hat, he made his way directly to the rear counter, where Cornelia was measuring out lengths of ribbon for a special order from the milliner.

After warning Aislinn to steer clear of her sister until she'd had a chance to prepare her for the news that they'd acquired an assistant, Dorrie had headed over to the hotel to see Eugenie. She'd gone after Aislinn's belongings, left behind in the dormitory, and carried messages for Liza Sue and Eugenie, but of course she was hoping for a letter from her Leander as well.

Mr. Kyle must have struck the counter with his fist, or even the butt of his pistol, for there came a sharp and sudden sound that made Aislinn jump and catch her breath. She pressed a much-coveted leather-bound copy of *The Lady of the Lake* to her heart, as if to keep that organ from bursting through her ribs in fright.

"Do you know what he's done, that brother of yours?"

Cornelia gave a sniff. "He's no relation of mine."

Afraid to breathe, let alone move, Aislinn was nonetheless possessed of such a sense of urgency that she took the risk of peering around one of the barrels. Mr. Kyle was leaning halfway over the counter, and he looked as though he might grab Cornelia by the hair.

"Shamus took him in, gave him a name, raised him as a son. As far as the law's concerned, he's as much your brother as if he'd been born into the family. If you know what's good for you, Miss McQuillan, you'll have a change of heart where young Shay is concerned. You'll press him to your bosom, forgive him for who he is and for every wayward action he's ever taken in his miserable life, and then you'll make him see reason and let Billy go before there's more killing than you can even imagine!"

Aislinn bit her lower lip and sat tight, waiting. She didn't know Shay well—there hadn't been time for that—but she would have wagered her small savings and all her prospects, such as they were, that nobody, least of all Cornelia, could turn the marshal from the course he'd set.

"He's not stupid," Cornelia admitted, in a grudging whisper. "He knows I have no use for him, and he'd see right through any attempt I made to mend fences at this late date!"

Kyle cupped Cornelia's chin in one hand, but the gesture was anything but tender. "Be persuasive," he said, with a softness that made Aislinn shiver. Then he released Cornelia with an angry flick of his powerful wrist, turned and walked away, leaving her staring mutely after him. Fear, fury and helpless frustration played in her face.

Aislinn ducked behind the barrels just in time to see Dorrie through the window, hurrying along with a bundle in her arms. Aislinn closed her eyes for a moment, offering a silent prayer that her friend would not reveal her presence by speaking to her or bringing up the subject of her hiring with Cornelia.

She did not fully understand the exchange between Cornelia and Mr. Kyle, but she was well aware that it was important. As soon as she was finished with her day's work, she would find Shay and tell him what had been said; it was up to him to decide what to do with the information, if anything.

Dorrie paused in front of the window, looked straight into Aislinn's eyes and winked. Then she waggled an envelope—a letter from the imprisoned Leander, no doubt—in one hand and went on by.

Aislinn held her breath again, awaiting discovery, but apparently Cornelia had not seen the exchange. Probably ten minutes had passed before Aislinn got up the courage to look around the nail barrel again, and when she did, she saw that the object of her dread was nowhere in sight.

Hastily, Aislinn got to her feet and took herself outside, where she stood on the wooden sidewalk, wondering what to do. She saw Shay come out of his office, sporting a gunbelt and an expression so grim that even the distance and the brim of his hat didn't hide it, and knew instantly that the time wasn't right for reporting that Mr. Kyle had practically ordered Cornelia to find a way into his good graces and talk him into letting Billy out of jail. She wasn't afraid of him—she knew he'd never hurt her, at least not physically—but he was obviously not in a receptive mood.

He stopped a man passing by, and they talked, though she was too far away to hear what was said. The man listened intently, then nodded and went inside the marshal's office, leaving the door open behind him. Shay looked up and down the street, then headed toward the livery stable. Aislinn was still standing in exactly the same spot, as undecided as ever, when he came out again, leading his horse.

If Shay had seen her, he'd given no indication. He swung up into the saddle and reined the gelding around. In the next moment, it seemed, he was beside her, looking down into her face.

"Did you sleep well?" he asked.

It was an improper question, but Aislinn had already let him kiss her in the dark, thrown away a perfectly good job, worn a prostitute's dress in public, marched into the Yellow Garter Saloon and spent a good part of the night in jail. Her reputation was beyond mending, so there was no sense in fussing over a point of etiquette. "Did you?" she countered, shading her eyes with one hand as she gazed up at him.

The semblance of a grin touched his mouth. "No, ma'am," he said.

She wanted in the worst way to ask where he was going—speaking of improper questions—but she managed to hold her tongue. She could admit to herself, if not to him, that he was one of the reasons she didn't want to leave Prominence.

He leaned forward slightly, resting one arm across the

pommel of his saddle. His eyes might have been windows on the sky itself, they were so blue. "How have you taken to storekeeping?"

The memory of Mr. Kyle's disturbing visit struck her with a visceral impact. "I'm sure I'll be very good at it in a day or so," she answered, because if there was one thing in the world she was sure of, it was her own ability to master almost any job. It was in the midst of that thought that she saw the marshal's gaze move back over her shoulder and fix on someone standing behind her.

After the briefest hesitation, he tugged at the brim of his hat. "Cornelia," he said, by way of a greeting.

"Shamus," Cornelia affirmed, in slightly brittle tones. "You and I must try to find common ground. Mama and Papa would be sorely grieved by our estrangement. Perhaps you might come to supper this evening?"

Shay's eyes narrowed for a moment; his surprise and suspicion were clearly visible. Then, bright as lightning on a dark day, and just as deadly, the grin flashed. "I wouldn't miss it for anything," he answered.

Chapter
7

S HAY AND TRISTAN SAT FACING EACH OTHER, their horses dancing skittishly, in the midst of a copse of birch trees, a hundred yards off the road. They would be visible to any passerby who took the trouble to look, but Shay didn't reckon that his brother cared about that any more than he did.

"It was Billy Kyle who robbed and killed those people," Shay said, bending to pat the gelding's neck.

Tristan leaned forward to rest one arm across the pommel of his saddle. His hat was pulled down low to protect his eyes from the glare of the midday sun in the same way as Shay's, and their clothes, while not exactly alike, were similar enough that they might have purchased them together. "That rancher's kid?"

Shay didn't bother to answer or even nod. The question, he knew, had been rhetorical.

"Well, it makes sense, I suppose. But why would a rich man's son take a chance like that? He'll hang for sure if he's convicted, and it's a rare jury that will countenance the murder of women."

Shay resettled his hat, but it still ended up at precisely the same angle as Tristan's. No need of mirrors; he could probably shave without cutting himself just by looking at his brother's face, and come out dapper as any dude. "If he admits what he did, or I find solid proof, I might not wait for a jury."

Tristan controlled his agitated horse with an expert, barely perceptible motion of the reins, which lay lightly in his left hand. "That wouldn't be the right thing to do," he said. "Still, it would be easy to forgive. All the same, you're not taking justice into your own hands if I have anything to say about it."

"You don't."

"I figure different," Tristan said calmly. "That was my stagecoach, my money." Maybe he'd intended to let that information slip, and maybe it had gotten past him in an unguarded moment. Either way, it was one hell of an announcement.

Shay gave a low whistle, and both horses pricked up their ears, did some sidestepping, then settled down again. "Why, brother, I believe you lied to me. You said you worked for the man who owned the line."

Tristan's grin was mildly cocky. "I do. I've always worked harder for myself than for anybody else, except maybe my pa, when I was still at home on the ranch." The sparkle faded from his eyes and his mouth took on a somber shape. Therein lay a tale begging to be told, Shay surmised, but it wasn't the time to dig for it. Tristan would talk about his adoptive family when and if he felt the need to do so.

As if in afterthought, he turned, opened one of his saddlebags, pulled out a small book bound in a tattered cloth cover and held it out to Shay. "Here. This will tell you a little something about our folks, the Killigrews. I've read it through a hundred times, so you can keep it if you want."

Looking down at that little, dog-eared volume, lying where Tristan had placed it on the palm of his hand, Shay dealt with separate and violently conflicting urges. He wanted to devour it, page by page, word by word, but he knew its contents, framed in careful feminine handwriting, had the power to change his most basic conceptions about himself and his life. His desire to fling the book into the brush or shove it back at Tristan was equally strong.

"A man needs to know who he is," Tristan said quietly, and Shay realized how much he'd given away, sitting there staring at that cheap remembrance book as though it had teeth sharp enough to sunder sinew from bone.

"I know who I am," Shay replied, but he wasn't so sure that was the truth. Not the whole truth, in any case. In retrospect, he'd often felt an odd, disjointed loneliness, throughout his life, as if some vital part of himself had gone, leaving him bereft. Perhaps his deeper mind had held on to some primitive, wordless impression of Tristan's presence, there in their young mother's womb, and had remembered him after he was gone.

Tristan let his gaze wander, giving Shay a chance to catch hold of his dignity. "You ought to take Aislinn for a wife, settle down, raise up some kids. It's time you had a place to lay your head, little brother. You might have passed most of your life right there in Prominence, but I do believe your spirit's been roaming the earth for a long while, looking for a home."

Shay cleared his throat, tucked his mother's journal into his own saddlebag. He didn't find the idea of setting up house with Aislinn all that hard to accept, as a matter of fact, but he had things to take care of first. "What are you, some kind of philosopher?"

Tristan chuckled. "No," he answered. "I'm the other side of the same coin, though, and like I've said before, I know about you because I know about myself."

That was more than Shay could claim, but then he hadn't had the advantage of being aware that he had a twin brother somewhere. He needed time to think matters through, where Tristan was concerned, and there was a lot of sorting and assimilating yet to be done. "You got a woman tucked away someplace?" he asked, wanting to know just how closely Tristan's inclinations resembled his own, with regard to Aislinn anyway.

Tristan smiled coolly, and the moving shadows of the birch leaves dappled his face and frame. "No, and to answer the question you haven't put to me, if you're fool enough to spurn Miss Aislinn's obvious affections, you can bet I'll be courting her quicker than you can draw that forty-five of yours."

Shay set his jaw. "That mean you plan to stay around here after we get Billy and the old man? What about your stagecoach line?"

"I like it here. In fact, I have my eye on a small spread south of the Kyle ranch—I was out there this morning, just before I ran into you. Good place to raise cattle, fine horseflesh and kids." He let that pronouncement sink in for a few moments before adding, "I've got the line sold, for all practical intents and purposes, but the deal is contingent on my getting to the bottom of that robbery and murder. The new owners aren't keen on taking over a business that can't be insured."

"What are you talking about?"

"The families of those murdered people had to be compensated," Tristan explained, surveying the white, peeling trunks of the birches that stood around them like whispering sentries. "The insurance outfit settled with them and repaid the stolen money, but they won't renew the company policies, for me or for the new owners, without some proof that justice has been done."

Shay frowned. "Can they do that?"

Tristan reined his horse toward the road. "They're doing it," he replied, and there was a shrug in his voice. "We're talking about a small fortune here, Shay. Insurance companies take a loss like that very seriously."

Shay followed his brother, left with little choice since Tristan had started out first. "How many stagecoaches have you got, anyhow?" They weren't so alike as some folks might think, Shay reflected; Tristan had a company, while he'd never made more than thirty-five dollars a month wearing a badge.

"Seven," Tristan answered, as lightly as if he were laying claim to so many matchsticks. "Not counting the one Kyle wrecked, that is."

The scene of the disaster came back to Shay in instant and vivid detail, like some kind of mental flash flood, as it always did when somebody mentioned what had happened. Except this time there was a new and very troubling element: he couldn't remember Grace's face. "Did you inherit money or something?" he asked, to distract himself. "A man needs a serious stake to start up a business like yours."

"I've been working since I was sixteen," Tristan said, gaining the road and turning to wait while Shay and the gelding descended after him, "and I've had as much good luck as bad. A man who puts his money by and watches out for opportunities can do real well for himself."

Shay polished his badge. He'd saved most of his salary, too, over the last few years, but it didn't amount to much. Anyway, he meant to reimburse the town council for what he'd been paid after Grace died. He hadn't rightfully earned a nickel of it, and he wouldn't have blamed them if they asked for his resignation. Their respect for Shamus, Sr.,'s memory was probably all that had prevented them from doing just that. "Or," he said, with some self-recrimination, "he can crawl into a bottle, curl up and wait to die."

"Takes a while to get over some things," Tristan remarked. "I explained how I came to be passing through those woods back there, but I can't rightly guess what you were doing. You have a couple of prisoners to guard, back there at the jail, don't you?"

Shay bristled a little, because no one had asked him for any kind of accounting in a long while, and he was out of the habit of giving explanations. "I was just trying to square some things away in my head," he replied, though grudgingly. He might have said Tristan had no call to worry about how he did his job, but he caught himself in time. The fact was, he couldn't make a case for himself, because he hadn't done his job for shit. "And I left a deputy in charge of Billy and O'Sullivan."

"You have a deputy?" Tristan grinned. "I'm impressed. Half the time, a one-horse town like this doesn't even have a marshal."

"If you think Prominence is so backward," Shay countered, unable to keep a defensive note out of his voice, "why the hell are you planning on settling down around here?"

Tristan pondered the inquiry for a while before giving his answer. They were riding slow and he was still taking in the countryside. "I've got family here," he said, in his own good time.

That comment shut Shay right up, and he spent the rest of the ride chewing on it. Meanwhile, Tristan turned talkative all of the sudden, spilling out plans and schemes to trap the Kyles and all their cohorts. Shay listened with half an ear.

Aislinn supposed it shouldn't have surprised her that Cornelia took the news of her staying at the house so calmly, given the woman's conversation with Mr. Kyle that afternoon, in the general store, but surprise her it did. They sat, she and Dorrie and Cornelia, in the fancy front parlor of the McQuillan house, sipping tea from bone china cups. When Dorrie said she'd hired Aislinn to work for them, and given her Shamus's old room as a part of her wages, Cornelia flushed a little, set her jaw, and smiled with all the welcoming charm of a gaping skull.

Cornelia's teacup rattled in its translucent saucer as she set it down on the table beside her chair. "Very well," she said, in shrill tones that had probably been meant to be melodic. "What's done is done. Have I mentioned, Theodora, that Shamus is joining us for supper tonight?"

Theodora? Aislinn took another sip of spicy tea to hide her smile.

Dorrie bent forward from the very edge of her chair, big-eyed and spindly-looking, like a baby bird perched on a branch that might give way at any moment. "You try to poison him, Cornie, and I'm going to know you were the one responsible!"

The elder sister rolled her eyes. She really was quite beautiful, but the coldness that seemed to seep through her very pores spoiled the effect. "I'm not going to do anything of the sort, Dorrie. Don't be ridiculous. I brought home a nice loin of pork—that's his favorite if I recall—and it's roasting in the oven right now."

Dorrie and Aislinn exchanged glances.

"What brought this on?" Dorrie demanded. She'd wanted Shay to be restored to his rightful place in the family, but naturally she was suspicious of her sister's motives. Aislinn could have told her that it was part of a scheme to jolly the marshal into letting Billy Kyle out of jail before he could be brought before a proper judge and jury, but she wasn't going to do that in front of Cornelia. The woman was vicious, like a peregrine trained to tear flesh with talon and beak, but with a difference: the falcon might have felt at least a twinge of remorse.

Cornelia squirmed a little, which indicated that she might have the suggestion of a conscience, if not the substance, locked up tight in some corner of her black soul. "We've been at each other's throats for too long, Shamus and I. I will never—*can* never love him, as one does a *true* brother, but I regret—" She paused, nearly choking. "I regret that I haven't shown more Christian charity toward him."

Dorrie got to her feet and smoothed the skirts of her greenish gown, which was only slightly more attractive than the brown calico she had given Aislinn. Her smile was dazzling, like sunshine on a Mexican silver hatband. "I'll get out Mama's good china," she said, with touching eagerness.

A protest took shape in Cornelia's mouth, but she swallowed it, with obvious difficulty, and rendered another parody of a smile. "Of course," she said. "Perhaps Aislinn wouldn't mind fetching a bouquet of flowers from the garden. Roses will do nicely, I think."

"A grand idea," Dorrie cried. Aislinn saw the corner of the letter she'd apparently gotten from Eugenie that morning peeping from Dorrie's pocket, and wondered if it contained tidings of Leander's triumphant return. Since it was plain that Shay was about as welcome in that house as a long-horned steer would have been, from Cornelia's standpoint anyway, there had to be another reason for Dorrie's exuberance.

Aislinn was in the garden, cutting prickly red roses with a scent that could make you drunk, when she sensed that someone was nearby and looked up to see Liza Sue watching her over the back fence. The maid's uniform, added to her scrubbed face and tidy hair, changed her appearance so much that Aislinn took an extra moment recognizing her.

"You landed on your feet, I see," said Liza Sue, without rancor.

Aislinn approached the fence, her arms full of fragrant, prickly-stemmed roses. "I have your dress upstairs," she said. "I'll fetch it for you."

Liza Sue shook her head. "Just burn it, or tear it up for rags. I won't have no use for it after this."

"How's Eugenie?"

"Mean as a bear. She misses you somethin' powerful, and she'd take you back if you asked her."

"I know," Aislinn said, and sniffled. She missed her friend, her space in the dormitory, the satisfying work that made the days pass quickly, but it was best to move on if she could.

"She sent me down here, Eugenie did, to watch for you and pass on a message. She'd like a visit, now and again, if you've a mind to be social."

Aislinn laughed, but the sound was part sob. Her relief was enormous; she might have lost her position at the hotel, but her friendship with Eugenie, which she valued a great deal more, was still intact. "I would enjoy that very much."

Liza Sue leaned over the fence a little way, and lowered her voice. "Is it true that Billy Kyle is in jail, and the marshal don't plan to let him out again?" Her eyes were wide, and shadows of fear flickered in their depths like specters.

"It's true," Aislinn confirmed. "You don't need to be afraid of Billy."

"You wouldn't say that, if you knew him the way I do. I'll be scared until I hear he's dead and see him in the coffin—him and his daddy, too."

The mention of the rancher made Aislinn take a step nearer the fence. She heard the threatening echo of Mr. Kyle's voice in the back of her mind, and knew that whatever Cornelia McQuillan's romantic hopes might be, she was as terrified of him as Liza Sue was. "Tell me about Billy's father," she urged, in a quiet voice. It was clear by the other woman's shudder that she'd touched a nerve, but that same sense of urgency she'd felt earlier was back again. "Please."

Liza Sue blinked rapidly, shaking her head. "He's bad," she said.

Aislinn reached out and grasped her newfound friend by the wrist, to prevent her from running away; she was strong from three years of hard work, but she took care that her hold on Liza Sue should not be hurtful. "Tell me," she repeated.

Tears brimmed in Liza Sue's eyes, and her nose reddened. "I can't," she said. Then, again, and more frantically, "I can't!" Fear gave her the strength to pull away, and she turned and hurried back toward the hotel, wiping her cheek with the back of one hand as she went.

Aislinn watched her until she vanished, then turned, with her fragrant burden of roses, and walked back inside the house. She wished she'd told Shay about the conversation between Cornelia and Mr. Kyle when she'd encountered him earlier, outside the store, but all was not lost. She'd make a point of speaking to him alone that evening, when he came to supper.

When the dinner guest arrived, his fair hair was shining and neatly combed and he was wearing a suit and a string tie. Even if he hadn't looked utterly accustomed to such fancy garb, Aislinn would have known the visitor wasn't Shay at all, but Tristan. The differences were subjective ones and as impossible to pinpoint as before, because on the surface the fine features, the breathtaking blue eyes, strong jaw and sensuous mouth, the physical grace and innate prowess, even the scent of the skin, were precisely the same.

While Aislinn hung back, there in the entryway of the McQuillan house, Dorrie and Cornelia greeted their "brother" very cordially, and neither seemed to suspect that they were entertaining an imposter. While the sisters were fussing in the dining room, Tristan paused beside Aislinn and spoke to her in a genial whisper.

"What gave me away?"

She smiled up at him. The deeper reasons were beyond her ability to explain. "The clothes. Shay probably hasn't owned a suit since he left home." Her amusement faded. "Where is he? He's all right, isn't he?"

Tristan was quick to reassure her. "He's busy looking after his prisoners. It seems they were a bit too much for the deputy he left in charge—the big one tried to hang the little one with one leg of his own pants. You're not going to tell them who I am, are you?" He tilted his head to indicate the McQuillan women, who were chattering as they bustled between the dining room and kitchen, carrying in platters and bowls, rearranging the lush, velvety roses in their mother's cut-crystal vase, moving silver candlesticks from the table to the mantel and then back again.

She linked her arm with his. "No," she said, hiding her disappointment that she would not see Shay that evening after all, unless she sought him out, which might be awkward. "It should be interesting."

"Which one hates me?" He was frowning at the two women buzzing around the table.

"The beautiful one, giving all the orders. Her name is Cornelia. Didn't Shay give you any instructions at all?"

"He said they'd probably serve something he hates."

"Pork roast," Aislinn confided. They had gained the threshold of the dining room then, and she was extra careful to keep her voice low.

Tristan's blue eyes sparkled. "Do I like that?"

She laughed, causing both Dorrie and Cornelia to turn and look in their direction. Dorrie's expression was indulgent, even benevolent, while Cornelia's smile was fixed and there was a pulse leaping spasmodically at the base of her throat. "It's your favorite," Aislinn answered, barely moving her mouth.

He gave a comical sigh of relief. "Thank God it isn't liver and onions," he said.

The meal was pleasant, and the food was plentiful. Aislinn had not enjoyed such a repast since before she left Maine, and even though she knew she was no more welcome in that house than the man the sisters called Shamus, in Cornelia's mind anyway, she ate heartily. The beautiful china, the starched white tablecloth from Ireland, the shining silver and the candlelight, all of it made for a very festive effect. Afterward, there was rich coffee, imported from Arabia, a little pyramid of chocolates served on a plate painted with lilacs, and the conversation, if superficial and somewhat on the brittle side, was lively. Not quite like eating in the hotel kitchen, with

Eugenie and the cook bantering back and forth over her head, but nice nonetheless.

The evening would have been close to perfect if the man with the elegant table manners and sophisticated opinions had really been Shamus McQuillan the younger. It was a testament to how little both Cornelia and Dorrie knew about their brother that they didn't seem to suspect anything. To Aislinn, who had not known Shay long at all, the contrasts were glaring.

"Perhaps Miss Lethaby wouldn't object to taking a brief stroll with me," Tristan said, when the evening began to wear on. Aislinn looked from Cornelia to Dorrie, unable even to imagine Shay speaking so formally, and certain that one sister or the other would take notice of the deception at last.

Neither of the women seemed even mildly suspicious. Cornelia had probably never paid a lot of attention to Shay, even while he was growing up in that house, preferring to pretend he didn't exist, while Dorrie had lived by means of distraction, keeping the realities of her life at bay by daydreaming of her reunion with Leander.

"Fine, fine," Cornelia answered, with a dismissive wave in Aislinn's direction. "Have a nice walk." The unspoken addition was as plain in its meaning as if she'd breathed sound into it. *Don't come back, and if you lose her somewhere along the way, that will be fine, too.*

The stars were out, the saloon was spilling noise and yellow light into the street as always, and Shay's office looked more like an armed camp than a small-town jailhouse. There were guards with rifles out front, and the back entrance was probably covered as well.

Aislinn was alarmed. "Is he expecting trouble?" she asked. She held Tristan's arm, and he squired her along the shadowy edge of the road with as much style as a gentleman escorting his lady through a park.

Tristan gave a little shrug. "It comes with the territory," he said. "He's a lawman, after all. Are you worried about him?"

She sighed. "Yes," she admitted. She thought he smiled slightly at that reply, but she couldn't be certain, since it was quite dark and she only caught a glimpse out of the corner of one eye. "Oh, yes."

He squeezed her arm reassuringly. "Shay's more than a match for Kyle, the boy and all their henchmen put together, but don't tell him I said so. I wouldn't want him to think too highly of himself." That time he did smile; she caught him outright.

"What brought you to Prominence? Were you looking for Shay?"

He seemed to be in no particular hurry to get back to the McQuillan house. Pausing across the street from the jail, he leaned one shoulder against a wall and struck a match to a cheroot. "I have business here," he said. "I confess that I wanted to see my brother, too."

"It must be a strange thing, to look at someone and see yourself."

Tristan nodded. "It's spooky, all right. But at the same time, it feels completely natural." He was silent for a few moments, his head tilted slightly back so that he could scan the star-bright sky. "We don't look alike to you, Shay and I, do we?"

Aislinn pondered the question, then shook her head. "It's a mystery to me, how I can tell one of you apart, because either of you might be the other's reflection."

"Maybe it's because you love Shay. You see him with your heart instead of your eyes."

She started to protest. She didn't know Shay well enough to love him—they'd danced on the hotel veranda in sweet, sultry shadows, and he'd kissed her, and as crazy as it sounded, the night she'd spent in his custody in that jail cell would probably be a fond memory until the end of her days. But those were frivolous things; when she gave herself to a man, the decision would be a serious one.

Tristan gazed toward the marshal's office as he drew on the cheroot.

"Shay cared for another woman," Aislinn told him. "Her name was Grace, and she was killed in a stagecoach robbery, along with several other passengers."

It was then that Shay came out of the building on the other side of the street, and Aislinn realized that Tristan had been waiting for his brother. That the forthcoming meeting had been prearranged.

"I know about Grace," he said quietly, watching his brother approach. "Losing her nearly destroyed him— he's been in some kind of trance since it happened, but he's coming out of it now. He's worth a little patience, Aislinn."

She was pleased by the prospect of an encounter with Shay, but when he stopped briefly to confer with a man passing by in a buggy, she looked up at Tristan and allowed him to see her worry. "Have you ever noticed how he polishes that badge of his? It's a habit with him, the way some men straighten their cuff links or hook a finger in the front of their collars. He'll never be happy in any other kind of work, but enforcing the law is danger-ous, and I would die a thousand deaths every time he strapped on that god-awful gun and stepped out of the house."

"You want a man who doesn't take risks, is that it?"

Shay was very near now, almost within earshot. She bit her lower lip. Her father had been a practical, quiet man, never given to taking chances, and he'd perished in the prime of life, along with her mother. Maybe there was no such thing as safety, no way to protect the people you loved. "I suppose that sort of man might be rather dull," she admitted.

Tristan laughed. "That's true. He'd be around to help

you raise your children, but you might find yourself wishing he'd take to the road now and again.''

"Good night, brother," Shay said pointedly.

Tristan grinned, inclined his head to Aislinn, and walked away, whistling, toward the Yellow Garter.

Aislinn had eyes only for Shay; when had looking at him gotten to be such a pleasure? He took her arm, and she didn't pull away.

"Why did you send Tristan to the house in your place?" she asked.

"It was his idea," Shay admitted. "And I had my hands full over at the jail. Did he fool you?" They were strolling slowly through the warm night, moving in the direction of the McQuillan house.

"No," Aislinn answered, without hesitation. "I recognized him right away. I don't think Dorrie or Cornelia suspected anything, though." Surely Shay's sisters had known he was a twin, though, if they had been nearly grown when he was adopted into the McQuillan family. It seemed odd that they'd never told him.

Too soon, they were at the gate in front of the house. Shadows gave them a degree of privacy, and Shay took a tender hold on Aislinn's chin and raised her face to his. His kiss was a gentle one, and yet it speeded up her heartbeat and sent heat racing through her veins. She was trembling when he finally let her go.

Amazingly enough, he looked as nervous as she felt. He took off his hat and thrust a hand through his hair. "When things settle down a little—well—I'd like for you and I to get to know each other better."

Aislinn was exulted and deeply touched by the shyness in his manner, in his voice. "I'd like that, too," she managed to say.

He leaned forward and brushed her forehead with his lips, ever so lightly, then reached around her to push open the gate. The air was redolent with the perfume of summer flowers. "You'd best go inside before I do something I shouldn't," he said. "Good night, Aislinn."

She hesitated briefly, then turned and started up the walk. When she reached the porch steps, she looked back, and saw that he was still watching her.

Dorrie waited just inside the house, holding a kerosene lantern and beaming as brightly as the light. "The evening went very well, don't you think? Cornie's gone to bed with a sick headache, but I had a perfectly stupendous time."

Aislinn smiled and secured the door while Dorrie prattled on. "Shay was charming, wasn't he? I've never known him to talk so much, about so many places and things."

"He had a great deal to say," Aislinn agreed, hiding a smile. "Dorrie, do you think I could take a bath?"

"Help yourself," Dorrie said. "There's still hot water in the reservoir beside the cookstove. I'll get the copper tub from the mud room and put it in the kitchen for you."

"I can find everything I need on my own," Aislinn said gently. She didn't want to put her friend to any more trouble than necessary. After all, Dorrie had already provided her with work, however tenuous, and a home, however temporary.

Dorrie took a candle in a brass holder from the entryway table, lit the wick from the flame of her lamp and handed the light to Aislinn. "I had a letter from Leander today," she said. "Would you like to read it?"

Aislinn didn't know how to answer. Dorrie looked so eager to share the contents of Leander's missive, and yet such things were private, like journals and keepsakes. "Is he coming back soon?" she asked, hedging. Something about the situation troubled her vaguely, though she couldn't have explained.

"Very soon," Dorrie said, with a nod. "I'm absolutely certain of that."

Aislinn smiled and impulsively kissed the other woman

on the cheek. "You'd better get your rest, then," she whispered. She stood watching as Dorrie nodded again and hurried up the stairs, happy as a child looking forward to Christmas. But as Aislinn made her way back through the large house, toward the kitchen, her heart still soaring from Shay's kiss, she felt fretful, too. Why was she suddenly afraid that Leander would never come back, and Dorrie would spend the rest of her days waiting for him?

Chapter
8

❧

$\mathcal{T}$HE RIDERS FROM THE POWDER CREEK RANCH stormed the town in the hazy dawn light of the following day, whooping like Apaches on the warpath and firing pistols and rifles and shotguns into the air. Although Shay had been half expecting them, the sights and sounds reverberated in his bones. Not a praying man, he offered a silent petition all the same, asking only that the citizens of Prominence, Aislinn Lethaby in particular, would stay in and stay down. That there would be gunplay he had no doubt.

Indulging in a quick, cautious glimpse out the front window of the jailhouse, he saw the flash of Tristan's silver card case, the prearranged signal, from the roof of the general store across the street. Lace curtains fluttered in the hotel windows, and he sensed motion in some of the other buildings, too, but except for the two guards out front, rifles cocked and ready, and the raiders from Powder Creek, now milling in front of the office, shooting holes in the sky, there was no one else in sight.

Old man Kyle rode to the head of the twenty or so riders, looking more like a circuit preacher than a prosperous rancher in his round-brimmed hat and dark, somber suit. A Remington with a polished wooden stock rested crosswise in front of him, and his expression was typically grim.

"Shamus McQuillan!" he snarled, never one to waste words. "Come on out here and maybe—just maybe—I won't have to shoot either of these fine men watching the door."

Shay was already on his way outside; he'd never planned on holing up inside until the danger was past. He glanced back at Billy, who was grinning at him through the rusting bars of the cell.

"Now don't get restless, Billy-boy," he said, "because your stay in our fine establishment is only beginning."

Billy's response was a confident curse; O'Sullivan, being older and perhaps a little wiser, hung back, looking like a man who wanted whiskey for breakfast.

Shay opened the door and stepped out onto the wooden sidewalk. He was armed, as always, but he hadn't bothered to draw the .45. He knew he had only to summon it with a thought and it would be in his hand and firing on command.

"Good morning, William," he said. If he'd been wearing a hat, he might have tipped it. "What brings you here, so early in the day?"

"You know damn well what brings me here, McQuillan. I want my boy back. He belongs at home, in the bosom of his family."

Shay sighed, polishing his badge with the cuff of his shirt. He was aware of the hired guards at his back, nervous and grim and probably as much a danger to him as the Powder Creek men, given their fidgety trigger fingers. It was Tristan he was counting on, lying on his belly over there on the roof of the store, with a pistol trained on the back of William Kyle's head. "I reckon we have differing opinions, you and I, on where young Billy belongs. He stays here until the judge comes through Prominence and says otherwise."

Kyle's foreman drew, and within the space of a heartbeat, he'd taken two bullets, one from behind and one from in front. Wearing an expression of indignant surprise, he fell forward from the saddle and landed on his face in the dirt, while the riders around him struggled to control their horses. Shay's .45 was still in his hand as he scanned the group to see if anybody else wanted to step into the crossfire. Several men had drawn, but they hesitated to shoot, and at the signal from Kyle, they holstered their guns.

"Pick him up," the rancher said, speaking of the dead man being trampled under the hooves of his own panicked horse, now barely restrained by the hold of another man's hand on the bridle. Someone at the edge of the group moved suddenly, and it was just enough of a diversion; Shay looked in that direction, and a rope looped over his upper body from the other side, pulled tight with such swift, muscle-severing force that he dropped the .45, his arms pinned to his sides at the elbows.

One of the guards behind him stepped forward, probably to come to his aid, and was immediately gunned down. Before Shay could turn and see for sure, he was jerked off his feet and dragged between the prancing, sharp-hoofed legs of a score of horses, helpless to free himself or even gain his feet.

He hoped to hell that Tristan was good in a crisis.

The dirt was packed hard and studded with more sharp rocks than he could have imagined, and as the horse dragging him picked up speed, its rider pulling the rope taut again with a wrench that fairly caved in his rib cage, he felt like he was being stripped of his hide. His mouth was full of dust and fine gravel and a few other things even less palatable, his eyes were veiled with grit, and he'd gotten the wind knocked out of him when he struck the road. None of that was as bad as knowing he was probably going to die with nothing much to his credit but a good childhood and eighteen months of self-pity and hard drinking.

He heard a shot, a hollow sound that might have come through a tunnel, followed half an instant later by another. Two shooters, since nobody could have gotten off a second round that fast.

Mercifully, the horse that had been dragging him stopped, but that wasn't necessarily a cause for encouragement, because Shay felt like some skinless creature, doused in kerosene and set ablaze. He rolled onto his back, blinking in an effort to clear his eyes, and looked up to see Aislinn kneeling beside him in the dirt, sawing at the rope with something that looked like a meat clever. Dorrie was at his other side, her face white as fancy foreign marble, except for two round blotches of color on her thin cheeks.

"Are you hurt?" his sister asked.

Now what kind of damned fool question was that? He'd just been roped and hauled half the length of Main Street behind a horse, and if he didn't die of broken bones and crushed organs and having no hide left on him at all, the wounds to his pride were probably enough to kill him on their own. He shook off Dorrie's concern and, when Aislinn had finally cut through the rope, struggled to his feet. His head swam, and he staggered a little.

The cowboy who'd been dragging him lay bleeding in the street a dozen yards away, and Tristan sat behind Kyle, on the old man's horse, the barrel of his pistol dug in deep at the base of the rancher's skull. Kyle looked to be reconsidering the whole situation, while everybody else gaped, now at Tristan, now at Shay. Eugenie, as fascinated as anybody there, nonetheless joined Shay and Aislinn and Dorrie in the middle of the street, still holding her fabled shotgun in both hands.

Shay might have grinned, if he hadn't been so mortified. Eugenie had fired one of the decisive shots, Tristan the other.

"Land sakes," said his female rescuer, "you look a sorry sight, Marshal." She spared him a pitying glance, then turned her attention to Tristan again. "If it weren't for all them bruises and all that dirt, I believe I'd think you'd done split yourself in two. Who the devil is that?"

Having caught his breath at last, Shay loosened the noose around his chest and arms and shrugged out of it. A couple of the Powder Creek riders were strapping the dead across their saddles, but everyone else was holding real still. If it weren't for the fidgeting of the horses and the rolling, shifting cloud of dust raised in the ruckus, the scene would have looked like some eastern painter's rendition of the wild and lawless West.

Tristan cocked the pistol at Kyle's head, his other arm wrapped around the rancher's middle. "Ride out, all of you," he said clearly, addressing the Powder Creek crew. "Now. If you don't, there'll be nobody left to count out your wages come payday."

"He won't shoot me," Kyle barked, his face and bearing hard as flint. "He's bluffing. Get Billy!"

Two or three men took the boss at his word and reached for their guns; Eugenie took one of them out of the saddle with a single shot, while Tristan blew off a hunk of the old man's ear. Blood flowed down over that custom-made suit like a river, but Kyle was no coward, you had to give him that. He was pale as curdled milk, and his head had to be ringing like a church bell in Boston, but he didn't acknowledge the pain, didn't even reach up to touch the wound.

Shay wrenched the shotgun out of Eugenie's hands and stalked through the center of the fray. Reaching the rancher's horse, he looked up at Tristan and his captive. "Mr. Kyle, sir," he said, hurting in every bone and joint, every muscle and pore, "it gives me genuine pleasure to arrest you. Your boy's been missing you something awful, but now you'll be right there to keep him company."

With that, he reached up and jerked the man out of the saddle. Kyle, awash in blood, landed on his knees and immediately got back to his feet, under his own power. His eyes settled on Shay and snapped with fury.

"This isn't over," he warned.

Shay grinned. He felt light-headed and queasy, and saw everything through a sort of murky veil, but he was still kicking. That was cause enough to celebrate. He was alive, and once this mess was settled, there was Aislinn to be courted and won. "Sure it is," he replied, shoving Kyle toward the jailhouse.

The doctor came out of the crowd, bag in hand. "You all right, Shay?" he asked, falling into step with the marshal and his prisoner. Behind them, the Powder Creek men hesitated, then wheeled their mounts around and rode out, but with none of the fanfare of their arrival.

"I'll be fine," Shay said, more out of habit than conviction. If anybody was going to be wiping his brow and dabbing at his wounds, he wanted it to be Aislinn, not the doc. "Mr. Kyle here, though, he seems to have lost a fair portion of his ear."

Inside the office, the doctor sat Kyle down in a chair, inspected his wound, stanched the copious bleeding as best he could, and applied a bandage. The patient refused the offered dose of laudanum and walked to the cell like some heroic king being escorted to the scaffold by traitors. "I'll see you lynched for this," Kyle vowed, looking straight at Shay.

O'Sullivan cowered in a corner of the cubicle, while Billy hovered, flapping his gums. "They shot my pa," he raved, over and over, like he couldn't believe what he'd seen, until Tristan finally carried over a bucket of water and doused him with it.

After that, things got hectic.

* * *

"He's hurt, Cornelia," Dorrie said, in response to her sister's protests, as Tristan and a deputy half dragged, half carried Shay between them, into the entryway of the McQuillan house. Aislinn was right behind.

"Look at him. He's—he's *filthy,*" Cornelia sputtered, attempting to bar their way, "and he's bleeding! Must I remind you that these rugs are Persian?"

Dorrie ignored her sister, addressing her words to Tristan and the deputy. "His room is up these stairs—I'll show you the way. Gently, now. Don't make matters worse by jostling him around like a sack of onions—"

Aislinn followed them to the base of the steps, a moving, breathing specter of herself, her lower lip caught between her teeth, her heart spinning and skittering like a flat stone on ice. Shay had remained upright until after Kyle was properly jailed, dictating the wires that were to be sent to surrounding towns, requesting an appearance by the circuit judge. Then, as he was crossing the floor of his office, his knees had given out, his eyes had rolled back, and he'd gone down in a heap at Aislinn's feet.

She'd given a little scream, certain that he was dead, that somewhere under all that dirt and blood was a fatal wound, and dropped down next to him, just as she had in the street, attempting to gather him in her arms. Tristan had lifted her gently back to her feet and set her aside, where Eugenie had waited to hold her upright.

Shay was unconscious, but as Tristan and the other man picked him up, each draping one of his arms over their shoulders, he came around just long enough to insist that he wasn't hurt, then passed out again. Moments later, he opened his eyes, shaking his head slightly, like a swimmer surfacing after a deep dive. Although he was standing, he was plainly dazed, and when he tried to speak, his words were jumbled and fractured.

Aislinn, last to gain the stairs, was wholly focused on Shay, and when someone grabbed her arm and stayed her progress, she was startled. Seeing Cornelia, she pulled free with a powerful, angry motion and hurried after the others.

The tiny room was hot and close and crowded, and while Tristan and the other man put Shay carefully down on the bed, Dorrie flittering here and there like a sparrow afraid to light, Aislinn flung up the window to let in a rush of clear morning air. Then she proceeded to the foot of the bed and carefully pulled off Shay's boots.

She was a doctor's daughter, and she had assisted her father in his surgery on occasion, when there had been a carriage accident, or some mishap on a nearby farm. She had seen all manner of injuries, but she had never been in love with the patient before, and that, she found, made a profound difference. Her hands trembled, and her stomach pitched, as though it would rebel at any moment.

"Hot water," she said. "We need lots of hot water, clean cloth and carbolic acid or alcohol for disinfectant."

Amazingly, Dorrie and the deputy obeyed her commands without question or hesitation, hurrying out to do her bidding. Only Tristan remained, speaking the occasional quiet, soothing word to his half-delirious brother while he helped Aislinn remove his brother's torn and bloody clothes.

Aislinn was an innocent, but the sight of Shay's bare body, magnificent as it was, did not move or shock her as it might have done in other circumstances. With Tristan's help, she examined him, and they concluded that there were several ribs broken and very possibly an injury to the spleen.

In due time, Dorrie and the deputy brought hot water in generous amounts, along with the other items Aislinn had requested. Dorrie said she'd go over to the doctor's office and see if he was finished patching up the man Eugenie had shot, and Tristan sent the deputy away.

Shay was unconscious, and Aislinn was struck by the careful way Tristan cleaned the dirt from his many cuts and abrasions. "Maybe you ought to leave this to me,"

Tristan told her, with a faint, crooked grin. "My brother will be fit to be tied if he finds out you were here looking on while he got his bath."

Aislinn straightened her backbone. "I'm not going anywhere," she said and, tearing off a piece of cloth and soaking it in fresh water, she began washing a nasty gash in Shay's right knee.

"The doctor'll be along presently," Tristan said, intent on a deep cut in Shay's shoulder. "Is that yardbird fit to operate, if the need arises?"

Aislinn's cheeks pulsed with frantic color. "No," she answered. "He's probably just a barber, calling himself a physician. I've seen him sit down to eat, over at the dining room, with dirt on his hands."

"You seem to know a lot about this sort of thing," Tristan observed thoughtfully, without looking up from his work. Shay groaned in pain as his brother probed for small stones and other debris, but did not open his eyes.

"My father was a physician," Aislinn said. "A good one."

"Your folks are gone, then." Not a question really, just an opening to step through.

Aislinn nodded. "They were killed in a fire, several years ago."

"And you've been on your own ever since."

She nodded again. "I've got two brothers, but they're very young. I've been saving my wages to bring them out here, but, well, I keep getting into trouble of one sort or another. I've lost my job at the hotel, through my own foolishness, and even though Dorrie is the very spirit of kindness, I'm not really welcome in this house or at the general store. Frankly, I don't know what I'm going to do next."

"There must be some solution to the problem," Tristan mused, still intent on what he was doing.

She shrugged. Wondering all the while how she could prattle that way with Shay lying there before her, broken and bleeding, maybe even dying, Aislinn poured out the story of how she'd put her brothers into a boarding school and traveled west, from job to job, saving practically every penny she earned.

Tristan didn't so much as glance in her direction. "A lot of women in your position would have stayed back East and married. Why didn't you?"

Aislinn reached for the bottle of sherry Dorrie had brought for disinfectant, doused a cloth, and prepared to advance on the worst of the tears in Shay's flesh. "I guess I wanted something that was our own, for Thomas and Mark and me. So we wouldn't be beholden. Besides, a woman should go to a man out of choice, not necessity."

"That's not always possible," Tristan observed, putting his hands to his brother's shoulders and pressing him back onto the soiled bedding when he would have risen up against the pain. Shay murmured something about bringing in firewood before the snow got any deeper and then lay still again, his eyes closed. "Seems to me women don't have as many choices as they ought to."

She sighed, reminded of Liza Sue and the stark lack of alternatives she'd had. Anything and everything was better to think about than what might be happening inside Shay's battered body. "No," she agreed. "You're right. I guess I've been luckier than a lot of people." After they'd bathed Shay, they would have to move him off the bed long enough to put on fresh linens. That enterprise called for extreme care, lest they make any internal injuries worse. Moving him at all had been a significant risk, but of course they couldn't have left him on the jailhouse floor. Tears pricked her eyes, like a shower of tiny needles, and she missed her father with a sudden and piercing intensity that fairly took her breath away. If only he were here now; he would know how best to help Shay, whether to perform surgery or simply wait for the healing process to run its course.

Tristan reached over then, to touch her hand, and she

realized for the first time that he himself was awash in dried blood—probably from Mr. Kyle's sundered ear. "Shay's tough," he said quietly. "He'll come through this just fine."

She sniffled, nodded, renewed her efforts with the sherry, causing Shay to flinch and curse beneath the keen bite of the alcohol. "What about the next time? Those men will come back—there must be a hundred hands on the Powder Creek spread, drifters and petty criminals most of them, and Kyle has money enough that they'd ride into the jaws of hell itself if he asked them."

"Billy and the old man are behind bars. As long as that's the case, we've got the upper hand." Tristan didn't seem the least bit worried. "Hush, now," he said to his brother, when Shay tried to roll away from the sherry, which must have felt like flames licking through his skin to the muscle and sinew beneath. The gruff affection in his voice made Aislinn's throat go tight. What must it have been like for them, to discover a nearly exact counterpart to themselves, after so many years?

"There aren't many men in this town who'll be willing to stand up to the Powder Creek outfit," she pointed out, after swallowing hard. "Aren't you even a little afraid?"

He smiled. "I'm an intelligent man, Aislinn. I've got sense enough to be scared. But this life is full of challenges that have got to be met, whether the folks involved feel up to the exercise or not. As my old daddy used to say, 'We've got it to do.'"

She looked at Shay and realized with a sense of abiding bleakness how dearly she loved him. "You won't abandon him to them?" It was no idle question; she was asking for a promise, a sacred oath, for Shay's sake and for her own.

"You have my word that I'll see this through," Tristan replied, looking directly into her eyes. "If they have to bury Shay, it'll be the day after my funeral."

"Thank you," she said. She might have kissed him,

such was her gratitude, if half the length of Shay's body hadn't been between them. There was a commotion in the corridor—the doctor had arrived, no doubt. She got up and hastened out of the room, in order to collect herself.

Tristan turned to his brother, who lay unmoving now, his eyes closed, his breathing shallow and slow. "For all that you're probably going to wish you were dead before this is over," he said, "you're a very fortunate man, Shay McQuillan."

The door creaked open and the doctor came in. He was a seedy-looking character and there were half-moons of dirt under his fingernails. His clothes smelled of sweat, whiskey and mothballs, and his skin was mottled with the broken veins of a drinking man. Tristan drew his pistol.

"Don't take another step," he said.

The mean-eyed spinster, Cornelia, slipped in behind old Sawbones. "Put that dreadful thing away. This is my house, that is my brother, and he will be seen by my doctor!"

Tristan didn't move, or lower the .45. "You're right about one of those things, ma'am," he said easily. "This *is* your house. But Shay is *my* brother—my face is proof of that—and nobody is going to lay a hand on him without my say-so."

"Go on out, Cornelia," the doctor said, with resignation and a thin shadow of something that might once have been dignity. "Leave us alone to talk this over."

Cornelia fulminated for a few moments, then left the room, shutting the door smartly behind her. The doctor shed his coat, went over to the washstand, poured water into the basin, and began to scrub his hands with a cake of yellow soap taken from his bag. The sharp scent of lye filled the room, temporarily blotting out the other smells.

"You can put that iron away, young fella," said the doctor. "I sized you up out there in the street, when you changed old Kyle's looks for him. You might shoot off one or two of my ears, fingers or toes, but you won't do me any lasting harm."

Tristan cocked the pistol, but the rum-sodden old man still didn't flinch. He did look back over one meaty shoulder, though. "My name's Jim Yancy. St. Mary's Surgical College, class of '65," he said. "I mean to have a look at the marshal, whether you care for the idea or not, so you might as well do any shooting you've got in mind right now so we can get on with this."

With a sigh, Tristan shoved the .45 back into its holster. "You don't look like much of a doctor to me," he said, but he had a grudging respect for the man's courage.

Yancy laughed. "I'm not, but right now, I'm pretty much all young Shamus there has, aren't I?" He took a brush out of his bag, gummed the bristles with soap, and began to scour his fingernails. When he was satisfied that they were clean, he rinsed his hands by dunking one and then the other into the pitcher, and dried them on a fancy white towel one of the McQuillan sisters had brought in earlier. "Move aside, and let me have a look."

Tristan moved, but he didn't go far. He watched as Yancy felt Shay's ribs, ran his hands over his limbs, poked and prodded at his middle.

"Make yourself useful and fetch me the stethoscope out of my bag," the doctor said.

Tristan found the requested item amidst a jumble of vials, a battered instrument case, a leaky whiskey flask and assorted tools of the medical trade. While Yancy was listening to Shay's heart and lungs, the door opened, and Aislinn slipped in, big-eyed and defiant, as though she expected somebody to try to run her off.

"How is he?" she asked.

"Broken ribs," the doctor answered, still bent over the

patient. "Going to have to bind them up tight. See if you can rustle up some clean sheets, sturdy ones, a sharp pair of scissors and one of those big, fancy brooches Miss Cornelia wears at her throat."

"Are there—internal injuries?"

Yancy turned to look at Aislinn curiously, surprised by the knowledgeable question. "I don't believe there are. Who might you be? You look familiar, though I can't quite place you."

She raised her chin and her eyes flashed and once again Tristan thought Shay was a lucky bastard, even if he *had* been bounced on the ground behind a horse with most of the town looking on. "I'm Miss Lethaby, from the hotel dining room," she said. Her gaze went, pointedly and with an utter lack of apology, to his hands, and widened a little when she saw they were immaculate. "My father was a doctor."

"Good," Yancy replied, after studying her for a few thoughtful moments. "Well, get those things I asked for, and we'll bind up the marshal's ribs, you and I. I daresay he'll be good as new, once those fractures knit themselves back together."

Aislinn cast a despairing and tender glance toward Shay, one Tristan would have given his gun hand to receive from such a woman. Then she nodded and went out.

Hard words were heard from below, but presently she returned, with the linens, a pair of sewing shears and a shining brooch studded with little jet beads and bigger than any Tristan had ever seen. Aislinn's resolute expression made him avert his eyes for a moment, like a man who's accidentally stumbled onto some intimate and private scene.

She proved an able assistant to the doctor, cutting the sheets into strips that matched his specifications perfectly, holding the cloth while Yancy wound it round

Shay's ribs and pulled it tight, like that cowboy's rope out in the street earlier. Tristan stood back, out of the way, keeping watch over it all.

Shay strayed in and out of consciousness during the ordeal, and it was plain to see that he was suffering, but he never cried out, never did more than groan. When it was done, and the doc clasped the bindings shut with that fancy brooch Aislinn had surely wrested from Cornelia, Shay opened his eyes. Seeing Aislinn, he winked and grinned, and that was when Tristan knew his brother would be all right for sure.

"You'd better give him a dose of this," Yancy told Aislinn, taking a brown bottle out of his bag and setting it down on the bureau with a thump. Laudanum. "He'll be hurting real good for a day or two."

Shay lifted his head off the pillow, saw the bottle, and shook his head. "No, sir," he said. "Keep that stuff away from me."

Aislinn crossed the room, sat down on the edge of the bed, and brushed Shay's hair back from his face with a gentle hand. She was smiling, and there was a radiance about her that put a man in mind of a stained-glass window. Tristan made hasty excuses and left, and the doctor was close behind.

Aislinn leaned forward and kissed Shay softly on the forehead. She supposed she might regret such an impulsive action later on, but just then she was too glad that he was alive to care about proprieties. "How do you feel?"

Shay chuckled, a gravelly sound from his throat, and for a moment his pain-filled eyes were alight. "I'm not sure. Do that again, though. I think it helps."

She laughed, but the tears came then, too, in a storm of terrified relief, and though she quickly put a hand to her mouth, it was too late. Shay reached up with one arm and drew her gingerly down onto his chest, where he held her.

"Here, now," he said. "It's over, and I'm all right."

She sobbed. "For now!" she wailed. "Until those men come back—until something like this happens again—"

"Shhh." He kissed her temple. "It was just bad luck, that's all. The circuit judge will come through any day now—he'll put Billy and the old man in prison, where they belong, and everything will settle down. You'll see."

Aislinn raised her head and looked into his eyes. "Nothing is ever that easy," she protested. "Especially not when someone as powerful and rich as Mr. Kyle is involved."

Shay brought her back down, brushed her lips with his own. "Hush," he breathed, and she was, against all reason and rationality, comforted by that simple, silly word. By the warmth of his mouth and the touch of his hands.

It wasn't until much later that the news reached Prominence: a peddler had found a man hanging, dead, from the lowest branch of an oak tree, several miles outside of town. The victim was soon identified as the circuit judge.

Chapter
9

*A*ISLINN MANAGED TO KEEP THE NEWS of the judge's murder from Shay for almost four days, during which he slept a great deal and dutifully swallowed the beef and barley soup she and Dorrie spooned into him at every opportunity. At his request, she read aloud from the journal his mother had kept, long ago on a wagon train, and his gaze, distant and blue as a mountain sky, stayed fixed on the ceiling while he listened.

Experiencing Mattie Killigrew's joys, tribulations and hopes for herself, through the fading, carefully shaped words inscribed on the thick vellum pages of that diary, Aislinn was glad Shay wasn't looking at her. That way, she was able to wipe away the occasional tear without his knowing.

On the fifth day, Tristan appeared for his usual morning visit, wearing a badge and looking so much like Shay that it seemed no great wonder a lot of the townspeople were mightily confused. Aislinn knew there was still a lot of speculation concerning who was whom, and some folks even maintained there were actually *three* brothers, all of them just alike. The unmarried ladies of Prominence were especially fond of that particular theory, which at once amused Aislinn and caused her to guard the door of Shay's sickroom like a mother bear with a cub.

Tristan gave Aislinn an apologetic glance as he entered, reached for a chair, and turned it back to front beside Shay's bed. He straddled the seat and regarded his brother with a cordial nod. " 'Morning," he said.

Aislinn stood with her hands knotted in front of her, holding her breath. Shay needed a lot more rest to recover from the injuries he'd sustained in the confrontation with the Powder Creek men, but the simple reality was that he'd been sworn in as a U.S. marshal, he had a job to do, and time had run out. If they kept the truth from him any longer, he would never forgive either of them.

Bare-chested, pillows plumped at his back, his bruised and abraded face cheerful, his hair in fetching disarray, Shay grinned. " 'Morning," he replied. "You know, that badge looks good on you. I might just let you keep it."

Tristan made a show of admiring the star gleaming on the lapel of his dark coat. "Pretty thing though it is," he said, "I'm not cut out to be a lawman. Too much politicking to suit me."

Aislinn bit her lower lip and held her peace, but it was hard. She wanted nothing so much as to interfere, to remind Shay of how close they'd become in the past few days, to speak of the tentative plans they'd made and the secrets they'd shared, to ask him straight out to turn in the badge and make another sort of life for himself. For both of them.

Shay assessed his twin through narrowed eyes. "Had a run-in with the town council, did you?"

Tristan chuckled, but Aislinn, who'd taken care to place herself where she could see both men's faces, saw that his expression was rueful. "The mayor paid me a visit this morning to suggest that we put the whole matter behind us. Forgive and forget, since old Will Kyle helped settle the area and found the town."

"Son of a bitch," Shay growled, already looking for his clothes. "It's worse than I thought."

"Much worse," Tristan said, getting up from the chair, finding trousers and a shirt and stockings in the bureau drawers, tossing the garments onto the bed, taking care to avoid Aislinn's eyes the whole time. "Somebody lynched the circuit judge."

Setting his teeth, Shay flung back the covers and sat up. He was as naked as the day poor Mattie Killigrew gave birth to him, but again it didn't matter, given the situation. Aislinn stood back, knowing there was nothing she could do to stop him from getting dressed and personally taking on every hooligan, drifter and outlaw on the Powder Creek payroll.

"I'll be damned if I'll give in now," he said, grimacing with pain as he grappled into his clothes. Wisely, Tristan too kept his distance, even when Shay gained his feet, teetered like a fence post in a shallow hole, and righted himself just in time to keep from crashing into the washstand. "Billy and the old man *are* still in jail where I left them, aren't they?" His blue eyes were snapping.

Tristan nodded, a grin playing at the corners of his mouth. "They are," he answered. "I don't figure they've drawn closer in their time of trouble, though. They've been at each other like a couple of castrated cougars since you locked them up."

Shay got his gunbelt from under the bed with a little unwilling help from Aislinn—he'd insisted it be kept within reach during the whole of his confinement— buckled it on and drew the pistol, popping the cylinder open with a practiced thumb and giving it a spin. Even Aislinn, who knew little of such things, could see that the gun was fully loaded.

Only then did he allow himself to meet her eyes. The plea she would not offer aloud must have been plainly visible in her face, because he shook his head in grim refusal. Then he was out of the room, clattering down the rear stairs.

Tristan waited in the doorway for Aislinn, who could not bring herself to follow just yet. He spoke her name as a gruff question.

She turned, looked at him. "Yes?"

"Pray," he said. Then he, too, was gone.

She sat on the edge of the narrow, rumpled bed for a long while, mourning all that she had lost, and all that she might lose in the hours and days ahead. Then, with a sigh, she got to her feet and left the room where she had spent the better part of a week, and didn't bother to close the door behind her.

She could not make herself go into the general store, knew she would only be underfoot at the jailhouse. Thus it was that Aislinn presented herself at the door of the hotel kitchen, where she found Eugenie on the step, enjoying a mug of the strong coffee she favored and a rare respite from hard work.

"How's Shay?" she asked, with the rough geniality that was typical of her. "I don't need to ask after you, 'cause I can see by your face and the way you carry yourself that you're plum tuckered out."

Aislinn sat down on the step below Eugenie's. "He's out of bed and determined to get himself killed as soon as he can."

Eugenie gave a grim chuckle. "He'll be all right, Shay will." She paused, and when she went on, her tone was more serious. "You've got to believe that, because believin' has an effect on things."

"I'm in love with him," Aislinn said, with as much gravity as if she were confessing a mortal sin to a priest. "Dear heaven, Eugenie, what am I going to do?"

"Marry him?" Eugenie suggested. "He'll give a woman good, strappin' babies, a man like that, and show her a fine time in the process."

Aislinn blushed wretchedly. She hadn't allowed herself to think of bearing Shay's children, not consciously at least, but now all the attendant images rushed into her mind in vivid detail. "He hasn't asked me to marry him."

"Maybe you'd better ask him, then," Eugenie said, sounding utterly serious. "You wouldn't want to let him get away, like poor Dorrie's Leander."

Grateful for a change of subject, however tenuous, Aislinn picked up the thread of Eugenie's statement and followed it. "She offered to show me that last letter you gave her," she said, with a sigh. "She's expecting him back shortly."

Eugenie made a sound that was both sorrowful and skeptical. "It's pitiful," she said. "The way she's kept sendin' off them letters all this time, and never a one back. The man's probably dead."

Aislinn frowned. "But she got one just recently——"

The older woman look a sip of coffee and savored it, her gaze fixed on something long ago and far away. "He wasn't worth much, poor Leander. A weak-minded man he was. And a rounder. Old Shamus was right to run him off, though it broke the girl's heart."

"But you yourself gave her the letter," Aislinn protested.

Eugenie sighed. "That was from some lawyer, back East."

Aislinn put a hand to either side of her head, drew and expelled a deep breath, and tried to slow her thoughts down. The love Dorrie cherished, indeed lived for, was fraudulent, imaginary. And yet her expectations were very real. "You're not saying she's mad?"

"Just a mite strange," Eugenie said tolerantly. "She wouldn't be the first spinster to build herself a pretty dream to live in."

Aislinn bit her lower lip, miserable.

"Is there somethin' wrong?" Eugenie wanted to know.

"Dorrie's not pretending," Aislinn said. "She's all but packed her bags."

"Land sakes. I'd best get this straight with her right now. Drat it all, I knowed she shouldn't be livin' a lie that way, but poor Dorrie was so brokenhearted after her pa brought her back here—" Eugenie was on her feet, ready to go in search of her friend, but before she could take a step, Cook called to her from inside the kitchen.

"Eugenie, you better come quick. One of them girls of yours is bent over a commode in one of the rooms, sicker than a saloon dog."

Clearly, Eugenie was torn, but she chose the most immediate duty and went to look in on her ailing employee. Aislinn, on the other hand, set out for the general store at a brisk march.

Fortunately, there was no sign of Dorrie, but Cornelia was at the dry-goods counter, taking payment for ten pounds of flour and some canned meat from a worn-looking woman in a calico bonnet and colorless dress. A man in a fancy suit was examining a box of cigars with intent concentration, while a farmer ran a loving, callused hand over the handle of a new plow.

The smile Cornelia offered Aislinn was brittle, and too bright by half. "So there you are. I was beginning to think you were being paid for mooning over my brother instead of helping out here in the store."

The woman in calico accepted her purchases, gave Aislinn a look of helpless sympathy, and scurried away. Aislinn leaned over the counter and spoke in a soft voice.

"Why have you let Dorrie go on making believe that Leander would come back?" she demanded.

Cornelia looked taken aback for a moment, but she recovered quickly. "I don't have to answer your questions, you ungrateful little snippet. In fact, I've had quite enough of you. I'll thank you to get your things and leave my house and my place of business!"

The cigar man and the farmer turned around at this shrill outcry; Cornelia treated them to an icy, unfocused smile that skimmed over them both but never actually landed.

"I would rather sleep on the street than accept anything from you," Aislinn said truthfully, keeping her tones mild and melodious. She didn't care enough about Cornelia McQuillan to hate her. "Shay is very fond of Dorrie. He'll help her, if you won't."

Color surged into Cornelia's face, then receded again, leaving a bloodless shore of white in its wake. This time, she made an effort to keep her voice down. "Of all the impertinent—" She paused, huffed out a fiery breath, hot as a dragon's. "I let my sister play her silly games because it kept her occupied. She was in despair. The whole town was whispering about her, snickering behind her back, after Papa went and fetched her back here. I thought it best to leave her be."

Aislinn stared at Cornelia. Sandwiched between the woman's protests of concern for Dorrie was the staggering truth: she, Cornelia, had been embarrassed by the gossip and the scandal. "You simply didn't want to be bothered," Aislinn accused. "You were *ashamed.*"

"Nonsense," said Cornelia. "It's kept her calm all these years, my going along with her delusions. Kept her from making a fool out of herself all over again."

Before Aislinn could respond, Dorrie stepped out of the storeroom behind the counter, looking white and shaken. She had one hand pressed to her mouth, and tears glistened in her eyes. "Leander isn't coming back?" she asked, in a child's voice.

Cornelia recovered first. "Are you happy now?" she asked, practically baring her teeth at Aislinn.

Aislinn was looking at the other sister. All her concern was for her friend. "Dorrie, please, listen to me—"

Aislinn rounded the counter and put an arm around Dorrie's thin waist, felt her trembling. Again she was reminded of a bird, a wounded one this time, fallen from a high nest and irretrievably broken. "Come along," she said gently. "I'll see you home. Make you a nice cup of tea."

"Don't you set foot in my house, Aislinn Lethaby," Cornelia warned, shaking her pointing finger. "If you dare, I'll—I'll—"

"You'll what?" Aislinn asked calmly, raising an eyebrow. "Have me arrested?"

"Tea won't bring Leander home. I don't want any tea," Dorrie protested.

"Yes," Aislinn said. "You do. I mean to add some sherry to it, too." With that, she led Dorrie down the center aisle and out into the sunshine.

"Leander is dead," Dorrie said.

"I think so," Aislinn replied. She wanted to weep with pity and with sorrow, but she would do that later, when Dorrie didn't need someone strong to lean on.

"But she'd convinced me that I wasn't wrong to think he'd return. That he truly had loved me."

"Oh, Dorrie, I'm so sorry."

"I'm not sure I will ever forgive her. It's like she gave Leander back to me just so she could take him away again, the spiteful thing. She never liked him any better than Papa did."

Aislinn didn't speak except to make encouraging noises. Dorrie prattled on as they walked toward the McQuillan house, but she wasn't rambling. She was quite sane, whatever anyone else thought, and talking was her way of sorting through the wreckage of a collapsed dream.

"She did something awful, you know," Dorrie whispered, when they entered the kitchen. While Aislinn pumped water to fill the teakettle, she sat at the round oaken table in the middle of that spacious, sunny room. "Cornelia, I mean."

"What?" Aislinn asked. Dorrie was probably referring

to her sister's relationship with Mr. Kyle, a tidbit Aislinn had forgotten to mention to Shay, for all the time they'd spent together during his recovery.

"I'll show you," Dorrie said. There was a strange, hunted glimmer in her eyes, but she wasn't mad, Aislinn was convinced of that. Dorrie got up and led the way to the top of the cellar stairs, where she took a kerosene lantern down from a hook and lit the wick with a wooden match.

Aislinn glanced back over one shoulder and shuddered. She might not be afraid of Dorrie, but she wasn't keen on the idea of letting Cornelia sneak up behind her.

The old steps creaked mightily as they descended, and the air was dank and moldy-smelling. Dorrie led the way through a labyrinth of chests and crates and shrouded pieces of furniture, finally coming to an old wooden trunk draped in cobwebs and piled high with dusty blue-green fruit bottles.

Dorrie handed the lamp to Aislinn and began clearing the surface of the chest. The hinges shrieked when she raised the cover at last, and Aislinn felt a shiver wind its way down her spine. For a moment, she could almost imagine that they were about to peer into a coffin.

Covered in cobwebs, Dorrie took the lamp back and looked inside the old trunk. Something skittered in the bottom. "There it is," said Dorrie, in a state of harried, fragile triumph. "Hold the lamp again, will you?" When her hands were free, she reached inside to retrieve some object Aislinn couldn't see. It turned out to be a heavy strongbox—the sort merchants and other business people used to store valuables and important documents.

The pit of Aislinn's stomach wobbled a little. "Dorrie, I don't think—"

Dorrie had already hunkered down on the floor to fiddle with the catch on the box. Curiously, there was no padlock, but whoever had hidden it probably hadn't thought such a precaution would be necessary, given the difficulty of reaching the hiding place.

The top of the box fell back and revealed stacks and stacks of currency; there must have been thousands of dollars there. Aislinn gasped and pressed her free hand to her heart, nearly dropping the lamp. "Good heavens, Dorrie," she choked out. "You shouldn't keep such a sum at home—it isn't safe!"

Dorrie looked up. "It's not my money. Nor is it Cornelia's."

"Then—?"

The other woman's eyes gleamed in the gloom, feral and bright, and Aislinn was forced to review her prior appraisal of Dorrie's sanity. "Billy Kyle took it from the stagecoach, that one that fell down in the ravine. Grace died that day. She was a sweet thing. Real sweet, and pretty, too."

Aislinn swayed slightly, reached out to grasp the edge of the chest to hold herself upright. "What does Cornelia have to do with what happened?" she asked carefully.

"She knew how Shamus loved Grace. She wanted to take away his reason for staying here in Prominence."

"My God in heaven," Aislinn murmured.

"You see, Papa loved Shamus the best of us all. He left him the house and the store—all of it. He knew he could trust him to look after Cornie and me. Shay didn't have much interest in any of it, though, until he met Grace. Then he started to talk about settling down."

Aislinn groped for a crate and sat, unable to trust her knees to support her any longer. "Dorrie, you're talking about murder, here. Not just robbery, which is bad enough, but *murder*. If you knew these things, why in the name of all that's holy didn't you tell someone?"

A tear shimmered in the light as it slipped down Dorrie's cheek. "I wanted to pretend it wasn't true. Like I wanted to pretend about Leander."

Aislinn knelt beside the other woman on the cold dirt floor and wrapped her arms around her. The lantern sat nearby, within reach. "Oh, Dorrie—Dorrie."

Dorrie began to cry, and the sound was heart-wrenching, childlike and at the same time as ancient and elemental as rain. "Papa should have left us alone, Leander and me. If only he'd left us be."

"Shhh," Aislinn said, weeping too. "It's all right. Everything will be all right."

A spill of daylight from the top of the steps made both women turn their heads and gave the lie to Aislinn's assurances. Cornelia stood in the doorway above, a shadow, a figure rimmed in fury. "Theodora, what have you done?"

Aislinn stood, hauled Dorrie up, too. *God help us,* she thought.

"I've told, that's what," Dorrie cried defiantly. "Aislinn knows what you did, how you got Billy to blow up that bridge when the stagecoach was passing over it and kill all those people. Shay's right to hold that monster and his father in jail, but you should be in there with them!"

Cornelia didn't say a word. She merely took another lantern down from the wall, lit the wick and tossed it to the bottom of the stairs. Flames flared instantly to life, gobbling the rotting cloth that covered the furniture, catching easily on wooden boxes and even on cobwebs draped from the ceiling in great looping scallops.

Through the smoke and blazes, Aislinn saw Cornelia shut the upstairs door, heard the bolt slam into place. Dragging Dorrie by the hand, she looked wildly around for a path of escape.

A fire. She had worked so hard and come so far, only to perish in an inferno, precisely as her parents had. Her brothers would truly be alone in the world now; in time they'd be dismissed from their school, sent to live in an orphanage or even turned out onto the streets to make their own way as best they could. Worse still, she would never see Shay again, never lie down with him, never carry his baby in her body.

"Is there an outside door?" she shouted to Dorrie, over the din of the fire, reasoning that if the entrance to the kitchen had a bolt, there must be a way into the house from the yard.

Dorrie was coughing violently, and the heat of the flames was already blistering. "Cornelia had it boarded over a long time ago," she choked out. "She said she didn't feel safe of a night, after Papa was gone."

"Get down," Aislinn cried, remembering something her father had once told her, about how the air was better down close to the floor, since smoke tended to rise, like heat. Crouching, she turned to look into Dorrie's face. "A window—Dorrie, is there a window?"

They were surrounded by flames by then; tongues of fire danced all around them like demons, consuming the air, licking at the support beams overhead. Dorrie did not answer, but simply collapsed in a spasm of coughing. Aislinn searched frantically for a way out, but the smoke made it impossible to see clearly.

It was in that instant of her greatest despair that she heard the blessed sound of shattering glass, heard her name shouted. Shay. The voice belonged to Shay.

"Here!" she cried out, and the word seemed to scrape her throat raw, like the rusty bristles of a steel brush. "Over here!"

He was a figure, a shape and nothing more, moving through the shifting smoke; she saw his hair, saw that he wore a bandanna over his nose and mouth, bandit-style. He took Dorrie's arm in one hand and Aislinn's in the other, and headed back through the fire. Aislinn felt herself being lifted, was aware of hands grasping her from outside the window casing. Gloried in the cool, soothing sanction of fresh air.

Someone—Eugenie, she realized after a moment— wrapped her in a blanket; she had not known her clothes

were smoldering until then. "Shay—" she gasped, raising her head, looking for him. All she could see was legs
and boots and tall grass.

"There's Miss Dorrie out safe," Eugenie said. Then she
smiled. "And here's Shamus. He's a mite singed, but
pretty as ever."

He was beside Aislinn in a moment, Shay was, bending
over her, sooty as a chimney sweep. His blue eyes stood
out vividly in his blackened face, still bruised and swollen
from his ride behind that cowboy's horse. "Are you all
right?" he rasped, and from his bearing and his tone and
the look of him, her answer was the most important thing
in the world to him.

She nodded. It was hard to breathe, and she'd suffered a
few minor burns, but she was going to be fine. She
coughed and tried to sit up; he grinned and pressed her
gently back down.

"Hold it," he said. "Now you get to be the patient, and
I'll be giving the orders. You just lie there a minute, until
you catch your breath."

Tears smarted in her eyes, happy ones. She was alive,
and so were all her dreams. "How did you know?"

"One of my deputies went over to the store to get a bag
of tobacco and found it locked up tight, right in the
middle of the day. When he told me that, I knew
something had to be wrong, because Cornelia won't miss
a chance to make a nickel if she can help it. So I came
over here, and found smoke billowing out from under the
porch."

"But you knew Dorrie and I were downstairs."

"That was a guess. Cornelia was sitting on the front
porch, rocking in Mama's old chair and smiling like she'd
misplaced her wits. I left her for Tristan to tend to and ran
inside, yelling and looking in every room in the house. By
that time, there was smoke coming up between the
floorboards, and the paint was blistering on the walls.
When I got to the kitchen, I saw that the cellar door was

bolted, and that was all I needed to know. I tried to get to you that way, but the stairs were gone, so I went outside and broke out that window.''

She closed her eyes, absorbing all those images, reveling in the blessed rhythm of her own heartbeat and the rising and falling of her chest as she drew in breath after delicious breath. Then, when she could delay it no longer, she told him what Dorrie had shown her.

''The stagecoach money is in there,'' she said slowly. ''Cornelia put Billy up to the robbery and the killing. She was afraid you would want the house and the store, since you were going to be married.''

Shay thrust a hand through his hair and swore. Only then did Aislinn become aware of the commotion all around them, of the townspeople battling the fire.

''I'm sorry,'' Aislinn said. She found his other hand, clasped it tightly in her own.

He leaned down, kissed her lightly. ''You're here,'' he said. ''I'm here. That's enough. I love you, Aislinn. I want to marry you.''

She laughed.

''That's funny?'' He tried to look injured, but his blue eyes were dancing.

''No,'' she said. ''I'm just happy, that's all. I thought I was going to have to propose to you, and you would never have let me hear the end of it.''

His grin was bright and broad. ''Well? Is that a 'yes'?''

Aislinn nodded. ''It is indeed,'' she answered.

He frowned. ''I'm not going to turn in my badge,'' he warned. ''That's got to be understood, right up front.''

''I understand,'' Aislinn said, with a little sigh. She was ready to sit up then, and that time he didn't try to stop her. The house fire seemed to be out, and she immediately caught sight of Dorrie, blackened and singed like Shay, but sitting under a tree, calmly sipping water from a ladle held by Liza Sue. The rest of Eugenie's girls were there, too, helping out in various ways.

Shay curved a finger under her chin and brought her back to face him. "I have things to do," he said. "You're sure you're all right?"

She wished they were alone, so she could put her arms around his neck and kiss him. Then she decided the circumstances were special, given that both of them had nearly died, and kissed him anyway. He tarried until Tristan came along and reminded him that there were prisoners at the jail and the judge's killers were still out there somewhere, waiting to be caught.

Cornelia was taken to the doctor's office, being in some kind of trancelike state. Eugenie took charge of both Dorrie and Aislinn, squiring them over to the hotel and installing them each in a room of their own. Dorrie was overwrought, Liza Sue reported later on, and had been given a sedative and put to bed. Aislinn, having come so near to death, felt exuberantly, exultantly alive, full of hunger and happiness.

She took a bath in tepid water, soaking away the smell of smoke, and shampooed her hair with lavender soap. She ate ravenously from the tray of cold chicken, bread and spiced pears Cook sent up from the kitchen, chattering while Liza Sue towel-dried and then combed her hair. Liza Sue smiled as she listened and wound the still-damp tresses into the customary plait.

A black skirt and pristine white shirtwaist were brought from the general store, a spontaneous gift from Tristan, and they were a perfect fit. Aislinn was standing in front of the mirror, imagining herself as a bride, when the blast came, rattling the window, shaking the walls, causing the very floor to tremble beneath her feet.

Chapter
10

*T*HE EXPLOSION SPLINTERED THE WHOLE FAÇADE of the jailhouse, bellying the windows outward, like the sails of a ship, before they shattered, sending the deputies posted by the door hurtling into the road in a shower of clapboard and glass. Horses from one end of Main Street to the other pranced and whinnied and pulled at their tethers, eyes rolling, while a cloud of smoke rose against an otherwise placid blue sky.

Shay saw the whole thing from the window of the hotel dining room, where he and Tristan were seated across from each other, eating the early lunch Eugenie had insisted they accept.

"Shit," Shay cursed, knocking his chair over backward in his haste to leave the table.

"I hope you've got the back door covered," Tristan put in, rising with a little more grace and somehow managing to get to the sidewalk before Shay did.

The deputies were just picking themselves up, with a little help from cautious bystanders, as Shay ran past them. One had a splinter the size of an ax handle embedded in his shoulder, but they were standing upright and breathing. For the moment, that was all that concerned him.

From behind the jail, he heard the sounds of retreating horses. He yelled for someone to fetch his gelding from the livery stable and picked his way into the ruined building, moving carefully through the wreckage toward the cell at the rear. He'd expected the prisoners to be gone, and was startled to find the rancher kneeling among the debris, his bandaged head bent, clasping Billy's limp body in his arms. They were both covered in mortar dust, which gave them a peculiar aspect, like ghosts, or statues come partway to life.

"He's gone," Kyle said, disbelieving.

Shay knew at a glance that the rancher was right; his son had perished in the blast that was probably intended to set them both free. "I'm sorry about that," he said, and he meant it.

Kyle was silent for a long time. Then, as Shay stepped over the fallen bars of the cell and began tossing aside beams and boards, he spoke again. "He would have hanged."

"Yes," Shay agreed quietly. "Did you order that circuit judge killed?"

The rancher stroked the boy's head, which lay back over his arm at an angle that suggested a broken neck. "No," he said, and Shay believed him. People didn't usually lie in circumstances like these. "I reckon the boys thought that's what I'd want, though." Somberly, he surveyed the damage around them, then lowered his gaze to Billy's face. "They meant to help. All the same, I'll cut their fool livers out if I ever catch up to them."

Tristan was making his way toward the center of destruction, pistol drawn, as were several other men, the doctor among them. Reluctantly, the aging rancher surrendered his son's body to them, let Shay help him to his feet after they walked away.

"Why?" Shay asked quietly.

Kyle didn't pretend not to understand what he was asking. He stood proudly, a shorn Samson in the ruins of the temple, his big, meaty hands loose at his sides, his head encircled in a dirty bandage. "I didn't know about the stagecoach until after it was all over," he said. "Then I wanted to protect Billy."

"And Cornelia?" He knew the truth, had learned it from Aislinn, but he wanted Kyle to confirm the tale of his own accord.

The rancher smiled humorlessly. "She put him up to it, looking to drive you away from Prominence once and for all. You didn't think Billy had the imagination to come up with a scheme like that on his own, did you?"

Shay shook his head. He would form a posse and ride after the Powder Creek men, of course, but essentially the case was settled. He felt no triumph, just an overwhelming sense of sadness and loss and, yes, pity. Pity for Billy, who'd done what he had out of stupidity, mostly, and a need to impress the world with his manhood; for the old man, whose actions, though undeniably wrong, were also understandable. He even felt a little sorry for Cornelia, whose reasons were the cruelest, coldest and most pointless of all—selfishness, jealousy, fear.

Tristan laid a hand to his shoulder. "You all right?" he asked quietly, as two members of the town council took William Kyle into custody. The rancher would be locked up in a storeroom at the livery stable until they could figure out what to do with him.

Shay nodded and raised his eyes to see Aislinn standing at the edge of all those fragments of boards and bricks, her hands clasped in front of her, her face anxious. He moved toward her.

"Are you hurt?" she asked.

He shook his head. "Billy's dead, though. And from the looks of Kyle, he won't last long enough to stand trial." He glanced back over one shoulder, saw Tristan helping some of the other men clear away the heaviest beams. "It's been a hell of a day, hasn't it?"

She slipped her arm through his. "What now?"

"I'll wire every marshal and sheriff I can think of to look out for O'Sullivan and the others, but by now they've scattered in every direction."

Aislinn's face was translucent with hope. "You aren't going after them?"

"I don't know," he answered. "I imagine the mayor and the town council will have an opinion on that. Right now, I've got to find out what kind of shape Cornelia's in, and Dorrie, too."

"Eugenie said the house wasn't too badly damaged," she told him, still holding his arm as he started in the direction of the doctor's office, which was down near the Yellow Garter. He recalled the bucket brigade that had formed while he was getting Aislinn and Dorrie out of the cellar. "Tristan recovered his money, too. It was just a little scorched."

Shay managed a crooked smile. "He didn't mention that. But, then, things have been a little wild around here this morning."

Entering the doctor's office, they were met with a disconcerting sight. Billy Kyle's body lay uncovered on a table, the glazed and lifeless eyes staring up at the ceiling, while Cornelia occupied a chair next to the wall. Her fists were clasped in her lap and she rocked back and forth, as though filled with energy she could not contain, but when her gaze rose to meet Shay's, he knew she was as sane as anybody.

She'd known full well what she was doing when she arranged Grace's death, the deaths of the others aboard that stagecoach. And when she'd tried to kill Dorrie and Aislinn, too.

"I didn't want your goddamned money," he said. "Or your house or your general store."

Cornelia averted her head, but there was no remorse in her, he knew that. She regretted being caught, that was all. If it served her, she'd do all the same things over again, right down to shutting two human beings, one of them her own sister, up in a burning cellar. Fearing the emotions that rose up in him, Shay turned blindly away and went outside, where he gasped for fresh air.

"What will happen to her, Shay?" Aislinn asked, when he'd had some time to collect himself. "What will happen to Dorrie?"

"I don't know about Cornelia," he answered presently, without meeting her gaze. "Dorrie will probably stay on in the house and run the store. At least, I hope she will. She's really got nowhere else to go."

He touched Aislinn's face with the back of his hand. "You haven't changed your mind, have you? About marrying me, I mean?"

Her smile was brilliant, dazzling, casting light into all the dark places inside him. "I haven't changed my mind," she said.

He kissed her, right there on the street, but only lightly. "When's the wedding?" he asked.

"As soon as my brothers arrive. I'll send for them tomorrow—things are pretty frenzied over at the telegraph office just now. And of course I'll need a dress."

The sound of someone clearing their throat interrupted the conversation, and Shay turned to see Tristan standing a few feet away, wearing that insouciant grin of his. "This is lovely, Marshal," he said, "but while you two are making wedding plans, those polecats are getting away. We ought to at least *try* to get them, don't you think? I've rounded up a dozen men to help."

Shay sighed. It was an exercise in futility, going after O'Sullivan and the others, but it was also the right thing to do. He gave the borrowed star pinned to Tristan's coat a pointed glance. "You're taking that badge a little too seriously, brother," he said. He turned to Aislinn, with an apology on his lips, but she met his gaze with a steady smile.

"Be careful," she said.

He nodded his promise. There was so much to say, a

whole lifetime of words to be exchanged, but it wasn't the time and he knew it. So he simply walked away with Tristan, headed toward the livery stable, where he would collect his horse.

Aislinn found Dorrie much recovered when she returned to the hotel to look in on her. The other woman read her expression as she stepped over the threshold, her face flushed with relief. "It's true then, what Eugenie said. Shamus wasn't hurt in that dreadful explosion."

"He's fine," she said. She didn't add that he'd gone after the riders who'd blown up the jail, nor did she say that Cornelia was in custody and would probably be charged with conspiracy to commit murder, among other crimes. Dorrie had enough to worry about as it was. "We're going to be married, Shay and I."

Dorrie's face, glistening here and there with burn salve, lit up. "That's wonderful. You shall have Papa and Mama's room, and we'll run the store together, you and me."

The idea of living in the spacious McQuillan house and working in the general store appealed to Aislinn very much, but she would be half of a partnership after her marriage to Shay, and that meant consulting with him before she made any promises or agreements. She smiled, glad that Dorrie had plans, that her sister's deception and the terrible events of that day had not broken her after all. "I'll need a wedding dress," she said.

"I know just the one," Dorrie replied eagerly, throwing back the covers and swinging her legs over the side of the bed. She was wearing one of Eugenie's nightgowns. "The ivory silk. It came in last week, on the stagecoach. Where in blazes are my clothes? I can't be lying around here all day. I want to see Cornelia, for one thing. And we'll need workers to start repairing the house as soon as possible."

Aislinn didn't attempt to protest; she just got out of Dorrie's way.

Cornelia had vanished by the time they reached the doctor's office; at some point, she'd simply slipped away, and nobody knew where she'd gone, though Dorrie seemed to have her suspicions. She headed straight for the safe in the office of the general store and found it open and empty.

"Good heavens," said Aislinn.

"Good riddance," said Dorrie.

It was later proved that Cornelia had added horse-thieving to her other offenses, helping herself to William Kyle's own gelding, heretofore detained in the livery stable pending its master's release or hanging, whichever came first. Aislinn waited nervously for Shay, well aware that any one of those men would shoot him dead without thinking twice about it.

To her relief, he returned before sunset, with Tristan and the posse and three prisoners, Mr. O'Sullivan among them. Aislinn stayed carefully back, but she heard a deputy telling his wife about the chase: the others had gotten away clean, but these were the ringleaders. They were bound, hand and foot, and would be under guard in the livery-stable storeroom with Kyle until a new judge arrived.

It was Dr. Yancy who met Shay in the street with the news that Cornelia had escaped Aislinn heard his words clearly, though she still kept her distance. Face set in grim lines, Shay moved immediately to rein his horse around and set out in pursuit, but Tristan stopped him by taking a firm hold on the gelding's bridle. He spoke in softer tones that eluded Aislinn, and Shay flushed as he listened, but he settled down a bit.

As he dismounted in front of what had once been his office, Tristan rode out of town without a backward glance. Shay stood watching him go for a few moments, then went off to attend to his prisoners.

Aislinn left him to his business, although she wanted nothing so much as to throw her arms around him, tell him that she loved him, that she was glad, so glad, he'd come back safe.

She had to wait until that night, when he joined her and Dorrie for supper in the dining room of the McQuillan house. Although the place smelled of smoke and the floorboards were buckled, it was a gracious gathering. Shay ate his fill of boiled turnips and roast venison and walked Aislinn back to the hotel, where she would stay until they were properly married.

He walked her as far as the lobby, where Eugenie was waiting with folded arms, her expression dour, and one eyebrow raised. "I guess I'd better not kiss you," he said, in a whisper. "I don't mind saying, though, that I'd like to do a great deal more than that."

A pleasant rush of anticipation swept through Aislinn; she wondered if it was normal for a bride-to-be to look forward to her wedding night with delight instead of maidenly dread. For her own sake, she changed the subject. "We have a lot of decisions to make, Shay."

He cupped her chin in his hand and cast a sidelong wink in Eugenie's direction. Aislinn did not dare to look and see how it was received. "We'll live where you want to live," he said. "If you want to work with Dorrie at the store, that's all right by me. I've only got one stipulation, and here it is: Don't you be giving me grief about turning in my badge, because I won't do that. Not even for you."

She swallowed, then nodded. "Fair enough," she said.

He traced the shape of her lips with the pad of his thumb, sending an achy heat all through her, and she trembled to think what it would be like, surrendering to him. "Good night," he said, his voice hoarse.

Aislinn was stricken by the depth of her love for this man; the simplest of looks or caresses could move her so profoundly. She just stood there, watching mutely as he turned and walked away, stepping through the doors of the hotel and vanishing into the lively noise of Prominence.

Eugenie startled her with a touch on the arm. "He'll be all right, your Shamus," she said. "Come along, girl. We'll have a cup of tea. Should have the kitchen to our own selves at this hour."

One lantern was burning in the large room at the back of the hotel, and the water in the kettle must still have been hot, because Eugenie had the tea brewing in no time.

"I wish there were a way to love him less," Aislinn confided, from her seat at the trestle table. She sat forlornly, with her chin propped in her hands. "I'm scared, Eugenie."

"Don't be a damn fool," Eugenie scolded, her motions impatient as she moved about. "You go ahead and love that man, girl—you love him like there wasn't gonna be no tomorrow. You love him as hard and deep as you can, at full throttle, like one of them steam engines with the boiler red hot and clankin' fit to blow. No, ma'am, don't you go savin' back love, or measurin' it out, like it was white sugar or somethin' that can be used up. You give Shamus all you got, and you take just as much back from him, every day of your life, and you count yourself lucky for havin' the chance."

"That was quite a speech," Aislinn said, when she'd had a moment to recover. "Who was he, Eugenie? The man you loved that way? Did he love you back?"

Eugenie set a chipped china teapot down in the middle of the table with a telling thunk, added cups and a sugar bowl and a little jug of milk. "He was a lawman, like your Shamus. His name ain't important; you wouldn't know it anyhow. He died in a shoot-out, a long while ago, back in Missouri. Happened the day after we was supposed to be married."

Aislinn bit her lower lip. Waited.

Eugenie sat down across from her and briskly poured herself a cup of tea, adding copious amounts of sugar and milk and stirring the mix with a loud clatter of spoon against china. Her expression was ruminative in the lamplight. "I stood him up at the altar," the older woman said gruffly, and at great length. "I was afraid to hitch up with a gun-totin' man, you see. Some folks might say I was proved right, him bein' killed just the way I was afeared he would, but I was wrong, Aislinn. I loved that man more'n my own soul. I gave up somethin' precious when I didn't take his name and whatever time the good Lord saw fit to give us."

Tears of sympathy burned in Aislinn's eyes; she looked away for a moment, blinking rapidly in a vain effort to hide them from Eugenie. "I'm so sorry," she said, finally.

Eugenie reached across the table to pat her hand. "Don't be. I ain't had such a bad life. But you take my advice, girl. When it comes to lovin' a man like Shamus McQuillan, you don't hold nothin' back. There ain't many like him."

Aislinn smiled and sniffled. "Well," she said, "there's one. Tristan."

To her surprise, Eugenie frowned, her bristly brows coming together. "That one," she said ponderously. "Now, he ain't exactly who or what he says he is." A smile broke through. "But that's no never-mind to you, so don't you go frettin' about it."

Aislinn's mind and heart were full of Shay, and wedding plans, full of her brothers, who would join her at last, just a few weeks hence, and of images from Eugenie's heartbreaking tale of love found and lost again. There was simply no room left for Tristan. The two women finished their tea in companionable silence, and Aislinn mounted the stairs to the room Shay had taken for her, and the bed that seemed too big and too empty.

EPILOGUE

ONE MONTH LATER . . .

*L*ACE CURTAINS FLUTTERED AT THE WINDOWS of the best room in the hotel, and there was only candlelight to push back the gathering darkness. A bottle of fancy wine jutted from a silver cooler, and petals from the last roses of summer were spread over the bed. Aislinn Lethaby McQuillan, new bride, surveyed the scene from her husband's arms as he carried her over the threshold.

A tremor went through her. She'd been anticipating this night for weeks, and she wouldn't have turned back for anything, but all of a sudden she was thoroughly, painfully aware of how very little she knew about the intimate rites of marriage.

Shay kicked the door shut with his heel, and the slam must have resounded throughout the hotel. The message was as clear as any DO NOT DISTURB sign would have been. He tasted Aislinn's lips teasingly before setting her on her feet.

"Doubts, Mrs. McQuillan?" he asked. His eyes twinkled with a sort of tender mischief.

She shook her head. They had been married for two hours, and the celebration was still going on, over at the house, where Thomas and Mark were happily ensconced in Shay's old room. Dorrie was probably still presiding over the festivities, as she presided over the general store, though she was teaching Aislinn the business. Cornelia was surely halfway around the world by then, with no intention of returning—Tristan had tracked her all the way to a shipping office in San Francisco, where she had bought passage under her own name—and Mr. Kyle and his consorts had been taken to Sacramento to stand trial. The new jailhouse was under construction, and it would have four cells, as well as space for a couple of deputies.

"No," she said. "No doubts."

He laid his hands on her shoulders, drew her to him. "Come here, then," he said, and bent his head to kiss her.

Again that shock of sensation went through her, stealing her breath, making her sway back onto her heels, so that Shay had to steady her. He chuckled.

"I want you, Mrs. McQuillan," he said, "but we're going to take this slow—real slow. I'll show you the way."

She moistened her lips and nodded, trusting him with her soul as well as her body. He put his arms around her, but loosely, and began undoing the clasps at the back of the ivory silk wedding gown she'd bought at the general store, with her own money. The fabric fell away gently, seemed almost to melt, like a fog under warm sunshine, and then she was standing before him in her white eyelet camisole, woven through with pink ribbon, her petticoats and drawers, her stockings and soft slippers.

She wanted a garment in trade, and took off his coat, tossing it aside. Then, emboldened, she loosened his string tie, unbuttoned his vest. He reciprocated by undoing the ties of her camisole, baring her breasts, admiring them with his gaze and with the light passage of his hand.

"Lovely," he breathed.

Her nipples jutted against his palms, eager and hard, as he weighed her. Bent his head to kiss her again, more hungrily this time, more fiercely.

She wanted fierceness from him, wanted to conquer

and be conquered. Wanted more, much more, of what he made her feel, holding her that way, as though she were precious and fragile.

He gave a low groan, caught her up in his arms, and carried her to the bed, where he laid her down gently and surveyed her, his eyes catching the wavering glint of the candlelight. He pulled off her slippers after a while, and rolled down her stockings one by one. Divested her of the petticoats and finally the drawers, and all the while she lay there like a willing captive on a sultan's couch, deliciously helpless and wanting nothing of power.

"You are," he said, shedding his vest, "too beautiful to be real." He shoved down his suspenders then, pulled his shirttail out of his trousers.

Aislinn watched him in fascination, thinking quite the same thing. He was a fairy-tale prince, or some kind of primitive god, but surely not a mortal man. He was made too perfectly for that; he was a golden savage, shaped by the hand of some mythical sculptor. "Lie down with me," she enjoined him softly.

He finished undressing and stretched himself out gracefully on the bed beside her; she reveled in the restrained power of him, the heat and weight and substance, the uncompromising masculinity. He kissed her tenderly, then with more fervor and still more, until she was tossing beneath him, full of need.

"Now?" she whispered.

He grinned and shook his head. "Not yet," he said. "Not for a long, long time." And then he kissed and nibbled his way down over her jaw and along the length of her neck. He tasted her collarbones, traced them with the tip of his tongue, while his hand made slow, soft circles on her belly and the tops of her thighs, always avoiding the place that strained for him, wanted most to be touched.

When he took a nipple full into his mouth and took suckle, Aislinn cried out in startled pleasure, her back

arching off the feather-filled mattress. His chuckle reverberated through her breast, and he was greedy, there and
in other places.

He took his time, loving her, just as he had said he
would do. She thrashed and whimpered and pleaded and
still he made free with her, teasing, touching, bringing
her to the brink of release over and over again, leaving
her to tremble there, and then letting her fall once more,
back into the heated ministrations of his hands and his
mouth and his whispered promises.

She was limp with wanting and slick with perspiration
when he finally parted her legs and poised himself over
her. He was big; she'd seen and touched his erection, but
feeling him at the entrance of her body gave new
meaning to the concept of size. She tensed and widened
her eyes.

He brushed her lips with his own. "We'll take this slow,
Aislinn," he said. "Just like I promised. Trust me?"

She nodded and raised her hips, seeking to admit him.
It was going to hurt; he'd told her that, so had Eugenie, in
her brusque, shy way, during one of their talks. But
because Shay was Shay, and because they loved each
other, pleasure awaited, beyond the pain.

He eased inside her, just a little way, and she started to
panic.

He stopped, kissed her, reassured her. Took her by
inches, with a patience she marveled at. Gradually, her
body expanded to receive him, and an ancient drumbeat
began, quickening her responses, causing her to move
beneath him, to move with him. She seemed to exist,
during those long, fiery minutes, only in the widespread
pulses of her body; she felt a tearing sensation as he
breached her virginity at last, but by then she was lost in
the heart of her need. Fevered, she flung herself upward
to meet every thrust of his powerful hips, her fingers
buried in his hair, her thumbs learning the shape of his
cheekbones. Their mouths were joined, their tongues

sparring, when the final, highest pinnacle was reached; they rocked together, their cries echoing one inside the other, descended to lesser peaks, one after another, and finally fell in an exhausted tangle to the mattress, arms and legs entwined.

"I love you," Shay said, when a long time had passed. He still sounded a little breathless.

"And I love you," she answered, twining one finger in a lock of his hair. "Do you suppose we made a baby?"

He raised his head, looked into her eyes, and grinned. "Twins, probably," he said. "But maybe we'd better try again, just to make sure."

She laughed and put her arms around his neck, drew him close for her kiss. "You're right, Marshal. Let's not take any chances."

"Ummm-hmmm," he agreed, with a look of sober concentration. "Can't be too careful." He moved over her, and it all began again, the kissing, the stroking, the teasing, the slow heating of the blood. Stretching forth one arm, Shay turned the lamp down until the flame winked out.

Two Brothers

For years, bestselling author Linda Lael Miller
has delighted readers with her passionate,
evocative stories of life and love in the Old West.
Now, with this innovative pair of novels, she creates
two gripping stories of identical twin brothers,
separated at birth, but drawn to each other's side. . . .

The Gunslinger

Now that he's finally found his twin brother, all Tristan
Saint-Laurent wants is to be a peaceful rancher. What he
gets is Miss Emily Starbuck, a determined package of
trouble from back East. Tristan knows he should tell Emily
and her aggravating sheep to move along, but he doesn't
have the heart. Suddenly this man of danger is dreaming of
weddings and babies. But the life he's left behind may yet
come between him and the woman he's growing to love.

Emily Starbuck is making a fresh start by raising the sheep
she's bought with a meager inheritance. She's willing to
fight every cattleman in the West, but she can't resist
Tristan. His handsome face and lean, strong body make her
knees buckle, and her thoughts move to sharing a blissful
ranch life with the man. But what Emily doesn't know
about Tristan could jeopardize their dream of happiness.

The Gunslinger

❧

1884

Tristan

❧

Chapter
1

◈◈◈

JUNE 1884

*H*E OUGHT TO MOVE ON, that was all. Bid Shay and his sweet, enterprising wife a fond farewell, saddle up his horse, and ride out of Prominence without looking back. There were a thousand places he might go—up to Montana, where he'd left a thriving cattle operation in the care of hired men, southward to San Francisco and certain women who professed to find him fair. Maybe even back East, to Chicago or Boston or New York—a man with funds to spend and invest might further himself in any of those cities, while enjoying the singular pleasures and graces of civilization.

He sighed and heaved another bag of oats up into the bed of his wagon, a small but sturdy buckboard acquired as part of the bargain when he'd purchased a local ranch nearly a year before. His brother stood watching as he worked, arms folded, one side of his mouth slanted upward in a self-satisfied grin. Shay's badge, a silver star, gleamed with all the splendor of something netted from a night sky. Shay'd been married for some time now, and the match was a contented one. He'd be a father at any time. He was proud as a rooster, and although Tristan usually found his twin's blatant good cheer cause for shared celebration, on that particular day, it chafed some

tender and previously unrecognized place inside him almost raw.

"You might lend a hand," he groused, hoisting up another sack of feed from the pile of bags on the sidewalk, "instead of just standing there, watching me sweat."

Shay didn't flick an eyelash or twitch a muscle; right down to that grin—which was all the more irritating for the fact that he'd worn it on his own face often enough—he stayed the same. He didn't point out that he'd spent many an hour on Tristan's land, roping and branding calves, rounding up strays, digging post holes, stringing lines of barbed wire, driving nails into shingles on the roof of the ranch house. He didn't say anything at all.

Tristan shoved past his brother and hurled the oats into the buckboard with such force that the springs bounced and the horses, a mismatched pair of roans better suited to sod-busting, pranced and nickered and tossed their heads.

"Aislinn wants you to come to supper," Shay announced. The expression of quiet understanding in his eyes was harder to take than most any other emotion would have been, save outright pity, that is. "She's frying up a couple of chickens. You know how those brothers of hers eat. No doubt, there'll be gravy and biscuits. Mashed potatoes, too. Green beans, I reckon, boiled up with bacon and onion."

Tristan's mouth watered; he swallowed. He was tired of the food at the hotel dining room, passable though it was, and wearier still of his own sorry bachelor cooking. While he didn't lack for invitations to take evening meals and Sunday dinners in various households thereabouts, he was reluctant to accept, since such doings generally occasioned the presentation of a marriageable daughter, niece or sister. Although he fully intended to take a wife, when he found the right woman, he did not enjoy being pursued, maneuvered, manipulated and arranged. "Biscuits?" he echoed, weakening.

Knowing he'd won the skirmish, Shay pushed away from the frame of the door, took up a bag of feed and flung it into the wagon. "Biscuits," he confirmed.

Tristan swept off his hat momentarily and thrust a hand through his hair, which felt damp and gritty. He hadn't shaved in a few days, and he probably smelled of sweat and horse manure. "I'm not fit to dine at a lady's table," he said, and he heard a woeful note in his voice that shamed him not a little. He wasn't about to start sympathizing with himself at this late date.

Shay arched an eyebrow as he assessed the sad state of his brother's grooming. Then he glanced up at the sun, squinting against the glare. When his gaze returned to Tristan's face, he'd sobered some. "You have time enough to get yourself bathed and barbered, and I can lend you a suit of clothes."

Tristan pulled off his hat again and slapped his thigh with it. There was something about this situation he didn't care for, though he couldn't say precisely what it was. He narrowed his eyes as the nebulous sense of trouble tightened into plain suspicion. "You aren't planning to include some female in this little do, are you?"

Shay laughed. "Well, Aislinn will be there," he said. "Dorrie, too, probably. And maybe Eugenie."

"You know what I mean, damn it. Just because marriage agrees with you and Aislinn, you believe, the pair of you, that everyone *else* ought to be hitched to somebody, too."

Shay shook his head, made a clucking sound with his tongue and put a curled fist to his chest, as though to pull out a still-quavering dagger. "To think my own brother, the only real kin I have, doesn't trust me."

"You're damn right I don't."

After consulting the sun again, Shay lifted the last of the feed bags into the rig. "You're getting prickly in your old age," he commented mildly. "If you don't have a care, you might turn into one of those crusty codgers who spit tobacco in the churchyard and go around with egg in their beards.

See you at seven o'clock. You need a clean shirt and a pair of pants, you know where to find them."

"Thanks," Tristan said, in a tone that might have been counted surly if it hadn't been entirely justified. He climbed into the wagon box and took up the reins, setting his face toward home. His ranch house was about three miles out of town, on a high bank overlooking Powder Creek, surrounded by a thousand acres of good grassland. To the north was the Kyle property, a vast spread that he coveted with an unholy longing.

Upon his arrival, he drove the rig into the barn, climbed into the back, and unloaded the oats before jumping down to unhitch the lamentable team and settle the animals in their stalls. After feeding those broken-down creatures and the gelding, then filling all the water troughs, he made for the house, a rambling log structure, with a good rock fireplace at either end. The kitchen, dining room and parlor were all one large room, but there were four bedrooms upstairs, good, spacious ones, with lace curtains at the windows and rugs on the wide pine-plank floors. He'd taken the best and biggest for himself; it had a good wood-burning stove and a nice view of the mountains, but it was a lonely place, for all its creature comforts and uncommon size, and he passed as little time there as he could.

He carried water in from the pump in the dooryard and filled the reservoir on the stove, then built up the fire. He looked around him and sighed, wondering when he'd developed this aversion to his own company. He'd spent much of his adult life on the trail, often traveling for days with no other companion than his horse, and it had never bothered him, but instead afforded him welcome opportunity to order his thoughts. Now, even though he had work to do, hard, outdoor labor that used all there was of him, body, mind and spirit, and that he loved, now that he had money, even a family of sorts again, and should have been satisfied with his lot, he felt instead like Cain, marked

and condemned to wander footloose until the end of his days.

Taking up the buckets, he went outside to pump more water, and as he walked, he whistled under his breath, grinning a little. Like as not, he was taking too solemn a view of things. He'd wash up, shave, put on clean clothes, and ride back to town. A dose of Aislinn's fried chicken would raise his spirits.

In time, he had a good bit of water heated, enough to fill the copper washtub, and he stripped down until he was naked as God's truth and gave himself a good scouring right there in the kitchen end of the house. Figuring he needed rinsing, he wrapped a sheet of toweling around his middle and headed for the yard again, meaning to douse himself with a bucket or two at the pump.

That was when he first heard the sheep.

Head dripping, one hand clasping the towel in place, Tristan stood absolutely still and listened. Yes. That bleating sound, growing ever nearer, was unmistakable.

He looked around and saw dust rising against the eastern sky in great, surging billows, like the aftermath of some apocalyptic eruption. The din was louder now, and he made out the barking of a dog, woven through in uneven stitches of noise.

The flock came over the rise behind his house then, a great, greasy-gray mob of complaining wool, heading hell-bent for the creek. Before Tristan could deal with his indignation at the intrusion, they were all around him, carrying on fit to rouse the mummies of Egypt, brushing past, raising enough grit to ruin the effects of his bath.

He watched, hot-eyed, as the sheepherder came toward him, mounted on a little spotted pony. He was a small man clad in a battered slouch hat, butternut shirt, dirty serape, indigo denim pants and scuffed boots, about as unprepossessing as he could be. The dog, some type of long-haired mix, paid Tristan no mind at all, but continued driving the

sheep toward water. God knew, the beasts were probably too stupid to find it on their own.

"I guess you didn't notice the fence," Tristan said moderately, taking a hold on the pony's bridle, when the shepherd would have ridden right past him.

The trespasser's face was hidden by the shadow of his hat brim. The sheep were still spilling over the rise, and raising such a cacophony that Tristan thought his head would split. That was probably why it took a moment for the soft timbre of the stranger's voice to register on his senses.

"Let go of my horse. It's thirsty and so am I."

Tristan held on, frowning. Took a tighter grasp on the towel. "That fence—"

The slouch hat fell back on its ties at a toss of the shepherd's head, revealing a head of honey-colored hair, wound into a single plait, a pair of brown eyes, thickly lashed and snapping with furious bravado, and a wide, womanly mouth. She was perhaps twenty years old, and about as ill-suited to the task she'd undertaken as it was possible to be, by his reckoning at least. Her features were refined, her bone structure was delicate; no, indeed, she was not fitted for the occupation she had chosen.

"I pulled down the fence," she said, without apology, patting a coil of frayed rope affixed to her saddle. "I won't be kept off my own land."

Tristan, still dealing with the fact that the shepherd was a woman, and the finest he'd ever seen into the account, for all that she was in sore need of tidying up, was a beat behind. The towel around his waist had taken on a whole new significance, now that his perception of the circumstances had been so drastically altered.

"Who are you?" she demanded.

He grinned, standing there in his dooryard, covered in goose bumps and sheep dust and damn little else. "That is an audacious question," he said, "given the situation. My name is Tristan Saint-Laurent, and this is *my* land."

The change in her face was barely noticeable, just a slight faltering of an otherwise resolute countenance. "You are mistaken, sir," she said. Her gaze strayed over his bare chest, took in the loincloth arrangement, and careened back up to his face. A flush stained the smooth skin beneath all that trail dirt. "Or perhaps you are simply a squatter."

"I have papers to prove I'm neither," Tristan answered, not unkindly. He was beginning to feel a little sorry for the woman, which was a laudable change from feeling sorry for himself. Of course, if she'd been a man, he might have shot her by now.

He took in the sheep, still trampling the grass in their migration to the creek, and then looked up at her again. "This is cattle country, Miss—?"

"Starbuck," she said, grudgingly. "Emily Starbuck."

He scanned the horizon, now a ragged scallop of lingering dust. The dog had gone back to collect the stragglers, but there was no sign of another horse, a wagon, or a herder on foot. Still up to his ass in sheep, Tristan was nonetheless distracted from the immediate problem. "You're not traveling all by yourself, are you?" he asked, bemused.

"Of course not," she answered, with a brittle, impatient little smile. "I've got Spud with me." With a toss of her head, she indicated the hardworking dog, then leaned forward slightly to pat the pony's gritty neck. "And Walter, here. Now, if you wouldn't mind getting out of my way, I'd like to water my horse at my stream."

Issues of ownership aside, Walter was a mare, Tristan had observed that right off, but he concluded that maybe it gave Miss Starbuck comfort to call the animal by a masculine name. "Go ahead and attend to your mount," he said. "Then you'd better come inside, where we can talk this out."

She eyed him, letting her gaze stray no lower than his breastbone this time, and blushed again. "I'm not stepping

foot over that threshold or any other in the company of a near-naked man," she said with conviction, casting a glance back over one slender shoulder at the house. "Have you got a wife in there? Or a sister, at least? Somebody to serve for a chaperone?"

"No," Tristan answered, "but you're perfectly safe all the same. I am a gentleman."

Her glance was skeptical. His hold having slackened on the bridle, she reined the horse away and rode past him, through what must have been four acres of bawling woollies, toward the water.

He might have been amused by the whole situation, if it hadn't been for those blasted sheep; if they got onto his range, they'd crop the grass off flush with the ground, leaving nothing but stubble for his cattle. Those he hadn't already lost through the gap in the fence, that is. He had to get rid of Miss Starbuck and her flock, soon, whether he liked the prospect or not.

Suddenly self-conscious, Tristan hurried into the house and up the stairs to his room, where he dressed hastily. His bathwater was still sitting near the kitchen floor, and he was almost as dirty as if he'd never taken a bar of soap to his hide at all, but expediency precluded all other considerations.

He nearly collided with the Starbuck woman when he wrenched open the front door and burst through it with the full momentum of urgency behind him. He gripped her shoulders, lest she fall, and in that tiny fraction of time, the merest shadow of a moment, something eternal happened. He released her as instantly as if she were made of hot metal, but it was too late. He knew he wasn't the same man who'd taken hold.

"Come inside," he said.

She seemed as shaken as he was, and he wondered if she'd felt the same strange, elemental tumult he had. "All—all right." She looked a lot smaller, now that she was down off that horse. Tristan figured she'd feel as fragile and fine-

boned as a bird, if he were to touch her again. Which, of course, he wasn't about to do. Not yet, anyway.

There were no makings for tea in his bachelor's cupboard, but he did produce coffee, in fairly short order, while Miss Starbuck—he already thought of her as Emily, though he supposed that was presumptuous of him—sat primly at his plain pine table, her hands folded in her lap, her outsized hat resting on the floor beside her. The infernal babble of her sheep seeped through the chinking in the sturdy log walls of the house, serving as an irritating reminder that women were women and business was business. And sheep sure as hell were sheep.

"This *is* the Eustace Cummings place, isn't it?" Emily inquired, at some length, when Tristan set a mug of steaming coffee before her.

"It was," he answered. "I bought it from him a year ago. Are you hungry? You look a little peaky."

Great tears swelled and glistened in her eyes, but she blinked them away, simultaneously shaking her head. Although she sat with her head high and her backbone rigidly straight, her despair was evident. Her hands trembled as she pulled off her leather gloves and shoved them into a pocket of the serape. "I have a marker here," she said, and stood a moment to pull a folded document from the pocket of her denims. Intrigued by the concept of a woman in pants, Tristan started wishing she'd remove the serape, and had to bring himself back to the moment by force of will. "Mr. Cummings put this place up as collateral for a debt," she went on, handing him the paper. "He defaulted, as you can see by this paper, and ownership was transferred to my uncle—"

He was touched by the earnestness of her expression. "Your uncle," he prompted, somewhat hoarsely, when she fell silent in the middle of the sentence.

"He died a month ago. But he left me this land and those sheep out there." She shoved the document toward him and he scanned it, and was more convinced than ever that it was

a forgery. Eustace Cummings had been illiterate, but the paper bore a flowing signature. "They're all I have in the world." This last was no bid for pity, but instead a clear warning against such sentiments, should he be harboring any.

Tristan wondered if there was a blade of grass left on the acre surrounding his house; like as not, he wouldn't be able to walk to the barn without sinking to his ankles in sheep shit. He was strangely unconcerned, given how much sweat, money, hope and calculation he'd put into the place.

"You've been cheated," he said, very quietly. He wished he had some tea to offer her; the stuff seemed to perk a woman up. His mother had always taken orange pekoe when she felt melancholy, and Aislinn generally brewed the like for Dorrie, if she got to pining for her lost love, Leander.

She sat even more stiffly than before, looking miserable. Her white, even teeth were sunk into her lower lip. Presently, she said, "You will be called upon to prove that assertion, sir."

"Stop calling me 'sir,'" he ordered. "This is not a cotillion or a box social, and we're casual out here in the countryside. Where are you from, anyway?"

She sighed. "Minnesota."

"You came all the way from Minnesota driving that flock, with just a dog to help you?"

That was when she smiled, and if Tristan had been standing, he'd have rocked back onto his heels. He damn near turned his chair over as it was, such was the impact of a simple change of expression. "I did not acquire the sheep until I reached Butte," she replied, and the smile was gone as quickly as it had arrived. The effect of its absence was quite as dramatic as that of its appearance, though in the opposite way. "You see, my uncle was my only remaining relative, and I was his ward, after a fashion. He contracted consumption, and summoned me to his side, but by the time I arrived, he was gone."

"I'm sorry," Tristan said, and he wasn't just talking. He had no blood family but Shay, and even though he'd really only known his brother for a year, he didn't like to think what it would mean to lose him. He didn't realize until she looked down at the tabletop that he'd laid his hand over hers.

She withdrew none too hastily. "Your proof?"

Tristan was momentarily baffled. "I beg your pardon?"

Emily tapped the document with the tip of a grubby index finger. "You claim to own my land. I should like to see on what authority you base your declaration, sir—er—Mr. Saint-Laurent."

"Tristan," he said, getting up. "You might as well call me by my Christian name, because I fully intend to address you as Emily."

Once again, she colored, but she let the remark pass.

He was grinning a little as he crossed the long room to the plain wood table he used as a desk. It was situated near the fireplace, a handy thing on cold nights. He took a deed from the single drawer—there was another just like it in the bank vault in town—and came unhurriedly back to where Miss Starbuck waited. Outside, the sheep continued to raise a mournful dirge.

She read the deed and if it hadn't been for the dirt covering her face, she'd have had no color at all. She swallowed hard. "Do you suppose Mr. Cummings deceived my uncle?" she asked, when an interval had passed, chopped off second by second, one tick of the mantel clock at a time.

Tristan knew only that his title to the land was legal. Looking at Emily Starbuck, sitting there in her oversized clothes, needing a bath and one of Aislinn's hearty meals even more than he did, he almost regretted his advantage. "It's possible," he said. "Cummings wouldn't be the first to cover a debt with a worthless note."

Emily sagged a little, inside all those clothes, and Tristan braced himself to catch her, fearing she was about to swoon.

Instead, she rallied, her spine straight as the handle of a pitchfork. "We shall have to carry this matter before the law," she said decisively.

Tristan pointed out the date on her marker, which fell a full six months after his own cash purchase of the ranch, but he could see that even an obvious prior claim did not convince her. "I've got a few acres up in the hills where you can put those sheep," he heard himself say. "Just until everything's been decided, I mean."

She looked at him steadily for a few moments, but he knew nonetheless that she was doing everything she could to keep from breaking down to weep. He put away an urge to take her into his arms and assure her that things would work out, he'd see to it. She stood.

"That's kindly of you," she said. "If you'd just point the way—"

He was on his feet. "I'll lead you there myself." He intended to talk her into putting the sheep in the dog's care, just long enough to come to town with him and tuck into some fried chicken at Shay and Aislinn's place.

"I couldn't abandon them," she said, when he had made the suggestion, indicating the ocean of moving, baaing wool with a nod of her head. He was mounted on the gelding, and she was beside him, riding the mare she called Walter. "One cannot merely leave them to wander and round them up whenever you want. Sheep are not like cattle, Mr. Saint-Laurent."

"I do know that, ma'am," Tristan agreed good-temperedly. "And it's Tristan." He adjusted his hat and sighed, looking up at the twilight sky as he spurred the gelding into an ambling trot. The smell of live mutton filled his nostrils like an itch. "There's an old man in a line shack up ahead; I'll get him to keep an eye on the flock for you. You can't spend the night up there alone anyway."

Emily did not turn to look at him, and her face was hidden, once again, in the shadow of her hat brim. "I have

not been sleeping in grand hotels since I left Butte," she said reasonably. "Spud and Walter and I, we like making our beds under the stars." She sighed. "I did expect a house to take shelter in when we arrived, though."

Tristan felt like the worst kind of brute, though he was fairly certain that hadn't been Emily's intention. "You can stay at my place. I'll bunk in the barn."

She spared him a glance. "I'll sleep near my sheep," she said. "Like I told you, they're all I have."

Tristan's attraction to this woman was equal only to the exasperation she caused him. "You can't do that. Between the bears and the mountain cats, your common drifter and some of those outlaws holed up on the Powder Creek spread, you wouldn't be safe."

"I'm not certain I'd be any better off in your ranch house. If indeed it *is* yours." She rubbed the back of her neck with one hand. "I am weary of rough accommodations, though, I must confess," she said.

They didn't speak again until they'd reached the line shack, where Tristan permitted an old hermit named John S. Polymarr to reside, in return for the occasional bit of information concerning the goings and comings of the riders up at Powder Creek.

Polymarr stood in his doorway, wearing an undershirt and a pair of baggy trousers held up by suspenders, watching the sheep move up the draw in a noisy V, driven relentlessly by the dog.

"You better get them critters out of here before Kyle hears tell of 'em," he said.

Tristan dismounted and removed his hat, more out of habit than real deference. His adoptive mother had been a stickler for manners. "Kyle is in the state penitentiary," he replied. "He won't be offering an opinion anytime soon, one way or the other."

Polymarr spat, let his gaze move to Emily, still mounted on her horse. "I don't hold with no sheep, myself," he said.

"I don't either," Tristan answered. "All the same, I meant to offer you five dollars to look after them for a day or two. The lady there has business in town."

The old man squinted in the gathering darkness. "That's a lady?"

Tristan felt Emily stiffen, despite the distance between them, and was glad she couldn't see that one corner of his mouth had developed a slight and intermittent twitch. He said nothing, but simply waited, thinking that she was an incredible woman, traveling all that way with only a dog and a mare and a flock of sheep for company.

"Five dollars?" Polymarr asked, and spat again.

"Two now, three more in a couple of days," Tristan said. It was a ridiculous amount of money to pay, just to get Miss Emily Starbuck to pass an evening in town with him and spend the night under his roof, but he would have given a lot more to achieve his purpose.

Polymarr rubbed his beard, only pretending to ponder the offer. The acquisitive light in his small, rheumy eyes virtually guaranteed his compliance. "Well, all right," he said, in his own good time. "But you just remember, St. Lawrence. I don't hold with no sheep."

Tristan didn't bother to correct the old man's mangling of his name, even though he greatly valued it. "Whatever your opinions," he said, placing a pair of silver dollars in the codger's hoary palm, "the count had better tally when I come back to collect those woolly wretches, or I'll take the difference out of your hide."

"Let me get my gear," Polymarr said, and went back into the shack. When he came out a few minutes later, he had a haversack over one stooped shoulder and a blanket roll under his arm. Tristan took note of the ancient pistol in the old man's belt. "What about that damn dog?" the old coot complained. "He bite or anything like that?"

"He'll tear the throat out of anything or anybody that tries to carry off one of my sheep," Emily said, without turning a hair. Tristan felt a wrench of tenderness, looking at her, thinking once again of all the miles she'd traveled

on her own. It was God's own wonder she wasn't lying beside the trail someplace, dead, the world being that sort of place.

They proceeded up into the high meadow, Polymarr plodding along behind, cursing in the midst of all those caterwauling sheep, and the moon was up by the time Emily had given him instructions and commanded the dog to stay. The animal yawped and ran a few paces after her as they rode away, she and Tristan, but in the end his sense of duty kept him with the flock.

"Tell me where we are suppering," Emily said, when the sheep and Polymarr and the dog were well behind them. "I've forgotten."

"There's no fault in your memory," Tristan replied. "I don't believe I've said where we're headed. We're joining my brother and his wife in town." He hoped Aislinn had held the meal, for he did relish her fried chicken, but if she hadn't, he would take Emily to the hotel dining room. What was it, he wondered, that made him want to feed her, protect her, scrub her down and buy her every length of lace and ruffle between there and San Francisco? There were other things he wanted to do, too, but the time to think of them had not yet come.

He cleared his throat. "You didn't truly come clear from Montana all alone?"

"I did," she answered, and sounded pleased with herself, too.

"Why?" He bit the word off, like a piece of hard jerky, his head full of ugly images. He'd seen the handiwork of renegade Indians and outlaws before, along the trails and on isolated homesteads, and although he admired her grit, it galled him that any woman would take such a risk.

"Why?" she echoed, her tone somewhere between incredulity and mockery. "Because it was the only way to get from there to here, that's why."

"I've made the trip myself. It isn't an easy one."

She looked at him; he felt her gaze even though he

couldn't see her eyes for the hat brim. "It's been my experience," she said, "that not much is easy in this life. Some things, though—well, some things are worth fighting for."

He agreed, and it was clear to him that there was a battle ahead, sure enough. He smiled to himself. There was nothing like a good skirmish.

Chapter
2

❦❧

*J*UST LOOKING UPON THAT STURDY HOUSE in town, with its windows spilling light into a yard where flowers surely grew, Emily thought her heart would burst with wanting such a place for her own. She had kept her spirits up all the way from Butte, more from necessity than courage, though she had her share of that to be certain, but now, all of the sudden, weariness descended upon her, wings spread and talons bared. She had been wearing the same clothes since leaving Montana, and hadn't managed more than a few washings in streams and rivers along the way. She'd probably forgotten the manners she'd taken such care to learn over the years, having lived roughly for so long, and she was bound to disgrace herself somehow.

"I can't." She didn't glance toward Tristan, but she was aware of him there beside her, all the same, sitting that gelding as though he'd been born a part of it. Her face felt hot and her chin wobbled.

"Sure you can," Tristan countered easily, just as if he knew beyond all doubt that she could. Out of the corner of her eye, she saw him swing down from the saddle and tether his mount loosely to the picket fence.

Before she could rustle up a retort, the screen door

23

creaked open and two middle-sized boys erupted through the opening, whooping like red Indians.

"Thomas and Mark," Tristan explained. He reached up and took Emily by the waist before she could deliberate further, lifting her down, setting her lightly on her feet. "In point of fact, they're in-laws, but I think of them as nephews, most of the time."

"And the rest of the time?" Emily asked, smoothing her trousers as though wishing and touching could make them into skirts of fine velvet, or at least clean calico. She took off the slouch hat and pegged it onto Walter's saddlehorn, then smoothed her hair with unsteady hands.

The boys were hurtling toward them over the dark grass. "The rest of the time," Tristan answered, "I pretty much accept that they're savages."

The screen door opened again, and a woman appeared. Her hair gleamed dark as onyx in the lamplight from inside, and her dress, though simple, draped her figure gracefully, for all that she was plainly with child. Once more, Emily felt the ignoble sting of envy; she turned and would have scrabbled back into the saddle and made a dash for other parts if Tristan hadn't stopped her by taking a soothing grasp on her arm.

Thomas and Mark had gained the fence and, for a beat, they were quiet, peering at Emily in the faulty glimmer of a waning moon. "Who's that?" one of them inquired.

"Miss Emily Starbuck," Tristan said, as formally as if he'd been presenting her at some grand ball, "meet Thomas Lethaby, there on the left. That's his brother, Mark, on the right."

"You're a girl?" the one called Mark wanted to know. He seemed skeptical.

"Howdy," Thomas said, simultaneously elbowing his sibling in the ribs.

"Boys! Come inside, this minute," the dark-haired woman commanded, with loving authority. She stood partway down the walk, and the children obeyed her reluctantly, casting backward glances as they went, while Tristan opened the

gate and stood aside to let Emily precede him. She had to force herself through for, drawn though she was, a part of her still wanted to bolt.

"Are we too late for supper?" Tristan asked, addressing the woman. There was a smile in his voice, and a degree of caring too pure and quiet to be without meaning. He'd swept off his hat, as well, holding it loosely in one hand.

The lady of the house laughed. "You know you could turn up in the middle of the night, looking for a meal, and never go away hungry." She put out a hand to Emily. "Good evening," she said. "I'm Aislinn McQuillan."

Emily responded with a handshake and gave her name shyly.

"Won't you come in?" Aislinn asked. By that time, she'd curved an arm around Emily's waist and was gently propelling her toward the house. A man stood on the porch now, leaning with his hands braced against the whitewashed railing, the warm light glowing golden in his fair hair. Although Emily could make out only the outline of his frame and a general sense of his manner, she recognized right away that he was a twin to Tristan.

Emily was secretly mortified by the state of her person, particularly her clothing, as she passed along the walk, up the steps, into the house. She regretted letting Tristan persuade her to accompany him here and, at one and the same time, yearned to be taken into the laughter, into the light, if only for a single evening. Like a ragged and piteous wayfarer, warming her hands at a friendly fire. "I've been traveling for many weeks," she said, in an effort to explain the trousers, the serape, the collarless shirt made for a man.

"With sheep," Tristan added, in the entryway.

The other man gave a low whistle of exclamation.

"This," Aislinn said, smiling as she turned to indicate Tristan's precise replica, "is my husband, Shamus McQuillan. We call him Shay."

"Sheep," Shay marveled, as though he'd not heard of such an animal before.

A table was set in the dining room, with candles and

china and silver shining fit to dazzle the eye. There was nary a sign of Thomas and Mark; Emily suspected they were looking on from some hidden vantage point, though. She couldn't help a small smile, nervous as she was.

"This way," Tristan said, before Emily had to ask for a place to freshen up. He took a light hold on her arm and led her on through the dining room into the spacious kitchen behind. After fetching a basin and a ladle from the mud room, he lifted a lid on the side of the huge black cookstove, trimmed in gleaming chrome, and soon there was hot water. Soap.

Emily yearned toward those plain refinements just as she had toward the house itself; she removed the serape, at a gesture from Tristan, and washed her face and hands as sedately as she could. Her every instinct bade her plunge into that basin, splashing exuberantly and shouting for joy, so welcome was the prospect of being even moderately clean again.

When Tristan led her back to the table, where his brother and sister-in-law waited, talking in low voices, she felt almost presentable. She had decided that, in this one instance at least, she would suspend all thought of her troubles and allow herself to enjoy a pleasant meal in this merry and benevolent place. For much of her life, she had lived in the future, plotting and planning and worrying, anticipating and preparing, but tonight, by conscious choice, she would confine herself strictly to the moment.

It proved dangerously easy to pretend that she had a place in the midst of this glad gathering, that she truly belonged. She forgot her dreary life in Minnesota, where she had been the child bride of a man her uncle's age, and subsequently a widow, forgot the difficulties she had had to face on her arrival in Butte, and the long, lonely and perilous trip overland to Prominence. For a little while, in her mind at least, her clothes befitted a woman, her future was a thing of bright assurance, and she had every right to enjoy the laughter and talk crisscrossing the table.

Only when the evening was drawing to a close, and the

four of them were taking rich coffee from china cups, did the subject of sheep come up again.

"There will be trouble when the ranchers hear about that flock," Shay predicted. Although he was looking at Tristan when he spoke, Emily knew the comment was directed at her. After all, the sheep were hers.

"I believe Emily expected to run them on her own land," Tristan said. His glance touched her, from across the table, as effective as a caress. "She was cheated—probably by Eustace Cummings himself."

Shay sighed sympathetically. "That old swindler," he said, with a sort of desultory affection. "The church was packed to the shingles at his funeral, but I suspect most folks just wanted to make sure he was really in the box."

"Shay!" Aislinn scolded, but her husband merely grinned and covered her hand with his, the thumb playing over her knuckles. She blushed prettily, but made no move to pull away.

Once again, Emily felt envious. In four sterile years of marriage to Cyrus Oxlade, she had never been touched so gently. Indeed, she had been a servant, not a wife. A possession, not a companion. Aislinn, she could see, was a full partner to Shay, and he clearly adored her.

"In any case," Tristan said, "Emily expected to find a house and land waiting for her here. Instead, she found me."

The words gave Emily an odd little thrill, though they shouldn't have done. She couldn't have spoken then for anything; it was as if she were strangling on her own tongue. *Instead, she found me.*

Aislinn passed her a kindly, knowing look. "Well, what will you do now?" she asked, in a practical tone, bare of prejudice or any preconception of justice.

Emily found her voice, but it came dry from her throat. "I guess I'll speak with a lawyer," she said uneasily. It amounted to a bald challenge, but still, it was the truth. She wasn't going to take Tristan Saint-Laurent's word that the ranch was his; she couldn't afford to do that. She had, after

all, nowhere else to go, and some two hundred sheep to look after.

"You're welcome to stay here with us," Aislinn said, her friendliness undiminished. "Until everything is decided, I mean. We have plenty of room."

Emily did not dare to look at Tristan for fear of what she might see in his face. "Mr. Saint-Laurent has been kind enough," she said boldly, "to offer me the use of his—of the house, temporarily."

"'Mr. Saint-Laurent'?" Shay echoed, in the same half-amused tone in which he'd said "Sheep?" earlier.

There was a short silence, then Tristan pushed back his chair and stood. "It's getting late," he said, "and I'm sure Emily is tired."

"I'm sure she is," Shay agreed mildly, standing too. Being nearest, he drew back Emily's chair before going on to perform the same service for his wife. Emily could not decide whether or not she liked Shamus McQuillan, and though she knew him to be almost an exact duplicate of Tristan, physically at least, she saw marked yet not easily definable differences between the two men. As alike as they were, she was sure she would have no difficulty in telling them apart.

"Thank you," Emily said earnestly, to Aislinn, as Tristan ushered her quickly toward the door. "I can't think when I've had a finer meal, or a more congenial evening." That much was certainly true.

Aislinn was looking at Tristan, and a small smile lurked at one corner of her mouth. "I daresay we'll be seeing a great deal more of each other, Miss Starbuck," she said, a moment before her gaze slid back to meet Emily's. There was a merry sparkle in her eyes, part mischief, part welcome.

"I'll be quite busy with my sheep, I expect," Emily said, with some regret. They were on the walk by then, and she was a little breathless, keeping up with Tristan's pace.

"Good night," he called, without looking back.

Perhaps half an hour later, they arrived at the ranch house Emily had expected to own, by virtue of her uncle's bequest.

The Gunslinger

It was dark, and the moonlight was thin. Tristan led the way inside, entering by the front door, and lit a lamp waiting on a table pushed up against the wall.

Emily hesitated on the threshold.

"Come in," Tristan said patiently. Quietly. "I'm harmless, I promise you."

Instinct told Emily that he was *anything* but harmless—he wore the .45 on his hip with too much ease for that, and his smile alone was a weapon—and yet something deep within urged her to trust him, in this one instance at least. She stepped through the opening.

He cocked a thumb toward the stairs. "Take the big room, at the end of the hallway. I'll bring up a couple of buckets of hot water and be on my way."

She yearned for any semblance of a bath, and the thought of a real bed to sleep in made her throat tight with gratitude and wonder. "Why are you being so kind to me?" she asked. "I still believe this is my land—my house." She had to keep believing, because without that, she had nothing.

He gave her another one of those devastating grins, and as far as Emily was concerned, it constituted an unfair advantage. "I see no reason to be *un*kind," he said. "If it turns out that you have a legal claim on this ranch—which you don't—I'll concede the point gracefully. In the meantime, you need somewhere to be."

She had gotten as far as the base of the stairs, and she paused there, one hand curled around the top of the newel post. "I could have stayed in town, with your brother and his wife," she reminded him.

He sighed, lit another lamp, and handed it to her for the ascent to the second floor. "You would have been too far away from your sheep," he said, and it sounded so reasonable that Emily had nodded and covered most of the distance between the foyer and the door of the assigned bedroom before it struck her that Tristan's concern for the welfare of her flock was at plain odds with his own interests as a cattleman.

Not that Emily believed that sheep and cattle could not

coexist, as many ranchers claimed. Granted, rams and ewes chewed grass right down to the roots when they grazed, but if the flock was confined to Emily's own acreage, there was no cause for her neighbors to be concerned. Unless, of course, she didn't *have* any land, in which case she did not know what she would do.

She turned the knob and entered the room Tristan had offered. He had told her it was his, and yet she was unprepared for the dizzying sense of intimacy that swept over her when she caught sight of the spacious bed where he slept, the wardrobe where he no doubt stored his clothing, the washstand where he performed his ablutions, night and morning. . . .

The lamp trembling a little in her hand, Emily closed the door carefully behind her. She set the light on a bureau, bare except for a hairbrush with an ivory handle and a small photographic likeness of a man and woman standing in front of a log house. At variance with most such subjects, they were both smiling, and each had an arm around the other.

The sight made Emily smile, too, and filled her with a strange, poignant affection. As a defense, against that ungovernable emotion rather than against Tristan himself, she carried the room's one chair to the door and propped it under the latch.

She pulled the serape off over her head and hung it carefully from a peg on the wall, then went to sit on the edge of the thick mattress. She wondered uncharitably if the bed belonged to Tristan, or if it might properly be viewed as a part of the Eustace Cummings estate. A brisk knock at the door interrupted her musings, and she stiffened, as though caught in some act of wrongdoing. "Yes?"

Tristan spoke from the hallway. "There was some hot water left in the reservoir," he said. "I'm leaving it out here. You'll find towels and soap in the cabinet under the washstand, and you're welcome to use one of my shirts for a nightgown if you want."

Emily stood, somewhat shakily, her face warm. She was glad for the door between them, not just for virtue's sake, but because it served to hide her state of renewed embarrassment. The prospect of wearing a garment belonging to Tristan against her bare skin, of sleeping on sheets that might still bear the invisible imprint of him, the scent and the shape, nearly overwhelmed her.

She would have been far better off, she concluded, too late, to pass the night on the ground, with her sheep nearby and only Spud to protect her.

"Thank you very much," she called, in a tone as even and steady as she could make it. She moved the chair but stood pressed to the door, waiting, listening for his retreating footsteps. When she heard him descending the stairs, she stepped quickly out into the hallway to collect the two buckets of steaming water.

Half an hour later, scrubbed and clad in a clean cotton shirt that reached almost to her knees, Emily sat cross-legged in the middle of the bed, grooming her hair with Tristan's brush. The rainwater scent of him was all around her, just as she had feared it would be, but the reality proved comforting, rather than worrisome. She had no sensible reason to be frightened; if her host had meant to take unseemly advantage, he'd already had more than ample opportunity to do so. No, it was not him she was afraid of, but something in herself. Some longing, some unmet need she could not define. Her marriage had done nothing at all to prepare her for what she felt in the presence, even the *shadow* of the presence, of Tristan Saint-Laurent.

After re-plaiting her hair, she turned down the wick on the lamp until the light was snuffed out, then crawled beneath the covers and stretched. She did not expect to sleep, but exhaustion must have claimed her right away, for the next thing she knew, sunlight was prodding, red-gold, at her eyelids.

It was another moment before Emily fully realized that she was not lying on the hard, cold ground, fully dressed

and tangled in her bedroll, but upon a nest of the softest feathers. And sheets—cool, clean, linen sheets, still crisp with newness.

Tristan Saint-Laurent's bed. The quilt might have been ablaze, so quickly was she out from under the covers and standing on the hooked rug, her breathing rapid and shallow, her heart pounding.

She closed her eyes. Instructed herself to be calm. It wasn't as if Tristan was *in* the bed, after all, or even in the room.

Hastily, she shook out her clothes and dressed, wishing for more hot water in which to wash her face. Moving the chair from under the knob, she peered out into the hallway, in one direction and then the other. No sign of anyone.

She made her way downstairs, saw that there were cheerful blazes crackling in the fireplaces at either end of the long, sparsely furnished room. Tristan was nowhere in sight, although she found a pot of fresh-brewed coffee waiting on the stovetop. She took an enamel mug from a set of open shelves and, using the tail of her serape for a pot holder, poured a generous portion. Her stomach rumbled, but she tried to ignore it. Bad enough that she was beholden for supper and a night of shelter, not to mention the engagement of Mr. Polymarr to look after her flock. Breakfast could only make things worse. Besides, she fully intended to take the matter to law, and when the judge decreed that this land was hers, she would thank Tristan for his cordial treatment, then ask him to pack his belongings and leave immediately.

The door opened while she was still mired in these thoughts, and Tristan came in, carrying an armload of wood, which he tossed into the box beside the stove with an exuberant clatter. His grin was winsome. "I brew a fine cup of coffee," he said. "Unfortunately, that's all I can make that's fit to offer company."

"I can cook," Emily was flabbergasted to hear herself say.

"Good," Tristan answered, dusting his hands together. Before Emily could correct any misimpression she might

have given him, he was out the door again, leaving it open behind him. She stood on the threshold watching him walk toward what was probably a springhouse. *Her* springhouse, she reminded herself, but it didn't help much, staking mental claims. She was having a very hard time thinking of this man as an opponent, let alone a prospective enemy, but in reality he was both. This was probably her one chance to have a real home, and he had the power to thwart that dream.

Momentarily, he came out of the little outbuilding, carrying a lidded stoneware crock under one arm, along with something wrapped in cheesecloth.

"Eggs," he said, tapping the side of the crock for emphasis. "I bought them yesterday at the general store." He indicated the gauzy package with a nod. "And this is bacon."

Emily's mouth watered. She'd been living on hardtack and beans since she'd left Butte, and she'd counted herself lucky to have that much, given the state of her late uncle's finances. He'd had nothing but the sheep and a marker for a thousand acres of land—this land, on which she stood. She turned and went inside to set a skillet on the stove, telling herself that cooking one meal for Saint-Laurent was the least she could do, given the hospitality he'd offered.

"Please cut that bacon into thin slices," she said, over one shoulder. "And wash your hands first, if you don't mind."

Tristan executed a salute that might have seemed cocky if it hadn't been for the smile in his blue eyes. "Yes, ma'am," he said. She heard him leave, watched through the window while he scrubbed at the pump, using bright yellow soap.

Twenty minutes later, they were seated across the table from each other, sharing a meal. Emily felt a bit dizzy, and for a brief and unnerving interval, she could not recall how she'd gotten from the decision to leave without accepting anything else from her charming adversary to this present, companionable moment. It was as if she had been bewitched.

"What did you do in Minnesota?" Tristan asked. He'd

eaten with good appetite, but now he seemed to have lost interest in the food.

Emily drew a deep breath and let it out slowly. "I was married," she said.

He considered her in silence for a while. Why, she wondered, did she want to tell him everything—how Cyrus had never been a real husband to her, how she'd sometimes felt so lonesome in the night that she'd curled up in a ball on her bed and held her belly with both arms, like somebody dying?

"What became of your husband?" he asked. His tone was easy, moderate, but he cared about her answer, she could see that in his eyes.

Emily looked down at her hands. Even though she wore leather gloves every day, her skin was callused and red-dened, her nails broken. "He died," she said. "Just collapsed one day, out in the fields."

"I'm sorry," Tristan said, and for some reason it shamed her, his sympathy.

She met his gaze. "It's your turn," she told him briskly. "You and Shay McQuillan are clearly twins. Why do you have different names?" *Who is that smiling couple in the daguerreotype upstairs?*

"That's a long and rather remarkable story. To be brief, Shay and I were born on a wagon train, somewhere in the Rockies, to a young couple making their way west. Our father—his name was Patrick Killigrew—was killed by Indians the same day we came into the world, and our mother, Mattie, died that night. A family called McQuillan took Shay in, while I went on with the Saint-Laurents."

It was indeed an amazing tale. "Did you know where he was while you were growing up?"

Tristan shook his head. "My mother—my adoptive moth-er, that is—told me what had happened when she took sick a few years back, and gave me a remembrance book that belonged to Mattie. I found out where Shay was by other means, but I might never have come here if I hadn't been looking for somebody else." For the first time since she'd

met him, and then just for the briefest moment, Tristan looked uncertain. "I meant to move on, once I'd taken care of business."

Emily felt uncomfortable. Although Tristan Saint-Laurent seemed affable, and even boyish, she sensed that there were uncharted depths to his nature, knew somehow that the currents could be dark and treacherous. "Business?"

His smile was dazzling, like a sudden show of sunshine on a cloudy day. "I got what I came for," he said. "And I found out I liked having a family again."

Emily waited. She wouldn't ask about the likeness in the frame on Tristan's bureau top, wouldn't ask if he'd ever had a wife and children of his own.

"Shay and I butt heads on a fairly regular basis," he went on, and a rueful light danced in his eyes. "All the same, it's a fine thing to have a brother. Were you close to your uncle?"

The question caught Emily quite unprepared. She had never really been close to anyone, except for some of the characters in the books she read and the made-up people she turned to when she was alone too long, or scared. "Well, no," she said, in a surprised tone. "My father died before I was born, and my mother passed on soon after. I boarded on a neighboring farm—that's where I learned to cook." She blushed. "I don't usually talk so much." At least she hadn't blurted out that the farm was Cyrus's, and she'd joined the household to take care of his ailing wife, Mary.

He laughed and glanced at her empty plate. "Or eat so much, I reckon."

Now it was Emily who laughed. She'd consumed twice as much food as Tristan had, and she could have eaten more, if the platter between them hadn't been scraped bare. The ease she felt frightened her more than all those nights alone on the trail had done, and she composed herself, bit her lower lip, sat up very straight in her chair.

"What is it?" Tristan asked, his voice quiet. It might be her undoing, that gentle voice.

She stood, managed a wooden smile. Tristan rose, too, and faced her over the table. "I must get back to my sheep,

Mr. Saint-Laurent. I appreciate your generosity, but we are adversaries, aren't we?''

"Are we?'' he countered.

She retreated a step, for no other reason than that she wanted so much to draw nearer to him. "Yes,'' she said, and the word came out sounding strangled and dry. "Yes.'' With that, she made for the door, open to the crisp midsummer morning.

"Miss Starbuck,'' he said.

She looked back, saw him standing in the kitchen doorway, arms folded, one shoulder braced against the jamb. "You'll need your horse,'' he said reasonably.

She stopped, glanced questioningly toward the barn.

Tristan pushed away from the door frame and ambled toward her. He had left his hat inside, and the sun caught fire in his hair. "I put Walter out to pasture,'' he said.

"What?''

"The mare is worn out, Emily.''

Through difficulty after difficulty, Emily had kept her chin up and her eyes dry. Now, in the face of Tristan's determined goodwill, she felt like bursting into tears. "Walter is a mare?'' she asked, partly because she wanted to know, and partly because she needed a few moments to shore up her backbone.

"Yep,'' Tristan answered, with another crooked grin. His arms were folded again, and his eyes were narrowed against the cool brightness of the morning. "I don't mind making you the loan of a horse,'' he said, "if you'll take one of the nags that usually pull my buckboard.''

The loan of a horse, like breakfast, was more than she wanted to accept, but she knew Walter must be exhausted. God knew, she was, but she had sheep to see to, Mr. Polymarr notwithstanding, and Spud, her one true friend, would surely be wondering where his mistress had gone. "I suppose it's too far to walk,'' she said.

Tristan laughed again. "Not if you don't mind spending half the day making the trip,'' he replied.

Emily was beginning to understand the concept of killing

with kindness. "All right!" she cried, in humorous consternation, flinging up her hands. "I'll borrow a horse!"

Tristan shook his head, and although he made an effort to look solemn, amusement lingered around his mouth. He cocked a thumb toward the barn. "Help yourself," he said. Then he turned and walked back to the house, whistling under his breath, while she stood in her tracks, staring after him.

Chapter
3

✧

*A*FTER SADDLING ONE OF THE PLODDING ANIMALS she found in the barn—neither of them looked fit to ride, if you wanted her opinion—Emily set out for the sheep camp in the hills. She might have been a greenhorn in every other respect, but she had a fine sense of direction, and she remembered each turn and twist in the trail that led up into the hills, where her flock was grazing.

For all her skill at finding her way, the ride took almost an hour. Emily was captivated, and kept stopping to look back over the land and admire the sparkling ribbon of water that was the creek, the stout and spacious log house with its mortar chinking and double chimneys, a mansion by frontier standards, the abundant, waving grass, miles and miles of it, it seemed, rippling and flowing in the breeze like some fragrant green sea. Tristan's cattle dotted the landscape as well, but she didn't begrudge them space in the promised land. In their way, they belonged as surely as the trees and stones, the ground and sky.

It was Tristan who didn't fit, Emily reasoned, with some sorrow. When Spud came streaking toward her, barking a joyous welcome and setting the sheep to bleating, she turned from her worries and jumped down to ruffle the dog's pointed ears.

Mr. Polymarr, who had been stretched out under a tree, pondering the inside of his ancient hat, scrabbled to his feet, roused by the ruckus, however belatedly, and cursing like a sailor. Spud, ever the gentleman, growled in disapproval.

The old man waved a dismissive hand at the dog as he trundled over to where Emily stood. "Mornin'," he said, miser-like, as though it cost him to part with even that one word.

"Good morning, Mr. Polymarr," Emily said, amused. She scanned the sheep, knew in that one practiced glance that they were all there, safe and well, if considerably spent from the long trek south. They would need all that was left of the summer grass to prepare for the long, snowy winter awaiting them, she reflected, but in the spring the lambs would come and, soon after, the adult animals could be sheared, their wool sold. A few, but only a few, were to be sold for mutton.

She had by no means forgotten that the cold months, not to mention Tristan Saint-Laurent and a host of other problems, stood between the difficult present and the first profits.

"I didn't expect to see you for a while," Polymarr said, rubbing his white-bristled chin, then spitting. "How do you tolerate these critters, carryin' on the way they do?"

Emily laughed. "They'll quiet down in a few minutes," she said. "Hearing Spud barking like that, they probably thought they were going to be moved again, poor things."

Polymarr sidestepped along beside Emily as she approached the grove of trees where he had made camp the night before. "I was kind of hopin' to stay on, at least until St. Lawrence gives me them other three dollars I got comin'."

The view from the knoll was breathtaking, just as Emily had expected. She stood gazing at it, stricken to the heart by an unrecognized emotion, neither joy nor sorrow, but something made up of both, and as intense as either. One hand shaded her eyes from the sun. "I suppose I could use

your help," she said, her throat thick. She imagined the valley in autumn, rimmed in gold and crimson and orange, and in winter, muffled beneath a layer of clean, glittering snow. Spring would bring the first pale grass, the crocuses and dandelions and a riot of wildflowers. How could she turn her back on such a place?

"You may stay if you wish. Just be warned that I cannot—and will not—pay you the same exorbitant wages you're getting from Tristan."

Polymarr squinched up his bulbous nose, baffled. "Tristan?"

"Mr. St. Lawrence," she said, with a little laugh, aware that if she said "Saint-Laurent" he wouldn't know who she was talking about. "I'm offering twenty dollars a month, and you won't see any of that before spring."

"What I *don't see* is, I don't see no wagon. I ain't takin' to the trail with no means of shelter. 'Round about October, it'll commence to snowin', and it won't let up much afore April." He studied her with a sort of hopeful speculation. "'Less you're headed south, o' course."

Emily sighed. "I'm not going anywhere," she said, gazing toward the distant ranch house. "I intend to settle right here, on this land. If you choose to hire on, you can either stay in the line shack or make a place for yourself in one of the outbuildings on the ranch."

Polymarr's Adam's apple went up and down, galloping the length of his neck like an ostrich in a trench. His filmy eyes were narrowed, and he pointed one scrawny and none too clean index finger at Emily. "You couldn't keep sheep around here, miss, even with St. Lawrence's say-so. The other ranchers won't put up with it for a minute. Fact is, I've been expectin' 'em to come in here shootin' since last night, and I got nary a wink of sleep for imaginin' my demise and sayin' my prayers, lest my soul go astray 'twixt here and heaven."

"I see." Along her slow route down from Montana, Emily had encountered quite a few ranchers, some with small

spreads, some with large. They'd watched her coldly as she passed through and by their towns, sometimes touching a hand to a hat brim in acknowledgment, but never smiling or extending any kind of welcome. The women had kept a careful distance, always, peering at her from behind fluttering curtains, as though she were an oddity, too dangerous to approach. Once or twice, men on horseback had surrounded her and the sheep, "escorting" the flock through their territory without even a pretense of friendliness. She'd been an outcast then, and it seemed now that things would be no different in Prominence. Her dejection was profound, for she wanted nothing so much as a home, though she wasn't precisely surprised.

"You got a gun, miss?" Polymarr pressed. "Somethin' to protect yourself with?"

She showed him the .38 caliber pistol in the holster under her serape. She had a cartridge belt, too, but she dreaded having to shoot anyone or anything, for she'd taken little practice, being possessed of a Christian aversion to violence. Anyhow, the noise of gunfire invariably upset her nerves.

"Not much of a weapon," the old man said. "Still, I guess it'd be better'n nothin'. You mean to stay around these parts, ma'am, you best get yourself a rifle. One of them carbines, maybe, like they use in the army."

Emily shuddered. "Maybe," she agreed, somewhat forlornly. She hadn't dared to attempt the long southward journey unarmed, but she had no plans to become another Annie Oakley, either. Her dearest hope was to make a place for herself in the valley by peaceful means; she wanted a home, like Aislinn McQuillan's, a place of love and laughter, of light and warmth, with bright, pretty dishes on shelf and table, and plenty of hot water always near at hand. It didn't seem like so much to ask, but she had met with discouragement too many times in her life to believe that dreams were ever assured of coming true, however plain and ordinary they might be.

She drew a deep and somewhat shaky breath. There was nothing to do, as far as she could determine, but press on.

Sure enough, at least fifty yards of his fence lay flat, the posts pulled right up out of the ground. From the looks of the tracks in the dirt, half his cattle must have been on the lookout for a chance to make for Powder Creek and mix in with the Kyle herd. They'd practically stampeded, those miserable animals, completely obliterating all sign of the sheep Emily had driven in from the other direction.

Until then, Tristan had run the operation alone, except for occasional help from Shay and old John Polymarr, but it had become clear to him of late that he'd have to hire on a couple of cowpunchers if he wanted to make any real headway. He preferred his own counsel, being a man with secrets to keep, and independent into the bargain, but he'd reached a pass where a choice had to be made. He could take to the trail again, or he could stay and put down roots for the first time since leaving the home place in Montana, after his folks died.

Muttering a curse, he spurred the gelding over the broken fence line and began following the trail of hoofprints. About a hundred yards along, the path began to fan out in every direction but back toward home. Tristan held to the center, moving toward the high meadow that lay ahead and above. He was out in the open, leaning into the climb with the horse, and he would have preferred not to be so vulnerable. The cattle hadn't been accommodating enough to choose a way that would have suited him better.

He sensed the riders before he saw them, drew the .45 and let it rest easily in his hand. There were two of them, one on a black and white paint, one on a bay stallion, and they'd probably been watching him for a while, because they carried their rifles across the pommels of their saddles, instead of in the scabbards, as peaceable men might do.

"This is private land," one of them said. His tone was neither neighborly nor threatening, and he had a long, solemn face, like an undertaker or a preacher fond of hellfire.

Tristan sighed. He supposed the prudent thing would have been to stop where he was, but they were on top of the rise, and he was damned if he'd let them have that advantage. Reaching the top of the hill, he nodded a greeting, the .45 resting loose in his hand.

"I guess you don't hear too good," said the man on the paint. He was hefty, and not without vanity, if his waxed mustache and slicked-down hair were any indication. The ruddy flush under his skin vouched for an uncertain disposition. "My partner here said this is private land."

Tristan repressed a sigh. Even though he was practically lounging in the saddle, he could have dropped both men before they managed to raise their rifles, and he felt the old, not-unpleasant quiver of excitement in the pit of his belly at the prospect. It was not a thing he liked knowing about himself.

"Some of my cattle've strayed onto the Powder Creek spread. But I expect you know that." He paused. "I've come to fetch them back. I expect you know that, too."

The ranch hands looked at each other. By tacit agreement, or perhaps long habit, Handlebar sat there choking on his tongue, while his companion did the talking. "You ain't got no cattle here," he said, with a slight motion of the rifle. *Get out,* the gesture said, clear as rainwater.

Undaunted, Tristan cocked the .45 and swung the barrel forward in a motion as natural to him as turning over in his sleep. "I'm not looking for trouble," he said evenly. "On the other hand, I don't mind a lively skirmish now and again, and I'm a pretty fair shot. Wouldn't it be simpler—not to mention safer—to let me look for my stock and ride out again?"

"Shoot him for trespassin'," said Handlebar. Evidently, he just couldn't withhold his opinion.

"His brother's the marshal," the other man pointed out.

"And this here's the fella that shot off half the boss's ear and got him sent away to the state penitentiary." Handlebar regarded Tristan with genuine hatred.

"Now, don't give me all the credit," Tristan protested affably. "Shay did his part, along with twelve good men and a sensible judge."

Veins bulged at the heavy man's temples, but his companion, having the cooler head, prevailed. "We've got a score to settle with you, Saint-Laurent, and with your brother, too. Billy's dead on account of you, and the boss is doin' hard time—an old man like him—and we ain't gonna forget that. But we'll have our day, right enough. Meantime, we'll check our herds for your brand, and cut out any that might have strayed."

"I'd like to go along," Tristan said. It wasn't a request, of course, even though it might have sounded like one, but a statement of intent. A man who didn't protect his stock, whatever the risks, would soon be out of business.

The other riders lowered their rifles, but Tristan waited until both guns were tucked into their respective scabbards before putting away the .45. He was watchful, but in his long career he'd learned to predict what a man meant to do next, and he was fairly certain these two didn't intend to put him to the test. At least, the smart one didn't.

He rode between them, and a little behind, the three horses moving at an easy trot. For some reason he couldn't put a finger on, Emily Starbuck came to mind, and he reflected that predicting a man's actions was one thing, and divining a woman's was quite another. He'd explained to her that the land south of Powder Creek was his, and showed her the proof, but that didn't mean she'd take her square mile of squalling mutton and strike out for new horizons. Even though he would have willed those sheep to perdition if he could have, he half hoped Miss Starbuck would stand toe-to-toe and fight.

He had no doubt that he'd come out the winner, in the

long run, but in the meantime the competition would be a spirited one, and thus very entertaining.

He smiled in anticipation as he and the cowpunchers rode through a stand of birch and aspen trees, still climbing, though the slope was gentler now. When they reached the crest of the hill, the high meadow was visible, and William Kyle's sprawling stone house loomed, with the mountains and the sky for a backdrop.

Tristan did admire that house, and where before he'd tormented himself with impossible images, in which Aislinn was its mistress, and he its master, that day he couldn't think beyond Emily. She was the one he envisioned, presiding over the place, wearing a fancy dress, her hair pinned loosely at her nape. He could even picture her carrying a child, his child, her face glowing with health and pride.

He'd made inquiries in town, with Kyle's lawyer, where the property was concerned—the old man wasn't likely to need the place again, and he'd left no heirs—but it didn't seem prudent to mention the subject in the presence of his escorts, them being so prickly and all.

An Indian woman, beautiful despite her barrel body and moon-shaped face, stepped onto the porch to shake out a rug. She looked at Tristan with bland curiosity, then went back inside the house. By then his presence had drawn notice from other quarters, and he thought it judicious to pay closer attention to the men watching him from the corral fence. That there were other eyes looking on as well, he did not doubt, but there was no fear in him. His adoptive father had always said he could have done with a few more qualms, where confrontations were concerned, but there had been something reckless in him in those days, and he hadn't mellowed overmuch in the interim.

He had no conscious wish to die, but he'd done a few things in the past that made him wonder if some part of him wasn't courting death. While he was ruminating on that possibility, he kept an eye on the men around him, prepared to summon the .45 if the need arose.

"Our good neighbor here claims some of his cattle have found their way onto Mr. Kyle's land," said the lean-faced man, to the half-dozen cowboys who drew nigh, all of them mounted and armed. Tristan had already figured out that he'd been at Powder Creek for a long while and, given his air of authority, he was almost surely the foreman. "You boys look after him, and make sure he don't meet with calamity whilst he's in our care."

The ranch hands didn't respond. They were sizing Tristan up, which was fair enough, because he was taking their measure, too. They looked like no-accounts to him, collecting wages, passing through, but having no particular loyalty to Kyle himself. He was always careful not to put too much stock in hasty judgments, but he trusted his gut far more than his eyes and ears, and so far, it hadn't offered an opinion. Which probably meant they weren't dangerous, unless you were stupid enough to turn your back on them, of course. Tristan admitted to a fair number of shortfalls in his nature, but stupidity was not among them. As before, he rode a pace or two behind, and presently found himself overlooking a considerable herd.

There were three riders to his left, three to his right. The youngest, a doe-eyed kid barely out of knickers, wheeled his horse around and approached, taking visible care not to make any sudden moves.

Tristan bit back a smile. He supposed the boy valued those shell-like ears of his, and didn't want their shape altered.

"What's your brand?" the kid asked. He sounded testy.

The mark was a crescent moon, and Tristan said as much, though he was sure it was common knowledge. Prominence wasn't all that big a place, and there were no more than a dozen ranches within a fifty-mile radius.

"You just stay right here," said the lad, "and we'll cut out your cattle."

"Like I said before," Tristan replied dryly, "I plan to take an active part in that process, thanks all the same."

There was no further argument, though the boy was

plainly simmering with opinions to which he didn't quite dare give utterance. He swept off his hat, dragged a forearm across his brow, and spurred his horse toward the cattle grazing placidly below. The other riders followed at a slower pace, and Tristan fell in behind them.

They cut out forty-odd head of beef over the course of two hours, and while Tristan suspected there were more, he decided to content himself with what he'd recovered, for the moment at least. The boy, who grudgingly admitted that he was called Fletcher—he didn't say if it was his first name or his last—was nominated by the others to help Tristan drive the cattle back over the broken fence line onto his own land.

"You like working for that outfit?" Tristan inquired. He was setting up the posts Emily had pulled out by that time, using a flat rock to pound them into the ground. Fletcher lingered, without saying why, still mounted and looking fretful.

The boy shrugged. "It pays a decent wage," he answered. "I get my grub and a place to sleep."

Tristan spoke calming words to the gelding, who'd grown fitful from the pounding, before pausing to look up into Fletcher's face. "I could use a good hand around here, if you're interested."

No smile. "I might be. How many men you got workin' for you now?"

Tristan grinned. "Just you, I'm afraid. You'd have the bunkhouse all to yourself."

Fletcher glanced back over one shoulder as if to see if he'd been trailed from the Powder Creek spread, then met Tristan's gaze straight on. "What makes you think you can trust me?" he asked.

"I didn't say I trusted you," Tristan answered and, tossing aside the rock, he gripped one of the fence posts in both hands and gave it a good wrench, to make sure it was stable. It was. "I said I needed help. Either you want the job, or you don't. That's all we have to discuss right now."

"I'd have to have a horse. This one belongs to Kyle."

"I'll provide a cow pony."

"I can shoot, too."

Tristan suppressed a grin. "That's fine," he said, "but I hope you won't have use for that skill." He murmured a few soothing words to the gelding and mounted, anxious to be gone. Miss Emily Starbuck was very much in his mind; he wanted to see her. Find out what mischief she'd made in his absence. He tugged affably at the brim of his hat. "We start at dawn. I'll see you then."

Fletcher swallowed, nodded, then turned and rode away. Tristan headed in the opposite direction, driving those knot-headed cattle ahead of him, toward his own herd. The noon hour had come and gone by the time he'd ridden back to the house, splashed himself relatively clean, brushed his hair and put on a fresh shirt. He set out for the hills in a hurry he didn't want to consider too carefully, and found Emily there, with her sheep. She was sitting on a grassy knoll, watching them clip the grass to the roots, the dog resting beside her. Polymarr and Walter the mare were nowhere in sight.

"Still here?" he said, as though surprised. But he'd taken his hat off, and he was conscious that his hair was still damp from washing, and bore ridges from his comb.

The dog growled and sprang to his feet, and his dusty ruff stood out around his neck.

"Hush," Emily said, stroking the animal's head, and Spud made a whimpering sound and lay down again, muzzle on paws. Her attention turned, belatedly he thought, back to Tristan, and he felt a sweet sizzle somewhere behind his navel, just to look at her. "I live here," she told him, as though that settled all disagreement.

He sat down beside her, letting her remark pass, and set his hat on the grass beside him. "This must be the sorriest way to make a living I've ever seen."

The corner of her mouth quivered, but she didn't smile. "I don't mind it," she said, after an interval of consideration. "It's an easy job."

Tristan rubbed his lower lip with the back of one hand. He sat cross-legged on the soft ground, enjoying the sweet, mingled scents of Miss Emily and the summer grass. "Yes, ma'am," he agreed, with a brief glance at Spud. "If a dog can do it, I reckon it is."

A slight flush climbed Emily's slender neck, and she wet her lips with the tip of her tongue, a gesture that was vengeance enough in its own right, if only she'd known it, but she didn't rise to the bait. "Spud," she said, "is a very smart animal."

He laughed, then looked around, squinting. "Where's Polymarr?"

"I sent him down to get his things out of the line shack. He's moving into the bunkhouse at the ranch."

"Is he, now? And here I told young Fletcher he'd have the place to himself."

Her flush deepened prettily and she cleared her throat in a delicate fashion. "I suppose it seems audacious, my hiring Mr. Polymarr away from you—" She fell silent, wretchedly embarrassed and, at the same time, determined to press for what she wanted.

Tristan was utterly charmed, though not ready to show it. "Listen, Miss Starbuck. If you want to live on the ranch and spoil whatever reputation you might have made for yourself, that's your business. Quite frankly, I would enjoy your company, but if you think I'm going to pack up and leave on your say-so, you are woefully mistaken."

"I could pay you something—some sort of compensation, I mean—after the shearing next spring."

Tristan barely refrained from rolling his eyes. "Even if I were willing to put up with those miserable sheep of yours—which I'm not—the other ranchers won't be. Once the word gets out that they're here, and that won't be long, believe me, the place will be under siege."

She blinked back tears, quickly, but not quickly enough. "We have to be somewhere," she said, evidently referring to herself and the sheep, and Tristan wanted to put his arms

around her, though for the sake of her pride, he refrained. *"Somewhere,"* she repeated, so softly that she might have been talking to herself, or to God.

He ran his tongue along the inside of his lower lip. "You could sell the sheep," he said. "There must be somebody who'd want them." He knew he sounded doubtful, but there was no helping that. He wouldn't have given a beer token for the whole band.

She kept her head turned away, dabbed at one cheek with the edge of her grubby serape. "I'm not going to sell my flock," she said fiercely, when she'd recovered herself a little. Her eyes were puffy, but they flashed, and her nose, while reddened, was pitched at a stubborn angle. "If I have to fight to defend it, I will. It's all I have."

Mingled with the admiration he felt for this woman, and the very elemental attraction toward her, was a quiet annoyance. *"You'll* fight? One woman and an old man against half a dozen ranchers and their hired hands?" He thrust a hand through his hair. "I hope you don't plan on making a hell of a lot of headway, Miss Starbuck, because the two of you won't be much of a match for those outlaws."

"I'll do what I must to hold on to what's mine," she said.

He let out a ragged sigh. "Maybe you *want* to get yourself killed. Is that it? Life is just too hard and you're giving up?"

He'd been trying to exasperate her, but when she spoke, she sounded haughty as a duchess at high tea, which was amusing, in an irritating sort of way, her sitting there in men's pants and a serape that smelled pungently of sheep, acting fancy. "I assure you, my life is precious to me. If I was going to give up, it would have happened long before this."

The words intrigued him; he wondered, not for the first time, what sort of past lay behind her. Since he wasn't ready to talk about his own, however, he didn't raise the subject. Instead, he stood and dusted off his pants with both hands, then bent to retrieve his hat. In the process, he

nearly bumped heads with Emily, and the desire to kiss her came over him with such sudden force that he felt unsteady.

She had fixed her attention on the .45. "Are you good with that?"

The question might have caught Tristan off-guard if he hadn't been paying attention. "Fair," he replied, and cleared his throat. He was not a shy man, not by any stretch of the imagination, but there was something about this woman that made him feel as awkward as a schoolboy in short pants.

"Have you ever killed anybody?"

He pretended not to hear. "I've got work to do," he said, moving toward the gelding. "I'll see you this evening." He mounted, tipped his hat and rode away.

Chapter
4

$\mathcal{R}$ETURNING TO THE BIG HOUSE THAT EVENING, after a long, dirty, hungry day, Emily felt her confidence slipping. Light glimmered through the windows of the kitchen, as she made her way toward the back door. After a moment's hesitation, during which she considered walking right in, regarding the property as her own the way she did, she knocked instead.

"In," commanded a good-natured voice, from the other side. From the place of light and warmth and belonging.

Emily entered, and found Tristan at the stove, cracking brown speckled eggs into a pan. He flashed one of his wounding grins at her. "I'm afraid this is all I know how to make," he said. "Never been much of a cook."

She hoped he hadn't heard the rumbling of her stomach and raised her chin. "I'm obliged," she said.

He gave her a look that seemed to take measure of her very soul, though there was nothing unseemly in it. "Are you?" he asked, his voice soft.

Why did she find this man's presence so soothing and, at one and the same time, so disturbing? He was fine-looking, yes, and he certainly had charm, but Emily had been practical all her life, and therefore not susceptible to such allure. Or so she'd thought.

She took a basin from its hook on the wall, carried it over to the stove. The eggs looked and smelled like ambrosia to her, though he'd nearly ruined them. "May I?" she said, indicating the water reservoir, with its chrome-handled lid.

"Be my guest," he said, removing their supper from the fire and setting it, skillet and all, in the center of the table.

Emily filled the basin and carried it outside, to the bench, where she found soap and a towel that smelled pleasantly of fresh air and Tristan. Hastily, she scrubbed her hands and face, fretted a moment over the sorry state of her hair, and went inside.

While other men would have gone ahead and begun the meal without her, Tristan had waited. He sat down only when she was seated, and nodded toward the strange mixture of over- and undercooked eggs.

She murmured her thanks and scooped out a healthy portion. It took all her willpower not to gobble the food, so ravenous was she, and she was halfway through when she realized Tristan wasn't eating.

"This stuff is terrible," he said, shoving his plate away.

Emily agreed, but she was starved, so she kept on, taking slow bites when she wanted to bury her face in the skillet, like Spud would do. "Yes," she said, refilling her plate. "Dreadful."

He laughed. "You are a woman of contradiction, Emily Starbuck," he told her.

The desperate hunger had finally begun to abate, and Emily laid down her fork at last, finished chewing, and swallowed, at a loss for a reply. She had been too busy surviving, of late, to ponder what sort of woman she was, and suddenly it was something she very much wanted to know.

Tristan got up and brought coffee to the table—coffee, that luxury she had gone without for so long—and set a cup in front of her.

"How," he began, in the same moderate tone as before, "did you manage to drive all those sheep from Montana to California by yourself?" He was standing a few feet away by

then, at the stove, the blue metal coffeepot in his hand, and his quiet regard was a great if inexplicable solace to Emily. She felt a peculiar need to take shelter in his arms, to rest her head against his shoulder, to share her hopes and secrets with him.

She stiffened, determined not to venture down a path that could only lead to degradation and heartbreak. Men like Tristan Saint-Laurent, handsome and prosperous, fitting easily into whatever place or circumstance in which they found themselves, merely dallied with women like her. And Emily did not intend to be dallied with.

"I didn't have a choice," she answered straightforwardly. She was tired to the core of her being, yearning for bath and bed, and yet there was an ember burning somewhere in her depths, a wanting for something else entirely. "I had inherited the sheep, and this land." She paused to let the latter part of the statement sink in. "I had nothing else, nowhere to go."

He studied her narrowly, standing next to the table with one foot braced against the bench, his own mug of coffee in hand. In anyone else, that would have been a breach of manners, but Tristan managed to look stately, and very much at ease. "You could have remarried."

She felt color sting her cheeks, looked away, then met his gaze again, fiercely proud. "I had one husband—that was enough."

"You must have been unhappy. I'm sorry."

"Don't be," she replied.

Tristan gave a low, exclamatory whistle. "I guess the poor bastard must have frozen to death," he said, after a few moments spent weighing the matter privately.

"It was not a love match," Emily said, her face still hot. She did not reach for her coffee, as her hands were trembling.

"All the same, you might be expected to at least *like* the man."

Emily did not look away, but neither did she reply. She had not felt anything for her late husband, except the

devout hope that he would never, ever touch her. After his death, she had not even kept his name.

Tristan expelled a sigh. "All right, so you didn't even like him. Why in hell did you hitch yourself up to the man in the first place?"

There was within Emily a longing to know and be known, and for a brief interval that desire did ferocious battle with her pride. In the end, the former prevailed, a surprise in itself, for she had kept her spirit alive all these years by nurturing her dignity, that being pretty much all she had. "I needed a place to live. He needed someone to look after the house, after his first wife died."

Tristan was quiet for a long while, and when he spoke, there was no condemnation in his tone, no judgment. He was merely reflecting aloud, or so it seemed to Emily. "Why didn't you just hire on as a housekeeper?"

The question struck Emily like a slap, even though she knew it wasn't hostile. "He would have had to pay me then," she said evenly. "Cyrus didn't spend any more money than he had to."

"You'd marry a man just to get a place to live?"

Emily rose, swept over to the cast-iron sink and set her plate inside. "I suppose I could have joined a brothel," she said, fully intending to shock him, and out of the corner of her eye she saw that she had succeeded, if the hardness of his jawline was any indication. She began scooping hot water from the reservoir to wash the dishes. "I was not trained to teach, and there were no fancy houses in our part of the country, where a maid might be wanted. So I married the first man who asked."

Tristan stepped into her path, stopping her fevered progress back and forth between the stove and the sink, taking the small bucket out of her hands and setting it aside with a thump. "I want to be the second," he said.

It was a good thing Emily wasn't holding the hot water any longer, because she would have dropped it and drenched them both. "What?"

"I need a wife. I think you'd do as well as anybody. You'd

have a home and half-interest in this ranch. Our property dispute would be settled, too."

Emily stared up at him, stunned. Her first husband had been well past his virile years, God be thanked, but this one was young and vital, of an age to father children. He would make demands—intimate ones. "You can't be serious," she said, though some part of her hoped he was. "We're strangers. How do I know you're not a mean drunk, or even an outlaw?"

A tiny muscle in his cheek flexed, and Emily wondered distractedly if it was the word "outlaw" that had perturbed him. She saw a counterquestion take shape in his eyes, but with visible effort he quelled it, and spoke carefully. "I guess you'll just have to take me at my word," he said.

She raked her teeth over her lower lip. The offer, outlandish as it was, was not one she could afford to dismiss out of hand. While she felt certain that her claim on the ranch was just, she could not assume that a judge would agree. This was cattle country, after all, and Tristan had a foothold here. She had already experienced enough prejudice, because of the sheep, to know her position was a tenuous one, be it right or wrong, and while the injustice of that galled her sorely, she had to take it into consideration.

"What about my sheep?" she asked.

"Sell them. Tuck the money away someplace—I won't make any claim on it." He sounded so sure of himself and his ideas. What was it like, she wondered, to walk boldly through the world the way Tristan did, with that apparently innate sense of his own value, his right place in the scheme of things?

She balked. The sheep were all that she had, and much as she would have liked having a nest egg, the animals represented an asset with the propensity for renewing itself. Besides, whatever Tristan said now, as her husband, he could take the money away from her, with the full blessing of the courts. For that matter, he could sell, shoot or drive off every one of her sheep, with the same impunity. Once he

put a golden band on her finger, she would have about as many rights as Spud did.

Still, the pull of home and husband, not to mention the prospect of a brood of children, was strong. She couldn't help picturing herself going to church of a Sunday, wearing a crisp frock and a fine bonnet, or chatting with the other women of the town at a quilting bee or an afternoon social. Her need for those things was almost as compelling as the beat of her heart and the steady flow of her breath. Almost.

"I don't even know you," she protested, full of sweet misery.

Tristan cupped her chin in his hand, raised it slightly, and looked deeply into her eyes. "This is who I am," he said, and then he bent his head and brushed her lips with his own. Gradually, the contact deepened, until it was forceful and, at the same time, heartbreakingly gentle.

Fire shot through her; she felt her knees wobble, and her heart threatened to fly away like a frightened bird, but she stepped into the kiss, instead of drawing back, as a more sensible woman might have done. When it ended, she swayed on her feet, utterly dazed, and to her profound embarrassment Tristan steadied her by taking her upper arms in his hands. His grin was wicked, insufferable and totally irresistible.

"Well?" he prompted. "Are we getting married or not?"

She flushed. "I suppose we could," she said.

His eyes laughed, and his mouth seemed to hover on the edge of another grin, but somehow he contrived to look— well—polite. "When?"

"There are so many things we haven't settled. The sheep—"

"Never mind the damn sheep. We'll deal with the problem somehow." He guided her to the table, sat her down, and straddled the bench beside her. His being so near affected her almost as much as the kiss had done. She touched her temple, feeling dizzy; then she drew a deep breath, expelled it. "There's something else. I have to know

if you expect—if you will require—" Another breath, another exhalation. "Conjugal relations. Right away, I mean."

There was a tender quality to his smile, which made the mischief dancing in his eyes a little easier to forgive. "I'm not planning to fling you down in the tall grass the minute you say 'I do,' if that's what you mean."

How had this insane conversation begun? Emily began to rub both temples, and she was blushing furiously. "I will—would—need time. To get acquainted."

He grew pensive, considering his options no doubt, and then beamed another one of his grins at her. The impact nearly sent her spinning. "I want a real wife, Emily. But I'll give you a while to settle in."

"How long?" She could barely squeeze the words past her heart, which had lodged itself in her throat.

He made a magnanimous gesture with one hand. "Until I seduce you," he answered.

"Until you what?"

"Until I make you want to share my bed." There was that confidence again. That damnable certainty. "Fair enough?"

"You won't force me?"

He frowned. "I'll thank you not to insult me."

"You won't shoot my sheep?"

He raised a hand, like a man offering an oath. "Before God, I will not do those miserable creatures willful injury."

Emily wet her lips with the tip of her tongue, and the memory of Tristan's kiss pulsed in every nerve of her body, like an echo. "You'd better keep your promises," she warned, sustained by bravado and hope. "If you ever lay a hand on me or those sheep, I'll sew you up in the bedclothes while you're sleeping and beat you black and blue with a broom handle. And when those animals are sheared, come spring, and the wool and mutton has been sold, you'll be wise to leave my money be. If you try to steal it, you'd do well to take to the trail, because I'll shoot you for a thief if I catch up with you."

Tristan drew back in mock horror. "Those are mighty

imaginative threats, Miss Emily. Methinks you either keep fast company or read too many dime novels."

Emily blushed again. In truth, she'd read about just such a stitching episode in a penny dreadful, and the image, vividly drawn, had stuck in her mind. "Nonetheless, I mean what I say."

"I believe you do." He put out his hand. "I will treat you as honorably as you treat me. Do we have a bargain?"

Emily could barely hear over the pounding of her pulses. She hesitated for a fraction of a moment, then placed her palm against his. It was like being struck by lightning, but she managed not to flinch. "We do," she said, and could not believe her own ears.

"You're doing what?" Shay demanded. He was mounted, while Tristan worked at mending another broken fence. The boy, Fletcher, who had arrived at dawn, with his bedroll, was using his gelding to round up the cattle for a head count.

Tristan knew his grin was the ingenuous, smart-ass reflection of Shay's own, and it pleased him to see his brother scowl in irritation. "I told you. I'm taking a wife. I figure we'll tie the knot on Sunday morning, after church."

Shay leaned down a little, his voice a harsh whisper, though no one was close enough to hear the exchange. "You don't know this woman from Adam's great-aunt!"

"I have an opinion or two where she's concerned," Tristan replied easily. He stroked the long neck of his brother's horse with a gloved hand.

"Do you love her?"

"I don't know," Tristan answered. "I think I could."

"Suppose you're wrong?"

"Suppose I'm right? I want what you have, Shay. You ought to understand that better than anybody."

The mirror image softened a little. "I hope this isn't a mistake," Shay said.

"Believe me, so do I. Now. What brings you out here on this fine day?"

Shay swept his hat off and resettled it. "Two things," he replied. "I got a wire from the warden at the state penitentiary today, saying Kyle took sick last month and died two days ago. If you want to buy the Powder Creek spread, you ought to talk to his lawyer, Tom Rutledge."

"And the other thing?" Tristan prompted, when the silence had stretched on for a while.

"It's those sheep of Miss Emily's. Word's gotten around that they're here, and there's some fretting among the ranchers. Folks want to drive them out before they ruin the grazing land."

Although Tristan himself had no particular fondness for sheep, and although he wasn't the least bit surprised, had even predicted the problem, the bald-faced presumption of it got his back up. "They needn't vex themselves," he said, with a calmness that was only partly genuine. "It's my grass those bleating woollies are cropping off at the dirt. My cattle that could go hungry."

Shay leaned forward, bracing one arm on the pommel of his saddle, and sighed. "You know damn well it isn't that simple," he said. "The reasoning goes that if they let in one sheep farmer, there'll soon be a plague of them. There's been some pretty crazy talk already, and while most of those windbags are just jawing, a few of them have fallen on hard times lately, and they sound real bitter. You're going to have trouble if you don't get that flock back on the trail, pronto."

Nothing would have pleased him more, but if the sheep went, Miss Emily Starbuck would surely go with them. He could not, would not, let that happen. Furthermore, he'd given his word that the greasy beasts would meet with no ill fortune while in his keeping, which pretty much meant he had to look after them as if they were as good as cattle.

"I appreciate the warning. How's Aislinn? That baby on the way yet?"

Shay paled at the mention of the impending birth, though the light of joy and pride shone in his eyes. "Time's getting close," he said. "She stayed home from the store this

morning to sit in the parlor with a pillow plumped behind her back.''

For the ambitious Aislinn, that was unusual behavior indeed. ''You send word when it happens. I've never been an uncle before.''

Shay swallowed. ''I've never been a father. As far as I know, anyway.''

''You'll do just fine,'' Tristan answered. For him, that was sloppy sentiment.

''You look out for yourself, and that woman of yours,'' Shay said, reining his horse away. A moment later, he was riding back toward town.

Tristan went back to his work, but his mind was elsewhere.

The sheep were quiet, enjoying the sweet grass and the plenitude of water flowing from the spring, and the scene was so pastoral that Emily, keeping watch on the hillside, let down her guard and drifted off to sleep. Mr. Polymarr was somewhere far afield, hunting rabbits for supper, so it was Spud that warned her of the approaching riders. If it hadn't been for him, they might have trampled her, streaming over the knoll behind her the way they did.

She was on her feet in a trice, the aged .38 shaking in her hand and aimed for the middle of the lead man's chest. The sheep, startled, began to mill and cry, and Emily spoke quietly to the dog. ''Keep them together, boy.''

Spud was reluctant to leave her side, but at her command he darted off to drive the splintering sheep back into the band. There were six riders, and though the brands on the flanks of their horses were varied ones, Emily supposed they'd come from the Powder Creek place.

''What do you want?'' she asked, squaring her shoulders.

The desperadoes were tremendously pleased with themselves. ''We came to relieve you of them sheep, ma'am,'' said one. He carried a shotgun, as did several of his companions, and Emily knew she would be cut down if there was

gunplay. She could probably plug the leader easily enough, but in the next moment, she'd be dead, too.

She raised the pistol, extending her arm to its full length, amazed at how steady her grip had become, when her palm was slippery with sweat, and thumbed back the hammer. *Please,* she prayed simultaneously, *don't let this thing go off.* "You men just turn around and ride out of here," she said, "and everything will be all right."

They looked at each other, amused and quite undaunted. Between them, they could wipe out her flock, leave the sheep to rot; she'd heard of such things happening. She planted her feet and held her ground.

"You can't protect these pitiful critters, ma'am," said the spokesman, with a courtly touch to his hat brim, "if you'll pardon my sayin' so. Not by yourself, leastways."

It was then that a bullet struck the ground just a foot or so in front of his horse. The animal shrieked and skittered backward, rolling its eyes and tossing its head. Emily turned, expecting to see Tristan sighting in for another shot, but to her disappointment and relief, it was Mr. Polymarr and the boy, Fletcher.

"Ride out," Polymarr said. He looked like Methuselah's grandfather, but he was sprightly with a weapon, and you could tell by his stance and his tone that he meant business. " 'Tween the three of us, we can get every damn one of you 'fore you so much as wheel them horses towards home."

One of the men drew, partly hidden from Mr. Polymarr's view by the other riders, and before her next heartbeat, Emily had fired. By luck, rather than skill, the shot nicked the assailant's right wrist and sent his pistol clattering to the ground.

At that, someone cursed, and Emily watched with disbelief as the barrel of a rifle swung toward her, shining nickel glinting in the cool afternoon sunlight. It seemed to move slowly, as though the air had turned to water, but even before she could pitch herself to the ground, there was a second blast, and her would-be killer flew backward out of the saddle.

"I told you I'd shoot," Mr. Polymarr said, and spat.

The sheep were in a state of pandemonium by then, and Spud was barking wildly, frantically, torn between defending his mistress and keeping the flock together. In the end, he stayed with his terrified charges.

After recovering their fallen comrade, the riders turned and fled. Emily, watching them, had no doubt whatsoever that they would return. They'd just be more devious about it the next time, that was all. Bullies, every one of them. And cowards, too.

Mr. Polymarr and the boy rushed toward her, swung down off the ancient horses Tristan used to pull his buckboard.

"You all right, miss?" Fletcher demanded. His freckles seemed to stand out an inch from his face, but it was the gentle bleakness in his eyes that moved Emily. Young as he was, he'd experienced suffering firsthand; she could tell that just by looking at him.

"Yes," she said. She wanted to reassure the boy somehow, but his physical attitude did not invite familiarity. "Yes, I'm fine." She caught Mr. Polymarr up in her gaze. "I'm grateful to you both."

Fletcher was pale, though his freckles had settled back into place. He glanced nervously in the direction the riders had taken. "Those were Powder Creek men. They'll be back for certain."

Polymarr nodded, his knuckles going white with the strength of his grasp on the rifle he carried. He was red and sweating profusely, and his breathing was shallow and raspy, but Emily knew better than to inquire after his well-being. He would not appreciate special concern. "It's started, then." He turned his head and met Emily's eyes. "This here, miss, is just the beginnin'."

A weight of sorrow descended upon Emily, momentarily crushing her. She struggled to hold on to her dream. "They were no better than outlaws. Good men don't enforce their will with guns." But even as she spoke the words, she was recalling the ranchers all along the trail from Montana,

taking grim care that she didn't settle in their territory. They'd been law-abiding men, husbands and fathers, brothers and sons, but they'd plainly viewed the sheep, and Emily herself, as a threat. For her, the open range had been closed tight.

"We've gotta move these critters downhill," Polymarr announced, rubbing his stubbly chin. "Closer to the house and barn."

"I don't work with no sheep," Fletcher said.

Emily ignored him. "Tristan won't like that," she pointed out to Mr. Polymarr.

"Well, I don't reckon he will," the old man agreed. "But if you want to keep these animals alive till spring, you've got to do somethin'." He gestured toward Powder Creek. "Once it gets dark, miss, those fellers will be back, and they'll bring their friends and relations. These here sheep will be easy pickin's then, and it will be next to impossible to protect them, there bein' no place to dig in for a fight."

Before Emily could respond, Spud took to barking again, and she was braced for battle when Tristan came riding out of the brush. She was so startled that she nearly shot him out of pure reflex.

"What the hell happened here?" he demanded, swinging down off the gelding's glistening back before it had come to a stop. Clearly, he had heard the shots, probably at some distance, and made haste to discover their source.

"We've had ourselves a social call from the Powder Creek crew, that's all," Mr. Polymarr replied, with some relish and another stream of spittle. "Shot two of 'em—I got one, and the lady here got the other."

"Sweet God," Tristan breathed. It was the first time she had seen him falter, but then, she'd only known him one day, for all that he'd proposed marriage and she'd agreed. Then his jawline hardened and he took an ominous step in Emily's direction. "Are you willing to get yourself killed for these damned sheep?"

She didn't retreat, although she was secretly intimidated.

"Yes," she said. "They are every bit as important to me as your cattle are to you."

He yanked off his hat and slapped his thigh with it in exasperation, and in a sidelong glance, Emily saw both Mr. Polymarr and Fletcher move back, out of range. Tristan's hair gleamed like so much spun gold, for all that it was mussed and dusty. "Damnation," he growled, "but you are a foolish woman!"

"I want to protect what's mine. Just like you."

He closed his eyes briefly, thrust a hand through his hair. His struggle for patience was obvious. "It was bad enough that you brought sheep into cattle country. God only knows what will happen now."

"A range war, that's what," put in Polymarr, from a judicious distance.

"Are you saying I should have stood by and watched while they scattered or even killed my flock?"

"Of course not!"

"Then what should I have done? What would *you* have done?"

He opened his mouth to speak, closed it again without uttering another word. He simply whirled away from her, strode to his horse and mounted.

"What about these sheep?" Polymarr wanted to know, looking from Emily to Tristan and back again. "We might just as well plug 'em our own selves as leave 'em here."

"Put them in the lower pasture," Tristan snapped. His gaze was hot enough to warp hardwood. "I'll deal with the visitors."

Emily sprang forward, before he could ride away, and grasped the gelding's bridle. "No," she said. She swallowed, and her pride went down, but not easily, and not without pain. "Please, Tristan. They'll kill you."

Polymarr and Fletcher had begun to argue about moving the sheep, while Spud trotted tirelessly back and forth along the outer edges of the flock.

Tristan's eyes were like blue flint. "There's a good chance

of that," he replied. "But nobody—*nobody* rides onto my land and makes threats."

She laid a hand to his thigh, felt the muscles go taut beneath fabric and flesh. "Don't go alone. Ride to town and fetch your brother first. Please."

"No."

"He's the marshal—it's his job to settle disputes like this—"

"He has a wife, a baby on the way. Aislinn's brothers and Miss Dorrie, they all depend on him. I won't put him in danger."

"Then take me with you."

He glowered down at her for a long moment. "Go look after your sheep, Little Bo Peep," he said, with quiet bitterness. Then, as she watched in misery and fear, he rode off, headed toward Powder Creek.

Chapter
5

*T*RISTAN HADN'T GOTTEN FAR WHEN the gelding came up lame. Maybe it was Providence, maybe it was just plain sorry luck, but there was nothing he could do, for the moment, but turn back. He'd pay his respects at Powder Creek another time, and make a point of doing it soon.

Carefully, he pried a stone out of the animal's hoof, but the soft flesh was bruised. On foot, with the horse limping along behind him, he set himself toward home. Of necessity, he made slow progress, but not so slow that he didn't catch up with that squalling mob of sheep. The gelding turned skittish at the noise and the smell, and it took some doing to calm him down.

He and Emily exchanged a look as he came alongside the flock, but neither made any attempt to speak. It would have been futile anyhow, with all that fuss-and-fidget going on.

A gentleman, he reflected, would help drive the stupid creatures to their new pasture, but that day he wasn't feeling very gracious. He'd asked the woman to marry him—he still wanted her more than he could admit, even to himself—but since then he'd begun to question his sanity.

Oh, plenty of hasty weddings took place, especially out

West, where women, handsome ones in particular, were at a premium, and babies had a way of coming ahead of schedule, but Tristan had always envisioned a different scenario for himself. He'd planned on abstaining from private pleasures, once he'd chosen a bride, and courting her properly, though with dispatch, wooing her with flowers and pretty words, bedding her only when she was his lawful wife. The first child, he'd always figured, would come after a full nine months had passed, that there should be no scandal attached to the boy's name—he wanted a son first, so there'd be someone to look after his daughters when he wasn't around.

Now, here was Emily, and abstaining was the last thing he wanted to do. It seemed plainly impossible, and after all, they would be standing up before a preacher come Sunday.

Reaching the barn, he took the gelding inside, took up a pitchfork to muck out a stall and put down fresh straw. That done, he cleaned the wounded hoof and treated it with salve. Meanwhile, Emily, Polymarr, the dog and the boy—who had turned sullen but was helping nonetheless—were herding the sheep into his best pasture to graze right alongside his cattle. Shaking his head, he muttered a curse and strode toward the house.

He'd clean up, he decided, and when Fletcher and the old man got through playing sheepherder, he'd take one of the old plow horses they were riding and go to town. For one thing, he needed more horses, and more men, if he was going to run the operation right. And it had occurred to him, during the long walk down the hill, that there was another way to handle his grievance with the raiders from Powder Creek. He could buy the place, and send the lot of them packing.

Meeting the price, undoubtedly high, wouldn't be a problem; he had plenty of cash, thanks to the wise investment he'd made a few years before, in his own stagecoach line, since sold at a hefty profit. He preferred not to

ruminate too much on where the seed money had come from; those days had dissipated into nothing, like thin smoke, and he had no desire to resurrect them in memory.

He was smiling as he filled a couple of buckets with hot water from the stove reservoir and carried them outside to the bench, where he liked to wash, since he always indulged in considerable splashing. He stripped off his shirt, hung it on a wooden peg, and reached for the soap. He was all lathered up when Emily startled him halfway out of his hide by sneaking up on him from behind.

He swore again, though more moderately than he might have done in other company.

"I am glad to see that you've come to your senses," she said. "Those men might well have killed you."

Tristan poured a bucket of water over himself, to rinse off the soap suds, road grit and sweat. "I'd be there now," he said pointedly, "if my horse hadn't picked up a rock." Her color flared a little at the challenge; he loved it when that happened—seeing it was like laying down a high straight in a game of cards.

"Then you're a fool," she said.

"I won't argue that." He reached for the other bucket and doused himself a second time. His trousers were wet through, and he was hard, and there was no hiding it. He wasn't sure he even *wanted* to hide it. "I'll speak to the preacher while I'm in Prominence. Unless you've changed your mind, that is."

She looked away, looked back. "I haven't changed my mind," she said, pinkening up again, real bright. Blessed God, she was stubborn, and he loved that, too.

He extended one arm to brace himself against the sidewall of the kitchen, deliberately capturing her gaze and holding it, just to prove that he could. "Listen to me," he said, and for all his easy stance, he was deadly serious. "If anybody comes looking for trouble, you leave those sheep to their fate and hightail it for the house. You might be foolish enough to die for a lot of mutton stew and woolen under-

wear, but that's too much to ask of Fletcher and the old fellow. Do I make myself clear?''

She swallowed, nodded. It made him mad that she didn't seem to place as much value on her own safety as that of two virtual strangers.

He kissed her forehead, just lightly. "I'll be back as soon as I can. Is there anything you want from the general store?"

She scrounged up a dusty smile. "Something for supper— besides eggs. Mr. Polymarr went rabbit hunting this morning, before those outlaws came along, but he didn't have much luck."

"I'd say he had more than his share of good fortune, just getting out of there alive. So did you. Be careful, Emily. I mean it.''

She nodded, and he headed into the house, mounted the stairs to his bedroom and put on dry pants and a clean shirt. After combing out his wet hair, he went outside again, and found Fletcher waiting with the nag he'd been riding all day. He was leading Polymarr's horse by the reins.

"I thought maybe you'd want some company," the boy said.

Tristan was touched, though of course he took proper care not to show it and embarrass the kid. "You'd best stay here," he said brusquely, taking the reins of the second horse and climbing into the saddle. "Look after Miss Emily and the old man."

Fletcher gulped down a protest, then gave a glum nod. "You're going to need a hell of a lot more men than just me and Polymarr if you mean to keep those sheep from being slaughtered," he observed. "And it'll be hard getting help, cattle-folk being like they are."

"You're right about that," Tristan admitted, with a sigh of resignation. "But I'm going to get the hands I need, that much is certain. Sweep out the bunkhouse, because I plan to bring home some company."

He asked himself, as he rode toward Prominence at the best pace the horse could manage, which wasn't impressive, why he'd ever let himself get knotted up in this predicament with Emily in the first place. He was a cattleman himself, and thus he sympathized with the ranchers' position. He had no use for sheep, except in the form of good, serviceable wool. Still, the answer wasn't hard to calculate: one look at Emily Starbuck, in her ragbag serape and slouch hat, and he'd lost every ounce of good sense he'd ever had.

Emily owned one dress, a blue calico, and it was rolled up and stuffed into the bottom of the small leather kit bag that held the few possessions she'd collected over the years—an old tortoiseshell hairbrush with bent bristles, a frayed camisole and a pair of drawers of butternut linen, and a copy of a dime novel about a handsome outlaw and a fancy Eastern lady. There were pages missing now, but that was all right; she'd read through it so many times that she could have recited the story without once referring to the print between its tattered covers. She particularly liked the part where the heroine sewed the villain into his own bedsheets and pounded him like berry pulp in a flour-sack dish towel.

When Spud, Mr. Polymarr and Fletcher had gotten the sheep to settle down, and she'd scanned every horizon for another batch of raiders, Emily went inside, built up the fire in the cookstove, and commenced pumping water to refill the near-empty reservoir. While it was heating, she shook out the tattered frock and hunted down a round copper washtub. By the time she'd carried that upstairs, into one of the spare rooms, purloined soap, a washcloth and a towel from the washstand in Tristan's bedroom, and carried half a dozen buckets to the tub, a precious hour had passed.

After propping a chair under the latch of the spare-room door, she stripped to the skin, stepped into the shallow but still-steaming water and sank down into it with a sigh of

well-earned contentment. There was no time for lounging—Tristan might come back at any moment—but that didn't matter. It was luxury enough, just to be clean.

Later, clad in the calico, she half carried, half dragged the tub down the stairs and outside, through the kitchen, to empty it off the side of the stoop. She rinsed the receptacle and returned it to its place in one of the sheds, then went back up to the spare room to brush her hair and wind it into a braid. After a glimpse into Tristan's shaving mirror—although she had slept in that room the night before, she had not been comfortable with the idea of bathing there—she pronounced herself presentable and returned to the kitchen.

A thorough search of shelves, bins and cupboards yielded the makings for baking soda biscuits, and she was rolling the dough out on the freshly scrubbed table when Fletcher rapped lightly at the open door. "Ma'am?"

She smiled at him, but some of her good cheer faded when she remembered the sheep and the men from Powder Creek, who were probably plotting revenge at that moment, if they hadn't already settled on a plan. "Is everything all right?"

"Yes, ma'am," Fletcher said, and even in that short stretch of words, his voice broke a couple of times. He was even younger, Emily realized, than she'd thought. "Polymarr, he sent me to see that you were safe." He took in her dress and tidy hair. "You sure do look different. I would hardly have knowed you."

She suppressed a second smile, but he turned red anyway. "Thank you," she said. "I think."

Fletcher remembered his hat with a painfully obvious jolt, and snatched it off his head. "I was making a compliment, right enough," he said, his Adam's apple bobbing.

Emily made a point of looking away for one merciful moment. "You're very kind," she told him softly. "I'll bring you some supper, when it's ready." She didn't qualify the promise, but it did depend on Tristan's timely return

and his good memory. Given the perils they all faced, though, she'd be happy if he merely came back, with or without supplies.

The sun had set and the lamps were lit when she heard a commotion outside, snatched up the .38 and hurried to investigate.

Tristan had arrived, with eight stout horses, each one ridden by an Indian. Grinning, he loosed a burlap bundle tied behind his saddle and handed it down to her. "There're two chickens in there, along with some other things." He cocked his thumb. "You don't need to fix for the new sheepherders—they prefer their own cooking."

Emily held the bundle of goods tightly, almost overcome with relief, not because there would be fried chicken for supper, but because there were no holes in Tristan. Because he was home, safe and sound. "Is there news of Aislinn?" she asked, after her heartbeat had played leapfrog with itself for a few long seconds.

Again, the grin flashed, brilliantly white in the thickening twilight. "The doctor's with her now."

"Is she well?"

He got down from the saddle, spoke briefly to one of the Indians, who nodded in reply, and turned back to her. "She's in better shape than Shay is," he replied. "If I didn't know for certain I'm his twin, I'd think he was beside himself."

Suddenly it seemed too personal, their discussing the coming of the McQuillans' child, out in the open and in plain hearing of eight Indians. Sparing Tristan only a nod, she lowered her eyes, spun around, and fled into the house.

She opened the parcel on the table, and found the chickens inside, plucked and dressed, along with a tin of lard, some yeast and spices, a packet of tea, a dozen potatoes, several tins of green beans and four dime novels, carefully wrapped in butcher paper and tied with string. Her eyes filled with tears, just to suppose, for the briefest interval of time, that they might be intended for her. She couldn't

remember the last time she had received an actual gift, although she was not ungrateful for her inheritance, uncertain as it was.

Try though she did to imagine Tristan immersed in stories bearing titles like *Vivian and the Sultan* and *The Loyal and Tender Heart*, quite without success, it was simply too reckless to hope for such a present. He owned a number of books, and she had already examined those, running her hands over the fine leather bindings in reverence and envy. He seemed to prefer history, mathematics and classic literature.

She busied herself with the making of supper, and when the meal was ready, she went to the door and called to Tristan. It was a bittersweet pleasure, doing that homey thing—sweet because she could pretend to be part of a family, and bitter for precisely the same reason: it was merely pretense.

Tristan washed up outside, and when he came back, Mr. Polymarr and Fletcher were with him, hats in hand, faces red from scrubbing, probably with cold water pumped from the well. Emily, who had been filling two plates to take out to them, smiled and made places for the men at the table instead.

It was a feast, that meal, made up of crisply fried chicken, potatoes and biscuits, thick gravy and green beans. For a long time, the men ate in silent earnest, made hungry by their hard work, and Emily took pleased satisfaction in their enjoyment, for she was a proud cook, and it had been a long while since she'd had the makings of so fine a dinner.

Presently, Mr. Polymarr wiped his mouth on the sleeve of his shirt, helped himself to the last biscuit, and warned Tristan, "You'd better watch them Injuns real close. They got a long, cold winter comin' on, and a lot of mouths to feed. Could be them sheep'll look mighty good to them."

Tristan met Emily's gaze, and she saw a teasing smile lurking in his eyes. "I can always hope," he said.

She thought of how she'd be married to this man, come Sunday, of how they'd live alone together in this house, sharing meals and plans and problems. Eventually, they would share a bed, too, of course. She felt shy, all of a sudden, and got up to clear the table.

In a moment, Tristan was beside her, holding his own empty plate. He'd done credit to the meal, though he hadn't eaten as much as either of their hired men. "Leave this for me to do," he said.

Emily had never known a man to wash dishes before, never even heard of one doing so, but of course he must have done. He'd been living alone, at least for a while, and the whole place was tidy.

"Go on in there and sit by the fire a while," he said, nodding to indicate the stone hearth at the other end of the house. He set his plate and Emily's in the sink, then retrieved the dime novels from the sideboard, where she'd put them earlier, to keep them out of harm's way. "The storekeeper—her name's Dorrie McQuillan—said these just came in last week, on the stage from Sacramento." With that, he put them in her hands.

She stared at them, her throat tight with an indefinable emotion.

He tapped at the books with an index finger, and there was a note of gentle amusement in his voice. "I'd like to read the one about the servant girl who becomes a trick rider in a Wild West show and then marries a count. That's quite a range of experience."

Emily met his gaze, and only when it was too late did she realize there were tears standing in her eyes. "I don't know what to say. Besides—besides thank you."

He set her back on her heels with that wicked flash of a grin. " 'Thank you' will do," he told her. Then he collected the plates Fletcher and Polymarr had left behind—at some point they had both fled the kitchen without her noticing—and put those in the sink, too. "I'd better go out there and make sure the new men are comfortable."

She merely nodded, since no reply came to mind that wouldn't sound foolish. She was glad he'd referred to the Indians as "the new men," instead of using some cruder term, as Mr. Polymarr had done.

Tristan touched her face with the backs of his fingers, then gave her braid a light pull that tugged at something far deeper and more mysterious. "You look real pretty," he said, and the simple words, spoken in a soft, hoarse tone, had the effect of an accolade.

Emily bit her lower lip. She might have been draped in velvet and dripping diamonds, instead of a hand-me-down calico frock, the way he made her feel, and while she reminded herself that he was a charmer, very clever with words, it didn't do much good.

Just when she thought she would succumb and throw her arms around his neck, he turned and left her standing there, in front of the sink, with the dime novels in her hands. She didn't stir for some time.

The Indians, splinters from a number of fractured tribes, had set up camp at the edge of the pasture. They had a good fire going, and the aroma of roasting meat mingled with the scents of smoke and grass and sheep. If they were having mutton for dinner, Tristan reasoned, that was fine with him.

The dog fell in beside him, gave a friendly yelp, and licked the heel of his palm. Tristan greeted the animal with a quiet word and a pat on the head.

Polymarr appeared out of the gloom, carrying the shotgun he was rarely without. It was sobering, the image of this crotchety old man wandering around in the dark with a loaded gun. Next to that, the prospect of entertaining a bunch of angry riders from Powder Creek seemed downright agreeable. "Them damn savages is cookin' up a dog or somethin'," he muttered.

"Never mind the supper menu," Tristan replied, irritated. "Have they posted guards around the sheep?"

Grudgingly, Polymarr nodded. "Fact is, there ain't much for me and the boy to do."

"You've earned yourself a rest anyway. Why don't you head for the bunkhouse and get some sleep."

"And risk gettin' my hair lifted?"

Tristan laughed. "Not much of a risk," he said, "since you don't *have* any hair to speak of."

Fletcher joined the party. He wouldn't meet Tristan's eyes; not surprising, given the way he'd looked at Emily during supper. Tristan couldn't blame him; she had been a sight to fasten on.

"You think it's smart, lettin' those Injuns have guns?" the boy asked.

"They'd have a hell of a time fighting off any night visitors without them," Tristan answered. "Just mind your business, and let them tend to theirs, and things will be fine."

Polymarr looked skeptical, and gave a great sigh. "I reckon I *am* a mite on the weary side. You sure I ain't gonna get my throat cut while I'm sleepin'?"

"I guess that depends on whether you snore or not," Tristan answered, and went on, the dog accompanying him, while the other two men headed for the bunkhouse. He walked the perimeter of the flock, found sentries in their proper places and returned to the house, where his thoughts had been all along.

Inside, he filled the sink with hot water and washed up the dishes, but all the while he was watching Emily, at the edge of his vision, sitting next to the fireplace, absorbed in one of the books he'd bought for her. He thought it ironic that she found the lives of fictional characters so fascinating, when her own included a fair amount of adventure. How many women could drive a flock of sheep all the way from Montana to California, with only a dog to help and protect them? How many could face down a pack of gun-toting thieves the way she had, that very day, up in the hills?

He shook his head, bemused. It seemed to him that Emily Starbuck ought to be writing those books, instead of just reading them.

Twenty minutes later, when he joined her at the other end of the house, she looked up from the pages at last, eyes wide and luminous. "How did you know she was going to become a trick rider and marry a count?" she asked, in a breathless way that set something to quivering inside him.

For a moment or two, he was confounded as to what she might be talking about. Confounded about a few other things, too, come to think about it. But then it struck him that she was referring to the plot of the dime novel. "I skimmed it while Dorrie was filling my order. She'll be bringing some other supplies out tomorrow, by the way."

Her eyes went wider still. "You read it?" She glanced at the shelves of leather-bound volumes he cherished. "This?"

"Sure. A book's a book. I like them all. That one has a bang-up ending."

Suddenly she laughed. It was a soft, musical sound, wholly feminine, and it roused an uncharacteristic shyness in him, an aspect of his nature that he had not recognized before. The sound of an approaching rider saved him; he found that his usually glib tongue was tangled, and the visitor gave him an excuse to leave the house.

Strapping on his .45 with hasty, practiced motions, he wondered if his neck had gone red. The identity and intentions of the rider were lesser concerns, which only went to prove that the right woman could set a man's brain to rattling around his head like a peach pit in a tin can.

Fortunately, when he went outside, he found Shay there, glowing like he'd swallowed the moon whole. "It's a girl," he said jubilantly, as he jumped down from the gelding.

Tristan responded with a happy exclamation and a slap on the shoulder. Then, more seriously, he asked, "How's Aislinn?"

Shay's face softened at the mention of the wife he adored. "She's the most incredible woman," he said, and from his reverent tone, one might have drawn the conclusion that nobody else had ever borne a child before. "Hell, I'd rather let a blind man dig a bullet out of me with a butter knife than go through what she did. But there she is, sitting up in bed, holding the baby and looking pretty as an angel. To see her now, you'd think she never broke a sweat."

Tristan smiled. "I'd offer you a drink in celebration, but you'd probably rather get back."

Shay glanced toward the house, and from his expression, Tristan knew Emily was standing in the doorway. He glanced back, saw her framed in an aura of soft light, and thought to himself that Aislinn wasn't the only one with the look of an angel about her.

"Things are a little tense in town," Shay admitted, lowering his voice. "Tristan, the ranchers aren't happy about those sheep. Some of them say you've sold them out."

He folded his arms. "I can't much help what they think," he said evenly. Then he grinned. "When can I have a look at this little girl of yours? And what's her name going to be?"

"You're welcome anytime," Shay said, as though surprised by the question. "Aislinn wants to christen her Mattie."

Mattie. The name of the young woman who had given birth to them only hours after being widowed in an Indian attack and then dying herself. "That's a fine choice," he said, and cleared his throat.

Shay was preparing to mount up again. He nodded toward Emily. "Come and see us as soon as you can." The vaguest suggestion of a grin touched his mouth. "Bring your friend."

Tristan promised to visit, asked his brother to convey his congratulations to Aislinn, and watched as Shay disap-

peared into the night. He felt a pang of fear, looking after him, and hoped that badge he prized so much wouldn't get him killed.

"The baby's arrived?" Emily asked, when he was inside the house again, his earlier embarrassed bewilderment forgotten.

He nodded. "A girl. They're going to call her Mattie." He went to the pine cupboard beside the fireplace, took out a bottle and a glass, and poured himself a whiskey to mark the occasion. "I'm an uncle."

Emily watched as he raised the glass to his lips and took a sip, but because of the shadows he couldn't make out her expression. "You're worried," she said. "Why?"

He couldn't tell her that he was afraid his brother might get caught in the range war that was almost sure to come about because of those blasted sheep. It wouldn't have been fair to lay such a burden on her, even if she had brought the flock to Prominence. Whatever his own feelings about the stupid critters might be, she obviously valued them, and she had that right.

In the end, he told her part of the truth. "There's some mean talk in town," he said, after another sip of whiskey. "The boys from Powder Creek aren't the only ones, Bo Peep, who find your sheep objectionable."

She turned her face toward the fire, and he saw in its glow that her cheeks were bright with indignation. The dime novel lay in her lap. "What do they expect me to do?"

"Move on," he replied.

Her gaze sliced to his. "Is that what you want?"

He considered the question, though he'd long since made his decision. "No," he said, "but I could do without the sheep."

She sighed, one finger curved to mark her place in the book. Once again, she was staring into the crackling fire, and its light danced along the length of her shining hair. Tristan wanted to touch her, but he restrained himself. Sunday—their wedding day—was not far off. That night, when she was officially his wife, he would begin his

campaign to bed her, but he would be patient, whatever the cost. His honor depended upon that.

"Is it true that cattle and sheep cannot coexist?" she asked, after a long time. Her voice was small and fragile, but he knew that she was one of the strongest people he had ever encountered.

"No," he said, with weary resignation. "If a man's got plenty of range land, he can move the flock from one pasture to another, so the grass has time to grow back. It isn't the animals that can't get along, Emily. It's their owners."

She stood, slowly, proudly, elegantly. "That flock is all I have," she said.

He wanted to tell her that wasn't so, that he meant to give her the world, but it wasn't the time for encouraging speeches, so he kept his mouth shut.

"You'll be sleeping in the barn again?" she asked, when he didn't speak right away.

He thrust out a hard sigh. "Yup," he said, and finished his whiskey in one gulp.

Chapter

6

⟨ↄ◊ↄ⟩

*T*HE WEDDING BAND GLEAMED IN THE LAMPLIGHT of the barn, a small golden circle in the palm of his hand. Tristan closed his fingers around it for an instant, as though it were a talisman, and then shoved it back into the pocket of his pants. Trying to calculate how long it would take, after the wedding on Sunday, to have his way with Emily, he put out the light, lay down in the hayloft and made up his mind to sleep.

Instead, he imagined Emily giving birth to their child, sometime in the not-too-distant future. He knew she'd be brave, as Aislinn had been, but he expected his own reaction would be similar to Shay's. Stoic as he might appear on the surface, inside, he'd be in a frenzy.

Mentally, he worked his way backward from that momentous day, and inevitably came to the time of conception. The pictures were so vivid that he groaned. He was in a bad way, and feared he would not soon see an improvement in his situation. The hell of it was that his personal code would not allow him to find his ease elsewhere; from the moment Emily had promised herself to him, he'd been committed.

He spent the next hour or so tossing and turning, but the day had been a long and difficult one, and he was tired, so

presently he lapsed into a shallow, fitful sleep. The sound of the dog whining at the base of the ladder awakened him, some time later, and he raised himself onto one elbow.

"What?" he snapped, and started down the ladder.

Spud whimpered, and there was an all-too-familiar coppery smell, mingling with the usual ones of hay and horse manure and sweaty animal hide. Blood.

Tristan felt his way to the lamp that hung from one of the low beams, struck a match, and lit the wick. The dog looked up at him with doleful eyes, and whined again, apologetically. Squatting in the straw, Tristan examined the animal and found he'd been torn up pretty badly in a fight of some sort. Probably, he'd tangled with a raccoon or a badger, maybe even a bobcat, prowling around waiting to make a swipe at the sheep, but one thing was definite: he'd come up the loser.

As gently as possible, Tristan lifted the dog in both arms and headed for the house. The Indians keeping watch were shadowy forms in the darkness, and their campfire blazed a bright warning to all intruders, whether they had two legs or four. Spud must have wandered a fair distance from the flock, a strange thing in and of itself.

Inside, he set the dog in the center of the kitchen table and started lighting lamps. Spud made sorrowful complaint, and the sound must have awakened Emily, for she appeared while Tristan was filling a basin from the hot water reservoir. Not that he'd tried to be all that quiet.

Seeing the dog's blood-matted fur, she gasped and went white. She was wearing one of his shirts for a nightgown, and he tried not to notice that her legs were showing. And fine legs they were, too.

"What happened?" she cried, rushing over to stroke the animal's head with a loving hand. For all that something had practically shredded the poor creature's hide, Tristan envied him a little, just then, wanting that tenderness for himself.

He got liniment and a clean cloth from the shelf where he

kept such supplies, accidents being a fairly common occurrence on a ranch. In the past, though, he'd only had himself for a patient. He dampened the cloth with pungent medicine and began to clean the worst of the dog's wounds, a six-inch gash on his left flank.

Spud showed his teeth and growled, no doubt prompted by the pain, but Emily spoke to him with a sort of stern compassion, and he quieted down a little. Tristan figured he might have been short a finger or two by then, if it hadn't been for her.

"Will he die?" she asked, when the job was nearly finished, and Tristan realized that she'd been working up her courage to pose the question all along.

"Probably not," he answered. "He won't be much use with the sheep for a while, though. These wounds are sure to get infected if he doesn't stay clean until they've closed up."

Emily shut her eyes and rested her forehead against the crown of the dog's head for a moment, and Spud made a low sound in his throat, reveling in her sympathy. Tristan was moved by the depth of the bond between the two of them and, once again, he felt a mild twinge of envy. When at last she turned to face him, he was stricken to see tears in her thick lashes.

"He's been a fine friend to me," she said. "For so long, there was nobody to talk to but him. I don't think I could bear it if he—if he died."

Tristan would have touched her, if his hands hadn't been dirty. More than anything in the world, he wanted to reassure her, and give her whatever comfort he could. "He'll be all right," he said hoarsely, and lifted Spud carefully off the table and set him on the floor. The animal retreated to the kitchen hearth, where he lay down on the hooked rug with a whimper of self-pity and closed his eyes.

When Tristan came back in from scrubbing off the liniment and blood at the wash bench, he found that Emily had scoured the table, added wood to the stove and set a

kettle of water on to heat. Now, she was merely measuring tea leaves into the chipped crockery pot that had come with the place, nothing more spectacular than that, but the sight of her in that shirt, with her braid dangling down her back, set him afire inside. Never, at any time in his life, had he wanted a woman as he wanted this one. He saw clearly that the secret feelings he'd cherished for Aislinn had been nothing more than shallow daydreams; this was something real and right. Something monumental.

And yet he barely knew her.

"I guess I'd best get back to the barn," he said. The words seemed to scratch his throat raw.

She looked at him in shy surprise and, unless he was mistaken, hope. "Won't you stay a few minutes?" she asked. "I don't think I can go back to sleep right away." She poured steaming water into the teapot. "Sometimes a cup of tea helps, though it's said to be a stimulant—"

"Emily."

She stopped, looked at him again, waiting.

"This is improper, my seeing your—your limbs and all."

Incredibly, she laughed. "Day after tomorrow, we'll be married. And it's not as if we're, well, *doing* anything."

"It's the prospect of *doing something,*" he retorted pointedly, "that I can't stop thinking about. Seeing you like that doesn't help, believe me."

Her mirth faded, though a spark of it lingered in her eyes. "Oh," she said, and the sound was small, hardly more than a breath.

He considered showing her the ring he'd bought earlier that day, at the general store, but if he did that, she might think he was trying to make her feel obliged. After all, he'd said, straight out, that he planned to seduce her. "I'd best go," he reiterated, and when he'd passed over the threshold, he stood looking up at the stars and silently cursing himself for every kind of idiot.

He returned to the barn, climbed up into the hayloft, and stretched out again. After a few minutes, he realized that he

could still see the stars, the cracks in the roof were that wide. One good rain and the horses and all the hay would be drenched.

He went to sleep making a mental list of things he'd need to make the necessary repairs.

Emily took her time over her solitary cup of tea, convinced that she wouldn't get a wink of sleep even if she went back to bed immediately. Her mind, her senses, her very soul it seemed, were all full of Tristan—Tristan's mouth, Tristan's hands, Tristan's powerful shoulders and lean midsection.

Sitting at the kitchen table, where he had so skillfully attended to Spud's wounds only minutes before, she spread her fingers over her face and groaned. Then, peering through a space at the dog, she said in mock accusation, "How could you? I'm the one who feeds you and scratches you behind the ears and throws sticks for you to fetch. And what do you do when you get into trouble? You go to *him* for help!"

Spud gave another low whine, as if to make excuses for himself, but did not raise his muzzle from its position on his outstretched forelegs.

Emily finished the first cup of tea and poured herself a second one. There wasn't a grain of sugar in the house; Tristan didn't seem to use the stuff at all, but she hoped there would be a supply among the things the storekeeper had promised to deliver. Many of her best dishes required sweetening—rhubarb pie, for instance. She'd found a patch of the stuff growing in the deep grass out behind the barn, and wanted to put it to good use before the first hard frost.

Thinking about cooking calmed her nerves a little, and soon she put her cup in the sink, along with the teapot, put out all of the kitchen lamps but the one that would light her way upstairs, and retired to the room she would be sharing with Tristan after Sunday.

The idea stopped her in midstride. He had sworn he wouldn't force himself upon her, and she knew he would

keep his word, as much for his own sake as for hers. But she hadn't asked if sleeping beside him was part of the bargain.

In the middle of the stairway, she laid her free hand to her bosom, fingers splayed, and tried to recover her composure by drawing and releasing slow, deep breaths. The thought of lying in Tristan's bed, with him right there next to her, maybe *touching* her, either by accident or by design, sent a terrifying surge of pleasure rushing through her. Suppose she saw him naked? He hadn't promised to behave modestly, after all. . . .

Wide awake again, Emily went back downstairs to get her book. It was, she thought ruefully, going to be a very long night.

Emily was pleased, the next morning, to meet the storekeeper, Dorrie McQuillan. As she began unloading the wagon full of supplies, the woman explained cheerfully that she was Shay's older sister. Her manner was so open and friendly that Emily felt completely accepted, and that was a new and delightful sensation.

Emily introduced herself and set to helping with the carrying. She was feeling guilty, staying inside the house that day, dressed in calico, while Mr. Polymarr and the Indians looked after her sheep. Tristan was on the roof of the barn with Fletcher, making repairs with a hammer and nails and scraps of wood he'd found in one of the sheds.

"It's time he found himself a woman," Dorrie said, with a nod toward the barn, where Tristan's shirtless form was disturbingly visible. Emily hadn't worked up the courage to ask him if he expected to share the master bedroom and walk around in a state of undress.

"It's a business arrangement," Emily felt compelled to say. There must have been a dozen boxes in the back of that wagon; Dorrie climbed up, agile as any man in her practical riding skirt, and began shoving them into reach.

"Sure it is," Dorrie replied, without sarcasm. Still standing in the wagonbed, she looked Emily over critically. She was a plain soul, too tall and too slender by common

standards of beauty, but she radiated some inner quality that made Emily want to know her better. "I reckon those ready-mades Aislinn sent along will fit you just fine," she said.

Emily was suddenly self-conscious, uncomfortably aware of her shabby dress, and though it chafed her pride sorely to accept charity, she could hardly wait to see what Dorrie had brought. "How is Aislinn? And the baby?"

"They're both just fine," Dorrie said, getting out of the wagon as nimbly as she'd gotten in. "Baby's delicately made, like her mama, but she's strong, too. There's so much life in her, you can feel the heat of it, little scrap of a thing that she is."

They took the last of the wooden boxes into the house.

"Will you stay for tea?" Emily asked. She would be frightfully let down if Dorrie refused, but she tried not to show it.

"I can't be gone long," Dorrie said, as she took a seat at the table, casting a curious glance at Spud, who was still languishing like an invalid on the hearth. "I'm running the store all by myself, with Aislinn in her confinement. Shay's right; it's time we hired on some help."

"Confinement" seemed a strange term, to Emily, for such a wonderful experience as bringing a child into the world. Busily, she rummaged through the groceries until she found a good-sized sack of sugar, and set the tea to brewing. Later, she would bake the rhubarb pies, to serve with supper, but for the moment there was nothing to offer Dorrie but tea.

"Where's home?" Dorrie asked. By then, Spud had crept over to rest his head on the bench beside her, and she was gently stroking his head, but her kindly gaze was fixed on Emily.

She didn't know exactly how to answer the question. She'd never in her life had a real home, until now. "Here," she said, at some length, and in such a quiet voice that Dorrie leaned forward a little to hear it. As far as she was concerned, the ranch was indeed hers, whether she became Tristan's wife or not.

Dorrie seemed satisfied with the reply. "Looks like this dog met up with a bee-stung grizzly," she observed. "Poor creature."

Emily recalled how Tristan had taken care of Spud, touching him gently and murmuring soothing words, even when the animal growled and bared his teeth. "Tristan says he'll be all right," she ventured.

"Of course he will," Dorrie confirmed.

After that, they drank tea and chatted a while, and Dorrie told the whole story of Shay and Aislinn's courtship, complete with dynamite and gunfire. It was, Emily thought, better than one of her books.

Perhaps an hour had gone by when Dorrie stood up and said she had to be on her way. She'd locked up the store before she left, and folks were bound to be breathing on the windows, which were impossible to keep clean, with all those fingers and noses pressed against them every day. And that was reckoning without the dust from the road which, according to Dorrie, never seemed to settle.

From the doorway, she pointed to a large brown-paper parcel, tied with twine. It was resting on the far end of the table, fat and intriguing. "That's from Aislinn," she said.

"Please thank her for me," Emily said.

Dorrie nodded and was gone.

Sorry to see her company depart, Emily set herself to unpacking the provisions and putting them in their proper places. There was flour, coffee, tinned vegetables, sacks of potatoes, turnips and onions, and a lot more besides, so the task took a long time. Emily saved Aislinn's package for last, and approached it cautiously when everything was done.

"It won't explode," Tristan remarked, from the doorway behind her, startling her by his presence. He'd put his shirt back on, at least. That was a mercy, because seeing him without it did unseemly things to Emily's insides.

She turned back to the package and took a step toward it. She was expecting a plain dress or two, well-worn and probably out of fashion, but her sense of anticipation was

tremendous all the same. She wanted to draw out the experience as long as she could, even though it shamed her not a little to accept a gift of that sort. She wanted so much to provide for herself, but there was scant hope of that until the wool and mutton were sold.

After another glance at Tristan, she removed the string and folded back the heavy paper, slowly and very carefully. What she found inside made her draw in a sharp breath— dresses, *beautiful* dresses that showed hardly any wear at all. There was a white one, embroidered with tiny pink and green sprigs, and a black one, made of crisp, rustling sateen, softened by a collar and cuffs of delicate ivory lace. Another was bright yellow. There were lovely linens, obviously new, and stockings as well.

Emily was all but overwhelmed. Her knees went flimsy and she had to sit down on the bench next to the table to recover herself.

Tristan's hands came to rest on her shoulders, and though she knew he had meant to comfort her, the contact had an electrifying effect, rather like taking hold of a lightning rod during a storm. When she stiffened, he released his grasp, to her regret, but did not step away. She was very conscious of him, as hard and warm as the wall of a blast furnace. "I've got some business in town later today," he said. "Would you like to go along, and pay a call on Aislinn?"

The suggestion was a welcome one; she turned to look up into Tristan's face, smiling. "You don't think we'd be intruding?"

"Shay will be insulted if we don't make a fuss over that baby, and he'll be looking for us. Why don't you wear that yellow dress?" The blue heat in his eyes drew a flush to her cheeks, and she barely kept herself from covering them with her hands.

"I was going to bake some rhubarb pies," she said, and immediately felt stupid.

He grinned crookedly. "We won't be leaving for a few hours," he told her. "I've got things to do here."

She swallowed, and nodded, and was both relieved and bereft when he finally left the house to return to his work.

The rhubarb pies were cooling on the table when Tristan returned, in the middle of the afternoon, to say he was ready to head for Prominence. He'd evidently cleaned up in the bunkhouse, because his hair was damp and freshly combed, his boots were shined, and he was wearing a fresh cotton shirt and black trousers. The ever-present .45 rode low on his hip, an ominous reminder that there was a dark side to his nature.

Emily had changed while the pies were in the oven, and she was encouraged by the light she saw in Tristan's eyes as he looked at her. She grew flustered by his attention, however, and her hands trembled as she reached up to make sure her hair, wound up in a careful coronet at her nape, was firmly in place.

"Best put those pies away," Tristan said, with amusement in his voice. "If Spud doesn't get them, Polymarr or the kid will." He didn't wait for her to do it, but instead wadded up a pair of dish towels to protect his hands and stashed them, one at a time, inside the oven, which was now barely warm.

"Do you think they'll be safe here, with the sheep? Mr. Polymarr and Fletcher, I mean?" In some ways, Emily had been holding her breath, figuratively speaking, ever since the confrontation with the Powder Creek men. She almost wished they'd attack, and get it over with.

"Black Eagle and the others will look after things," he said. He had a lot of confidence, it seemed to her, in people he didn't know very well. Like her, for instance. Was he assuming that she was giving up her claim to the ranch by marrying him? Was that the true reason for his hasty proposal?

"Why should they?" She knew little enough about Indians, and she certainly sympathized with their plight, but she'd heard plenty of stories about their propensity for stealing.

His expression was grim, even hard. Here again was the dark Tristan, the inner twin to his normally sunny persona. "Because they've got families on the reservation, going hungry. They need what they earn."

Emily felt as though she'd been reprimanded, but that was of no consequence next to the starvation of a displaced and cheated people. "You care about them."

"Somebody ought to," he replied. "Are you ready, or not?"

Not for the first time in her life, Emily wished she'd kept her observations to herself. She followed him outside and hurried to keep up as he strode toward the buckboard, which was already hitched and waiting beside the barn. "I care, too," she protested, setting spaces between the words because he was moving so fast that she practically had to run to keep up.

"Do you?" He helped her into the wagon seat, went around behind, and climbed up beside her. "Then give them some of those damn sheep."

Emily was silent while he disengaged the brakes and brought the reins down lightly on the horses' backs. The buckboard lurched forward, and she hung on to the hard wooden seat with both hands. Finally, she found the words to form a reply. "I'll give them as many as they need," she said, "*if* you hand over the same number of cattle."

His blue eyes were narrow with suspicion as he looked down at her. "Do you mean that?"

She swallowed. She thought of the money she'd lose in wool and mutton sales, and mourned it, but the specter of starvation was far worse. She wouldn't be able to put a bite of food in her mouth, knowing that others were going hungry, practically at her elbow. "Yes," she said.

A grin broke over his face like a sudden sunrise. "Good," he said, "because I gave them twenty head this morning."

The true meaning of sacrifice impressed itself upon Emily. "You did not."

"I did," he insisted, fairly bursting with appreciation of his own generosity.

Emily sighed and bid a score of perfectly good sheep a silent farewell. "Will it be enough?" she asked, at great length. "To sustain them, I mean?"

Tristan was solemn again. "Probably not," he said. "They'll share with all their friends and relations. That can thin down the stew quite a bit."

After that, Emily was quiet, her mood dampened.

It was only when they reached the edge of town that her spirits rose a little. She hadn't been a part of a community since before the sheep came into her life, and it was lovely to see people striding along the wooden sidewalks, leaning in doorways, talking in front of the livery stable. She couldn't help noticing, though, that a few of them pointed fingers in their direction, and that Tristan's jaw was now set in a hard line.

They soon arrived at Shay and Aislinn's gate, and Emily thought the place was even more beautiful in the bright light of day, though it didn't have the same sturdy substance, she decided, as the ranch house did.

Shay called to them as Tristan was lifting Emily down from the wagon, and she saw him crossing the street from the marshal's office. His star-shaped silver badge gleamed on the lapel of his knee-length black coat, his hair was ruffled, and his grin was wide.

"Aislinn will be pleased," he said, coming to an easy stop before them. He nodded politely to Emily. "Ma'am," he acknowledged.

"Emily," she corrected.

He beamed. "Emily, then," he replied. Then he headed for the gate, unhooking the latch and standing back so his guests could pass. When they entered the front parlor, Emily was amazed to find Aislinn out of bed and neatly dressed in a black sateen skirt and starched white shirtwaist, the baby making a little bundle in her arms.

Her dark hair was swept up and held in place by tiny ivory combs, her brown-amber eyes sparkled, and her face glowed with happy color.

"Tristan—Emily—I'm so glad you came to call."

Tristan bent to kiss Aislinn's forehead. "All right," he said, with a soft gruffness that Emily might have begrudged, had the situation not been special, "let's have a look at this niece of mine."

Proudly, her eyes shining with motherly pride, Aislinn drew back the edge of the blanket to reveal a small, downy head, covered in fair hair. The child was delicate and lovely and yet, as Dorrie had said, there was a lively vitality about her, a distinct presence, even though she was but one day old.

Tristan lowered himself to one knee beside Aislinn's chair and grinned up at his brother. "Now *here*," he said, "is a breaker of hearts."

Aislinn laughed tenderly. "No," she said. "She will be kind, our Mattie. Kind and generous and sweet."

"And smart," Shay put in, taking Emily's arm lightly in one hand and ushering her to a nearby chair.

"Well, that goes without saying," Aislinn replied. Tristan got up, and she held the baby out to him. "Will you hold her?"

Tristan blushed and retreated a step, something Emily could not have imagined him doing before that moment. "I don't think I'm ready for that quite yet," he said.

"Coward," Aislinn challenged.

He would not be moved by insult, good-natured or otherwise, and perched on the edge of the settee, hat in hand, as if ready to bolt for the door. Within a few minutes, he and Shay went outside together, ostensibly to enjoy a celebratory cigar.

Aislinn smiled at Emily as warmly as if they'd been friends forever and said in a conspiratorial tone, "They're hiding out there."

Emily laughed. "Yes, I think you're right," she said. Her heart was warm and full. She looked down at her lovely yellow frock. "Thank you for sending me some of your things."

She assessed Emily thoughtfully. "That gown is very nice

on you. When I wore it, I looked as though I had jaundice.'' Her face was soft with love for her husband and child. ''What about you, Emily? Would you care to hold Mattie?''

''Oh, *yes*,'' Emily said, and got to her feet.

Aislinn handed over the child with an easy trust that Emily would always cherish. She held the baby carefully, and sat down, and could not have explained why her eyes suddenly stung with tears. Silently, she offered a fervent prayer that the baby would always be loved and kept safe.

''Shay tells me you and Tristan are to be married on Sunday.''

Emily looked up and met the other woman's gaze, blinking in vain. Her tears must have been obvious to Aislinn. ''Yes,'' she said.

Aislinn's eyes sparkled with innocent pleasure. ''Good. Tristan will make a fine husband. Reformed rogues usually do.''

It came as no surprise to Emily that Tristan had been a rascal. He was handsome, and possessed of a potent sort of personal charm. Such men were popular with women, and generally took full advantage of the fact.

Her expression tender, she admired the baby, so small and solid in her arms, and yearned for one of her own. ''He's a good man,'' she agreed. Then she remembered the broader situation and concern welled up inside her. She forced herself to look at Aislinn again. ''How do you feel about sheep?'' she blurted.

Aislinn stared at her, clearly baffled. ''Sheep?''

''I have a flock. It's my understanding that the ranchers and a good number of the townspeople despise the poor creatures.''

Aislinn rose, took the baby from Emily's arms and placed her carefully in the cradle that stood nearby. After covering her, she sighed and turned back to her guest. ''These are honest, hardworking people,'' she said. ''Give them time, and they'll come to their senses.''

Emily squared her shoulders and raised her chin. ''I've

had experience with 'honest, hardworking people,'" she answered with some bitterness. "They acted as though I'd brought some dreadful plague into their midst."

Aislinn came to stand beside her, and rested one hand on her shoulder. "Was there no one to take your part?"

Emily shook her head, afraid to speak for fear she'd burst into wailing sobs, wake the baby, and make an utter fool of herself.

Aislinn's fingers tightened slightly. "Well, you have a family now. Things will be different."

Chapter
7

*T*RISTAN HAD BEEN GONE A LOT LONGER than it should have taken to smoke a cigar, but Emily didn't mind. She and Aislinn exchanged life stories while the men were away, and a lasting bond was formed between them.

When Tristan did return to collect her, he had a thick packet of papers in the back pocket of his trousers and he was sporting an almost insufferable grin. He was pleased about something besides being an uncle, that was plain, but apparently he did not intend to confide his news any time soon. He said fond good-byes to his sister-in-law and niece—Shay was off making his rounds—and squired Emily outside to the wagon without a word.

Unsettled by the silence, benevolent though it was, she tried to make conversation when they were outside of town and moving toward the ranch at a good pace. "Shay and Aislinn are lucky to have that beautiful baby," she said.

"Yup," Tristan agreed, still grinning. He didn't even spare her a sidelong glance.

She cleared her throat and made another, more daring attempt. "I suppose you'll want children."

He made a clicking sound with his tongue to speed up the horses. "Yup," he repeated, and began to whistle softly through his teeth.

Emily gave up, but only temporarily. Whatever his secret was, she was bound to discover it in time. That it was probably none of her business anyway was wholly irrelevant.

Reaching the ranch, she was relieved to see that the sheep were grazing peacefully and that Fletcher and Mr. Polymarr were still in possession of their scalps. She began to hope that the danger from the Powder Creek men and others was past, though she knew that was overly optimistic. The animosity between cattlemen and sheep owners ran deep, and was by no means specific to Prominence and the surrounding area.

Holding the skirts of her prized yellow dress high, to avoid soiling the hem, Emily made her way to Black Eagle, who stood still as a statue in front of a cigar store, his sinewy arms folded. He smelled of smoke and leather and some sort of animal grease. There was no expression at all in his face as he looked down at Emily, but the marks of suffering and sorrow were etched deep into his flesh and bearing. He was gaunt, defeated, but still proud.

She smiled uncertainly, full of pity and well aware that that was the last thing he wanted or needed from anyone. How, she wondered, could she offer the man twenty head of sheep without sounding pompous? "You seem to be doing a fine job overseeing the flock," she said.

He didn't speak, and his features remained blank. She wished she'd consulted Tristan before approaching Black Eagle, at least asked how he'd given the tribe a score of cattle without injuring its collective dignity, but he'd been hardly more communicative than the Indian ever since they'd left town.

"Where is your village?" she persisted. Men were cussed creatures, it seemed to Emily, whatever their race, creed or color.

Black Eagle stared into her eyes for a long time, and she stared back. She'd approached him in good faith, the flock was hers, down to the last lamb, and she would not be

intimidated. When he saw that she meant to stand her ground, he pointed to the west.

"There," he said.

Emily was mentally winded, just from the effort of pulling that one word out of him, but hers was a hearty soul, and she greeted it like a flash flood of scintillating conversation. "Do you have a wife? Children?"

"Three wives," Black Eagle responded, in perfectly clear English. There went the theory that he didn't speak the language. "Ten children."

Emily was taken aback. "That's—impressive." A great many mouths to feed, she reflected, and there might well be elders in Black Eagle's household as well, and indigent relatives. Most distressing of all, the group represented just one family, out of dozens or even scores. She was about to plunge in and offer him the pick of her sheep when Tristan interrupted.

There had been a profound change in his disposition since she'd seen him last. He was scowling, his eyes were narrowed and his jawline was clenched. Emily gaped at him, dumbfounded, with no earthly idea what she'd done to make him so angry.

It was Black Eagle who broke the uncomfortable silence. "Your woman talk plenty," he said.

Emily flushed with humiliation. She was about to protest that she was her *own* woman, and no one else's, that this was her land they were standing on, when a look from Tristan stayed her tongue.

"She raises sheep," he said, as though that explained her every shortcoming. His gaze had never left her face. "Go back to the house, Emily," he said crisply. "Right now."

Plainly, it would only make matters worse to argue, but she intended to blister Tristan's ears the instant they were alone. The very idea of his ordering her about that way, like a—like a husband! She would clear *that* little matter up, in no uncertain terms. Snatching a better hold on her skirts,

she whirled and flounced off toward the sanctity of the kitchen she had already begun to think of as her own.

Tristan watched his future wife's departure with undisguised appreciation. Lordy, but she was a little hellcat, all hiss and claw. Taming her might take years, and he looked forward to every moment of their life together, good, bad and middling. In time, he might even grow to love her, whatever that meant.

"Indian woman no talk," Black Eagle said firmly.

Tristan didn't see any reason to point out that Emily wasn't an Indian; that much was obvious. He heaved a great sigh of pretended resignation. "I guess I'll have to beat her," he said, though he'd never laid an angry hand on a woman before and never intended to do so.

Black Eagle nodded sagely. "It plain why white man take only one wife," he observed.

Tristan laughed. He knew Black Eagle had three mates, and the idea of Emily in triplicate was certainly enough to give a man pause, all right. "God help us all," he muttered, and steered the discussion in the direction he'd intended in the first place. "I bought a considerable spread of land today," he said. "I'll need all the men you can spare to help me run it. To seal the bargain, I'll give you twenty head of these sheep, your choice."

The Indian beckoned to one of the others and said something to him in dialect. The younger man nodded grimly, and the process of selecting the promised animals began. Tristan watched for a few moments, then turned on his heel and went back to the house, well aware that Emily would probably strip off a patch of his hide when he got there.

She was stirring something in a large kettle, her strokes powerful enough, in her dudgeon, to churn watered-down milk into butter. She glared at him and waited in obstinate silence for his apology.

He had no intention of offering one, but he was grateful as hell that she hadn't been there to hear his bluff remark

about beating her. "When you give an Indian a gift," he explained, folding his arms, "he feels obligated to give you something in return. If he can't, he loses his honor, and honor is just about all these people have left."

Her fury dissipated, but she set the bowl down with a thump. Tristan saw cornmeal batter inside, and his mouth watered. "You might have mentioned that before," she said, still huffy.

"It didn't come up in conversation."

She narrowed her gaze, suspicious again. "What did they give you, for the cattle?"

"Firewood," he said. "Enough to keep us warm until the turn of the century, probably. The women and kids are gathering it now."

She bit her lower lip. "I'm sorry."

He allowed himself the semblance of a grin and pointed at her in mock surprise. "You?"

"I almost made a terrible blunder. I was about to say to Black Eagle that I'd heard the people in his village were starving, and that he should take his pick of the best ewes." She pressed the back of one hand to her forehead and heaved a frustrated sigh. When she looked at Tristan again, her eyes were bleak. "Isn't there something the government can do?"

Tristan spat out a contemptuous laugh. "The government? No Indian in his right mind would trust a politician or a soldier. Not after being lied to so many times."

The idea must have come to her out of the blue; he saw it take shape in her expressive face. "Will you take me there?"

"Where?" he asked, though he had an awful feeling that he already knew the answer. Not for the first time, he wondered what forces had shaped this remarkable woman into the person she was.

"To the Indian village, of course," she answered, confirming his suspicions.

He ground his back teeth, making an honest effort to show patience. "No," he said, and it came out sounding like a bark, though he hadn't meant for that to happen. The

ragtag band occupying the small village a few miles to the west was largely peaceful, but there were always renegades, and they played by their own rules. Like as not, if some of them were to come along and carry her off, the others would not interfere.

Her eyes widened. "Why not?"

"Because it's no place for you, that's why."

"You'll have to give me a better reason than that if you expect to persuade me."

What was it about this woman that made him dig in his heels? "I'm not trying to persuade you. I'm *telling* you not to go near that camp."

"And I'm telling you that I'm not one of your men, obliged to take orders from you. Have you forgotten that I have a valid claim on this land? It seems to me that I should have something to say about how things are done!" She picked up the bowl again, grabbed the wooden spoon and stirred with a vengeance. He hoped the cornbread would still turn out, because he had a powerful hankering for a good-sized piece, slathered with butter.

He deliberated for a few moments, then gave a little ground, though he told himself it was mostly for the sake of supper. He'd deal with the domestic property dispute later. "You might carry some sickness to them," he said. "They're vulnerable to things like that—especially the children."

She put down the bowl again and dusted her hands on the printed flour sack she'd tied around her waist for an apron. Her brown eyes had gone round again, and he knew he'd swayed her, though he wasn't particularly proud of the fact. Anyway, it was true that the tribes had been decimated by smallpox, cholera and typhoid, all plagues they rightly dreaded. "But I'm fine," she said.

He spoke quietly, his mind full of the horrors he had seen in his travels. "That doesn't mean they couldn't catch something from you. Or me. Or any of the rest of us. It's better to leave them be, Emily."

She sighed. "It doesn't seem right," she said.

He wanted to put his arms around her, but he was afraid

to do that because then he wouldn't be able to resist kissing her, and who knew where that might lead. He didn't doubt his ability to turn away, but the price of restraint was high. He'd suffer for his chivalry, and he was more than miserable as it was. He was not used to that particular sort of sacrifice.

Without making a reply to her remark, he took his leave, still hoping there would be cornbread for supper. A minor consolation, but a consolation all the same.

Mr. Polymarr and Fletcher came inside to eat, just as they had the night before. Emily was touched by their attempts to groom themselves for the occasion, and she made them welcome, filling their coffee mugs repeatedly and making sure they got a share of the cornbread she'd baked to compliment the meal. Tristan consumed more of the stuff than four men could have held.

When she served the rhubarb pie, all three men took generous portions and surrounded them with ease. It struck Emily that cooking meals on a ranch might be a career in itself.

Presently, murmuring their thanks, Mr. Polymarr and Fletcher left the house, and Tristan insisted on washing up the dishes, just as he had done the night before. She went in to sit by the front-room fire, still brooding over the Indian women and children, their hunger and hopelessness vivid in her mind's eye. She could well understand Tristan's bitterness on their behalf, and it raised him in her estimation that he cared at all. Many white men spoke of the natives with disdain, as though they were less than human, and treated their livestock with more charity.

So far did Emily's thoughts carry her that it made her start when Tristan spoke. "I have something to show you," he said, in a quiet, almost shy voice.

She looked up at him, standing over her, his hair full of firelight.

He dragged the other chair over and sat down facing Emily. Then he handed her the packet of papers he'd been so secretive about earlier in the day.

Confused, she unfolded them, and drew in a sharp breath. The documents represented the deeds for the Powder Creek ranch, which the late owner had evidently acquired in parcels. "This represents a great deal of money," she said, for she was frightened of debt and nothing more sensible had come to her.

"I *have* a great deal of money," he replied, without arrogance. He seemed to be merely stating a fact. "We'll move up to the big house as soon as I've gotten rid of the present crew of ranch hands," he added.

To her, the house they were *in* was big. Furthermore, it was hers, by rights. She wasn't sure she wanted to leave it, even though she had been there a very short time, and although she moved her lips, she found herself utterly unable to speak. The Powder Creek place was probably very grand; suppose he came to regret taking her to wife, instead of a woman with elegant manners, money of her own, and all the attending social connections?

He squinted. "What's going on in that extraordinary brain of yours?" he asked.

Emily raked her lower lip with her teeth, searching her heart for the courage to answer him. "I'm wondering if you'll change your mind about me one day."

He leaned forward and kissed the tip of her nose. The gesture was wholly innocent, and yet, like all his other caresses, it shook her somewhere far within. "I don't believe I will," he said, as though that closed the discussion. "Do I have to sleep in the barn again tonight?"

Her pulses began to pound, an inner drumbeat that warmed her blood. "We must come to an understanding about that," she said bravely. Her voice was a mere squeak.

Tristan arched one eyebrow. "What sort of understanding?"

"I was—well, I was wondering whether we're going to sleep in the same bed. After we're married, I mean."

He couldn't quite suppress the grin that lifted his mouth at one corner. "Don't all married people share a bed?" he

asked, and though she knew he was teasing her, that did nothing to calm her racing heartbeat.

She looked away, looked back. "We didn't. My husband and I."

That announcement struck him with a visible impact. "Not ever?"

Emily shook her head. "He was old. He wanted a servant, not a wife."

"Then you're a virgin?"

"Yes," she said, straightening her spine. Her dignity, such as it was, was all she had to cling to at the moment.

"That," he said, cupping her face in both hands, "is good news. Not that I would have thought less of you, because I wouldn't have. But I do like knowing that I'll be the only man who has ever taken you to his bed."

She was afraid he would kiss her, afraid he wouldn't. If he did, she couldn't be certain *what* she might say or do. She felt his breath fan warm and sweet over her mouth, setting her lips to tingling. "I don't—I don't know how," she faltered.

He brushed her lips with his own. "I'll teach you," he promised.

A hot tremor went through her. "You'd better go now," she said, pulling away from him and bounding out of her chair as though there was a hot coal on the seat.

He caught hold of her hand. "You don't have to be afraid," he told her. Then he pulled her down onto his lap, and she did not have the will to resist him. His tone was low, rumbling, mesmerizing. "The first time can be uncomfortable, but I'll never hurt you. I swear it."

She couldn't say anything, and though she tried to summon the will to pull away, it simply wasn't there to draw upon.

"I'll make it good," he went on. With the back of his knuckles, he lightly, ever-so-lightly, brushed the fabric covering the hard points of her breasts. "Let me show you, Emily."

Her head was swimming; the fire was a flickering blur on the hearth, and every nerve in her body was alive with a need so elemental, so primitive, that it frightened her. "Tristan," she whimpered.

He bent his head to her bosom and nibbled softly at one of the hidden nipples, and in that moment she became a part of the fire. Then he gave a raspy sigh and set her back on her feet, holding her by the waist for the several moments it took to regain her balance.

"I'm sorry," he said, and the legs of his chair scraped the floor as he stood. The deeds to the huge ranch bordering his lay scattered on the rug, and Emily bent to gather them up so swiftly that she nearly fell on her head.

He steadied her again, this time grasping her shoulders.

She handed him the papers, taking refuge among the last shreds of her pride. "Why apologize?" she asked, with a slight edge. "You did say you planned to seduce me."

He folded the documents, tapped them against the palm of one hand. "I wouldn't respect myself at all if I didn't try," he said. "Do you mind if I go upstairs for blankets and a set of long johns? It's cold in the barn."

She averted her eyes and gestured generously toward the stairs. "Help yourself," she said, and he laughed hoarsely as he left her.

Emily had expected her ardor to cool by morning, but when Tristan came in for breakfast, without Mr. Polymarr and Fletcher, her attraction to him was as strong as ever. She served him coffee and salt pork and leftover cornbread, and he watched her with a smile in his eyes while he ate.

"You'll be going to Powder Creek this morning?" The question had the tone of a statement. A sort of bleak resignation came over her. "Alone."

"Black Eagle and a few of his friends are going to ride along with me," he said. "And Powder Creek is the Double Crescent now. It's part of this place."

There it was again, that subject they were both avoiding.

It just seemed that there was always something more important to discuss.

"You're determined to get yourself killed," she accused, in a burst of fear, unable to keep up the pretense of being calm any longer. Tears burned in her eyes, and she blinked desperately to force them back.

Tristan rose slowly from the bench at the table and came to her, laying gentle hands on her shoulders. "On the contrary," he said, "I've never wanted to live more than I do right now. But there are times when a man has to stand up for what's his, and this is one of them."

She knew he was right, but that didn't make it any easier to send him off to deal with people who weren't above shooting him. She slipped her arms around his waist and laid her head against his chest, and he held her, tentatively at first, then with a sort of possessive strength. He placed a light kiss on her temple.

"I'll be back in no time," he said. Then he hooked a finger under her chin and raised her face so he could look into her eyes. "Don't fret, Emily."

She sniffled and nodded her head, and they both knew it was a lie. She *would* worry, terribly.

He'd only been gone for a few minutes when she hurried upstairs, put on the trousers and shirt she'd been wearing when she arrived a few days before, and made for the barn. Walter was there, in her stall, growing lazier by the hour in her idleness.

Emily pulled a bridle over the mare's head and mounted, not troubling with a saddle. Tristan and Black Eagle were well ahead, accompanied by five other men, and she followed, staying well behind them. Should Tristan spot her, he'd make her go back if he had to hog-tie her and throw her over a saddle, and she didn't doubt for a moment that he was capable of just such drastic action.

The ride grew steeper as she progressed, her heart thundering at the base of her throat. She was scared of what might take place at the former Powder Creek, and even more

frightened of not knowing, not seeing for herself what was happening.

Eventually, Tristan and his companions disappeared from view, swallowed by the dense woods that banded the hill in oak and fir, maple and birch. The leaves were bright yellow and russet, just beginning to turn. Emily kept her distance, guided by the trail of hoofprints pressed into the soft ground. Beyond the trees was a high meadow, and she was forced to rein Walter in and wait at the edge of the forest. If she went farther, she would be out in the open and certain to be noticed.

The house Tristan had bought was the largest Emily had ever seen, a magnificent structure of natural stone, with a score of windows and a veranda that wrapped around one side of it like a steamboat rail. A windmill turned slowly in the breeze, and she could see a massive barn as well, and a corral full of fretful horses. It was plain that, like Emily herself, they smelled trouble, even though there was no one in sight besides Tristan and Black Eagle and the braves riding a short distance behind them.

Emily was jerked off the mare's back, striking the ground hard, and before she could cry out, a callused hand clamped itself over her mouth. She struggled, and the assailant dug his thumb and forefinger into the hinges of her jaw, giving her head a painful shake.

"Settle yourself down, little lady," an oily voice hissed. "I don't want to hurt you, but I will if I have to." Emily was swamped with fear, but there was a quiet place inside her, a calm place where reason held fast. She obeyed the command and went completely limp, hoping her captor would think she had fainted and release her.

It didn't work. He stuffed a wadded bandanna into her mouth the moment he moved his hand away, and then tied another around her head to secure the first. He bound her wrists behind her, then hurled her up onto the back of a horse with such force that for a moment she thought she would swallow the bandanna and choke to death.

She still hadn't had a good look at the man who had ambushed her, but she didn't need to see him to know he was one of the riders who had terrorized her two days before, when she and Spud and Mr. Polymarr were looking after the flock.

He mounted behind her, and she felt his sloppy bulk, smelled sweat and whiskey and rotting teeth. He forced his hat down onto her head, and it was as effective as a blindfold. Emily's stomach roiled, and she fought the urge to vomit, knowing she might well strangle if she lost control.

After a while, revulsion gave way to sorrow. Tomorrow was Sunday, the day she was to have been married, and now everything was ruined. She might be dead by dawn, or wishing devoutly that she were. They would use her, these outlaws, as a weapon, or as bait for a trap. Once they'd drawn Tristan in, they would surely kill him.

Emily reminded herself that she must not panic. If she was watchful, an opportunity for escape might present itself, but hysteria—her first and most ardent inclination—could only work against her. And against Tristan.

Give me courage, she prayed, and centered her thoughts on the sanctuary she had found within herself.

The hairs on the back of Tristan's neck stood upright, and the horses pranced nervously. Black Eagle and his braves arranged themselves in a circle, facing outward, keeping their mounts under careful control.

Tristan drew his .45 and got down off the gelding. On the second floor of the house, he saw a curtain move, caught the glint of a polished gun barrel. Suddenly, all hell broke loose behind him, the Indians shrieking war cries and generally creating a disturbance.

Tristan used the distraction to make a run for the front door, and even then the ground behind him was peppered with bullets fired from the roof. He was glad to see, when he had a chance to look, that Black Eagle and the others had

taken cover behind water troughs and at the edge of the house itself, evidently unharmed. They had guns, and they gave back as good as they got.

Two men tumbled down from the roof, dead before they hit the ground.

Tristan pushed open the heavy front door, using it as a shield. "There's nowhere to go from here," he called. "Throw your guns out the window and we'll take you in alive."

The reply was another spray of gunfire, riddling the door.

"Hell," Tristan muttered, frowning at the damage. He'd probably have to send to San Francisco for a replacement, or even Mexico.

"Where's your bride, Saint-Laurent?" someone yelled from the upper floor. "You seen her lately?"

A chill trickled down Tristan's backbone like a drop of January creek water. He would have liked to believe the bastard was bluffing, but his gut told him this was no idle taunt. He held up a hand, palm out, signaling Black Eagle and the others to hold their fire.

"If you've got something to say," he shouted back, "say it straight out."

Silence.

A stir at the edge of the meadow caught Tristan's eye, and he let out a long breath when he recognized Emily's mare, riderless, reins dangling. Until then, he'd thought she was at home, with Polymarr and Fletcher and the rest of Black Eagle's crew to protect her. Now he knew she'd followed him, and they had her.

Bile scalded the back of his throat. Dear God, those sons of bitches had her.

He took a few moments to collect himself. Then he stepped into the spacious entryway and fired three shots through the ceiling. Overhead, somebody howled, and Tristan reloaded.

"Where is she?" he demanded.

"You loco or somethin', shootin' up your own house?" It

was an aggrieved bellow. Word of the purchase had gotten around, apparently.

"I'll burn it to the foundation if I have to," Tristan replied, and he meant what he said. He'd roast the truth out of them if that was what it took to find out where Emily was.

"How do we know you won't start shootin' as soon as we show ourselves?"

"You don't," Tristan replied. "Where is she?"

Chapter

8

◦⚬❧⚬◦

$\mathcal{W}$HEN THERE WAS A HITCH IN THE NEGOTIATIONS, Tristan
figured it was time to take decisive action. He found an old
newspaper next to a nearby fireplace, rolled it up, lit it with
a match, and set the drapes in the front parlor ablaze. They
made a dark, acrid smoke, and as the house filled, the two
men who'd been hiding out upstairs came stumbling down,
choking and swearing.

Tristan got them both by the collar and flung them out
the door. They pitched halfway across the veranda before
landing, and when they hit the floorboards, he was there to
send them flying again. They struck the dirt in a pile and
squirmed there, howling as loudly as if they'd been shot full
of arrows.

Several of the Indians rushed past into the house, presumably to put out the fire, while Tristan and Black Eagle stood
over the whining no-accounts. Tristan shoved his .45 into
the base of one man's skull, while planting a knee in the
middle of his partner's back.

"One more chance," he said, his voice hoarse from the
smoke inside the house. "That's all, and then there's going
to be a mess the likes of which this country has never
seen."

"We don't know where she is!" squealed the one in the

greatest danger of getting the back of his head blown off. "I swear to God, they never told us!"

Tristan got the other one by the hair and yanked. Coupled with the pressure of his knee in the middle of the man's spine—if indeed he *had* a spine—it got his point across. "There's a line shack somewhere up in the hills," he bawled. "It's north of the Indian camp!"

Tristan ground the bastard's face into the dirt. "She'd better be all right," he warned, in a voice that would have frightened him, coming from someone else. "My friend Black Eagle is going to keep an eye on the both of you until I get back. As God is my witness, if there's so much as a scratch on that woman, I'll jerk your insides out, set them on fire, and stomp out the flames." He stood up, and Black Eagle signaled two of his braves, who promptly bound the outlaws hand and foot with strips of rawhide.

"I ride with you," Black Eagle said staunchly, and Tristan could see by his expression that there would be no changing the man's mind. There wasn't enough time to work out an agreement anyway.

Tristan swung up onto his gelding and reined it toward the high country. Black Eagle was mounted as well, and he spoke to his men in an earnest undertone before catching up with Tristan.

"What did you just say?" He was only mildly curious as to whether or not the captives would be alive when they got back.

The Indian's black eyes glittered. "I tell them, if the woman-killers try to get away, shoot them." Black Eagle probably knew every fold and hollow of the hills above, and Tristan was glad to have his company, though he wouldn't have admitted as much. With this particular companion at his side, he had a much better chance of getting Emily back safe, though he would have preferred Shay.

He'd seen a half-dozen cabins in varying states of collapse while exploring in the mountains; some had housed miners, some the families of settlers who'd died out or given up long

ago. Some were line shacks, where cowboys riding a fence line could get in out of a storm. Emily could be in any one of them, or none.

"We need dog," Black Eagle said, and for a moment, Tristan, riding hell-bent for nowhere, couldn't grasp the meaning of the statement. Then he remembered Spud, and wheeled the gelding around in a wide circle, racing back toward his own ranch house.

It probably took thirty minutes to get there, and Tristan begrudged every second of that time, but if he was going to find Emily he had to have the animal's help. The gelding was still moving when he dismounted, bounding into the house, slamming the front door open, taking the stairs two and three at a time. In his bedroom he found what he sought: the tattered serape Emily had been wearing when she entered his life.

He didn't have to whistle for Spud; the dog, though injured, sensed calamity, and he was pacing nervously back and forth on the rug at the base of the stairs, making a sound somewhere between a snarl and a bark, when Tristan came down. He let the animal smell the serape, and the result was more than he would have dared hope for—Spud shot through the gaping door like a Chinese rocket, and Tristan went stumbling after him.

Both he and Black Eagle rode full out to keep up with the dog, and even then they probably would have lost him if he hadn't been forced to slow down on reaching the timber line. Of course, they couldn't travel as fast either, and time was passing, and Tristan was about as scared as he'd ever been in his life.

His greatest fear was for Emily, of course; her captors were just stupid enough to hurt or even kill her. Every atrocity he'd ever seen, and he'd seen plenty, replayed itself in his mind as he rode, with Emily as the victim. He felt stark, cold terror, and the messages rising from his gut were no comfort at all.

At last the dog paused, prowling along the edge of a ridge.

His ruff stood out in bristles, and he snarled and yipped like a wolf with prey in its sights, waiting impatiently for the pack to catch up.

Tristan might have ridden straight down into the gully if Black Eagle hadn't extended an arm and stopped him by taking hold of the gelding's bridle.

They dismounted, and Black Eagle led the horses farther back into the woods, after giving Tristan a warning glance. The shack below, a weathered board structure leaning far enough to one side that a stiff wind would blow it over, was clearly occupied. There were two horses out front, and a ribbon of smoke curled from the crooked chimney pipe, making a gray smudge against the sky.

Black Eagle returned, crouched beside Tristan. "No guards," the Indian said. By then, Tristan had to restrain the dog to keep him from flinging himself at the cabin, a pretty good indication that Emily was inside and probably alive, too, though there was no telling what shape she was in. He closed his eyes for a moment, and silently implored a God he had long since stopped believing in to protect her.

"Not worry," Black Eagle said, in a whisper. "She talk them to death."

He'd no more than uttered those words when the shack's rickety door creaked open and one of the Powder Creek men came outside, unbuttoned his pants, and took a long piss in the brush at the side of the cabin.

Tristan squinted, straining for a glimpse of Emily through the open door, and in that moment he relaxed his hold on Spud just long enough for the dog to break free and dash, growling ominously, for his target. The cowboy, still holding his pecker in both hands, was taken by surprise and gave a little whoop of alarm that might have been funny, under other circumstances.

The dog was on him, at his throat, when the second man came out of the shack. He had Emily crushed against him, facing forward, and his pistol probed deep into the side of her neck. She looked pale and understandably rumpled, but

otherwise unhurt, and Tristan's relief was so great that he almost forgot she was in imminent danger of being shot to death.

"Come on out, Saint-Laurent," the big man called, getting his name right, and Tristan recognized him then. Once a Texas Ranger, Elliott Ringstead had gone bad a long time ago, and made himself a reputation as a thief and murderer of no little imagination and enterprise. He was the one man Tristan had ever tracked in vain, and the bounty on his head had probably compounded half a dozen times over the years. "No sense hidin'. I know you're out there."

The man with his pants down was still wrestling with the dog, and shrieking like a frightened spinster all the while. Emily looked down and spoke to the animal in a quiet, firm tone. Reluctantly, Spud withdrew, but he didn't go far, and he kept looking from one outlaw to the other, awaiting his chance.

Ringstead cocked the pistol and thrust it harder against Emily's neck. "You gonna make me shoot her, Saint-Laurent? A ladies' man like you? Why, I don't believe it!"

"All right," Tristan shouted back. He stood and tossed the .45 down the hillside, and it struck the ground with an audible thump. "Let her go." He started the descent, his hands raised.

Emily's bright eyes widened with alarm when she saw him, then she squeezed them shut and shook her head slightly. Her lips formed a soundless word, once, then again. "No—no."

"You know, Saint-Laurent," Ringstead drawled, "I've always wished I had your way with the women. This one here's uncommon pretty—you outdone yourself this time, yes indeedy."

"I should have tracked you down a long time ago," Tristan said evenly. He met Emily's gaze and saw a reprimand there; she had not wanted him to come out of hiding. Of course, he couldn't have done otherwise, and right then her opinion on the matter was of little concern anyhow. "I

believe the posters read, 'Dead or Alive.' The first will do as well as the second.''

Ringstead laughed, showing a row of tiny brown teeth and a lot of gum. "Looks like you're goin' to be the one that's dead," he observed. With the toe of his boot, he gave his partner a nudge calculated to bruise. "Get up, Homer. In case you ain't noticed, we got the upper hand here."

Emily flashed a warning look at Tristan and then bit said hand with as much force as she could. Ringstead bellowed a curse, and she brought her heel down hard on his instep for good measure. Tristan made a desperate dive for Emily and flung her to one side, and during that interval Ringstead recovered enough to raise and sight in the pistol. He was so close there was no need to take aim; he simply drew back the hammer.

"No!" Emily screamed.

A shot was fired, and Tristan waited for it to hit him. And waited.

Ringstead went down instead, graceful as a dancer, despite his bulky, awkward build, a crimson stain spreading across his chest and belly. Tristan realized that Black Eagle had just saved his life, but a shout from Emily brought his attention to the fact that the partner, heretofore wriggling on the ground, twisted up in his own pants, had gotten hold of the discarded .45.

"Put it down," Tristan said calmly.

Emily had collected Ringstead's gun, and she was standing over the other man, the pistol steady in her hands. "If you pull that trigger," she told Homer, with bitter sincerity, "I will kill you."

The outlaw considered his situation and then handed the .45 over to Tristan, butt first. Tristan jerked the man to his feet and tossed him to Black Eagle, who was ready with more rawhide to secure the prisoner's hands and feet, but his attention, all of it, was fixed on Emily.

"Are you hurt?" he asked. They might have been alone, for all the notice he took of the world around him; it was

merely a pounding, blurry void, an aura of light at the edges of his vision.

She flung herself against him, hurled her arms around his neck and held on like a drowning swimmer. "They were saving me for after they killed you," she replied, trembling against him. "Oh, Tristan, thank God you're safe!"

He held her very tightly and closed his eyes for a moment, dizzy with relief. Then he thrust her to arm's length and looked her over again. His fear had crested and then ebbed, but his mind was still spinning in the backwash. He opened his mouth to tell her precisely what he thought of her reckless interference, but she was alive, and unhurt except for a few bruises and scrapes, and that made the rest of it unimportant. He wrenched her close again and buried his face in her hair.

Black Eagle leaned over Ringstead's body, peering at him curiously. "You knew this man?"

Tristan let Emily go at last and turned to look down at the dead outlaw. "I spent two years hunting him," he answered numbly.

Emily came to stand beside Tristan, gazing anxiously into his face. She was a tough little thing; many other women would have swooned, or at least burst into tears, during and after such an ordeal, but she hadn't given Ringstead's corpse a second look. "Hunting?" she echoed.

He had not wanted her or anyone else—not even Shay—to know about his years as a bounty hunter, little better than a hired gun. But the choice had been taken from him; he would have to tell the tale, admit that for most of his life he had made his living by tracking men like any other prey, dragging them to the authorities when they would surrender, killing them when they wouldn't. He had in fact enjoyed the hunt, the way he would a challenging chess match or a high-stakes game of cards, and as long as they'd been the first to draw, he hadn't minded killing them, either.

"Tristan?" Emily prompted, when he didn't speak. Didn't look at her.

Finally, she turned away to crouch down in front of Spud, ruffling his fur gently and praising him. He gave a series of happy yips and licked her face until she laughed and struggled back to her feet.

Only later, when Ringstead's body was strapped facedown onto his horse, and his more fortunate partner perched in his own saddle, with his hands bound to the saddle horn, did she press the point. Since she was riding behind Tristan, her arms tight around his waist, her mouth close to his ear, he could not pretend he didn't hear her question.

"Are you going to tell me who you are?"

"Yes," he answered, after a long time. "Later. At home."

Mercifully, she settled for that.

The ranch house was a blessed sight to Emily, for she had not expected to see it again. Near the kitchen door, Tristan handed her down from the horse's back without dismounting himself. Black Eagle kept a tactful distance, the exhausted Spud sprawled across his lap like a sack of grain.

"Shall I hold supper?" she asked.

He sighed and shook his head. "No." He indicated the dead man and the prisoner with a grim nod. "Shay will have a lot of questions, Emily. Black Eagle and I left a few bodies scattered around today, and that calls for some explaining."

She pressed her lips together briefly, biting back a protest, and then managed a wobbly smile. "Thank you for coming after me, Tristan. Even though it was a stupid thing to do."

He gave her a wry look. "We'll discuss stupid things to do when I get back," he said. "Save me a slice of that rhubarb pie, unless Fletcher and Polymarr have already gotten to it."

Her eyes burned, and she blinked a couple of times. Spud leaped down from Black Eagle's horse and limped over to her, dirty and sore and all but spent by the afternoon's heroics. "Hurry back," she said to Tristan, and started toward the house, walking slowly so the dog could keep up.

There was plenty to occupy her hands, but her mind was with Tristan while she washed Spud's wounds again, and treated them with medicine, while she took a sponge bath in

the spare room and changed into another of the dresses Aislinn had given her. Downstairs, in the kitchen, she peeled potatoes and turnips and put them in a pan of cold, salted water to be boiled later.

The sun was setting when Fletcher rapped shyly at the open door and found her sitting at the table, her hands folded in front of her, staring into space. She started, then summoned up a smile.

"I brung you these here grouse," he said, and held up a brace of birds, already plucked and cleaned. "They're good when you fry 'em in bacon grease."

Emily had not thought beyond the turnips and potatoes, and she was genuinely pleased by the boy's gift and the generous spirit behind it. "How wonderful," she said. "Thank you. If you'll give me half an hour, I'll have a meal on the table."

Fletcher swallowed, and she knew he was going to ask about Ringstead and his companion. There was no way to stem the question; it was a marvel that he'd waited this long to approach her. "Looked like there was trouble up in the hills today. Sounded like it, too."

Emily met his eyes. "Everything's fine now," she said soothingly, and hoped she was telling the truth. She had a feeling that her whole future depended upon what Tristan would say when he came home that night. "I'd better get busy," she said, with forced good cheer, "if we're going to have supper anytime soon."

Fletcher hesitated, then went out. Spud, back in his spot in front of the kitchen hearth, whimpered a comment, then closed his eyes for a well-earned rest.

Soon, the grouse were cooked and the potatoes and turnips were drained and steaming in the middle of the table, still in the cast-iron kettle. She went out to the pasture, where the sheep were bedded down for the night, watched over by their Indian shepherds as well as Fletcher and Mr. Polymarr.

Looking over her flock, Emily knew her problems were far from over. Maybe what Tristan was going to tell her

about himself would change things, and maybe it wouldn't, but either way she was still an outsider, land or no land, house or no house. A sheep owner smack in the middle of cattle country, a pariah of sorts. Would there never be a place for her?

"Time to eat," she said quietly.

"Them Injuns claim they're entitled to their pick of the sheep," Mr. Polymarr fussed. He would not have been happy without a crisis, but Emily was ready for peace. "Twenty of 'em, no less!" He squinted at her as they walked toward the square of golden lamplight that was the kitchen door. "That true?"

"It's true," she said and, to his plain disappointment, did not elaborate.

When supper was over and Mr. Polymarr and Fletcher had taken their leave, the former having made repeated and hopeful reference to his fondness for rhubarb pie, making it clear that he would welcome a second helping, all to no avail, Tristan had still not returned from town, and his interview with Shay.

Emily heated water, washed the dishes, and watched the clock. It was after nine when Tristan finally came in, looking weary and strained. He tossed his hat onto a side table and thrust a hand through his hair.

"I've kept your supper warm," she said. They might, she reflected, have been married for twenty years, such was the sense of ease and quiet acceptance between them. To her way of thinking, any trouble that fell to him would fall to her in an equal portion.

He nodded. "Thanks." He went outside to wash while she built up the fire in the cookstove to brew fresh coffee. When he came in, she took his plate from the warming oven, with its gleaming chrome front, and set it on the table.

The food looked a little shriveled, but Tristan didn't seem to mind. He ate with good appetite, saying hardly anything, and some of the familiar twinkle came into his eyes when he saw the generous serving of pie she'd saved for him.

She poured his coffee and waited and, in time, her

patience was rewarded. He pushed away his empty pie plate and looked at her steadily. She knew he was almost ready to tell her about his past, and braced herself to hear it.

"That was a good meal," he said. "Thank you, Emily."

She sat down across from him and folded her hands. "You're welcome," she said, and then lapsed into an expectant silence.

He heaved a heavy sigh. "Shay wouldn't let me out of his office until he'd gone through every wanted poster he had, in case I turned out to be a fugitive. I'm afraid things are a little awkward between my brother and I, just now."

"Are you?" Emily asked. "Wanted, I mean?"

A shadow moved in his eyes. "No," he said. "I always managed to stay on the right side of the law. I was a bounty hunter, and before you say that's a respectable trade, let me tell you that you're wrong. I was a gunslinger. I took a lot of men in alive, but I killed just as many. I thought I'd left that life behind, until today." He sighed. "I should have known better. I've got enemies out there—fathers, brothers, friends of the people I shot down or sent to prison. What happened today could happen again. And again."

She held her breath, then blurted, "I won't go, if that's what you're about to suggest."

"Emily, it isn't safe here. Never mind the cattlemen. *I'm* more of a threat to you than they are. I'll pay you for the land, for the sheep—"

She folded her arms. "Are you going back on your word?" she interrupted.

He stalled by reaching for his coffee and taking several sips. Finally, he had no choice but to answer. "Were you listening to me?" he countered, leaning forward. "I've *killed* people, Emily. Dozens of them. And it isn't over, because there's always going to be somebody like Ringstead, looking for revenge. Or just wanting to prove something."

She considered that statement. "I'll take my chances," she said. "It's not as if I expect an easy life, after all. Just a good one."

He looked bewildered for a moment; then he laughed

ruefully and shook his head. A mischievous smile touched his lips. "Does this mean I don't have to sleep in the barn?"

"I couldn't very well ask you to spend the night out there after the day you've had," she said, and watched as his eyes widened. "You can have your own bed back, and I'll sleep in the spare room."

His face fell slightly, but he was quick to recover. "You're very generous," he allowed. He raised both arms and stretched, and there was something so earthy and sensual, so masculine, in that simple motion that Emily was deliciously discomfited.

"Well!" she said brightly, getting to her feet and words spilling out of her and scattering as if someone had turned her upside down, like a milk can full of marbles, and given her a shake. "It's been quite a day, hasn't it? I believe I'll turn in. Good night, Tristan."

He reached across the table and caught her hand in his. Then, leaning forward slightly, he brushed a light kiss across her knuckles. "Good night," he said, in a low tone that lodged inside her, sweet and warm and spiky. The sensation was one of pleasure, rather than pain, but it left her even more shaken than before.

He held her hand a moment longer, clearly as aware of the charge passing between them as she was, then reluctantly let her go. "You take the main bedroom," he said, and his voice raked the smoldering embers inside her to full flame. "You have my word that I won't bother you."

Emily turned and fled, mostly to keep from blurting out that she wanted him to lie beside her, husband or not. It did not even matter to her that he was a self-professed gunslinger with a string of killings behind him.

She did not sleep well that night, and thus, when the delegation of ranchers arrived just after dawn, she was dressed and ready to face them. Quick as she was, Tristan, clad in hastily donned trousers and his undershirt, was there before her. His suspenders dangled at his sides and his hair was mussed, but he was wearing boots and the gunbelt that seemed such an integral part of him.

There were a dozen mounted men in the dooryard, all of them grim and armed with rifles. Their faces were shadowed by the brims of their hats, but they'd made no attempt to disguise themselves. Emily glimpsed varied brands as the horses fidgeted, sensing conflict the way animals do.

"We can't have them sheep in amongst our cattle," the lead man announced. He was probably in his fifties, with a gray stubble of beard and a lean frame that bespoke years of hard work. "You ought to know that as well as anybody, Saint-Laurent."

It angered Emily that the man would address Tristan, when the sheep were hers alone, but there were more important things at stake, so she held her tongue.

Tristan pulled up one suspender, then the other, giving each one a little snap for emphasis. Standing beside him, Emily saw that his gaze had locked implacably with that of the spokesman, and understood some of what the men he hunted down must have felt, facing that quiet, unbending certainty. "As long as these sheep stay on my property, I don't see where they're any concern of yours."

Emily felt a surge of pride and, at one and the same time, she was as frightened as she'd ever been in her life. Even with Black Eagle and his men, and Mr. Polymarr and Fletcher, Tristan was outgunned. It wouldn't matter much who won or lost, she reasoned, if he died in the skirmish. Nothing mattered as much as saving his life. She stepped in front of him, as if to form a shield.

"I'll move on," she said quickly, looking up into the rancher's shadowed face, trying to find a human being there. "I'll surrender my claim. I'll take my sheep and leave, right away. There's no need for any shooting."

Tristan set her aside, and she sensed both anger and respect in the way he gripped her shoulders. "She's not going anywhere," he said, "because we're about to be married. But Emily's right about one thing: there's no call to start a range war. You men get down off your horses and come inside. We'll have breakfast and talk this thing through."

Emily held her breath.

The ranchers argued among themselves for a time, but finally they dismounted. Although they sheathed their rifles in the scabbards affixed to their saddles, they were all wearing side arms. Tristan led the way into the house, and Emily trembled inwardly as she walked beside him.

The men took their places at the long table, filling up the benches on both sides. Tristan brought a chair from the other end of the house and sat at the head, as dignified, even in his undershirt and suspenders, as a judge calling a courtroom to order.

Emily busied herself brewing coffee and starting a batch of flapjacks, but she was alert to every nuance of word or movement at the table. She took note, with a degree of consolation, that once they'd shed their hats and long, dusty coats, the ranchers were but ordinary men, one or two well into their later years and graying, their faces weathered and rugged, a few just sprouting their first whiskers. Most, though, were someplace in between.

They were family men, almost without exception, fathers and husbands, brothers and sons. Seated at her table, with mugs of coffee steaming before them, they did not seem so fearsome as they had out front, mounted and carrying rifles at the ready.

"You ain't got enough land to run sheep and still keep 'em off the open range," a bearded man challenged.

Tristan sat easily in his place of command, his hands cupped loosely around his coffee mug, his tone and manner affable. "I own this place—" He paused and glanced at Emily. "—or at least, my future wife does. The Powder Creek spread is mine now. To my way of thinking, that's plenty of space to accommodate a band of sheep."

"Since when are you so fond of them woolly critters?" a younger man asked. "I thought you was a cattleman, like the rest of us."

"I am," Tristan said. His eyes met Emily's as she came to the table and began to set enamel plates in front of the men. She was shaking a little, marveling. He'd conceded that the

original ranch was hers. "The sheep belong to my bride here. Because they're hers, I'm willing to see them through the winter and protect them like I would my own stock."

A brief, pensive silence fell, then the ranchers began to stir and murmur again, and reminded Emily of a covey of old ladies gossiping over a quilting frame. Except, of course, for the guns on their hips.

"I reckon we can wait till spring," one man said, at last. "See how things go."

Emily's knees went weak with relief, and while she was cooking and serving up the pancakes, her heart sang.

Chapter
9

$\mathcal{T}$HE CHURCH WAS PRACTICALLY EMPTY that afternoon, when Emily and Tristan stood up before the preacher to exchange their wedding vows. Shay served as best man, while Aislinn lent her support from the front pew. Although she had insisted that she was well enough to stand beside Emily, her husband had insisted otherwise. For the sake of the peace, she had complied.

Emily was moved when Tristan produced a golden wedding band at the proper point in the ceremony and slipped it onto her finger. She promised herself that she would buy a matching ring for him, come the summer, when the lambing and shearing were done and there would be money to spend.

When the preacher pronounced the words that bind man and woman together in the sight of God and humanity, Emily nearly swooned with joy, excitement, and relief. Tristan took a steadying grip on her arm and they turned together to accept congratulations from Aislinn and Shay.

"I'll be a good wife to him," Emily said, when Shay planted a brotherly kiss on her forehead. Although he smiled, the expression in his eyes was serious, and she knew the strain between him and Tristan had not abated.

"I know," Shay answered gruffly.

Tristan had taken a seat beside Aislinn on the pew, and she was embracing him in gleeful celebration. Emily felt a tug in the region of her heart, looking at them, and hoped she would be in her sister-in-law's place one day soon, with a genuine marriage and a child.

A commotion outside distracted them all; Shay and Tristan exchanged a closed look that troubled Emily and headed down the aisle together. Both wore the ever-present gunbelt and pistol, and neither Emily nor Aislinn failed to notice that they'd thrust back their coats on one side, in order to draw unimpeded. They hurried after their husbands.

Outside, the sunshine was bright, the air crisply cool. More than twenty mounted men had gathered in front of the church, pistols in hand. Emily recognized some of them: ranch hands, formerly employed at Powder Creek. It was plain from their bloodshot eyes, flushed faces and unkempt clothing that they'd been consuming ardent spirits, and that the indulgence had not improved their general attitude.

A man spurred his horse through the center of the gathering and drew up within a foot of where Shay and Tristan stood, shoulder to shoulder, each with a hand resting on the well-worn butt of his .45.

"You think you can turn us out like so many Injuns and run sheep on Powder Creek land?"

"That's exactly what I think," Tristan answered. "The place is mine now, and I'll do as I like with it."

The man blinked, obviously confused as to who was whom. Then he glared blearily at Tristan. "We'll kill you if we have to," he said, and Emily's throat closed so tightly that she couldn't breathe. Aislinn gripped her fingers and squeezed hard, crunching the bones together.

"You're never going to get a better chance than right now," Tristan replied. They might have been discussing the price of oats for all the emotion he showed, and his hand was all too steady on the handle of his pistol.

"You can't get us all," another man put in.

"That may be so," Shay interjected, "but we can take a fair number of you with us."

Emily started forward at that, a protest on the tip of her tongue, but Aislinn jerked her back with surprising strength, for someone who had so recently given birth.

If she could have spoken, Emily would have cried out that the men could have her sheep, could do anything they wanted, if only they would leave Tristan and Shay alone. She did not wish to become a widow on the very day of her wedding, or ever, for that matter.

"Stay out of this," Aislinn whispered fiercely.

Emily's pulses pounded, and it took all the self-control she possessed not to wade straight into the center of the fray, but she was not without a measure of common sense. The situation was a powder keg, and one impulsive move could bring on an explosion.

A flash from an upstairs window of the hotel caught her eye, and Emily squinted in disbelief. An old woman was bending over the sill, sighting in a rifle with obvious expertise. Cowhands came out of the Yellow Garter Saloon, while other men appeared in front of the feed-and-grain and the livery stable.

Emily recognized several of the ranchers who had dined at her kitchen table that very morning. The group converged to form a broad half-circle around the angry riders.

One of them stepped forward and spoke in a strong voice. "Don't you boys go thinkin' you can shoot the marshal and ride out without takin' the consequences," he said. It was Elmer Stanton, the gray-haired fellow who'd eaten three stacks of pancakes. He served as the spokesman, just as he had earlier in the day. "You ride out of here and let us handle our own troubles."

"But they've got sheep!" one of the mounted men argued.

"Like I said, that's between them and us. It's got nothin' to do with you, now that you ain't part of the Powder Creek outfit anymore. And now, well, it's time you boys moved on

to someplace where you ain't got a reputation. We've got no use for you around here.''

Emily leaned against the doorframe, her fingers and Aislinn's interlaced as they waited. The golden wedding band, so recently donned, seemed to sear her flesh. She wanted nothing in that moment—*nothing*—but to go home with Tristan, her husband. To be alone with him, to lie in his arms, to lay her head upon his chest and hear the strong, steady beat of his heart. Knowing that any one of the men gathered in the street had the power to still that heart forever only made the prospect more poignant.

Tears burned in her eyes, and she blinked them back furiously.

"I ain't gettin' myself kilt over a few sheep," one of the younger riders announced, in a clear voice. "There's work up in Montana. I'm headed that way, if anybody wants to come along." With that, he wheeled his gray speckled pony away from the others, and the barrier of armed men who'd come to intercede parted to let him pass.

It was the lead man who shot him, square in the back. Emily saw a puff of smoke from the old woman's rifle before she heard the report of a second bullet, and watched in horror as the slayer fell forward, out of the saddle, dead before he struck the ground.

For a few moments, panic reigned; pistols and shotguns were brandished, and Emily was terrified that there would be more shooting.

Then Shay's yell rose over it all. "Damn it, don't anybody fire another shot! This thing has gotten out of hand as it is!"

Several of the first man's friends had gone to check on him; he was wounded, and there was copious blood, but when they hoisted him to his feet and shuffled him off in the direction of the doctor's office, it seemed likely that he'd survive. The second one, the ringleader, was not so fortunate. Tristan crouched before him and pressed two fingers to the base of the man's throat.

"He's dead," he said, addressing Shay.

"Damn it all to hell," Shay replied, irritated. Then he stepped toward the remaining riders. "Any of you fellows want to pass the night in my new jail? If you don't, then I'd advise you to get out of here before I lose my temper!"

Emily dared to glance at Aislinn.

"Isn't he wonderful?" whispered the latter.

Emily smiled, but she wasn't thinking about Shay, either; her mind was on Tristan. He was alive and unhurt. He was her husband. "Oh, yes," she agreed, and she wasn't talking about Shay. "There's no one like him, anywhere."

The riders scattered, however reluctantly, and Shay and Tristan went forward to confer with the ranchers who had come to their rescue. Emily, suddenly reminded of the strain her sister-in-law had been under, took Aislinn's arm. "We'd better get you home now," she said.

Aislinn nodded, and let Emily assist her to the house at the other end of the street, where the boys, Thomas and Mark, waited wide-eyed on the front step, while Dorrie looked after the baby inside.

"We heard shots," Thomas said, hurrying toward his sister. "Is Shay—?"

Aislinn ruffled her brother's thick chestnut hair. "He's fine. So is Tristan. There was some trouble, but things are fine now."

"Can we go see?" Mark wanted to know.

"Absolutely not," Aislinn answered. She was looking a bit wan, though Emily knew how strong she was, and figured she'd be right as rain after a few days of taking things easy. "You'll just have to wait until Shay comes home. He'll tell you the whole story, I'm sure."

The screen door squeaked on its hinges as Dorrie appeared on the threshold. "I see by your face that my brother is still among the living," she said to Aislinn, as coolly as if she'd been through the same ordeal a hundred times before. "The babe's sleeping like a little angel, but you look a mite the

worse for wear." She came outside and, between the two of them, she and Emily got Aislinn inside and up the stairs to bed.

In the large kitchen, Dorrie brewed a pot of tea and joined Emily at the round oak table. She glanced tellingly at the band on Emily's finger. "So he's taken a wife at last, has he?" she murmured, and for a few moments it was impossible to tell whether the older woman was pleased or displeased by this turn of events.

Emily twisted the ring round and round. Why didn't Tristan come and fetch her? Surely it was time to go home and—what *would* they do when they reached the ranch? She wished she were an experienced woman, knowledgeable in the ways of the flesh, but she was woefully ignorant in such matters.

A blinding smile broke across Dorrie's otherwise plain face. "It's time and past that Tristan Saint-Laurent settled down. He wants a family in the worst way, that young man. That's why he stayed on after he got his money back. His brother was here. He didn't want to leave Shay."

Emily bit her lower lip. She certainly understood Tristan's desire to be close to his only blood kin; it was not pleasant to be alone in the world, however self-sufficient one might be. "It would be a fine thing to have a brother or a sister," she said, and cleared her throat because her voice had turned rusty all of the sudden.

Briefly, Dorrie looked sad. "Usually," she agreed, and then her smile was back. "No sense in looking back," she said musingly, as though speaking to herself. She patted Emily's hand. "You have choices in life, for all that you're a woman. Choose to be happy, and you will be."

Aislinn had told Emily about Dorrie's lost love during their long conversation the day before, but she didn't want to ask about the choices the other woman had made.

Dorrie beamed. "You're wondering about me, aren't you? Whether or not I'm happy?"

Emily lowered her gaze briefly, embarrassed, and did not reply.

Her companion laughed. "Don't you fret, Mrs. Saint-Laurent. I've got a good life here in Prominence—Aislinn and Shay need me. There's the baby, and those mother-less boys, to look after. The store takes up a lot of my time, too. I reckon I've got more to be thankful for than most."

It was the first time anyone had addressed her by her married name; she loved being called "Mrs. Saint-Laurent." Her mind was eased, too, at least where Dorrie's welfare was concerned. Hearing Tristan and Shay entering at the front of the house, her thoughts turned to other matters. She swallowed and looked away.

Dorrie patted her hand again. "You picked a good man," she said, in a reassuring whisper. "He'll know when to be gentle and when to be rough."

"Emily?" Tristan's voice rang through the house.

After a farewell word to Dorrie, she went to find him. They met in the dining room, stopped about ten paces apart, like gunfighters meeting in the street.

"Ready to go home, Mrs. Saint-Laurent?" he asked. His voice was husky, and his blue eyes burned into her, making promises. It was only midafternoon, but autumn was coming on fast, and it would be dark in a few hours.

She nodded, suddenly shy. Tristan had sworn he would not force her into conjugal relations, and she trusted him wholeheartedly. Still, he had made it clear that he expected to lie beside her in their marriage bed, and he'd never been secretive with regard to his intention to seduce her. She wanted him, perhaps even loved him, but the reality was a fearsome thing. Suppose she was a disappointment to him? Suppose intercourse was painful and degrading, as some women hinted that it was?

Seeming to read her thoughts, he took her hand and smiled. "No hurry," he said softly, and led her outside. The wagon, left behind at the churchyard when the Powder Creek men came looking for trouble, had been

brought to the McQuillans' gate, where it waited, stately as a glass carriage come to fetch a princess back to her castle.

Tristan helped his bride up into the seat and then climbed up beside her. He released the brake with one foot and whistled to the team, and they were on their way home.

Twilight was falling when they arrived. Emily got down without waiting for help and hurried toward the house, while Tristan took care of the team and wagon. In a backward glance, Emily saw to her consternation that he was smiling to himself.

Mr. Polymarr and Fletcher were present at the evening meal, as usual, the man oblivious to the charge in the air, the boy awkwardly aware. Tristan ate slowly, moderately, without saying much, as he would have on any other night, but his eyes followed Emily while she pushed her food around on her plate with the back of a fork. And when she got up, in desperation, to begin a clamorous round of clearing and cleaning.

"Come on, old man," Fletcher said, when Polymarr would have settled back to light a pipe. "Let's go out and make sure them Injuns is mindin' the sheep the way they should."

Mildly befuddled, Mr. Polymarr rose, thanked Emily for a fine supper, and trundled outside. Fletcher lingered a moment, his color high, glancing from Emily to Tristan and back again.

"Good night," Tristan said, and while there was a point to his words, he did not speak unkindly. Emily thought he looked like some sort of pagan priest in the flickering light of the kerosene lantern behind him, in command of a rustic magic all his own.

Fletcher nodded once and fled, and for a moment Emily's heart followed him, sore with sympathy. He was so young, and could not know that the hurt he felt would soon melt away, like a mist at sunrise.

She took up the rest of the plates and utensils.

"Sit down, Emily," Tristan said quietly. "I don't expect you to wait on me like a servant."

She had already put dishwater on the stove to heat—the reservoir was nearly empty—and now she added soap and swirled it around once before adding dirty plates. Aware of Tristan in every part of her body and spirit, she turned to him at last, using the apron around her waist to dry her hands.

He patted the bench beside him. "Come here," he said.

Over by the fire, Spud gave an expansive, contented sigh. He was old, had spent his days working hard, and he deserved the easy life of a pet.

Emily patted her hair, as though it were elaborately coiffed instead of wound into a simple plait, then forced herself across the room. Now it would begin, the wooing, the seduction he had promised to accomplish. She sat on the very edge of the bench and held her breath, like someone about to be branded with a hot iron.

Tristan traced the outlines of her cheeks with the backs of his fingers. "Did he hurt you?" he asked.

She was taken aback by the question and for the briefest of moments she had no idea what he meant. Then it came to her that he was talking about Cyrus, about her previous marriage. She shook her head. "No," she whispered.

"Then why are you so scared?"

She let out a shaky breath. His caress, innocent though it was, ignited fires in the farthest reaches of her being, and echoes of heat boomeranged to consume her at the core. "Lots of reasons," she said. A sweet tremor went through her as he ran the pad of his thumb lightly across her lower lip, as though preparing the way for a kiss.

A smile flirted with his mouth, flew upward into his knowing eyes. "Such as?" he prompted.

She wanted to look away, but found she couldn't. She was

under his spell, as surely as a mongoose facing a cobra. Her voice came out scratchy. "You might— I've never done this before—"

He leaned toward her. "I might—what?" A whisper, nothing more.

She felt the blood rush to her face and pound there like thunder beating hard against the sky. "Be disappointed," she blurted miserably.

He chuckled. "That's not likely," he said, and kissed her lightly, teasingly, on the mouth. He stood, and what was a relief to Emily was also a tearing-away. "I've got a few things to do outside, then I'm going down to the spring to wash up." He glanced at the clock ticking loudly on the mantelpiece. "I'll be about an hour, I reckon."

Emily knotted her hands together in her lap and nodded. Tristan wouldn't be sleeping in the barn that night, or in the spare room, and he was reminding her of their agreement. They would share a marriage bed, and she was free to spurn his affections—if she could.

And now she wasn't even certain that she wanted to. What sort of woman was she? She had not known Tristan Saint-Laurent a full week, and husband or no, he was a virtual stranger.

She sat at the table for a long while, torn between running away and offering herself to Tristan like a wanton. In the end, she compromised and took the middle ground. She cleaned up the kitchen, went upstairs to the master bedroom and lighted the lamp on the bedside table. She wondered, as she stripped off her clothes in a corner of the room, whether or not Tristan could see the window, glowing with welcome, from wherever he was.

After a careful washing, she donned a prim nightgown, one of the garments Aislinn had given her, and carefully hung her bright yellow wedding dress from a peg on the wall. She had brushed her teeth and was lying in bed, waiting and reflecting on the events of the day, when the door opened and Tristan came in.

She drew the covers up under her nose and peered at him over the edge.

He grinned, kicking off one boot, then the other. His hair was damp and freshly brushed and even in the dim light, his eyes sparkled with mischief and amusement. Behind the sparkle, however, blue embers smoldered, just waiting to burst into a conflagration. "Tired?" he asked, as companionably as if they were an old couple who'd shared the same bed every night for years.

"Yes," she said, her voice muffled by the covers. Her gaze tracked Tristan as he unbuckled the gunbelt and crossed the room to set it on the bedside table beside the lamp, the .45 protruding ominously from the holster. Then he pushed down his suspenders, very methodically, and she noticed that his shirt was moist in front, where he'd splashed his bare chest with water and put the garment back on without using a towel. She did not dare to look at his trousers.

"Hmmm," he said, and pulled the shirt off over his head. After tossing that away, he reached for the buckle of his belt.

Emily commanded herself to avert her eyes, and found she could not. His chest and shoulders were overwhelming enough; she did not need to see the rest of him to know that he was as magnificent, as inherently masculine, as any stallion, wild or otherwise.

He stepped back from the side of the bed to push his trousers down over his hips, and Emily caught her breath. He was erect, and his size was intimidating; far out of proportion, she was certain, to its natural counterpart, her own feminine passage. Her eyes skittered to his face and she saw that he was utterly without self-consciousness; his expression was confident, but not arrogant, and amusement touched one corner of his mouth. He was, to Emily's consternation, glorious.

He turned the lamp down until the flame was almost out, and the room held more shadow than light. There was still enough illumination to see by, however.

"My turn," he said, and tossed back the covers to reveal Emily's nightgowned figure. He made a tsk-tsk sound with his tongue. "Unfair. Here I stand, wearing what God gave me and nothing else, while you're swathed to the throat in flannel."

Emily waxed defensive. "You didn't say I had to be—to be *naked.* You said we were going to lie down together, that's all."

"Take off the nightgown, Emily," he said patiently. "Let me look at you."

She squeezed her eyes shut and tugged at the nightgown, baring her ankles, then her knees, then her thighs . . .

Tristan stretched out beside her, and her knuckles went white, her fingers full of bunched flannel. "You're headed in the right direction," he prompted mischievously. "Keep going."

She could have refused him at any time, she knew that. But there was another part of her, hungry and eager, that would not countenance retreat. She pulled and, in one long, bumbling stroke, the nightgown was off, over her head. Away.

Tristan let out a low whistle, his gaze moving over her at a leisurely pace before returning to her face. "I knew you were beautiful, Mrs. Saint-Laurent," he said gruffly, "but it turns out that you're more than that. You're perfect."

Emily's throat was tight, and tears burned along her lower lashes. She had never heard such words before, from anyone, and they were an elixir, mending tiny, forgotten fractures within, though there was something else she wanted him to say. "This seduction," she said. "Does it involve touching?"

Tristan's grin flashed. "Oh, yes. Considerable touching," he assured her. Then, as gently as he might take up an injured bird, he cupped her left breast in the palm of his hand. "Like this, for instance."

Emily let out a soft moan as he teased the nipple into a

hard point with his thumb. Feverishly, she reached up to put her arms around his neck and draw him down to her mouth for the first of a series of ever-deepening kisses. All the while, he continued to fondle and caress her breast, rousing a new and piercing desire that was as elemental as lightning.

When he lowered his golden head and took her nipple full into his mouth, she cried out in a sort of exultant protest, plunging splayed fingers into his hair, pressing him closer. He nibbled, then tongued, then suckled her, and when she flung both hands back onto the pillow in surrender, he caught them together at the wrists and held them gently above her head. He made free with both her breasts then, until she was tossing on the mattress, needing more, and still more—without quite knowing what it was that she needed.

He lowered a hand to the nest of moist curls at the apex of her thighs, parted her, and began a light, swirling motion with his fingers. Fire shot through Emily; she might have come back from the frantic stupor he'd induced by enjoying her breasts so thoroughly, but she was utterly lost in that moment.

He buried his face in her hair, his lips close to her ear. "This," he said hoarsely, "is why it's worth a little pain the first time. Remember this when I take you, darlin'. Remember how it feels, and how it will be again."

With that, he kissed his way down her breastbone, pausing briefly at her belly, then proceeded to the place he had awakened to aching alertness. When he took her into his mouth, she was so stunned by the swift, searing pleasure, by the unexpectedness of the gesture itself, that she made a sound as wild and fierce as the cry of a she-wolf, half defiance, half submission.

He worked her until she begged, until she hurled her hips upward off the bed to meet him, until her entire body was slick with perspiration and her hair clung in tendrils to her cheeks, her forehead, her neck. Then, with a few teasing

flicks of his tongue, he sent her reeling, tumbling, end over end, into an inferno bright enough to blind her, hot enough to brand her forever, as his and his alone.

For a time, she was one with her own heartbeat, then there came a cataclysmic explosion, following which she was borne skyward upon a pillar of fire, only to descend slowly, slowly, in scattered, burning fragments. During the long fall, Tristan comforted her, held her, whispered sweet, senseless words against her damp temple. Transported, she was at the same time excruciatingly aware of the weight, heat and substance of his body, pressed against hers. Promising other, greater odysseys, deeper mysteries, still more breathless heights to be scaled.

She clung to him and wept, for she had never suspected that such pleasure, such abandon, was possible. He soothed her, stroking her gently along the curving length of her side, murmuring, occasionally kissing her eyelids, the hollow of her throat, her forehead and temples.

After a very long time, she settled back inside her own skin, and Tristan's shadowed face came into craggy focus. The flame in the lamp on the bedside table was struggling, about to gutter out.

He kissed her mouth lightly, briefly, but in a way that reawakened the needs he had so thoroughly assuaged before. "Well," he said, in a husky voice, "did it work?"

Emily knew what he meant—he wanted to know if his attempt to seduce her had succeeded. She stretched and crooned, rested, ready for another breathless climb. "Oh, yes," she said, and wriggled against him, reveling in what she had wrought. He was not the only one who could cause physical havoc, after all; the proof of his desire pulsed between them.

"You understand what I'm asking you, Emily?" he pressed, and she loved him all the more—yes, loved him— for his concern, for his restraint, which she knew was hardwon. "I want to take you, right now, and it's probably going to hurt some. There's no way around that."

"It can't hurt more than needing you does," she reasoned, drawing his head down for a hungry kiss.

He positioned himself, paused briefly to give her a chance to change her mind, then delved into her with a long, deep stroke. And there was some pain, though short-lived and, as the friction built, so did Emily's responses, and soon she had given herself up, once again, to the primitive forces that made her entirely female. Tristan, too, was lost, and as their bodies interlocked in ferocious pleasure, their spirits took wing, like magnificent birds, soaring into the star-speckled sky.

EPILOGUE

~

ONE YEAR LATER . . .

*T*HE BIG HOUSE WAS FILLED WITH LIGHT and music, and while the band—three fiddlers, a piano player and a washboard man—held forth, couples from farms and ranches for miles around danced round and round the big parlor. The furniture that usually graced that room had been carried out into the front yard, under a clear, starry sky, where children of varying dispositions and ages played house, musical chairs and tag.

Folks were still getting used to calling the ranch the Double Crescent, rather than Powder Creek, but all agreed that the place had benefited by changing hands. Tristan Saint-Laurent was making it pay, and to virtually everybody's relief, the missus had gotten shut of those sheep of hers, in midsummer, selling some, shearing some, and giving the rest to Black Eagle in trade for elk meat, herbal medicines and the odd bit of beadwork. Not that the sheep had really been so bad, for they hadn't eaten so much as a blade of range grass.

Now that Mrs. Saint-Laurent, she was a pure fascination, just like the marshal's wife, Mrs. McQuillan. Both of them in the family way and neither one making the slightest effort to retire from public view until their confinement was over. The two women were the closest of friends, but they

were also part of the community, speaking up at town meetings and clamoring for the vote.

As for the brothers, Tristan and Shay, well, they were so alike that it was nigh unto impossible to tell them apart. Once in a while, Tristan would put on Shay's badge and serve a whole week as marshal, with nobody the wiser until they chose to let the word get out. The women, Emily and Aislinn that is, could always recognize their own husbands, and claimed they were as different as any other pair of brothers. Just about anybody else in Prominence, Miss Dorrie McQuillan included, would have disagreed.

There were lots of rumors about Tristan, for by virtue of his growing up away, he was a stranger. Some said he'd been a bounty hunter once, some said a Texas Ranger, and some even maintained that he was one of the worst outlaws ever to strap on a gunbelt. The speculations had spiced up more than one conversation, and made for a favorite topic at the feed-and-grain and around the potbellied stove in the general store. Some of the old-timers said there'd be gunslingers along to challenge him, but so far none had appeared. Most people figured it would take a pure fool to mess with him or Shay, given their obvious prowess with those .45s they always wore. Funny thing, that—the way they'd grown up apart and still turned out pretty much the same.

Now, on the night of the party, the parlor crowd cleared, and Tristan Saint-Laurent and his beautiful Emily took the floor for a waltz, soon to be joined by Shay McQuillan and the lovely Aislinn. They seemed to glow, the four of them, each couple gazing into one another's eyes, as if oblivious to the rest of the world.

It was enough to make a person believe in fairy tales.